She crouched down and [...] one side. A human h[...] out. It lay on the grou[...] palm up, perfectly still.

Joanna screamed and fell back, rolling farther down the hill to crash to a halt up against a tree. It looked as if someone was trying to crawl out from under the boat.

She gathered her breath calmly and with nerves she didn't know she possessed, walked slowly back to the boat. She took a deep breath and placed both her hands firmly on one side. With a burst of strength pulled from heaven-knows-where, she threw the boat over onto its back. A flurry of activity erupted as beetles and mice scurried out of the unexpected light.

Old Luke lay facedown. She knew all along it was Luke. There were no visible marks but the black hair on the back of his head was thickly matted with a dark brown substance.

★

---

WHITEOUT

vicki delany

WⓄRLDWIDE®

TORONTO • NEW YORK • LONDON
AMSTERDAM • PARIS • SYDNEY • HAMBURG
STOCKHOLM • ATHENS • TOKYO • MILAN
MADRID • WARSAW • BUDAPEST • AUCKLAND

WHITEOUT

A Worldwide Mystery/January 2008

First published by LTDBooks.

ISBN-13: 978-0-373-26624-1
ISBN-10:   0-373-26624-3

Printed in U.S.A.

WHITEOUT

PROLOGUE

FOOTSTEPS WERE FOLLOWING HER. She was sure of it. Every nerve twitched as she stopped walking and strained to listen. Nothing. She laughed at herself, a quick embarrassed laugh. *Must be my imagination; imagine me being frightened like some kind of snotty-nosed kid.*

An ancient gray owl watched the girl's progress with contempt. It wasn't the owl that the human heard; the owl made sure to be sensed only when she wanted to be. No creature of that size was of the slightest interest to her. Her only concern at the human's passing was that the girl might disturb the mouse now sniffing the air with great hesitation prior to stepping away from safety. The mouse was expending an extraordinary amount of effort checking the environs outside of its hole beneath the enormous old white pine, afraid to venture out to begin the night's foraging, afraid to face the clearing and what might be found in it. At last the mouse looked as if he was set to make a leap into the darkness. The owl tensed, ready to launch herself off her perch.

The sound of the girl's heavy boots stomping through the decay of the forest floor cracked the mouse's courage and he dove back into his hole. The owl stared at the girl malevolently, then resumed her silent watch of the forest.

The girl heard nothing but the distant sounds of the party continuing on without her. *Stupid party anyway,* she thought in a vain attempt to cover up the hurt at being forgotten so quickly. At the thought that her so-called friends barely even noticed her distress as she slipped out of the circle of firelight to be swallowed up by the darkness of the deep woods.

She continued walking, whistling to herself. She was smart enough to know that the whistle was a futile attempt at reassurance, but she was powerless to stop it.

Then she heard it again: a dead twig cracking under a boot. She whirled around and shouted out in her loudest, most authoritative voice.

"Who's there? Are you trying to scare me? Come out where I can see you." To her horror her voice came out as a broken squeak.

"Hey, hold up there." A teenaged boy, older than her, perhaps seventeen or eighteen, stepped into the path. He was dressed in a Tommy Hilfiger jacket and excessively baggy jeans. Above the waistline of the pants she could see the rim of dirty underwear. The jacket was probably stolen. This boy could never afford something like that. He held his hands out in front of him, palms up; a gesture of peace, and stepped forward.

High above them the owl shook her head in disgust; there would be no hunting at this spot tonight. She glided on silent wings into the depths of the forest.

"Why'd you run off so quick like that?" he said. "I wasn't about to do nothing." He stepped closer.

The smell of too much beer and unwashed clothes almost made her gag. She took a step backward. "I didn't run off, I just want to go home. That party was boring."

"Yeah, you're right, it's a real bore. How about you and me make a party of our own, eh?"

The girl took another step backward. "No thanks." Despite her growing fear, she still tried to be polite, like her grandma had taught her. "I'm tired, I'm going home. See you later."

As she turned to leave, the boy reached out and grabbed her arm. She could smell the thick reek of beer on his breath. Beer and something else, something threatening and sinister.

"I thought you and me could party a bit more, how about it? A hot chick from Toronto like you ought to know some good party games."

She tried to pull her arm away but his grip was too strong. "Let me go."

"You a tease or something?" He leered into her face, beer fumes and bad hygiene enveloping her in a wave of nausea. "You think you can lead me on and not follow up. Is that it?"

"Look," she pleaded. "I didn't mean to lead you on. I'm sorry if you thought so. I just want to go home. Please let me go."

"I'll let you go home to Mama all right, but let's have some fun first." He released his grip on her arm and with both hands lashed out and shoved her to the ground. She landed on a soft bed of pine needles, but it was sprinkled with tiny sharp twigs that dug into her back. The shock of the landing shot up her spine and dazed her momentarily. She shook her head to clear it.

The boy loomed over her. Unaccustomed to power, his eyes swelled to monstrous proportions. He breathed deeply and rapidly through his mouth.

The fall shook the girl to her bones; she lay stunned on the forest floor. Too stunned to hear a soft, gentle moan breaking through the silence in the clearing. But the boy heard it, deep in his soul. It was his turn to be scared. The darkness surrounding the girl and boy shifted and moved. Black is black, but this black moved. It was darker than the blackness of the woods at night. The moan sounded again, a long, mournful vibration, a sound without meaning and a sound without hope. The blackness moved again. It drifted gently over the girl where she lay

on the ground. The blackness stopped in front of the boy. The
look of power had died in his eyes, it was gone and it would
never return. He turned and ran.

The girl stumbled to her feet and ran as fast as she could.
She ran toward home.

ONE

GRAY WATER AND GRAY SKY blended seamlessly together in the mist. There was no horizon, only a world of gray, unmarked by beginning or ending. *Like my life,* Joanna thought.

It had stopped raining but the air still hung thick and heavy with moisture. There was no wind; the water on the lake lay quiet and still. In the woods behind her the trees shook off a steady stream of rainwater.

Joanna stood on shore beside the dismantled dock and stared across the lake for a long time. The mist muffled any noises from lake or forest; serenity enveloped her like a soft wool cape. The haunting call of a loon broke through the silence and echoed across the lake, long and lonely and piercing.

She nodded to herself and smiled. *As omens go, that one is fitting. Life always goes on, after all.* She turned her back to the lake and walked up the hill toward the cabin. She hesitated before putting the key into the lock, took a deep breath, unlocked the door and stepped into her new life.

"Well, hello, world. Here I am." Joanna announced her arrival in a loud firm voice to the empty room. "First things first, then I'll stop to think." Bone chilling damp filled the cabin. It was only late September, but this far north in Ontario, September often meant wet, cool days and frosty nights. Fortunately a supply of firewood was chopped and neatly stacked beside the old iron stove, waiting for her arrival, a box of long matches lying nearby.

Although Joanna had no experience lighting a wood-burning stove, the instructions she had received over the phone were excellent and a strong fire was soon burning cheerfully.

She returned to her car and set about carrying boxes and bags into the cabin. She hadn't brought much from her old life to the new. It was surprising how little one really needed. A lifetime of accumulation reduced to no more than it takes to fill the trunk of a Toyota.

The cabin came fully furnished, she had put most of her belongings into storage not knowing or caring if she would ever have use for them again. She brought only her clothes, a few favorite cooking pots, some good sheets and towels and her best prints. Plus, of course, her library of books and the computer, which were the tools of her trade, and her CD player.

From the first box she carefully extracted three picture frames and placed them on the tiny table by the large front window, where she planned to set up the computer. She held each picture in her hand for a moment before setting it into place. Wendy posed solemnly in gown and mortarboard at her University graduation, trying so hard to be serious while inwardly shouting at the camera, "Look out world, here I come." James was laughing; sometimes it seemed as if James was always laughing, waving to her from the canoe he loved more than anything, that last summer in Algonquin Park. Alexis had been caught in a rare moment of peace, setting out for school on a warm spring day, clad in her regular uniform of dirty jeans, black T-shirt and overlarge flannel top; frozen in time as if all would be well once again. Tears filled her eyes and Joanna put the last picture down with a soft thud.

She walked around the main room, deciding where it would be best to put her things. She would drag the kitchen table over here to make the space her dining room as well as her office, for the window overlooked the forest of maples and pines and on down to the lake. At least she would have a panorama of the lake from here. It was dark now, only the first row of trees were visible in the light cast from the cabin windows, standing like ghostly sentinels against the nightly spirits of the Northern woods. As she wandered around her cabin, imagining how it would be all fixed up, she could feel the pall of anxiety lifting off her shoulders like a Victorian bride carefully removing her veil for that first, hesitant kiss. She had been crushed by despair, by depression and by responsibility for too many years. She believed she could now cast them off, like the bridal veil on the wedding night, and go on.

She finished unpacking, and opened a bottle of Cabernet Sauvignon she'd brought from the city and sipped it while preparing her dinner. An excellent bottle, far more than she would normally spend, or could afford, but she so wanted to mark this first night as something special. On the CD player Loreena McKennitt sang the haunting strains of "Greensleeves." She chopped onions and peppers and several cloves of garlic, put chicken into the oven to broil and a cup of basmati rice on to boil. While the chicken cooked she chopped more vegetables and ripped up red-leafed lettuce for a salad.

The shrill ringing of the phone cut into the quiet of the cabin like the alien presence it was. Instinctively Joanna put down her knife and crossed the room. The phone was a heavy black rotary dial, one the likes of which she hadn't seen for many long years.

I don't have to do this, she thought, putting the receiver to her ear. *If I don't want to answer the damn phone I don't have to. Not anymore.*

"Hello."

"Mom, how are you? Are you okay? Have you gotten settled in? What's the place like?"

"Oh, Wendy," Joanna replied. "I'm fine. I'm cooking dinner. The cabin is exactly as I thought it would be: small, plain and simple. I'll be fine." Fortunately the phone had an exceptionally long cord. She stretched it across the tiny room into the kitchen and stirred her vegetables with the phone propped on one shoulder.

"Are you sure this is what you want? You can always change your mind and go home."

"Please, Wendy, we've been through all this. This is what I have decided to do. And you know full well that I can't come home and I can't back out of this deal on the cabin."

"Robert and I have been talking about it," Wendy said.

I'm sure you have.

"And we think that you should come and stay here with us. At least until you find a place to rent in Toronto. You know how thoughtful Robert is. It would work out fine."

Wouldn't that be bliss, thought Joanna, *all three of us living in a graduate student hovel in Toronto. The ever-noble Robert wouldn't last a week.*

"No dear, I don't think so. Now I have to go, dinner is almost ready."

"I'll call you tomorrow to see if you're okay."

"No. No you won't. I don't want you checking up on me, Wendy."

"I really don't think its safe, Mother," Wendy insisted. "I've said all along, it's not safe, you living up there all by yourself. Suppose something happens to you. Suppose you have an accident and break your leg or something and can't get to the phone. You could lie out there for days and no one would know a thing about it."

Joanna rolled her eyes. "Maybe you shouldn't be living in downtown Toronto, Wendy, it's not safe. Suppose you are mugged one night walking home from class. Suppose some crazed drug addict breaks in when Robert isn't home and you're there by yourself."

"That's different."

It's always different for children. "I don't have an answering machine yet and I don't have voice mail, so don't be rushing up with the police if I don't answer the phone every time you call, do you hear me?"

"Yes, Mother. I hear you."

"Good night, dear."

"Good night."

Joanna shook her head as she hung up the phone. As annoying as that conversation was, it was nice to know that someone did care about her.

She placed a single tall silver candlestick on her table and lit the candle. A bunch of fresh flowers bought on a whim as she drove out of the old neighborhood was arranged in a drinking glass to serve as a centerpiece. She turned off most of the lights, poured herself another glass of the excellent wine and served up a huge portion of chicken and rice. The trees outside the cabin windows were barely visible, swaying gently in the shadows. The mist had cleared and a full moon was rising over the lake, casting a stream of light to dance gaily across the dark water up to her dock. All was still and quiet. For the first time in many long years she felt serenity settle around her. Loreena McKennitt sang on and she started to eat.

JOANNA AWOKE WITH A START, and for a moment she couldn't remember where she was. The fire in the wood stove had gone out and her bedroom was freezing. She pulled the quilts tighter under her chin and tried to settle back to sleep. She couldn't stop shivering and was soon driven to throw off the covers and pull on housecoat and slippers. Might as well get used to country living right away.

She padded into the living room and started the stove with logs and kindling chopped and waiting on the floor. *Perhaps I should chop some more firewood,* she thought. *This pile won't last much longer.* Not that Joanna knew anything at all about chopping wood, but how difficult could it be?

After lighting the fire she ground coffee beans and put them on to brew, then walked across the room to stand at the long window. A weak autumn sun was beginning its slow rise behind the cabin; the trees cast long shadows over the lake. Not a cloud marred the soft blue sky. She wrapped her arms around herself and snuggled further into her robe. She shivered once again, but this time it took a moment until she recognized the feeling. Not cold but joy, and joy had been a rare thing in her life for a long time. It felt good.

The rich, welcome aroma of coffee filled the cabin. It smelled wonderful, and even more wonderful was the simple fact that she had nothing in particular to do today. Once the machine ceased bubbling and the coffee was ready, Joanna poured herself a large mug and took it out to the deck. With the worn terry cloth belt of her housecoat she wiped a dry place to sit on the single bench. "Deck," she realized, was altogether too fancy a word for something that was no more than an old wooden porch on spindly legs.

The cabin had come cheap, the most that Joanna could afford. Once she had made up her mind to give up her job and leave the city everything happened almost at the speed of light. Her house rented so soon after she advertised that she was caught breathless by the sudden direction her life was taking. She didn't bother to inspect the cabin before renting it, just asked a few questions over the phone and signed the papers that arrived in the mail. Although she hadn't been expecting much, in the daylight she could see that she had received nothing more than she'd paid for.

The ad called it a "cottage," but it had none of the country home elegance that word implied. This was a cabin in the woods, plain and simple. It consisted mostly of one room, with a small room off the back to be used as the bedroom and a tiny, ancient bathroom. The kitchen was an alcove, open to the rest of the cabin. A wooden porch ran the full length across the front, affording a fabulous view of the lake and surrounding woods. As much as it was in need of a thorough sanding and a good coat of varnish, the long, wide porch stretching the full length of the cabin was certainly the best feature of the place. There was no garden, just a clearing in the woods with the cabin sitting in the center of it, and a rough gravel driveway running down the hill from the road. A small, largely overgrown path etched through the woods led down the hill to the water. The dock had been taken apart and stacked on the rocky shore for the winter, safe from the destructive power of packing ice. There was no garage or other shelter for her car. Joanna hoped that wouldn't be a problem. She had no intention of going anywhere with any great urgency. She was looking forward to being snowed in, with all the solitude and isolation that phrase suggested.

As she sipped her coffee, Joanna drew a mental picture of what the property could look like in the summer. She would dig a few flowerbeds for bunches of impatiens along the deck, perhaps some perennials around the sides of the cabin. With all the trees there wouldn't be much sun, so she would put in some hosta and other plants that didn't mind the shade. Pots of flowers, lots of big terra-cotta pots, overflowing with summer blooms in a riot of color to line the driveway, maybe some begonias and more impatiens. And smaller containers spilling across the porch railing, geraniums perhaps, in a lovely red. No lawn though, she smiled at the thought. No grass to cut. That would be true freedom. She would pull her lawn chair out of storage and set it out overlooking her new garden as soon as it was warm enough.

The lake was located too far north, too far from Toronto, to have many true cottages. While driving in yesterday, Joanna had seen only a few cabins scattered along the shore of the lake, not many of them any fancier than hers. No one would be coming up here for weekends away from the city. Which suited Joanna perfectly.

She hadn't brought much in the way of groceries, there not being any room left in the car after crowding in all of her possessions. So after a leisurely breakfast and still more unpacking and arranging of furniture, Joanna drove to the nearest town to shop. And to check out the locals.

Hope River, as it was called, consisted of not much more than a slowing in the speed limit and a collection of small stores, small being the operative word.

The signs were clear; the days of this town's prosperity were long past, if indeed they had ever been at all. The main, and as far as she could see, the only, street boasted a liquor store, a rundown old restaurant, a tiny grocery store, a hamburger stand with a hand-printed sign in the window informing one and all that they were "Closed for the Season," an antique "shoppe," a gas station long past its prime, and the ubiquitous T-shirt emporium. And that was it. Beyond the hamburger stand, the road curved and widened and disappeared back into the endless rocks and pine of northern Ontario.

Her first stop was the liquor store to stock up on red wine. Then the grocery store. She was impressed by the wide variety

of goods available in the shop: different types of pasta, vegetarian specialties, exotic teas. Even her favorite rice: basmati.
She wandered through the store, filling up her shopping cart.
It was a treat to be buying only for herself after all those years
of trying to please a family. Wendy was a strict vegetarian,
James grumbled if a "dead animal" didn't grace his plate at
every meal, and Alexis discussed in great detail the fat content
of everything that approached her mouth. Trying to please them
all was a nightmare, and she never seemed to end up preparing
anything she actually liked. With a frisson of guilt she tossed
a carton of whipping cream, a bottle of chocolate syrup and a
freshly baked pecan pie into the cart. Prices of fresh produce
were absolutely out of this world but she was surprised to find
that most other goods, particularly anything canned and
packaged, were comparable in price to the city.

As she strolled down the aisles, Joanna could see that the
woman behind the cash register was making no attempt to hide
her interest. She was about her age; considerably overweight
with a pasty tint to her skin testifying to a lifetime spent in front
of the TV, ample supplies of chocolate bars and bags of chips
for company. She was dressed in a smock of a highly unflattering pink. A shockingly bad blond dye job adorned her head.
Two inches of black roots screamed for a touch-up. Catching
sight of the clerk smiling at her as she headed for the counter,
Joanna hastily stuffed the two large bags of chips in her cart
back onto the shelves. She remembered that she was almost due
for a visit to the hairdresser. *God help me find someone any
good around here,* she thought.

"Just passing through, are you?" the woman asked as Joanna
unloaded her shopping cart and placed her purchases, one at a
time, on the counter.

Joanna hid a smile. The clerk must know full well that no

one in their right mind would stop in this hole-in-the-wall town just to go grocery shopping. "No, I've rented a cabin nearby for the winter. I expect I will be coming in here regularly."

"Is that so, what cabin would that be now?" The woman stopped any pretence of working and turned to face Joanna, ready to launch a full-scale inquisition. She was clearly delighted at this sudden break in her routine. Joanna was somewhat taken aback; in her experience store clerks were for checking out your groceries and nothing else. Of course there were no other shoppers in this store, so no one was likely to complain about being kept waiting.

The woman stood behind her cash register patiently, head cocked to one side, waiting for a reply. Joanna hesitated— she had no desire to advertise where she was staying, or to discuss her business with anyone—but the question was so direct, she simply did not know how to avoid answering. "Mr. McKellan's place. On Concession Road Five. By Black Lake."

"Jack, come meet this here lady," the clerk bellowed into the back.

A work-worn, middle-aged man emerged from the stock room, wiping his hands on a butcher's apron that stretched to the limit across his ample stomach. The apron was freshly laundered, but nothing could remove the residue of blood and grime that had accumulated over the years. He was almost completely bald with a few greasy hairs dripping down the sides of his head. Small black eyes stared over Joanna's shoulder in a total lack of interest. He said nothing.

"What did you say your name was, dear?" the clerk said.

"Joanna Hastings."

"Pleased to meet you, Joanna Hastings." The woman extended her hand.

Joanna shook it with some trepidation, overwhelmed by this woman's friendliness.

"I'm Nancy Miller, and this here's my Uncle Jack. My daddy and Jack own this store. Joanna's rented the McKellan's place," she explained to her uncle.

He grunted and returned to the stock room.

"Don't you mind Uncle Jack." Nancy smiled at Joanna. "He just don't like strangers too much." Joanna's sympathies were with Uncle Jack entirely.

"Where you from then? Toronto, I guess, eh?"

"Toronto, yes."

"You'll be finding our little town pretty small, after Toronto. I lived in Toronto once. Nineteen-seventy, I think it was. No, nineteen sixty-nine, I remember we watched the moonwalk on TV. It was just so exciting, being in Toronto I mean, although the moonwalk was exciting too. Everything was exciting in Toronto. I had a small apartment with my cousin Mary. Mary was going to the university, the University of Toronto. My dad didn't want to let me go. He thought I would just get into trouble. But my mom, she said I needed to get out of this town." Nancy stared vaguely into space and smiled at her memories. "She told him that things had changed; girls needed some experience of the world these days, she said. What fun it was. I got a job in Eaton's, working in the lingerie department. Such nice things they had."

The gentle smile disappeared and Nancy shook her head sadly. "But then my mom died, and I had to come home to help Dad and Uncle Jack in the store. Mary stayed at the university and got her degree. She lives in Vancouver now. She's an accountant. Have you ever been to Vancouver, Joanna?"

"What?" Joanna started guiltily. She hadn't been paying much attention. "Vancouver… Oh yes, I've been to Vancouver. I have friends there."

"It must be nice to travel."

"Uh, I really must be on my way," Joanna said. "Do you think perhaps we could finish here now?"

Nancy sighed and returned to punching numbers into the cash register. Only half the groceries had been checked before she paused again.

"Why would someone from Toronto want to live in the old McKellan cabin? It's just a shack you know. You'll find it isolated. Boring, I would think." She smiled at Joanna, once again waiting for an answer.

"I'm a writer. I've come up here to write."

"A writer." Nancy's eyes opened wide. "How exciting. What do you write? Do you write romances? I love romances."

Joanna groaned inwardly. "Yes, that's right," she lied, "and I really do have to be going now. Can you finish with my groceries please?"

Nancy continued as if she hadn't spoken. "Do you write under another name? Maybe I've read something of yours. I've read all the best romances. What name do you use?"

The door chime tinkled as more patrons entered the store. Saved by the bell. An elderly woman came to the end of the counter and waited patiently until Nancy finished helping Joanna while her teenaged companion moved languidly to the magazine rack.

Joanna stared at the girl. She was short and slight and fairly pretty, but everything from her slovenly posture to her gigantic flannel shirt and ridiculous purple hair screamed "attitude." The girl tossed her hair and selected a magazine. A silver nose ring caught the light. Joanna's heart ached.

"Maude, I'd like you to meet Joanna. Joanna's taken the McKellan cabin for the winter. Though I don't know why anyone would want that broken down place. Joanna, this is

Maude Mitchell. Maude has been living here in Hope River longer than almost anyone else."

"How nice." Joanna tore her eyes away from the teenager. "Can we please get on with this? I don't have all day you know." She jerked open her wallet without noticing that she was holding it upside down. Coins sprung from the change purse and a flurry of pennies, nickels and dimes clattered across the counter and onto the floor.

"Oh, for heaven's sake!" Joanna scrambled to pick up the money while Nancy finished checking her out. At last it was over and Joanna handed across what she owed. She wondered if she was being a touch rude, maybe she stopped taking the Prozac too soon.

"Bye now," Nancy said cheerfully, packing Joanna's purchases into white plastic bags. "I'm sure we'll be seeing you again. I'll look forward to talking to you some more. Would you like me to call Uncle Jack to help you carry out your bags?"

"Heavens no, I can manage." Joanna took one more glance at the teenager who was flicking though a magazine with a vacant air, not registering a word she saw.

"Well," Mrs. Mitchell harrumphed indignantly as they watched the door swing shut. "Don't think much of the likes of her. Pretty rude, if you ask me."

"Oh, I don't think so. I liked her. She's a writer you know, a writer of romance novels. She's really famous and has come here to Hope River to be alone and work on her next novel. It's going to be turned into a movie. Starring Tom Cruise. They might even film some of it here, she told me. Imagine Tom Cruise right here in Hope River."

"I'll believe that when I see it," Mrs. Mitchell said, "but for now I believe I'll have a pack of Du Maurier, please."

TWO

THE BRIEF NON-ENCOUNTER with the teenaged girl in the grocery store left Joanna tense and short of breath. She drove back to the cabin, much too fast, forcing her breathing to slow itself, forcing herself to calm down. By the time the car crunched to a stop on the gravel drive she managed to regain some semblance of composure. "This is absolutely crazy," she shouted to the interior of the car. "I can't be running off half-cocked like that."

She remained sitting in the car, giving her heart time to stop pounding and her breath to return to normal. The driveway ended at the top of the hill and the view was quite wonderful. In the summer the lake would no doubt be obscured by dense green foliage, but at this time of year most of the trees had only a smattering of red and yellow leaves still clinging to their branches.

It was a large lake, spotted with small islands. As far as her eyes could see there was no sign of habitation; nothing but thick stands of trees stretching off into the distance. A small motorboat sped through the channel between two of the islands and was lost from view. Long after it disappeared the roar of the motor vibrated in the still air.

She breathed deeply and let the peace of her surroundings work its magic on her jangled nerves. The air was heavy with the scent of rotting leaves and the timeless decay of the forest floor. An aroma rich with the promise of the renewal of spring sure to come.

A flash of movement beneath the largest of the white pines and Joanna turned her head in time to catch sight of a bushy red tail disappearing back into the cover of the woods. A fox: the first of her neighbors to come and pay a call. The heaviness of scant moments ago was forgotten. She smiled.

A line of churning black clouds was advancing in a steady line across the lake, moving in from the horizon. Joanna roused herself to carry her bags into the cabin as the first thick raindrops fell.

It poured all afternoon, a real storm with lashes of rain and heavy winds, rolling thunder and quick flashes of distant lightning. But far from dampening Joanna's spirits she found the chaos of the storm strangely comforting.

As nature railed outside her window she prepared her workspace. With enormous care, the computer was set on the wooden table that would be used as a desk, and the bookshelf arranged with precision. It took a great deal of resolve, but she managed to resist the urge to scatter her possessions every which way. A large part of Joanna's determination for her new life was to be neat and organized, something she had never quite accomplished in the past. She hooked up the modem to the single phone line and tested it with a call to her internet provider. Success on the first attempt. She was congratulating herself on a perfect set up when she realized that the printer cable was nowhere to be found. A search was initiated through all the now-empty boxes and under the desk. No cable.

Damn, where is that blasted thing? She shrugged on her raincoat and prepared for a dash into the elements. The rain was coming down heavier than ever and a gust of wind tossed a bucket of water straight into her face the moment she pushed open the cabin door. Despite the raincoat, by the time she got to the car she was soaked right through to the essentials. Drops of icy cold water dripped down the back of her neck.

The trunk and back seat were empty. She crawled into the car and felt all around on the floor. Nothing left behind. Abandoning the search, she ran down the hill back to the cabin. In her headlong rush to escape the strength of the lashing rain, Joanna failed to watch her footing. Her moccasins slipped on a patch of wet gravel, pitching her forward face-first into the mud. A sharp stabbing pain jolted up her arm into the shoulder as her left wrist took the full force of the fall.

"Hell and damnation," Joanna shouted into the wind. She struggled to her feet, slipping and sliding on mud and gravel. She fell once again as she hit a loose step on the rain-slicked wooden porch, tumbling backward to a crashing halt flat on her bottom at the base of the steps. She sat in a puddle in the freezing rain in her useless raincoat, the pain from her wrist shooting up her arm…and laughed. The release of the tension carried around like a ball and chain since the grocery store was almost too much to bear. She laughed and laughed. When the laughter eventually stopped Joanna struggled one-armed out of the mud to her feet and, with greater care this time, climbed the steps. Once inside she pulled hard to close the door in the face of the storm that was still struggling to get into the cabin. She leaned against the doorframe and watched the floor as a wet and dirty puddle spread outward from her feet.

She started up the stove and peeled off rain- and mud-sodden clothes. As she rubbed her hair one-handed with a towel, Joanna smiled at herself in the bathroom mirror. *Don't I look a treat? But I wanted solitude amidst the forces of nature. And that is certainly what I have.*

Once she was dry and a fire was burning merrily in the stove, Joanna opened a can of chicken noodle soup. Soup heated, a lettuce and tomato sandwich constructed, it was time to get to work.

She started up her word processing program and began to type, using her left hand gingerly. She could manage without the printer for a few days but would have to get a new cable soon. It was just too difficult to proofread properly off the screen; she needed to print out her work to check for spelling mistakes and typos.

Joanna had worked as a programmer, then a systems analyst and eventually project manager at a major computer company for more than 20 years. Unexpectedly, last month she came across an ad in a trade newspaper, looking for people to write technical documentation.

And she jumped at it.

Over the objections of most of her friends and family she quit her job, cashed in her company pension money and her retirement savings and rented out her house for one year.

The week before the move her closest friend invited her out for dinner. Joanna and Elaine had been best friends ever since they suffered through grade nine together. They had both been "nerds" with thick glasses and even thicker braces and A+'s on every test. High school was a torment. Only their friendship and their shared "geekdom" saw the two girls through the five long years until graduation.

Elaine had sipped her vodka martini carefully and looked Joanna in the eye. "After all you've been through, why would you give up now?"

"I'm not giving up," Joanna said quietly. "I'm going to do something new. Try something completely different."

"But you're a city girl, like me. You'll be lost up there in the back of beyond. It will be nice in the fall, hills covered in masses of colored leaves and rustic bonfires and all that sort of thing. Maybe you'll even meet a strapping young farmer on his way to milk the purebred Jersey cows—are cows purebred? But you'll hate it in the middle of winter, trust me, Joanna. It will be a frozen hell on earth. Imagine, no theater, no book readings, no wine bars." She shuddered at the thought. "What on earth will you do with yourself then?"

"I'll reconsider my options and do something else. But I don't expect to hate it. Don't worry about me, I'll be just fine." Joanna took a tentative sip of wine and picked a sliver of tomato off the brushetta on her plate, knowing that she was attempting to convince herself of the rightness of her decision as much as her friend. "I think that I can do without the book readings for a while. This isn't something out of nowhere, you know. This is something I've wanted to do for a very long time. All those years when things were so difficult, I kept everything together because it was always in the back of my mind that some day I could give it all up."

"I understand that, I really do." Elaine speared the olive in her drink with a colored toothpick and popped it into her mouth. Her long nails were perfectly polished as always, in the exact shade to match her pale pink lipstick. Her soft blond hair was gently touched with gray, just enough gray left to make the color appear natural. She was wearing a black Chanel suit with a cream, raw silk blouse, three-inch heels and tiny pearl earrings. Even in her own best dressed-for-success suit, Joanna felt like a country clod in the company of her elegant friend. She always did, yet she loved Elaine dearly.

"I do know what you have gone through," Elaine said. "I was there with you, remember? And I admire you for having survived with your humor intact." She looked down and scratched at a non-existent stain on the black jacket. "I don't want to see you have a relapse. Without me near to help you."

Joanna was deeply touched. She knew how much Elaine worried about her.

The restaurant was filling up rapidly; it would be a busy night. The maître d' glided past, leading a party of four to their table. A large red-faced man in a cheap polyester suit, chomping on the soggy end of an oversized Cuban cigar, lurched up against Joanna's chair, just as she lifted her glass of wine to her lips. She barely managed to save the front of her suit from a good soaking. The man burped in apology. His evening had begun quite some time ago. One frozen glance from Elaine wiped the words off his lips and had the man scurrying after his companions.

"Boor," she said with a sniff, signaling to the waiter for another round of drinks. "Okay, so you're going. I know that I can't talk you out of it. But your RRSPs." Elaine was a financial planner; the idea of someone taking the tax hit incurred by cashing in her retirement savings was tantamount to sacrilege. "Can't you hold on to them? The tax will absolutely kill you, you know." She snapped her fingers as the waiter foolishly attempted to ignore her.

"I don't have any other money. I quit my job, remember? That means I don't qualify for Employment Insurance. I have to live on something, at least until I start earning some money from my writing. The rent from the house will only cover the mortgage and property taxes. And that computer cost me a lot. It was important to get something really top of the line. Once I finish this first job and get paid then I'll be able to support myself again."

Joanna hoped that was true. So far she only had a contract to write one technical manual, for a household accounts program. If more work didn't start coming in over the winter she would be in trouble.

Elaine placed her hand on the table palm upward. "But won't you be lonely?"

Joanna put down her piece of bread and grasped the offered hand tightly. "I'll miss you very much, of course. But I really want to be alone for a while. I'm sure I'll make friends from the homes nearby."

At that moment the smiling waiter brought their plates of pasta: artery-clogging fettuccine Alfredo for Elaine who never worried for a moment about what she ate, and pasta primavera for Joanna. She picked up her fork, grateful for the chance to change the subject.

JOANNA WORKED STEADILY all through the next few days while the cold rain fell outside her window. Before she could write anything about the software, she had to learn how to use it. The program crashed her computer twice but she got it installed, eventually. She bought another personal accounting program, for comparison. Already she could tell that the other product was much superior to her own. At least she didn't have to try to sell it. Just write the facts, ma'am, just the facts.

A week after her arrival, Joanna awoke to the welcome sight of sunlight streaming in through her bedroom window. After only a few days of working and living all on her own she was getting restless.

Perhaps I'll take a day off and explore the neighborhood, she thought as she popped a sliced pumpernickel bagel into the toaster. It was time to discover the location of the nearest library. The pile of mystery novels for nighttime reading was getting perilously low. As was the supply of red wine. Time for another trip into town.

She poured her coffee, placed thin slices of tomato onto the bagel with a dab of Dijon mustard, and then carried her breakfast over to the table. She ate, watching the soft morning light play across the waters of the lake. Encouraged by the warmth of the sunlight, a few small creatures—squirrels and chipmunks and one enormously fat raccoon—ventured out of their hiding places and sniffed about on the rocks and under the trees.

After breakfast, mindful of her resolution to be tidy and well organized, Joanna washed up her single plate and coffee cup, dried them and placed them back in the cupboard. When she had lived in Toronto with three children and an overly packed schedule, she'd been a dreadful housekeeper. But up here in the cabin she was determined that things would be easier if she kept her small household under control.

Town and chores could wait; the sun and the forest were beckoning. She pulled on her heavy boots and raincoat, and for the first time since her arrival trudged up the driveway and down the road. The welcome sun was shining in a cloudless blue sky but the ground was drenched and the forest foliage saturated by many days of rain. So many drops fell from the trees that it might as well have been raining again. Joanna pulled up her hood, shoved her hands in her pockets and walked on.

To her city ears the silence in the woods was total. But slowly, gradually, like a beautiful butterfly emerging from the darkness of the cocoon, Joanna's senses tuned in to the rustle of wind through the trees, the shifting and settling of branches and the scurry of small animals in the undergrowth. Occasional flashes of sunlight dancing on the blue expanse of water shone through a thinning in the trees, but otherwise she was surrounded by the heavy stillness of the forest. She passed a few cabins, but encountered no other humans. The dark woods were thick with the sweet, rich scent of decaying undergrowth, mixing with a hint of wood smoke that drifted lazily from the chimneys of some of the properties barely visible through the thin, leafless trees. She breathed the fragrance in deeply, and kicked at piles of dead leaves underfoot to hear them crunch.

The beautiful emptiness of her surroundings was comforting and once again Joanna congratulated herself on making the move north.

As she walked, that strange, unnamable, prickly feeling of being watched touched the base of her spine. She stood still in the roadway, her breath caught in her throat and looked about, trying to appear casual. Nothing and no one were in sight.

A swift, cold wind whipped up the dead vegetation lying in the road so that the colored leaves swirled around and around in little eddies at her feet. The chill air, which only minutes ago had been sun soaked and warm, pierced through her raincoat. Then it was gone, the wind died and the leaves settled back to the ground. Joanna carried on with her walk.

Had she lingered a moment longer she would have seen a thickening in the woods, a place where the black shadows under the trees formed for an instant into something blacker, something with depth and movement. Then it too disappeared and the forest settled.

The furious barking of a dog announced the animal long before it rushed out of the woods to stand in the road howling. It was a good-sized animal, tall and muscular and heavily built. Part Malamute she guessed, with perhaps a bit of German shepherd thrown in. The eyes stood out in sharp contrast against the dark face, a strange, disconcerting color. A pale shade of ice blue.

The dog curled back its upper lip to show off an extremely impressive set of teeth and fangs, and growled low in its throat. Joanna stood stock-still. She had read somewhere that you were supposed to stare an aggressive dog in the eye…or was it avoid all eye contact with the threatening beast? She couldn't remember. Fortunately the dog dropped the aggressive posture and crept toward her, nose twitching and bushy tail wagging.

"Hello there," Joanna said. She was about to pat it behind the ears but hesitated. It could be wild.

"Rocky, Rocky, stop that! Leave the lady alone."

At the sound of the woman's voice the dog turned and eagerly ran back into the woods. It emerged again a moment later, this time followed by a tiny old woman. She wore a floppy yellow rain hat with matching slicker and a pair of thick boots that reached almost to her knees and were coated with a liberal covering of mud. A stout walking stick was clenched in one gnarled, liverspotted hand but her step was strong and firm.

"Well, hello. How nice to see you again, Ms. Hastings." The woman held out her hand. "Maude Mitchell, we met in town."

"Oh, yes." Joanna took Maude's hand firmly in her own.

"What a nice day. Are you out for a walk?"

"Yes."

"Getting settled in all right?"

"Yes. I really must be heading back." Joanna had a tinge of guilt at the thought of how rude she must sound to her elderly neighbor but she could not and would not do anything to stop it. She had come to the north to be alone and recover from clinical depression. She had no desire for anyone's company and certainly did not intend to worry about their feelings. "Good-bye now."

"If you ever need anything, my granddaughter and I live just through the woods here a bit," Maude called to Joanna's retreating back.

Maude stood in the road for a long time, watching until the other woman rounded a bend and was out of sight. "Not too polite is she, Rocky?" she said to her dog. "Won't last long around here."

Rocky, sniffing lazily at a spot in the road where a family of deer had recently walked, said nothing.

THE DAYS PASSED in a gentle scam of hard work and quiet contemplation. After a period of initial panic and some writer's block, the software manual started to take shape. Joanna didn't like the product but good documentation would help to smooth out some of the rougher spots. She only hoped that she could produce good documentation.

September moved into October, and as October faded the days were getting shorter and colder. The last scarlet and golden leaves fell mutely from the trees leaving the woods bare and vulnerable, sleeping restlessly as they waited for the first soft light of spring. Puddles of rainwater froze on the porch overnight and the roar of motorboats was no longer heard across the lake.

The supply of firewood stacked in neat rows beneath the cabin was dwindling at an alarming rate; with a great deal of trepidation Joanna eyed the axe leaning up against a scarred old stump, used, she assumed, for chopping.

She saw no one for days at a time, unless she ventured into town for groceries and wine. Some days, particularly if it was raining, Joanna didn't even bother to get dressed, but sat at the computer all day in her white terry cloth dressing gown, a gift from Wendy. After dinner she curled up by the stove engrossed in a novel.

Her oldest daughter continued to call a couple of times a week but to Joanna's relief she made no further mention of her mother returning to Toronto.

One evening, after a rare day of bright sunshine and warm winds, when the dinner dishes were all washed and put away, Joanna turned off the outside lights and stepped out on the porch. A combination of clear night and the moon not yet risen created perfect conditions for a display of the heavens. In the east?—west?—the blanket of stars in the Milky Way was so thick it was difficult to distinguish one individual star from another. But in the opposite sky, each star twinkled clear and distinct. The biggest of the stars reflected off the still waters of the lake far below like diamonds resting on a pane of flawless black glass. In the cabin the CD player came to the end and clicked off. The silence was complete. Too soon the cold crept through her thin sweater and Joanna was reluctantly forced back inside.

She curled up on the couch by the stove, and happily retreated into the delights of her mystery novel. She was reaching for a glass of wine placed strategically within reach on the coffee table when an abrupt gust of wind rattled the old cabin's joints. Joanna looked up in surprise to see sheets of rain cascading across the windows.

Now where did this come from? she thought. She placed her book aside and walked over to look out into the night. Trees swayed wildly under the force of the wind. Overhead she could hear the smaller branches tearing frantically at the cabin roof as if desperate to gain entry. Rain fell in torrents; a stream was already rushing down the hillside in a race to the lake. A flash of sheet lightning lit up the sky over the water; the roar of thunder sounding at the same instant.

Joanna tossed another log onto the fire. The temperature was dropping fast. She returned to her book, shaking her head in amazement: she had never seen weather turn so fast.

A light scratching at the front door gently pierced through the noise of the storm. She put her book down once again and listened carefully. *Must be imagining it.* She returned to her novel. There it was again. *Perhaps a neighbor's cat trying to get in out of the storm.* She struggled to her feet and stumbled to the door. The noise stopped. Cracking the door open, she peered out but there was no animal in sight. Joanna returned to her place on the couch. As soon as she was seated the scratching sound started again. Again it stopped the moment she got to her feet. This time she did not open the door.

She returned to the couch; the scratching resumed yet again, louder and more persistent.

Joanna put aside all pretence of trying to read. She wrapped herself tightly in a blanket in an attempt to ward off the cold that crept over her out of nowhere. She sat immobile, staring at the door, until the scratching stopped. At the same instant the wind died down and the rain ceased.

It was a few minutes before she gathered enough nerve to creep back up to the window. The clouds were rolling back as quickly as they had advanced. In minutes the stars again hung soft and radiant in the clear night sky. Heart pounding in her chest, she opened the door carefully and glanced down. In front of the door a tiny puddle of rainwater slowly disbursed into the wooden planks of the porch.

THAT NIGHT she dreamt about her cabin. But it wasn't really her cabin, at least not as she knew it. It was early autumn; the leaves were in full color, the air heavy with the promise of a few more nice days before the darkness of winter settled in for good. There were more outbuildings than Joanna had seen. A shed collapsing along one side so that the door couldn't fit to anymore but flapped aimlessly in the wind day after day; a bit of a lean-to where a car or truck must have parked; a chicken coop approaching its last days of useful life. In her dream she drifted lazily into the shed, the door swinging open long enough to permit her entry. The building was full to overflowing, mostly a collection of rusty, long-unused farm implements. Only a small clutter of garden tools looked to have performed any useful work recently. Mice and spiders went about their business, ignorant of the visitor watching them. Disembodied,

Joanna floated out again. A few chickens scratched around in the dirt outside of the small coop, which didn't offer much of a challenge to any foxes that might wander by. A small patch of garden lay outside the chicken coop, with rows of corn stalks recently stripped of their harvest, turning brittle and golden in the autumn sun. Tomato plants, staked with rough wooden posts and torn up rags, were desperately trying to ripen the last of their rich fruit before the first killing frost. Underdeveloped orange pumpkins and scrawny yellow squash huddled under thick green stalks catching the last of the sun's rays. A woman in a torn old housedress bent over the largest of the pumpkins and with a sharp kitchen knife sliced steadily at the tough stalk. At her feet, a filthy toddler, snot running in a steady stream from her nose, knees torn and bleeding, dress grimy with garden dirt, held a wriggling worm up to her face for closer inspection.

Joanna shifted and tossed on the couch as a rattling old pickup truck turned into the drive from the road. Clattering down the driveway as if it were only seconds away from giving up the ghost, it rattled to a stop right where Joanna's Toyota should now be sitting, and then a gaggle of teenaged boys leapt out of the back. Not much cleaner than the toddler in the garden, they swept down the path and into the cabin. One boy broke away from the others and joined the woman and little girl in the vegetable patch. He pulled the remnants of a clean handkerchief from the pocket of his much-patched pants and wiped at the girl's face. She smiled up at him and lifted her arms in anticipation. He did not disappoint her, but swung the toddler in a wide arc above the ground. She screeched with delight and the woman stopped her work long enough to smile at them.

Joanna drifted again and this time she had a good view of the cabin itself. Her cabin, but different. A wooden rocking chair sat on the front porch and a teenaged girl sat there. She

*tossed her shoulder-length dyed platinum blond hair, and
tucked one lock behind her ear. The hair was curled under in
a tight pageboy with a heavy section falling over her right eye
in the style of an old-time movie star whose name, even in her
dream, Joanna couldn't remember. The girl's face was thick
with pasty makeup and her lips were a slash of bright red. But
her bone structure was good and underneath the layers of
cheap foundation her skin was clear and she would have been
pretty, if she didn't try so hard. She was dressed in a heavily
washed dull green housedress, clearly a hand-me-down by the
way it bagged under the arms and across her skinny bosom and
thin hips. A red scarf decorated with swirls of blue flowers was
knotted carefully at the neck of the old dress, in a hopeless
attempt to give it a bit of color, a touch of style. She stared in
contempt at the stream of boys as they scrambled up the steps
and poured into the cabin, ignoring her in their single-minded
search for something to eat.*

*A middle-aged man, almost bald, heavily beer-bellied,
dressed in a pair of continually patched overalls and a thick
flannel shirt, climbed out of the old truck's cab and made his
way to the cabin. He stopped for a moment at the top of the stairs
to glare malevolently at the girl in the rocking chair. She stared
back, eyes blazing with a cool blue fire, until he looked away.*

*The woman in the patch of garden cut through the vine and
struggled to settle the misshapen pumpkin under one arm then
followed him into the house.*

Joanna woke with a start and a stabbing pain in her side. She
found herself lying on the living room couch clutching the thin
blanket to her chest. Her back ached as she rolled over and
swung her feet onto the floor. She was stiff and cold and sore
all over. She had fallen asleep reading.

She shook memories of the dream out of her head, stretched

her arms and clambered off the couch. As she did every morning, Joanna looked out the window to check on the weather. It was another dull, gray day but there was no evidence of last night's sudden storm. The front porch and steps were dry with not a trace of the creek that had formed instantly during the night. *What a strange dream,* she thought, walking stiffly into the kitchen to put on the coffee, one hand pressing into the small of her back. Two strange dreams. A lost cat must have been scratching at her door looking for shelter and her restless sleep inserted the poor animal into her dreams. She would keep her eyes open for the cat.

THREE

A MONTH AFTER HER ARRIVAL at the cabin, Joanna awoke to a world of white and silence. The sunlight streaming through her bedroom window had a cheerful intensity it could only get when reflecting off fresh snow.

She saw the tiny tracks of birds on the porch rail, marking where they gathered under the well-stocked bird feeder. As she watched, a lone chickadee landed on the step of the feeder, his brown head bobbing cheerfully in enjoyment of his breakfast. A tender gust of wind ruffled the branches of the big pine nearest her window sending a shower of white powder drifting gently through the air. Sunlight danced through the flakes like the lights of an enormous Christmas tree.

Definitely not a working day.

Immediately after breakfast Joanna walked the length of the driveway, tied on her out-of-fashion cross-country skis and set off down the road. At first her movements were stiff and jerky, signs of how much she was out of practice. But she soon settled into her stride, picked up the pace and glided, if not perfectly smoothly at least with what she hoped was a bit of grace, through the woods. The morning sun was warm and she was soon unzipping her jacket and stuffing woolen mittens into her pockets.

She dusted a thin layer of snow off a large rock to make a place to sit while enjoying a snack of granola bars and orange juice. She closed her eyes and turned her face toward the welcome warmth of the sun. It was so pleasant, just sitting there enjoying the snowy silence, but all too soon the biting cold of the rock reached tendrils through her pants and into her bottom, forcing her to her feet. She glanced at her watch. She had been skiing for almost two hours.

The return trip had barely begun before her arms and legs were complaining about the unaccustomed level of exercise. Joanna cursed herself. Any fool should know not to overdo it the first time out after so many years. A bank of thick, storm-tossed clouds blotted out the sun and an icy wind whipped against her cheeks. Her breathing was laborious and her fingers cold. Over the weeks since her fall she had almost forgotten about the sore wrist but the effort of digging the tips of her poles into the snow was becoming too much for the joint. Joanna was thoroughly miserable and swore at every laborious step.

She pushed away an unwanted image of herself buried beneath a mound of snow on the side of the road, nothing but a ski pole sticking up, forgotten until spring thaw. In the back of her mind she could hear Wendy's voice promising not to call to check up on her every day.

With a tiny shiver of delight she heard a car coming up behind her. At last, a sign of human habitation. The rushing warmth of relief coursing through her body caught her by surprise; she had been determined to get as far away from civilization as she could. She did not expect to welcome it back with quite so much enthusiasm. She skied over to the side of the road to let them pass. Instead the car slid to a halt and Maude Mitchell leaned out.

"You're quite a way from home, Ms. Hastings. I think it's getting colder, can I offer you a ride?"

Joanna accepted gratefully, stuffing her skis and poles into the back seat of the woman's battered old Chevy.

They traveled in silence most of the way. Now that she was returning home in comfort, Joanna was amazed at how far she had skied.

The old car clattered to a stop at the top of the hill overlooking her cabin. Maude switched off the engine and got out to help with the skis.

"Well, thank you for the ride."

"It was no trouble." Maude smiled but made no move to get back in her car.

"Uh, would you like to come in for a cup of tea?" Joanna forced herself to remember her manners. Particularly as it would appear that she couldn't exist entirely by herself up here, after all.

"Why yes, that would be nice."

"YOU'VE MADE THIS PLACE quite comfortable, Ms. Hastings," Maude said as Joanna placed her big pottery teapot and a plate of cookies on the scarred old kitchen table. "I was last in here about fifteen years ago. Just when old John McKellan started to go funny. It was sure a dump then."

"It's Joanna, please. How do you mean, funny?" Her interest was tweaked.

"Funny in the head, I mean. Nice tea this. His wife died about thirty years ago. I remember her clearly. Everyone liked her. It was hard on old John, very hard, he adored her. Never got over her passing. He wasn't interested in marrying again. Sent his son off to his sister in North Bay to raise. Just sat in this cabin all the day long." Maude shook her head sadly at the memories. "He did a few odd jobs to raise enough money to go drinking at O'Reilly's bar every Friday night. Other than that he didn't have anything to do with anyone. Being alone isn't good for a person. God didn't mean for any human being to live alone. People need other people around them. Finally old John went a bit crazy."

Joanna shifted uncomfortably in her seat; she wanted to live alone. "Where is he now?"

"Well, as I say he went a bit crazy. Didn't mean no harm to anyone, I'm sure. We all just left him be for many years, but then he started creeping around in the woods at night carrying a lantern. Scared a few folks half to death. Rachel Parmeter looked out her bedroom window one night and there was John staring in at her. Of course Rachel made a big to-do of it. Told everyone how John ought to be locked up. Rachel never could pass up the chance to be the center of attention."

"And…"

"Well, John's son came up from the city and put old John into an old folks home in North Bay. Poor old John, he must miss the woods something awful." Maude frowned at the thought. "It would sure be the death of me, to be taken out of these woods."

"You mean he's still alive?"

"Oh, yes. Last I heard. Stuck in some retirement home." Her upper lip curled as if she could taste the words on her tongue. "Like a worn out old slipper. Somewhere in the city with a room overlooking a parking lot, I wouldn't doubt. Not a fitting end for a proud man of the woods like John, let me tell you. John's son used the cabin as a summer cottage for a few years and then decided to sell the cabin. 'Course nobody would want to buy it. Too far away from the city, and no jobs around here anymore. So he cleaned it up."

"And rented it to me," Joanna said.

Maude peered into her teacup. "Any more tea in that pot, Joanna?"

She rose and poured more water into the kettle to boil and refresh the pot. She remembered the feeling of being watched that first time she walked down the road, the strange scratching the night of the storm. No lost cat had ever appeared. "Uh, does he ever come up here any more? To have a look at the old place I mean."

Maude looked up, astonished at the question. "Of course not. They're watched closely at those places I understand. And if he did get away he would have no way of getting here, too far to walk. You ski much?" She changed the subject abruptly.

"No, not now."

"But you did, before?"

"I was keen on cross-country once. I was on the team at university. Of course cross-country wasn't anywhere near as popular then as it is now. I mean thirty years ago you rarely heard of anyone doing cross-country just for fun. My coach said I had what it took. He said if I kept on training I might even be able to compete one day." Joanna's voice trailed off.

"So, what happened?"

"I got married."

"Were you sorry?"

"Later I was. Of course at the time it was just so exciting to be getting married. But I have always wondered what I could have done. I wonder what it would be like to compete at the Olympics?" Joanna pushed the thoughts to the back of her mind. Better not to think about what might have been. She didn't know why she was suddenly saying all this to a total stranger. Embarrassed at herself, she changed track abruptly. "I still have some work to do this afternoon. So if you don't mind…"

Maude failed to take the hint and nodded toward the now-boiling kettle. "Water's ready. What sort of work do you do?"

Joanna favored her right leg as she walked to the stove. She would be a physical wreck tomorrow. She poured hot water into the teapot and placed it on the table in front of her visitor. "I write computer documentation."

"Not romance novels?" Maude served herself another cup. Joanna grinned, sliding back into her chair. "Afraid not."

"Too bad." The old woman glanced around the room with interest. "I notice that you have quite a fancy computer over there. Do you know a lot about computers?"

"I know a lot about personal computers."

Maude stared thoughtfully into her tea for a few moments. The sound of wheels turning in the older woman's head was almost audible.

"My granddaughter lives with me. She isn't doing well at school and I'm worried that she won't be able to get into a university or community college anywhere."

"Is your granddaughter the girl you were with in the store that day?" Joanna gathered up the tea things and stacked them on the edge of the table. It was all she could do not to snatch the half-empty cup out of Maude's liver-spotted hand. As soon as the conversation turned to the purple-haired girl, it was time for the guest to be gone.

"Yes, that's Tiffany. I would like her to learn something about computers. If she has any chance of getting anywhere in this life, she has to be able to work with computers. Least that's what everyone says. I don't know much about life outside of this town myself any more." Maude sipped the last of her tea. "Could you teach her?" she asked, her voice low. Afraid to ask.

Joanna stared in horror. An image of the girl with her jeans falling around her hips, the hideous purple hair and the nose ring flashed into her mind. "No. No, I don't teach. Sorry."

"I would pay whatever you wanted."

"No thank you."

"Would fifty dollars an hour be all right?"

Joanna pushed her chair back and got to her feet. "I don't teach and I don't like teenagers. Thank you for the offer, but no."

This time Maude took the hint. "Well, if you change your mind, let me know. I would sure like to see Tiffany learn something useful. Let me jot down my phone number for you." Maude dug in her large handbag for a pen and scrap of paper. "You should really have my number anyway. In case of an emergency, I mean. We all have to look out for our neighbors up here, you know."

Joanna accepted the scribbled phone number with a twinge of gratitude and nodded her thanks. She realized now that it probably wasn't such a good idea to be totally isolated, as had been her original plan. A watchful neighbor would be nice, as long as she kept her distance.

She watched Maude walk up the path to her car and felt bad, really bad. The old woman was trying to be kind, no doubt about that. Joanna wanted to run after her, crying out apologies for her rudeness. But that would involve explanations and Joanna was never one to confide her private feelings to anyone, and certainly not to a near-total stranger. The girl, Tamara? Tammy? Tiffany was a sharp reminder of Joanna's own lost teenager and far too likely to probe at painful wounds that Joanna tried, and not very successfully at that, to keep buried very, very deep.

After Maude left Joanna limped stiffly into the kitchen to wash up the tea things. Her arms and left wrist were aching and her thighs felt like they were on fire. She pinned the scrap of paper with the phone number up on the corkboard over her desk, tossed the dishes into the sink and collapsed back into her chair.

THE MORNING'S SUN had disappeared under a blanket of heavy black clouds, leaving not even a memory of warmth. It was starting to snow again, not gentle fat flakes this time, but sharp brittle slashes of ice-filled pellets. The temperature in the cabin was dropping fast. Joanna struggled to her feet and lifted a log, which was about the weight of her car, to put into the wood stove. It was the last piece of firewood. With a groan she struggled into her snow boots and coat. A set of rickety steps led down the back of the cabin. The building stood on legs of concrete blocks so that it rested about four feet above the ground. A low alcove underneath the main building provided storage space for firewood, an old boat motor, a shiny new barbecue which looked to have never been used (at least by anything bigger than the spiders that lately had taken up residence), the hot water tank, and many assorted odds and ends. It also provided a nice dry home for (as well as the spiders), field mice, chipmunks and Joanna dared not think what else. Bent double she clambered under the cabin and seized a heavy log, then another. Every step ached as Joanna backed out of the alcove and crawled up the stairs with her burden. Lugging her load of wood up the steps, she fondly remembered her comfortable, warm, cozy home in Toronto. Central heating, air-conditioning, everything right there at the push of a button. For a moment she considered flinging the log aside and piling all her belongings back into the car for a mad dash to civilization. The thought of Wendy and Elaine's chorus of "I told you so" returned her to the task at hand.

On her last trip out she stood too soon and with a teeth-rattling crack her head met the underside of the cabin floor. She swore furiously and kicked a piece of loose bark at a squirrel that dared to laugh at her. Now there was no part of her body that didn't ache. She continued backing out of the enclosed space and hoped she would have enough wood to get through the night.

FOUR

"Sorry, Joanna. It's just that no one can make a decision around here anymore." Fred Blanchard, Joanna's old boss, sighed with frustration. "You know what things are like. Everyone who was worth anything in that department took a package and left long ago. All they do know is to strike committees to generate more paper. I'm doing what I can, you know that."

Joanna shifted the phone to her other shoulder and rubbed her arm. "Of course I know, Fred. It's so difficult, not knowing if this is going to happen or not."

"I think that you would be better off not to count on getting the contract. It still might happen. I know that the job needs to be done. But Hell may well freeze over before that bunch come to a decision."

"Thanks anyway, Fred. I appreciate what you're doing for me."

"Only because I know that you're the best person for the job. Gotta run now, the first of today's several meetings starts at eight. Seems like that's all I do anymore, go to meetings. Maybe I should come up there and join you, eh?"

Joanna laughed. "Too far away from the tennis clubs and the espresso bars for you, Fred."

"Bye now."

Joanna resisted the urge to fling the phone against the wall, instead placing it back in the cradle gently. Fred was, as always, charming, friendly, helpful, but she knew from long acquaintance that his veneer had as much substance as a single drifting snowflake. Fred did absolutely nothing that was not in his own best interest. It worried her, leaving her prospects in his hand, but as far as she could see, she had no choice.

When she left the company she had been all but promised the contract to write the documentation associated with a huge project now underway. It was a large job and there wasn't anyone else with more knowledge of how the company's computer systems worked. Joanna sighed. *"All but" just doesn't cut it in the business world.*

She picked up the printouts of the last revision of the home-accounting manual. It was looking good. She should be ready to e-mail the finished product to her agency later this week. Then what? She needed to make money, and soon. She didn't have another contract lined up yet. If she didn't get something she would be in trouble.

Of course she could consider the teaching offer from Maude. Fifty dollars an hour was extraordinary. She wouldn't have thought that Maude had that kind of money. This must be some awful kid. She made note of the phone number posted beside the window.

Maude was delighted to hear from her. "I'll bring Tiffany over this afternoon, and you two can talk about what you want to do and set up some sort of schedule. Would two o'clock be all right?"

"Yes, two is good. Uh, you did say fifty dollars an hour?"

"Is that enough?" Maude sounded anxious.

"It's fine. See you at two."

The prospect of some real money coming in helped to put Joanna's mind at rest and she made good progress on finishing up the latest section of the manual while waiting for her two o'clock appointment.

Right on the dot she heard the sound of the old car turning into the driveway. The visitors' boots crunched on the snow as they climbed the steps to the porch. As she reached to open the door, Joanna heard the whining.

"This is soooo stupid, Grandma. Computers are for boys and losers. What a waste of time."

Joanna threw open the door. Maude smiled brightly—her granddaughter pouted. The girl was still dressed in the uniform of discontented kids everywhere: massively oversized blue pants, heavy, black, Doc Martin lace-up boots and a huge flannel shirt. She was tiny, not much more than five feet tall and, from what anyone could see through the baggy clothes, thin and small-boned. Her winter coat was unbuttoned and her hands were already turning red with the cold. It was not cool, Joanna knew, to ever wear anything at all sensible such as mittens, scarves or a hat. At least, not until the temperature plummeted to at least minus 40 degrees. Her long hair hung straight across her face and down her back; it was dyed an amazing shade of purple. Dull brown roots peeked through at the top of her head. Her nail polish was black with silver sparkles. But her eyes were bright and her complexion was clear, with only the nose ring to mar the surface. Her arms were crossed tightly across her thin chest, her shoulders stiff.

"Joanna, this is my granddaughter, Tiffany Jordan. Tiffany, this is Joanna. She has kindly agreed to teach you a bit about computers, dear. That's very nice of her, isn't it?" Maude beamed.

Tiffany grunted.

"I won't be staying, I have some errands to run in town. I'll let you two get to know each other. I'll pick you up in an hour. How does that sound, dear?"

Tiffany grunted again. Maude took that as agreement for she turned and bustled down the stairs waving good-bye the entire way to the car.

Joanna and Tiffany stood at the door and watched as Maude backed out of the driveway. Joanna sighed, "Come in."

Tiffany grunted for the third time and shrugged her shoulders as she walked into the cabin. She showed no interest in her surroundings, just plopped herself down on the couch to gaze intently at her nails.

Joanna sighed again. "For starters why don't you tell me what you know already. So I have some idea of where to start."

"I don't know nothing."

"You don't know anything about computers?"

"No."

"But haven't you taken some computers in school?"

"That stupid country hick school? They've only got a couple of real old things. From the dark ages. But they think their computers are soooo special." Tiffany rummaged in her bag and pulled out a pack of cigarettes.

"Please don't smoke. Not in my house."

The teenager shrugged and stuffed the pack into her bag.

"Even an older computer has many of the features of newer models," Joanna said through gritted teeth. "You can still learn a lot on them."

"Well, they don't let me near them."

"Why not?"

The girl admired her nails. "'Cause I told them that I didn't want to use their stupid computers. So they said, 'Fine, don't then.' So I don't. My school in Toronto, they had good computers and lots of them."

"Why don't you tell the school that you would like to be allowed to use the computers again. Your grandma shouldn't have to pay for private lessons if you could be doing the same at school."

Tiffany looked directly at Joanna for the first time since her arrival. "I'm not going to tell them anything. I hate them all there. My grandma doesn't have to pay for me to come here. I told her I didn't want to come. Computers are for losers. I'm not a loser."

Joanna groaned inwardly. She wondered if she could be paid enough to deal with this angry child.

"Nevertheless, you're here now. Come over and sit by me and we can begin. But first take off your coat."

Tiffany rolled her eyes at the ceiling but dragged a chair over to the desk and shrugged out of her coat. She slouched in the chair, legs straight out, arms hanging at her sides.

"To begin with, you have to sit up straight to type. Can you type?"

"No."

"My children all took typing. Keyboarding they call it in the schools now. Didn't you have to take it?"

"Yea, but I failed."

Joanna was not surprised. "There is no point in starting any of the software packages if you can't even type yet. So I think that first I will have to teach you. I have a typing tutorial program in here somewhere. Move the mouse to where it says, 'Start.' That's right. That pulls up all the functions you will need. Move the mouse up here to 'Programs' and that will open another menu. Now choose 'Mrs. Beeton's Typing Tutorial.' You choose by clicking the left mouse button again."

"Have you got any games on this thing?"

"Yes, I have games."

"Can I play them?"

"No, certainly not. You're here to learn some skills, not play games. First let me tell you what kind of computer this is..."

"Not interested."

"Oh, fine. Just follow the instructions in the typing tutorial as they come up on the screen."

Tiffany poked at the keys lazily for about five minutes. Then she stood up suddenly. "I have to go to the bathroom."

"Past the kitchen, to the left."

The girl was gone for a long time. When she returned it was noticeable that she had reapplied her makeup.

"I don't think your grandma wants to pay me for my time while you fix your makeup, you know."

Tiffany shrugged. Joanna was getting tired of that shrug. It was a sharp, very painful reminder of her own troubled teenager.

"So, she has lots of money. She can afford it. She sure doesn't spend any of it on me." She wandered casually around the living room, looking at things. She stopped by the table with the photographs and picked up the picture of Wendy. "Is this your daughter?"

"Yes it is."

She put Wendy's photo back onto the table and picked up the next one. "And your son?"

"Yes."

Then she chose the photo of Alexis.

"Who's this?"

"My other daughter."

"What's her name?"

"Alexis." Joanna rose to her feet, her fists were clenched at her sides and she was trying to breathe steadily. "Put the picture down, please, and come back to work."

"How old is she?"

"Sixteen."

"Why doesn't she live with you?"

A cold fist closed over Joanna's heart. Tiffany had crossed the line into uncomfortable territory. "Put that picture down now."

"'Course I can see why she wouldn't want to live here. This town is such a dump. Everyone here is a loser. Alexis is lucky she doesn't have to live here."

Joanna rushed forward to grab the picture out of Tiffany's hand. The girl moved to snatch it back but instead knocked it flying across the room to fall to the floor with a crash. The sound of breaking glass echoed throughout the small room.

Joanna gasped and fell to her knees. She gently placed the broken frame to one side and frantically picked up the shards of glass.

Tiffany had the grace to sound embarrassed. "Gosh, I'm sorry. You can buy another frame anywhere."

"Look," Joanna said through clenched teeth. "You don't want to be here and I don't want you here. So I think you had better go."

"But it's not time yet." The girl shifted anxiously from foot to foot.

"Good-bye. You can wait for your grandmother on the road. Or better yet, walk home. Tell her that you're not interested in learning and I don't want to waste any of my time on you." Joanna sat back on her haunches and glared at the teenager. "Now get out."

Tiffany grabbed her coat and struggled to put it on. A large logo of the Chicago Bulls was featured prominently on the back. "Lady, I can see why your kids don't live with you. Lighten up. It's only a picture frame. I'm not interested in learning about your stupid computer anyway." She slammed the door on the way out, rattling the windowpanes.

Joanna sunk to the floor and carefully brushed broken glass out of the frame. She sat there for a long time rocking the picture in her arms as large silent tears crept down her cheeks.

FIVE

"YOOHOO, ANYBODY HOME!"

"Just a minute. Hold on, I'll be right there." Joanna rushed out of her bedroom pulling on her robe and trying to flatten her unruly bed-head of curls. To her surprise Nancy Miller, the grocery store clerk, stood smiling at the porch door. She wore a faux-fur coat that was the absolute latest in fashion in the 1970s, with a matching hat. Her face was ruddy from the cold but she was beaming brightly. She towered over the old man who stood stone-faced at her side, barely reaching her fake-furred shoulder. He was dressed in working man's clothes, well worn but clean, a cloth cap with pull-down ear covers protecting his head from the cold. A scruffy gray beard covered most of his face. He was so thin he appeared almost skeletal beside the larger-than-life Nancy.

"Bit early for a visit, isn't it?" Joanna asked.

"Is it?" Nancy waved her hands. "Sorry if we woke you. But I'm on my way into work and thought it would be a good time to stop by." She paused expectantly.

Damned if I'm going to offer uninvited guests coffee at seven a.m., Joanna thought. She stood firmly in the doorway and waited for Nancy to continue.

"This here is Luke Snelgrove. Luke lives further up the road. I know that you're out here by yourself like, and I thought that maybe Luke could help out a bit. You know, shovel snow, repair things, chop wood. That sort of thing."

Luke nodded. No expression crossed his face.

"Chop wood," Joanna echoed. "Please come in. Would you like a cup of coffee?"

They stepped eagerly into the cabin. Joanna went into the kitchen to put on the coffeepot while Nancy and Luke removed their boots and hung their coats on the wooden coat stand by the door. Luke sat at the table immediately but Nancy moved through the living room, eyeing everything.

"My, you've done this place up nice. Oh, here is your computer. Is it ever fancy. Is must be one of them PCs."

"Yes. It's a Pentium three with 633 megahertz, 256 megabytes of memory and a 20 GIG hard drive. It has a CD ROM and a 56 K Baud Modem." The instant the words were out of her mouth Joanna wished she could call them back. It was a condescending remark.

Nancy didn't seem to mind. She waved her hand. "Oh my, lots of numbers. Is this where you do your writing?"

"Yes."

"I would love to read something that you write some day. Maybe I could make some suggestions."

Joanna caught herself before she made another smart remark. "Perhaps you could. Coffee's ready."

She placed coffee mugs on the table along with a plate of bran muffins.

"This is wonderful coffee," Nancy said. She took a bit of muffin. "Umm, great muffin. Did you make it yourself?"

"Yes."

Nancy helped herself to another. "Now, I know that Luke would be happy to do any sort of odd job that you might have around the place. You can be sure he will charge you a fair price and do real good work."

"I need some wood chopped," Joanna said. "The stack under

the cabin is being used up faster than I thought it would and I was getting worried about having to chop it all myself."

Luke sipped at his coffee and nodded. He did not take a muffin.

"Would you like to start today, Luke?" Nancy asked.

Luke nodded.

Joanna smiled awkwardly. Couldn't he talk?

"How about if I just leave you here 'cause I have to be getting to work now. You can walk home when you're finished, can't you?" Nancy said.

Luke nodded again.

After a third muffin, Nancy pushed herself away from the table. Joanna walked her to the door. While Nancy struggled with coat, hat, mittens and scarf Joanna whispered, "Can't Luke talk?"

Nancy looked at her in surprise, "'Course he can talk. He just ain't had nothing to say, yet. Bye now. Bye Luke."

Luke waved.

The morning passed quickly as Joanna typed up letters to computer industry magazines outlining proposals for articles she would like to write and surfed the internet looking for contract positions. She enjoyed working to the steady thud of the axe chewing up logs outside. She sat struggling over the proper wording of one of her letters for several moments, then got up for another cup of coffee while she thought about it.

She stood at the kitchen window waiting for the coffee filter to do its magic and watched Luke hard at work in the back. For such a little, old fellow he was remarkably energetic.

She opened the back door to call Luke in for a coffee. His thanks were so effusive that she was glad she remembered her manners.

Again they sat down at the table—this time Luke accepted a muffin.

"Have you lived around here for long?" Joanna asked.

"Whole life," Luke replied. Without Nancy to speak for him Luke's conversation apparently consisted of the shortest possible sentences.

"Are you related to Nancy?"

"Sister's daughter."

They sat in silence for several minutes while Joanna sipped her coffee and tried desperately to think of something else to say.

Finally, Luke cleared his throat. "People in town are saying you're gonna teach Maude Mitchell's granddaughter to use the computer. That right?"

"Well, I'm not sure about that."

"Stay away from her. That girl is no good. She'll do nothing but break her old grandma's heart."

Joanna was taken aback at the vehemence in his voice. "A few computer skills might do her some good."

"Nothing'll do that girl any good but time in the county jail," Luke said. "Just the look of her is enough to tell you what kind of girl she is."

"Lots of teenagers dress like that these days, or worse. You should see them in Toronto." Unexpectedly she found herself coming to Tiffany's defense.

"Well this ain't Toronto. And that kind don't belong here. Thanks for the coffee. I'll be getting to work now." He slammed the back door on the way out.

Joanna remained at the table, stunned. What could Maude Mitchell's granddaughter have done to so rouse Luke's anger? Whatever it was, it was none of her business. Joanna resolved to keep as far away from Tiffany Jordan as she could.

MID-NOVEMBER AND another snowfall blanketed the landscape. This one was heavy and laid a white carpet across the country-side that would probably last until spring.

A few small contracts had come in, mostly from her contacts in the computer world. The work kept Joanna busy and her head above water—just—but she desperately hoped for a big job that would promise some steady income. Fred Blanchard continued to put her off. Work was apparently going very badly on the big job, several of the top programmers had quit all at once and they were scrambling to find replacements. But earlier in the week he had called to set up a meeting with the powers-that-be to discuss the documentation and manuals as well as additions to the company's web pages.

Joanna filled the bird feeder with seed and scattered a handful of leftovers onto the ground for the squirrels and anyone else who might be in need of a snack. Out of the corner of her eye she caught a glimpse of movement in the woods. She held her breath and turned her head, trying not to make a sound. She hoped that it was the fox she had seen only that once and had been looking out for ever since. She gasped in astonishment. A deer stood at the edge of the forest, sniffing the air carefully, not moving. Joanna stood in awe, watching the beautiful animal as she checked her surroundings for signs of danger. Then, with a flash of dappled brown and white rump, she dashed across the path that led down to the lake and was gone.

Joanna moved her head in a bow of good-bye, picked up the snow shovel and trudged through heavy drifts up the hill to her car. Because the radio had predicted "light snow of two to five centimeters," she parked the car close to the road last night so as not to have to shovel out the whole drive. This was no two to five centimeters, more like twenty-five, and certainly not light. The snow was thick and wet. Every shovel-full was an effort. She stopped frequently, placing a hand on her aching back and stretching backward to work out some of the kinks. A fierce wind was all that remained of the storm. The cold sliced through Joanna's mittens and snow pants and sent its cold fingers searching out openings in her scarf. Her fingers and toes were freezing and as she worked she gradually lost contact with the end of her nose.

At long last the top of the driveway was clear and she was digging out the car itself when she heard the groan of the snowplow making its slow progress down the road. The driver waved at her as he passed and she lifted her shovel in reply. Then she bent once again to dig through the packed snow deposited by the plow. When last in town Joanna noticed several flyers posted on telephone poles and on the grocery store bulletin board advertising shoveling or plowing of driveways, but she thought she would save money by doing it herself. She leaned on her shovel and wiped her brow with her mittens. She would reconsider the expense.

At long last Joanna was able to stand back and admire her handiwork. Lifting her shovel once more she fought her way back through the snow to the cabin.

She picked up the phone and trailed its long cord into the kitchen. She put the kettle on for a cup of hot chocolate and punched in Wendy's number.

"It's stopped snowing, dear. I'm going to have a quick dinner and then I'll be leaving."

"Oh, Mom, it will be so late by the time you get here. Perhaps you should cancel your appointment and come down another time."

"I can't do that, Wendy. They have been so hesitant to come to a decision about this that I have to strike while the iron is hot. I'll be fine. If it's all right with you I'll stay an extra night so we can spend some time together before I have to come back."

"That's fine."

"See you soon then, dear. Say hello to Robert for me."

"Uh, Robert's not here right now. He, uh, had to go away for a couple of days."

Very interesting, Joanna thought as she hung up the phone. Wendy's strong, confident voice changed tone as soon as her husband was mentioned.

Joanna fried two eggs and heated a can of beans. Time for a quick bite and then be on her way. The meeting with Fred was scheduled for first thing tomorrow morning in Toronto. Her plans were to leave for Toronto early this morning, have dinner with Wendy at one of their favorite restaurants and spend the night at the apartment, but the snowstorm had put an end to that. Now she would be driving through the winter's night, arrive late at Wendy's, tired and harassed, and then be irritable for her interview in the morning.

After her meal, gulped standing up over the kitchen sink, she headed out the door, power suit tucked into her suitcase. Out of the corner of her eye she saw Luke's battered old cap resting on the windowsill. The last time he was here, he placed it on the table while she counted out his pay, and left it behind. Joanna hesitated; she intended to take it back to him but never got around to it. Now she was going away for a couple of days. His cupboard was probably full of identical caps all lined up in a neat row; if he wanted it he would have come back for it, wouldn't he? She started to close the front door behind her, then ran back in and grabbed the hat. It would only take a couple of minutes to drop it off. She locked the cabin door and struggled up the hill with the heavy suitcase, the cap under her arm. The night was inky black. Thick storm clouds still covered the sky, blocking out any light from moon or stars.

She drove carefully, hoping that Luke would have shoveled his driveway. He hadn't. She couldn't even tell where the driveway was.

Joanna sat in the car, the cap on her lap. It seemed like an awful lot of trouble to try to wade through hip-high snowdrifts in the middle of the night just to return a cap. She could see the outline of the cabin from the road, no lights were on. Wouldn't want to wake him up.

Placing the car into drive she caught a quick flash of red light flickering through the coal-black night. Then it was gone. She narrowed her eyes and peered into the darkness. There it was again. This time the red light didn't disappear.

Joanna wrenched the gears back into park and leapt out of her car. She ran to the edge of the road. Tongues of flame leapt into the sky behind Luke's cabin.

SIX

"FIRE!" SHE SCREAMED, "Fire!" But there was no one around to hear. She grabbed her cell phone and started to punch the buttons before she remembered: there was no 911 in this god-forsaken part of the world and she didn't know the fire department or police phone number. They were pinned to the cork bulletin board over her desk. Fat lot of help that was now. She dialed the only number she knew. Fortunately Maude Mitchell's number was an easy one to remember.

"Please be there," she whispered while the phone rang on.

Someone picked it up. Joanna didn't even wait for them to say hello. "Fire," she shouted, "at Luke Snelgrove's place. Call the fire department. Hurry." She threw the phone back into her car and ran.

Her heart was pounding with enough strength to burst through her chest. Thick, heavy snow pulled at her legs, trying to slow her down. Before she took ten steps she was out of breath. The flames were higher now, long red tongues reaching up into the night sky. Joanna couldn't tell if the cabin was on fire, or something behind it. She ran on.

"Fire, fire." She pounded at the front door, gasping for breath. "Luke, Luke, are you there?" There was no reply. The curtains weren't drawn. Hands forming a cup around her eyes she peered through the window. The only jacket she had ever seen him wear was tossed over a chair. *He must be inside,* she thought, trying to control her rising panic. *He wouldn't go out without a coat.*

She kicked the door furiously, screaming Luke's name all the time. Luke's cabin was even smaller than hers. She could see right through it and out the back window. The fire was still confined to the outside, but she could see the flames licking hungrily against the window, seeking a way in.

The wood in the old door gave way under her foot. Joanna pushed at the broken panels and cleared a space large enough to squeeze through. The moment she crashed into the cabin, the flames broke through the back wall. The shack was filling up with smoke fast. She stumbled into the room.

"Luke," she cried, "for God's sake where are you?"

Then she saw a foot sticking out over the edge of the old torn couch in the middle of the room. The old man lay on his back, covered in a rough blanket, snoring as if he didn't have a care in the world.

Joanna pounded on his chest furiously. "Wake up, Luke, wake up. Your house is on fire."

She would never be able to carry him. The whole back wall was now a sheet of flame. If Luke didn't wake up NOW, she would have to leave him.

She almost cried with relief when he groaned and tried to push her away.

She grabbed his arm and pulled. "Get up, Luke. Now. Fire!"

His eyes opened. "Jesus H. Christ," he screamed at the sight of the back end of his home, consumed in a wall of flames.

Luke stumbled to his feet. He was dressed only in a set of dirty, torn long underwear. Joanna grabbed the blanket and tossed it around his shoulders. She supported his arms and together they dashed through the smoke. She pushed Luke across the broken door and then stumbled after him. Staggering into the middle of the clearing in front of the cabin Joanna felt safe enough to collapse onto her stomach. She rolled over and lay in the snow, sucking fresh, clean air into her lungs. It tasted so good.

Luke sat down heavily beside her. "Jesus, my place. Look at my place." The old man began to cry.

Joanna rolled onto her back. The silence broken only by Luke's sobs and the crackle of flame, they watched the cabin burn. "We'd better move," she said when she could speak again. "The trees might catch."

"No chance of that," he said through his tears. "They're full of snow."

For a long time the only sound to be heard was the roar of fire. Then cars came to a screeching halt on the road and doors slammed as men leapt out and ran toward them. In the distance Joanna could hear the piercing cry of the fire truck.

"Goddammit, Luke, what's happened here?"

"Are you okay, Miss?" Tight with concern, the face of one of her neighbors peered into hers. She could only nod.

The volunteer fire department ran up, dragging equipment, stumbling through the snow. They turned their hoses on the blaze but it was too late. With a crash and shower of sparks that had them all hiding their eyes, the roof collapsed.

She didn't look up again until a warm mug was pressed into her hands.

"Here you go, dear. I think you need this." Maude Mitchell crouched in front of her clutching a battered thermos. Joanna accepted the mug gratefully. Steam drifted into the night air and the welcome warmth soaked into her frozen fingers. Maude pulled another cup out from her pocket and poured hot chocolate for Luke.

"You two had better get to the hospital," Maude suggested. "I'll drive."

Joanna and Luke both refused her offer.

"I'm fine, really," Joanna said. "Just a bit shaken up."

"So you must be," Maude replied. "Come back with me to my place anyway. We better get you warmed up. Luke, I still have some of Harvey's old work clothes in the shed somewhere. You can't wear that blanket the rest of the night."

Gratefully Joanna allowed herself to be lifted to her feet and led to Maude's car. It was so nice to be taken care of, like a child allowed to stay up late to watch the Canada Day fireworks but then too sleepy to make it home without aid. One of the men assured her that he would look after her car.

Maude settled Joanna in front of her stone fireplace with a hand-knitted afghan wrapped around her knees and a glass of brandy in her trembling hand. Maude also managed to find a pair of men's pajamas about three sizes too big for Luke and tried to pack him off to bed. But he would have none of it, and instead paced up and down the living room. Rocky walked in rhythm with every restless step.

"Quite a night." Maude threw another log on the fire and went to answer the knocking at her front door.

The Volunteer Fire Department, representatives of the Ontario Provincial Police and assorted helpers and hangers on filed in, stamping their feet and spreading snow all over Maude's immaculate hardwood floors. Rocky rushed about the room, frantic with delight at all these unexpected visitors.

Maude tossed a towel to the youngest of the men. "Mike, you wipe up that mess. The rest of you come and stand by the fire and warm yourselves."

In no time Maude produced gallons of coffee and hot chocolate and plates of sandwiches and cookies for her midnight visitors.

The man who had offered to drive Joanna's car home handed her the keys. She smiled her thanks.

The chief of the fire brigade sat down beside Joanna. "You're a lucky man, Luke," he said. "Lucky Joanna here was passing by."

Luke stopped walking and collapsed into a chair with a grunt, embarrassed at being the center of attention.

"I just wanted to return his cap." Joanna shivered at the memory.

"Any idea what caused the fire, Chief?" Maude asked, bringing in yet another plate of cookies. Joanna wondered where they all came from. Did Maude have an entire supply of food ready for any old time about 30 neighbors would show up needing to be fed?

"Not yet," he replied. "But it started for sure in the tool shed out back. That was a rotten old building anyway, it's burnt right to the ground now."

"Goddamn Roy McMaster." Luke leapt from his chair. "He set my place on fire, he tried to fry me." He shook a bony finger at a man rubbing his hands in front of the fire. So disheveled, he obviously had been dragged from a warm comfortable bed and out into the snow to the site of the fire. "He's been telling everyone he's gonna kill me for years. Now he tried to do it. You arrest him, Roy McMaster's the one."

"Who's that?" Joanna whispered to Maude.

"Bob Reynolds. Ontario Provincial Police."

"Now, Luke," the OPP officer said, turning reluctantly from the fire. "Don't go saying things like that. Not unless you have proof."

"Don't need no proof," Luke mumbled, but he settled back into his chair. "Ain't he always been saying he's gonna get me some day?"

One of the men who had simply wandered in hoping to be part of the excitement elbowed the man beside him. "No more than Luke's been promising to get Roy," he whispered.

"Well, we'll look into it. I'll go and talk to Roy tomorrow," Reynolds said.

Maude interrupted, "Luke, you've had one heck of a night. Why don't you get off to bed and we'll go over it all tomorrow? Ain't no one going to do nothing tonight." Carefully she raised the old man to his feet. In the huge pajamas he looked like a large, wrinkled baby. All the fight went out of him. He wilted before everyone's eyes as he allowed Maude to guide him down the hall to her spare room.

The men watched him go. When they heard the bedroom door shut someone spoke up. "Do you think Luke took a lamp out to the shed, then forgot about it when he went in?"

"Maybe," the fire chief said. "But that don't seem likely to me. Luke may be old, but he's not careless."

The men all nodded in agreement.

"He was awfully hard to wake up," Joanna said. "I was wondering if he might have been drinking."

"That's possible. Luke's been known to go on a bender now and again. But I still can't see him being careless."

"He doesn't keep anything in that shed that would just go up in flames," one of the firemen said, a reasonably young and handsome one. As he spoke he tossed a cookie to Rocky. The dog caught it in midair and swallowed it in one gulp, then innocently looked about for more. "I was in it a few months ago, returning a hammer my father borrowed. No paint, or oil rags—nothing like that. Just his tools and some firewood."

"Don't you be feeding any more cookies to that dog," Maude chided, reentering the room and settling into a scarred old rocking chair that claimed pride of place in front of the fire. "He's getting much too fat and lazy as it is."

The cookie-thrower lowered his head. "Yes, ma'am," he mumbled.

"The fire inspection people will be nosing around tomorrow," the chief said. "We'll know more then."

The front door opened with a crash and Tiffany flew in with a gust of wind. Eyes wild, she searched the faces in the crowded living room until she found her grandma sitting in her rocking chair. The girl settled back into her regular sneer. "What's going on? What are all you people doing here?"

"Luke's cabin burned down," Maude told her.

"Oh." Tiffany shrugged. This didn't affect her. She took the last cookie on the plate and started to walk out of the crowded room.

Bob Reynolds of the police stepped in front of her. "Where were you tonight, Tiffany?"

"Out," she replied.

"Out where?"

"What's it to you?" she demanded.

"Maybe nothing," he replied. "So where were you tonight?"

"Just hanging with some friends."

"What friends?"

"No one you know."

"I know most people around here."

"Well, my friends aren't from around this stupid town."

Joanna looked around the room. Every eye was on Tiffany. The pain etched into Maude's face was palpable.

"Were you down the road earlier? Say, near Luke's place?"

"No, we weren't down the road. Who would want to go near Luke's shack anyway? What a stupid question." She snapped her fingers and Rocky rushed over for a scratch.

Tiffany bent to rub the dog's ears. Reynolds tried to look into her face, but she gave all her attention to Rocky. "Were you and your friends taking drugs tonight?"

"No, we weren't taking drugs, not that it's any of your

business. You can't ask me that." Dog at her heels, she stormed out of the room. They could all hear the bedroom door slam.

An uncomfortable silence hung in the air, people shifted in their chairs.

"Now Bob, you can't go accusing Tiffany of anything," Maude said, her voice high and anxious. "She goes out lots of nights, people's houses don't burn down just because some teenagers are out having fun."

"Girl's all drugged up, Maude," he said. "Her pupils are the size of saucers."

Maude stood. "I'm very tired, and I'm sure Joanna is too. I think it's time you boys were all leaving."

One by one the men filed out, muttering thanks for the coffee and cookies. Bob Reynolds was the last to go.

"Think about it, Maude," he said.

Maude turned to Joanna, a frozen smile pasted on her face. "You are welcome to spend the night, dear. With Luke in the spare room I can only offer you the couch, but it should be comfortable enough."

Joanna struggled to her feet. "No, thank you. I will be more comfortable in my own bed. I can walk, it's not far."

Maude snorted. "I'll drive you. And not another word."

They drove the short distance through the snow-wrapped, dark forest. It was as silent inside the car as out. Joanna was relieved to see her car safely parked in her own driveway. She hesitated before getting out. "I think that Mr. Reynolds was way out of line. He virtually came right out and accused Tiffany of starting the fire. Right there in front of half the county. You were right to stand up for her."

Maude grimaced. "There's a lot of folks in this town what don't like Tiffany much. She's a difficult girl. She's led a hard life in so few years and she doesn't have much reason to trust people. But she's not dishonest and she would never try to hurt anyone." Maude looked Joanna in the eye. "She's a good girl, if people would only give her a chance."

"Good night, Maude. And thank you very much for the coffee and brandy."

"Good night, Joanna. Sleep well."

SEVEN

JOANNA GROANED AWAKE in a haze of aching muscles and thick thoughts, a persistent buzzing sounding in her ears. She recovered her senses just enough to reach for the phone. The receiver slipped out of her hands and clattered to the floor. She hauled it up by the cord.

"Hello?"

"Mom, where on earth are you? I sat up until two a.m. waiting for you, then fell asleep on the couch. Fred Blanchard's call woke me up."

"Oh, God!" Joanna was suddenly awake. She fumbled with her watch. "What time is it?"

"Ten o'clock. He said you were supposed to be at the office at nine for a morning meeting. What on earth are you doing still in bed?"

Joanna sunk back into the pillows. "It's a long story, Wendy. But there was a fire last night. Not here, the house down the road. I was up half the night."

"A fire. Are you all right? Were you in it?"

"Don't worry, dear. I'm fine. It was just all the excitement. Half the town driving up and down the road. Fire engines, police cars, the whole story. No one was hurt, but the house was totally destroyed."

"Well, I'm sorry about that. But really, Mom. Surely you can see by now how dangerous it is for you out there all by yourself. What if it had been your house to catch fire?"

"Well, it wasn't. Good-bye, dear. I must call Fred now. Talk to you later."

Joanna pretended not to hear Wendy's cry of "Listen to me, Mother!" as she set the phone down. She looked up at the ceiling and exhaled. In all the excitement the meeting with Fred and the company directors had slipped her mind completely. Fred was an incredible stickler for being everywhere on time. For always following the rules, the perfect Company Man. She smiled grimly, remembering how it was with Fred. Tall and dark, with a Tom Selleck-as-Magnum P.I. moustache, she had been attracted to him at one time, and always thought that he felt the same way about her. Just as she was getting ready to make her move, to ask him out to dinner or perhaps to a see a play, he engaged in an incredible temper tantrum (privately, of course, it would never do to make a scene) over a colleague who arrived late to an important meeting. Joanna realized that he would never be able to fit in, no matter how peripherally, with her chaotic schedule and rowdy family life. So she did nothing. Six months later Fred married a department secretary, twenty-five years old, and the stars still fresh in her eyes.

She mentally prepared herself for the fireworks to come and dialed Fred's office.

"Blanchard."

"Fred, it's Joanna here. I…"

"Joanna, good heavens, are you all right? Where are you? When Wendy told me that you hadn't arrived last night…"

"I'm fine, Fred. Thank you for worrying. But I'm afraid that I won't make it in today." She explained about the fire with as little detail as told to Wendy. She was still braced for an explosion.

"Well, you must realize that the directors were quite upset at such a waste of their time. I tried my best to calm them, of course." *Of course,* Joanna rolled her eyes at the ceiling. "It will be difficult to get them together again."

She recognized the signs. If Fred wanted his ego stroked, she could be a champion stroker. "Oh, Fred. Please try, won't you? I'm sure you can explain the situation to them so that they will understand. They'll listen to you."

"Well, you see, Joanna…Some of them don't really know why you have gone to live up in…wherever it is you are. They are wondering how reliable your work for us will be."

You're wondering how you could trust someone who doesn't want to be under your suffocating wing, Joanna thought. But into the phone she stroked some more. "I understand, Fred. But I know that you really believe that I am the right person to do this job. If you remind them of that, then they'll understand."

"Perhaps, let me see what I can set up and I'll get back to you."

"Bye, Fred. My love to all there."

Joanna suppressed a screech as she hung up the phone. Fred sounded suitably pacified. But it was just such a waste of effort. Of course she was the only person for the job.

Every muscle in her body screamed to stay in bed as she swung her legs to the floor. She made her way across the room and into the shower, taking great care not to jar anything tender. The stream of hot water worked magic as it always did and got at some of the aches, but not all. She was painfully lifting one leg to put on a slipper as the phone rang once more.

She considered letting the infernal machine ring away to its heart's content. But, like any modern city dweller, she couldn't resist the siren call, and stumbled to her desk for the receiver.

"Hello."

"Is that Joanna Hastings?" It was a man's voice, deep and slow. One she didn't recognize.

"Speaking."

"You don't know me, but I was given your name by Maude Mitchell…"

"Yes?"

"Maude told me that you are quite a computer expert and I'm having a bit of a problem with mine. So I was wondering if you would be able to come over and have a look."

This was unexpected. She had absolutely no interest in setting herself up as some sort of computer repairperson.

"Uh, are you there, Ms. Hastings?"

"Yes, I'm here. But really, I don't know. I don't do house calls. What have you got?"

"A Pentium, I think."

"What level of Windows do you have?"

"Uh, Windows NT, I think. Would that be right?"

"Oh. Not many people have that on their home computers."

"Well, my brother is in the computer business. He set it all up for me."

"What's the problem?"

"I just bought a new desktop publishing package. It's the first thing I bought extra for the PC and I can't get it to print."

"Why don't you call tech support. You must have been given a number. Somewhere in the software manual will be a number you can call." Joanna tucked the phone under her chin while she struggled with the other slipper. God, her legs hurt. This business of saving lives wasn't all it was cracked up to be.

"I don't like talking to strangers on the phone."

Neither do I, Joanna thought. "Well, I don't know what I can do. I don't have any supplies of hardware or anything. If it's a hardware problem it would be a waste of time for both of us, me coming out to see it." Longingly she eyed the coffee machine standing empty and silent in the kitchen, just out of reach of the long phone cord. She wondered if she could use telepathy to fill it and start it working.

"I'll pay your going rate whether you can fix it or not, if you'll come out and have a look. Fifty dollars an hour, Maude tells me."

Joanna was caught up in dreams of a coffeepot that could start brewing all by itself. Maybe if that worked she could clean the cabin the same way, sitting in an easy chair directing the broom. Fifty dollars an hour. She dropped the attempted telepathic link. "Well, I suppose it wouldn't hurt to have a look."

"Great," he said. "What time can you be here?"

"How about two?"

"Sounds fine." He gave her directions. "See you then. Bye."

Joanna reached the coffee jar and carefully measured grounds into the pot. How had her "going rate" ever gotten to be fifty dollars an hour?

For the rest of the morning the phone continued to ring. Everyone and their dog had heard the news about the fire by now and was calling to a) exclaim over how lucky poor Luke was to be alive, or b) exclaim as to what a brave woman Joanna was to venture into the face of certain death to save a friend or c) exclaim as to how one didn't know what the world was coming to when innocent people could be roused from their beds in the dead of night.

Joanna didn't realize how many people knew her number. People she had never even heard of.

Nancy Miller called to express point b. "Heaven's sake, Joanna, I never thought, when I brought poor old Luke over to meet you the other day, that that would be the saving of his life. Suppose you didn't happen to be passing by? Poor Luke. It doesn't bear thinking about." Nancy thought about it some more. "Scares me to death, it does, just thinking about it. Imagine, being sound asleep in your own house while it's burning down all around you."

Joanna continued typing, the phone tucked under her chin.

She was writing an e-mail to her son James, away at the University of British Columbia. She debated telling him about the fire. She didn't want him to worry, but it was an exciting story. She grunted into the phone now and again while the keys clicked under her fingers.

"Arson, I hear it was. There was an arsonist—that's a person who sets fires on purpose—when I was living in Toronto in nineteen sixty-nine, or was it nineteen seventy? Anyway, no matter. It was on all the news. Terrible it was…"

"Umhmm."

"Bunch of teenagers been hanging around town lately. Scruffy pack they are. Up to trouble I'm sure. Drugs, everyone is saying…"

"Oh dear. There's my other line. Have to go now, bye, Nancy."

"Well, bye, nice talking to you."

Joanna hung up. That was definitely the last call she was taking today.

For the remainder of the morning Joanna resolutely ignored the ringing phone.

At two she promptly drove up to the house of her morning phone caller, clutching firmly to the slip of paper with scribbled directions.

The long circular drive was plowed clean. It led up to a house that resembled a Muskoka cottage more than any other on Joanna's stretch of the lake. It was old, but lovingly maintained. The walls were freshly painted dark gray with forest green highlights on the crisp gingerbread trim. A large wraparound porch covering three sides of the cottage looked out through the trees and over the lake. As she drove up Joanna sighed with envy. Such a beautiful place, and so isolated.

A man stood at the back door waiting for her. Once the car

came to a stop he smiled, raised his hand in a wave and walked over to greet her. He was dressed in an old plaid work shirt, heavily patched at the elbows, and a pair of paint-encrusted overalls that fit his bulky frame closely. Well over six feet, he was about the size of a brown bear. To complete the ursine image, a thick beard, black hairs liberally streaked with gray, covered the bottom of his face. But brown eyes twinkled merrily in a face deeply lined and permanently tanned from years in the sun. His hair was shoulder-length, clean and tied back loosely with an elastic band. He smelled of wood smoke, paint, strong soap and turpentine.

"Welcome, I'm glad you could come." He extended one massive paw as Joanna stepped out of the car. "Scott O'Neill."

"Joanna Hastings." His hand was large but his grip was gentle.

He bowed low and swept one arm back. "Welcome to my humble abode. Come on in." Normally Joanna clung firmly to an abiding air of cynicism, particularly where men were concerned. But this time, despite herself, she was charmed.

The building was beautifully furnished in true Canadian cottage style: plain wooden furniture, a scattering of colorful rugs, hardwood floor glistening with careful applications of urethane, masses of family photographs and a bright display of fabric art covering the walls. Logs and kindling were systematically laid but not yet lit, in an enormous stone fireplace. The long wall of the main room consisted of a huge window with a breathtaking view of the snow and ice covered lake beyond.

One corner of the room was nothing but a jumble of canvas, easels, paint and brushes, jars of dirty water and rags. All the canvases were either blank or had their faces turned to the wall.

"Oh," Joanna said. "You're a painter." She bit her tongue. What an infantile observation. Obviously the man was a painter.

"After a fashion."

"Can I see some of your work?"

"No," he said abruptly. As if realizing that he may have sounded a bit rude he smiled in apology. "No, nothing personal, but I never show unfinished work to anyone. And I don't have anything finished here. The computer's this way."

Joanna followed, charmed still further by his embarrassed recovery.

After the beauty of the living room, this office was a disappointment. It was small and plain, sparsely furnished with only a table for the computer equipment and a single bookshelf. One screw was half out of the wall and it looked as though the laden shelf would collapse at any minute. It was very dark; there were no windows or natural light. The same wooden beams and brick facing that worked so well in the living room gave this space a cold and unwelcoming gloom, shut in and dark.

The centerpiece of the room was the computer. It was obviously new and hardly used. The keyboard looked as though it was yet to be soiled by the touch of human fingers. An expensive laser printer sat on a small table beside it.

Joanna pulled a chair up to the desk and lovingly ran her fingers over the computer. "A nice machine," she said approvingly. "It looks new."

"It is new," he said. "I bought it from my brother who's in the business. Not that bought is the right word, more like agreed to take it and pay at some future date because he kept pushing it at me. He keeps telling me how I've got to keep better track of my expenses and my sales—if I ever make any, that is. He suggested I buy this software package." He held the box up. "I installed it according to the directions but I can't get it to work."

Joanna flicked the "on" button and the computer whirred softly as it started up. "Show me what the problem is."

"I typed up a flyer, for the show I hope to have in the spring.

Maybe I just get too frustrated. It looks real nice on the screen, but this is what it prints like." He grimaced as he held up a stack of pages of closely packed computer characters.

Joanna laughed. "I can tell you what the problem is right away. You haven't printed anything else, have you?"

He shook his massive head.

"Quite simply, your printer isn't set correctly. Look here, where you select what printer you want to print to. Your printer is a laser. But you've told the computer that it's a dot matrix. So you're getting all the characters it uses to try to print to a dot matrix. Didn't your brother set up the printer for you?"

He shook his head again. "I bought it separately. It cost a lot, but I wanted the best to advertise my work."

Joanna smiled, now she was on comfortable territory. "Do you still have the packaging the printer came in? There should be a set of diskettes."

"I never throw anything out. Good thing some times." He reached under the desk for a large box. Joanna sorted through the packaging materials and found the envelope of diskettes.

In no time the printer was correctly installed and tested. She printed out his flyer and proudly showed it to him.

"Here you go," she said, getting up from the chair.

"Wow, that was easy." He grinned from one ear to the other. "Thanks. Do you think this works okay?" He held up the flyer for her inspection.

Joanna considered it carefully—should she nod appreciatively or be honest? In business it sometime didn't pay to give your true opinion. But Scott looked the down-to-earth sort that would appreciate honesty. "Well, frankly, I think that it's a bit busy. Too cluttered. I would suggest fewer graphics, and a crisper font."

He studied it intently. "I knew that something was wrong.

Just couldn't put my finger on it. Maybe you're right. Advertising isn't my strong suit. I'll work on it a bit more."

Joanna moved toward the door but he was blocking the way. "Well, if that's all, I think I'll be going now."

"Oh, sure. Sorry." Flyer forgotten, he stepped aside. "Would you like a cup of coffee or something before you go?"

Joanna was tempted. He was certainly attractive, in a rustic sort of way. But if this was a business visit, it was important that she keep it that way. "No, I don't think so. Thank you anyway."

Joanna slipped into her boots and coat while Scott grabbed his checkbook from the solid wooden table by the door. He signed a check, tore it out with a flourish and handed it to her, smiling.

It was such an insignificant job that for a moment she considered refusing payment. But she reminded herself that she was in business now, that she must value her own skills if she was to survive; women are too used to helping others for free. Nice, but it doesn't pay the rent.

He walked out with her to the car.

"This is a great place," she said. "Not like most of the houses around here. Is it yours?"

"My parents'. My dad really hated people. He wanted to retire to someplace as far away from the city as he could get. I think he would have built on Baffin Island, but after a lifetime of agreeing to everything he said my mother put her foot down at last and this was as far as she would come." He smiled at the memory. But the smile faded all too quickly.

"Mom and Dad died in a car accident last year. My brothers and sister are fighting about selling the place and dividing up the money. I'm the only one who ever really loved it here. It's too far away from the city for them."

"It's very beautiful. You can't buy them out?"

He shook his head. "No way I could afford everyone's share.

I sure would if I could. I'll be sorry to see it go." He sighed at the thought. "I can't afford to work in this sort of luxury anywhere else. Maybe I'll be lucky and no one will want to buy it. Well, thanks very much for coming."

"No problem."

"I have your number. If I need anything more I'll give you a call."

Joanna suddenly felt uncomfortable. A warm flush crept up her neck and she hoped it didn't show in her face. Hurriedly she circled the stand of trees and drove off. She wondered what exactly Scott meant by "anything more."

EIGHT

SUPPLIES OF GROCERIES were perilously low. Joanna was reluctant to head into town, expecting that she would be stopped by everyone she saw, all wanting to talk about the fire. But the frightening prospect of a peanut butter sandwich dinner, the sole remaining ingredient in her kitchen, made up her mind for her. The day after her visit to Scott's lovely cottage she ventured into town once again.

She pulled open the door to the grocery store just as Nancy Miller came bustling out.

"Joanna," Nancy cried, "so nice to see you. Are you feeling all right after all your adventures?"

"Yes. I'm fine. I just came in for a few things."

"Oh, you shouldn't have. You should have called me. Uncle Jack'll deliver anything you want."

"I wouldn't dream of putting you out." She tried to squeeze past Nancy to get into the store, but the larger woman stood firm.

"I'm going across to the restaurant for a coffee on my break. I would love it if you would join me, Joanna."

"Sorry. But I have to do a bit of shopping and then I need to be getting home."

Nancy stood her ground. "I only have fifteen minutes. Uncle Jack is real sticky about me only taking fifteen minutes. It would be so nice to have company," she added wistfully.

Against her better judgment Joanna agreed. How bad could it be, if Nancy was up against a deadline?

They crossed the street to the town's one tiny restaurant. From the outside Joanna was reminded of a saying of her mother's: this place looked the absolute definition of a "greasy spoon." The restaurant was empty. Nancy determinedly led the way to the largest booth, one in the very back by the washrooms.

Slipping into the booth, Joanna took a quick look around. A long counter stretched almost the length of the room, with stools pulled up, facing an open grill. Nothing was cooking at the moment, the cooking surface was cold and scrubbed, patiently waiting until it was time to swing into action for the lunch crowd, assuming there was a lunch crowd. Several glass-covered platters containing a variety of pies and cakes in various stages of consumption covered one end of the counter. A souvenir clock marking someone's visit to the mining city of Sudbury (10 minutes slow) and a calendar from the Jones Brothers' Auto Body Shop featuring a variety of classic cars in mint condition, hung over the grill, the only wall decorations in the restaurant. A row of high-backed booths covered in red vinyl lined the other side of the room, leaving a very narrow passageway for customers and serving staff.

The linoleum on the floor was cracked and peeling, several initials were carved into the table at Joanna's elbow and she felt a spring give way under her bottom as she lowered herself onto the stiff plastic seat. But despite the air of seedy decline, the small room was well scrubbed and freshly painted.

An elderly waitress dressed in a well-mended old house-dress, clean white apron stretched across her ample bosom, shuffled on arthritic knees to their table. She patted the hairnet covering thin, gray hair, but smiled broadly. "Morning, Nancy. What'll you have?"

"What's your pie today?"

"Blueberry."

"Oh great. I love the blueberry pie here. With ice cream. And a coffee. Joanna?"

"Just coffee thanks." The waitress carefully wrote their order in longhand on her pad. Her tiny wrinkled hand was dotted with liver spots.

"Isn't this nice," Nancy smiled.

They talked of the weather for a few minutes, then the waitress returned with a tray bearing two mugs of coffee, sugar, cream in a real glass pitcher and a huge chunk of blueberry pie topped with a generous scoop of vanilla ice cream.

Joanna sipped her coffee. It was delicious, hot and fresh. Maybe she should have had some of the pie after all.

Nancy soon switched to the topic most on her mind. "Some people are saying that the fire was started on purpose. By that bunch of teenagers that passes through sometimes, most likely."

"I think that we should wait for the official report, don't you?"

"Oh yes. I'm just telling you what everyone is saying. Poor Maude, it will break her heart if Tiffany is involved."

Joanna bristled but controlled her tongue. Mother of teenagers herself, one of them very troubled, it always angered her when people automatically associated "teenager" with "Columbine High." Or "single mother" with "bad kids." Instead she took another taste of her coffee. "Why does Tiffany live with her grandmother? She told me she hates it in this town. I can understand why any girl her age would. Not quite the center of the universe, is it?"

Nancy dropped her voice and leaned closer to the table. Her grocery store smock was in imminent danger of dipping into blueberry pie. "She doesn't have anyone else, poor little thing. Maude doesn't talk about it much. She only had one daughter,

Bev. Harvey Mitchell died a few short months after Bev was born, terrible thing. I remember my mom and dad talking about it. He was working on a farm down south for the summer and was caught in a threshing. Bled to death, my mom said."

Joanna shivered and took a quick gulp of the hot coffee.

The door swung open bringing with it a blast of cold winter air. A group of workmen flowed into the restaurant like a small river swollen with spring snowmelt, breaking over its banks. They clambered into stools along the counter and boisterously shouted for attention.

The elderly waitress bustled over, arthritis forgotten, eyes sparking with flirtatious delight.

Nancy glanced up at the commotion, then returned to her story. "They were really in love, Maude and Harvey, Mom always said. Bev was the apple of Maude's eye. Maude loved that girl so much. Maude was so brokenhearted about Harvey that she never remarried, although lots of men would have been glad to have her. Not just because she was such a beauty, but she was an only child herself, so she inherited all her daddy's property when her own parents died. But she didn't want to remarry so she raised her child all by herself. Bev was a bad seed right from the get-go. Of course, Maude couldn't see it."

The waitress bustled back and forth, cutting and serving cake and pie and pouring coffee. The men teased her with loud voices and much laughter and she blushed like a schoolgirl.

Nancy dropped her voice even lower until it was barely a whisper. "Bev moved away as soon as she was old enough. These days most of the kids leave this town the minute they can. She went to Toronto and married a man named, what was his name now?" Nancy chewed thoughtfully on her last piece of pie and scraped at the ice cream drips with her fork.

She shook her head. "Can't remember. Anyway, he took off right after Tiffany was born. Never heard a word from him again. To this day, Tiffany doesn't know whether her daddy is alive or dead. So Bev tried to raise Tiffany herself, just like Maude raised her. But Bev, she was never like Maude. Too weak, if you ask me. She couldn't hold down a job, fell into some bad company." She licked the ice-cream covered tines of her fork.

"Maude went down there a couple of times. To look after Tiffany and help out a bit, so Bev could get a decent job. But she never stayed long. She couldn't get along with Bev anymore. Of course Bev didn't want her there, there was always one boyfriend or another hanging around."

"More pie, Nancy?" The waitress was back.

"I really shouldn't, but I guess this is a special occasion," Nancy giggled. "Yes, please. With ice cream. That was great. And more coffee."

The waitress eyed Joanna.

"Yes, please, another coffee." Joanna would have loved to try the pie. She cursed herself for being a stuck-up city snob, but she simply couldn't bring herself to eat in the shoddy diner.

Once again the woman laboriously wrote their order onto her pad. Nancy was silent until the waitress was behind the counter pouring the second round of coffee. The group of workmen laughed at an off-color joke. They had made a serious dent into the platters of cake and pots of coffee.

"Well, last year Bev just upped and disappeared. Put Tiffany on the bus to Hope River with ten dollars in her pocket and moved out of her apartment. Ran off with the latest boyfriend I suspect. And Maude hasn't heard a word from her since."

It never failed to amaze Joanna how thoughtless people could be toward their own children. "How terrible for Tiffany."

With a clatter the plate and cups were placed on the table, along with the bill. Joanna reached for her purse but Nancy stopped her. "Let me treat you, Joanna. It has been so pleasant chatting with you."

"That's very kind of you. Thanks. Has Maude tried to find Bev?"

Nancy attacked her pie with gusto. "She went to Toronto and asked at Bev's old apartment. But no one there knew anything. She went to the Tim Horton's where Bev was supposed to be working, but they hadn't seen her for three months. Didn't know what else to do. So she just came on home and tried to do her best for Tiffany."

"How sad. No wonder the poor girl is so angry."

"It's been real hard for Maude. Not many of the people in town like Tiffany. They think she's a bad girl. My Uncle Jack, he tells everyone that Tiffany's just like her mother. She'll never amount to anything, he says. It hurts Maude a lot, what people say about Bev and Tiffany. But Maude's so proud; she'll never let on. I've tried to be friendly to Tiffany, but she's just rude back. It's real hard, but I keep trying."

"I know it's hard." Joanna gripped her coffee cup tightly. Her eyes welled up and she fought to control it. "But you're right to keep trying. Some kids you'll never get through to, no matter how hard you try. But sometimes you will. Then it's all worthwhile."

Nancy looked at her. Her eyes gleamed with understanding and a long-dormant intelligence. "You have children of your own, don't you, Joanna? How are they?"

"Fine, just fine. Hadn't you better be getting back to work? We've been sitting here for over half an hour now."

Nancy shrugged. "Uncle Jack will be mad. Who cares?" But she swallowed the remains of her coffee with a quick gulp and carefully counted out the exact change to place on the table alongside their bill.

Joanna did manage to get her shopping done. When she left the store carrying bulging brown paper bags to her car a group of teenagers were lounging on the restaurant steps watching the non-existent traffic.

It looked like three boys and two girls, but it was hard to tell in their uniform of oversized jeans, baggy coats and hair either long and straight or cropped almost bald. They passed a pop can around and were all smoking. Only one of the group noticed Joanna as she packed her trunk with groceries. Tiffany raised her hand lazily in what Joanna interpreted as a wave. She waved back and Tiffany turned away.

She left the car in the grocery store parking lot and walked up the hill to the liquor store. It was very cold and she took long deep breaths through her mouth, savoring the sharp taste of the air.

The street seemed very busy all of a sudden; a small crowd was descending on the liquor store and disappearing around the back. She could hear shouting and the murmur of excited voices. Drawn by nothing other than curiosity, Joanna went to see what was going on.

A group of about fifteen people stood in a circle in the parking lot. She could see two old men facing off against each other, feet apart, fists bunched. One of them was Luke.

"You bastard, you burnt down my home," Luke shouted, his face red and contorted in anger.

"I never," the other man replied. He was of similar age as Luke, equally work-worn although taller and much heavier. His many-times broken nose was a bulbous red, the sign of a lifelong drinker. This must be Roy McMaster, whom Luke had accused the night of the fire.

"You been waiting to get me my whole life, you bastard," Luke shouted. "Now you gone and done it."

"You stupid old man. If I wanted to get you I would take you on like a man, not sneak up behind your house and start a fire in the night. That's the work of a coward."

The crowd murmured in agreement. Roy's statement made sense to them. But Luke wouldn't back down.

"Well that sounds just like you to me, don't it? I know you been having wild parties out in the woods on my property, you and your no account friends. Hanging around watching the girls, probably."

Roy growled. The shot seemed to have hit home. Then he snorted. "If I was gonna have a party, I can think of better places to have it than that run-down old dump of yours. And I sure ain't seen any pretty girls round your place lately."

No one moved to intervene. Surely they weren't going to simply stand by and let two old men come to blows? There was no aura of tension among the onlookers. Presumably they never expected the altercation to come to an actual fistfight. After a few minutes of both men looking nothing but ridiculous, Roy relaxed his fists and took a step backward. The crowd murmured in appreciation. Joanna crept away. As she rounded the corner, one of the onlookers invited everyone to meet at the bar in North Ridge, to commiserate with Luke on his misfortune.

JOANNA DROVE HOME deep in thought. As soon as she walked in she picked up the phone and called Maude before she could change her mind.

"Maude, it's Joanna. I would like to ask Tiffany to come back and continue with the computer lessons. We got off on the wrong foot, but I think we could work something out."

The relief in the older woman's voice was almost physical.

"That would be wonderful. I know that Tiffany wasn't very polite to you the other day, but that's just the way she is. She really is a nice girl." Maude's voice trailed off.

"I do know. I know exactly what you mean. How about after school three times a week?"

"Thank you, Joanna. Thank you very much."

"Tell Tiffany to be here tomorrow. We'll start then."

Joanna put down the phone. What had she done?

THE NEXT MORNING she was sitting down to breakfast when she heard a car stop on the road, soon followed by a sharp knock at the front door. She peered out the window. It was Luke.

"I didn't expect to see you here today, Luke."

"Why not? You asked me to fix that back step what's coming loose."

"I thought that you might be too tired and upset, after the other night."

"Work's got to be done. No matter what." He shuffled his feet and twisted his cap in his hands. "I have to thank you. You saved my life. Thank you." He was in an agony of embarrassment.

"It was nothing. Come in and have a cup of tea before you go out back." She stepped aside to let him in.

"I'm so sorry about your place," Joanna said as she placed a massive pottery mug and a plate of chocolate-chip cookies on the table. The front of the mug was handcrafted into a face with thick brows, bulging blue eyes and a foolish expression. She never noticed before just how much the face on the mug resembled Luke. She hoped he didn't think so.

"Yeah."

"And all your things as well. Have you been living there long?"

"My daddy built that cabin. I was born there."

Joanna couldn't imagine living in one town, never mind the

same house, all your life. How devastating it must be, to lose it. "Where are you staying now?"

"With my brother, Larry, and his wife, over by North Ridge. They said I could live there now, long as I like. Larry drove me here today. He'll be back to pick me up in two hours. So I guess I'd better get to it." Luke finished his tea in one gulp and wiped his mouth with his sleeve. He looked wistfully at the cookie plate.

Joanna took the hint. "Would you like to take some cookies outside with you? To have a break later, perhaps?"

He smiled shyly as he slipped the remaining cookies into his coat pocket.

"Do you have any idea what happened?" Joanna walked Luke the few steps to the back door. "What caused the fire, I mean?"

He shook his head sadly. "Wasn't me, that's for sure. I ain't been out to the shed for a couple of days."

"Have you had any visitors or anything? Someone who might have started it by accident, I mean."

"No. People have been in the woods a lot lately, though."

"What do you mean, 'people'?"

"Kids, you know. Hangin' around, makin' noise, playin' loud music. I seen that no account Tiffany Jordan out with that bunch, sassed me right out when I told her to get off my property. For all I been friends with her grandma goin' on fifty years." He shook his head. "Stupid kids. Don't know why they'd be out in the woods at night, no how. Weather as cold as it's been lately." Luke shrugged.

"When did you see them last?"

"Week or two, I figure. I finally caught one o' them. Told him I'd have my shotgun out next time I found him on my property. Ain't seen them since."

"Have you reported them to the police?"

"I can take care of my own business. Don't need no police."
The door slammed shut and Luke stomped down the steps to
begin his work.

AT THE REQUEST OF the fire department, outside investigators
were brought in to investigate the matter of the fire at Luke's
home. They visited Joanna and asked a great many questions.
There wasn't much she could tell them. She saw flames; the
place was on fire. That was it.

In due course their report was released to the volunteer fire
department and in a matter of minutes the whole town knew
every detail.

The inspector's report concluded that liberal quantities of
gasoline had been sprinkled throughout Luke's woodshed and
ignited. Luke insisted that he had never spilled anything out in
the shed and the town believed him.

NINE

TIFFANY SAT AT THE COMPUTER, her regular sullen expression locked firmly in place. Joanna resolved to ignore it.

Joanna called up Mrs. Beeton's typing tutorial. Tiffany poked at the keys; her body language screamed, "Boring!"

"Let's make a deal, Tiffany," Joanna offered. "If you can put a bit of enthusiasm into doing these exercises, you can play with one of my games."

Tiffany's eyes flickered with interest, but she tossed her purple hair. "Games, oh, goody. We get to play games."

"I mean computer games. I have Tomb Raider. Have you ever heard of it?"

"Yes, I've heard of it. One of the rich chicks at school has it. The kids all say it's really cool. But I've never seen it."

"Well, do the tutorial and I'll show it to you."

The girl straightened almost imperceptibly in her chair and her fingers picked up their pace.

Joanna hid her smile. She just might be getting somewhere here. It was a nice thought.

As she hoped, Tomb Raider and Lara Croft were a big hit.

"Cool," Tiffany exclaimed as the graphics unfolded on the screen. "How do they get all those pictures and movement into the computer?"

"Now that's something I don't know. But it looks wonderful, doesn't it?"

She started Tiffany off by explaining the various key combinations, to run, to jump, to move forward and backward. The girl picked it up instantly. It was nice to watch her delight as she successfully maneuvered the buxom Lara through her own home in the introduction to the game.

She played for just a few minutes before Maude arrived to drive Tiffany home. The girl's enthusiasm dried up the minute she rose from the computer table. Her shoulders slouched and the sullen expression returned.

"Did you have a nice lesson?" Maude asked as Tiffany pulled on her boots.

"It was okay."

From Tiffany that was a ringing endorsement. Joanna and Maude smiled at each other over the girl's bent back.

"See you on Wednesday," Joanna said.

"Maybe," Tiffany grunted.

But right on time on Wednesday Tiffany was standing at the cabin door.

After an hour and a half of finishing homework assignments with Word, Joanna stood up to stretch. "You've done very well," she said. "Why don't we put on Tomb Raider for a while until your grandma comes."

Tiffany enthusiastically agreed. "Joanna, do you think maybe on Friday I could ask Grandma to come a bit later? So I could play for longer. If I wouldn't be in your way, that is?"

"That's a great idea. Friday night I don't usually do much work anyway. So you can have the computer for as long as you like. I'll tell Maude that I'll drive you home when we're finished. That way she won't have to worry about what time she should come to get you."

Joanna was extremely pleased at how well things were going with Tiffany. The girl was obviously very bright. All she needed was a little respect and encouragement.

LIKE A CAT STRETCHING every inch of its body, the kinks worked themselves out of the muscles in Joanna's arms and legs. It felt really good to be back on her skis. She had warmed up carefully before starting out and was keeping a close eye on her watch to ensure that this time she didn't go farther than her middle-aged body would take her.

She wanted to explore a different route this morning, so instead of continuing along the main road she turned off and skied down a small path cutting through the woods to another lake. This was a summer road, not plowed in the winter. The snow was thick and heavy under her skis but the absolute quiet and the splendor of open blue sky and sun shining on pristine snow was well worth the extra effort.

Joanna delighted in her surroundings. It was the dream of her life to come back up north, and now at last she was here. When she was young her parents owned a cottage on Lake Rousseau, in the very heart of Ontario cottage country. She remembered idyllic summers filled with dives off the dock, long swims as the melting sun turned the water orange, roasting hot dogs and dripping marshmallows over a roaring bonfire down by the water and lazy boat rides just to see what was happening on the rest of the lake. But one day it ended, as she came to believe that all good things must end, and her beloved father was killed in a freak water-skiing accident when she was thirteen. The driver of the boat had consumed far too many martinis, but no one worried much about that sort of thing, whether boating or driving, in those days. Showing off to the waving admirers standing on the dock, he veered too close to the shore. Joanna's dad crashed into the low-lying rocks hugging the water's edge, and flew into the dock headfirst.

Fortunately, he had barely enough life insurance that Joanna's mother was not forced into the uncomfortable position of destitute widows everywhere, to look for work for which she had no skills, no aptitude and no training. But she sold the family cottage to the first person that made an offer, and soon after that the large comfortable home in upscale Forest Hill. Joanna didn't mind the move to a small bungalow in the suburbs, but the loss of the cottage was like her father's death all over again. When she was young she was angered beyond reason at her mother's refusal to accept kindly extended invitations by close friends and relatives to spend weekends at their cottages. But with insight that only arrives with maturity, after years of anger she was able to recognize her mother's aloofness for what it was. Returning to the lakes would have been just too painful, too much a reminder of all that was lost, so she preferred to spend the summer in the sweltering city. The children were packed off to day camp, and sent swimming in the over-chlorinated, overcrowded town pool on the weekends. Now that it was much too late, Joanna wanted to tell her mother that she understood.

The road wasn't long and ended abruptly at a small summer cottage sitting high on a rocky hill overlooking the lake. She skied over to the edge. The lake lay beneath her, an unbroken stretch of snow reaching to the hills beyond. Not a single footprint or the marks of a snowmobile broke the surface.

She pulled off her skis and settled comfortably into a rock to eat her snack before heading home. A chipmunk ventured out from behind a tree, wiggling its nose timidly at the sight of food. Joanna broke a small crumb off her sandwich and held it out to him. "Come and get it."

The tiny body quivered with excitement and the nose twitched furiously but the animal dared venture no closer.

"Very wise of you, I think," she laughed, tossing a piece of bread onto the snow.

The chipmunk never reached his meal. It turned on its heels and bounded back into the safety of the woods as a crash echoed from the cottage. More clatter broke through the silence of the woods, followed by the soft tinkling of broken glass.

Two figures jumped out of the cottage and ran up the road. Joanna crouched down closer to her rock, trying to make herself as invisible as the chipmunk. They were laughing wildly as they ran, zigzagging from one side of the clearing to the other. In each hand they held a bottle, liquor by the look of it. They were dressed alike in oversized winter jackets, one bearing the loud logo of the Chicago Bulls on the back, and both wore thick brown work boots and black woolen toques. All she could tell from her vantage point on the rock was that one was tall, the other very much shorter.

They didn't look back and soon the wild laughter died away and Joanna's heart returned to its normal rhythm. She left her skis and backpack at the top of the hill and walked cautiously up to the cottage.

It was similar to Scott's cottage but smaller. A wide deck wrapped around the front of the building, overlooking the lake far below. Joanna climbed the steps and peered in through the large hole where a boarded-up picture window now gaped open. Shards of glass and chunks of broken plywood littered the carpet. The door of a small cabinet hung half off its hinges, revealing the rows of liquor and mix bottles filling the shelves. Joanna backed away quickly. She didn't want to be here if they came back for a second load. Blowing snow drifted lazily through the broken window, a layer as fine as icing sugar already dusting the beautiful carpet.

Joanna grabbed her backpack and snapped her boots into the ski's bindings. She traveled up the path at a steady pace, concentrating intently. She had no worries about rounding a corner and running into them, whoever they might be. Judging by the amount of noise they were making she would hear them long before they came into sight.

But she saw no one and made it home without incident, although she did travel much too fast for the comfort of her arm muscles.

She called the police, made a cup of hot chocolate and settled down to wait.

The police officer who arrived at her door less than a half an hour after her call was an older man, a few years short of retirement, with the vein-lined red nose and prominent belly that bore witness to many hours spent in the neighborhood bars and donut shops. He listened to her story thoughtfully, jotting down notes in a small pad as she spoke.

"Why don't you come with me, ma'am?" he suggested. "They'll be long gone by now, I don't doubt. Then you can show me for yourself what you saw."

Joanna again struggled into her heavy coat, scarf, mittens, boots and hat and rode in the cruiser with Constable Jenkins. As much as she liked winter, it was a chore getting dressed to go outside.

"Don't get much vandalism up here," he said. "Too far from the city, I guess. People feel pretty safe leaving their homes and cottages around here. This sort of thing gets people all upset."

They were forced to leave the car at the top of the summer road and walked in. The tracks of her skis cut a good trail through the snow. Two sets of running footprints veered wildly down the lane.

Dense, gray clouds replaced the pleasant sunshine of just a short while ago. The snow was falling faster and thicker as they walked.

"These tracks will be covered up pretty soon," Jenkins observed, "but those look like pretty big boots. And I guess the ski tracks belong to you?"

Joanna nodded.

"Can you describe the people you saw?"

She thought for a moment. "Not very well. I only saw them from the back. They were all bundled up in the usual winter paraphernalia. I couldn't tell anything at all about their shape. But one was a good bit shorter than the other. That's it."

"What sort of clothes?"

"Big jackets, with some kind of team logo on the back, jeans, black wool caps."

Jenkins nodded at her story. Joanna felt inadequate, as if her description should be more concise. "I can't tell you much, I spent most of the time trying to make myself invisible."

The cottage was as she left it. Joanna waited on the deck while Jenkins climbed in through the broken window.

He examined the interior of the cottage quickly, then knelt down by the liquor cabinet to inspect the damage. In her first panicked look inside Joanna hadn't noticed the piles of broken bottles littering the carpet in front of the cabinet. The nauseating smell of spilled booze filled the room and drifted out to reach Joanna on the deck.

"Quite a mess." Jenkins hauled himself across the windowsill once again. "But looks like nothing else taken or broken. They were only after the liquor. Looks like they drank a fair bit of it as well. Though it's hard to tell as so much soaked into the carpet. Could have been worse," he said solemnly. "You were lucky they didn't see you."

The walk back up to the main road and the cruiser was long and tense. The considerably overweight Jenkins huffed and puffed the entire way.

"I'm sure I would have been all right," Joanna said, pulling her scarf tighter around her neck. They were walking into the wind this time; it bit savagely at her nose and cheeks.

"You never know with kids these days," Jenkins said, shaking his head, "they can turn on you in a minute."

"What makes you think they were kids? Isn't that jumping to conclusions?"

"Who else would break into a place like this after the liquor? Sounds like the way these kids dress, too."

"Lots of adults commit crimes as well, Mr. Jenkins. And everyone around here wears winter coats and jeans."

"Still sounds like kids to me." Jenkins hesitated before getting back into the car. "Let's see where these tracks go."

They followed the running footprints around the next bend. The snow was chewed up by the spinning wheels of a car.

"Too bad I didn't get here sooner," he said. "Looks like they had a bit of trouble getting their car out of this ditch. Well, they're long gone now. I'll put in a call for everyone to be on the lookout for a couple of drunken kids driving around, but I don't think we'll catch them this time. Nancy and Jack up at the store in town know most of the summer folk around here. They might have a phone number for the people who own the cottage. Someone had better call them to come up here and fix that window. Else they'll have a place full of drunk mice and melting snow by spring."

They rode back to Joanna's cabin in silence. Jenkins let her out at the top of the driveway.

"Thanks for calling us, ma'am. I'll let you know if we catch anyone."

She got out of the car and was walking down the driveway when Jenkins called her back.

"Another thing, ma'am. I'd think twice about going out into these woods by myself if I was you. Anyone could be out there these days. You should ask your husband or a friend to go skiing with you next time."

Joanna thanked him through clenched teeth.

"Ask my husband, indeed," she marched into her home in a red rage. "Fat lot of good that would ever do," she shouted to the uncaring wind. "I didn't move all the way up here so I could cower under the covers waiting for the big, strong man to say I can go outside to play." She slammed the door with such force that the windows rattled in agreement.

TEN

As CAREFUL AS SHE HAD tried to be, every muscle in Joanna's arms and legs screamed their disapproval the next morning. She moved through the early day routine with care, grumbling to herself with every painful movement.

She turned on the shower and stood under the hot water, sighing with relief as the warmth cascaded over her aching body. All too soon the hot water turned cold and Joanna turned the taps off in annoyance. As she reached for her towel, the soap fell out of the soap dish onto the shower floor. Before she could stop her forward movement, she planted a foot firmly on the slippery bar and plunged forward. She threw her arms out to protect her face and fell with the full weight of her body resting on her left hand, unfortunately the same spot that absorbed the tumble when she first arrived at the cabin. Her wrist took the full force of the fall and she landed heavily on her side. She gasped and gripped her hand, writhing on the shower floor. "Oh, oh. That hurts," she shouted at the uncaring walls.

The shrill ringing of the phone broke through her moans of self-pity, then the answering machine picked it up.

"Mom, Mom are you there?" Wendy shouted into the phone after the machine had invited her to leave a message. "It's seven o'clock in the morning—you must be there."

"Yes, yes, I'm here. I was just in the shower." Joanna held the phone in her right hand, jumping up and down as the waves of pain receded slowly from her left wrist. She gripped the phone, stark naked and dripping wet. She was freezing; the stove had not yet fully fired up to provide enough heat for the day.

"Oh, well, I won't be long then. Are you all right? Your voice sounds a bit strained."

"I was up late last night, working on a new piece, that's all." Joanna poked at the feeble fire, trying to encourage a few embers to respond with some sort of enthusiasm.

"I haven't been up there to see your place yet. I would really like to. How about if I come up this weekend?"

"How would you get here, without a car?"

"I can borrow one from my friend, Marie. You haven't met her, but she has the same faculty adviser as me and we've really struck up a great friendship. She hates Professor Blenkhorn as much as I do. I was telling her all about you moving up there to the back of beyond and she offered to lend me her car for the weekend. How about it?"

Joanna groaned inwardly. She would love to see her eldest daughter. But until she could ascertain the state of her wrist she didn't want to risk Wendy discovering that she was hurt. "Not this weekend. I have a prior engagement. Sorry, dear. Maybe another time. How about next weekend?"

All Joanna could think of was that she was slowly freezing to death and she wished her arm would drop off. She didn't hear Wendy struggling to keep the disappointment out of her voice. "Well, I'll have to see if I can get the car then. I'll call you next week. Bye, Mom."

"Good-bye, dear."

Joanna struggled to make her breakfast with the use of just one hand. She kept telling herself that she only needed a bit of time to let the wrist relax and it would be fine. She sat down to the computer to work but gave up after a few minutes of laboriously struggling to keep the left hand synchronized with the right.

By noon, it was getting increasingly hard to ignore the fact that, compared to the right, the left wrist bore a close resemblance to a watermelon. Joanna pulled over the thin phone book for Hope River and Environs, and looked up the number of the nearest doctor. It came as no surprise that there wasn't one listed for Hope River. She eventually found a doctor in North Ridge who could see her that afternoon.

The town of North Ridge was about a half an hour of careful driving from Joanna's cabin. It boasted a few more amenities than Hope River, including a couple of bars and a fairly elegant looking restaurant. She found the professional building without much trouble.

Doctor Richardson's office was bright and modern. The waiting room was painted a fresh peach, with pale green furniture and good, cheerful prints decorating the walls. She happily lost herself in a stack of up-to-the-minute women's magazines while waiting her turn.

With some disappointment Joanna tore herself away from an article on the fate of licensed day-care in Canada under the present government when the smiling receptionist called her name.

Doctor Richardson was young and attractive with an eager smile and an engaging chatty manner. She was surprised— most new doctors avoided remote rural practices like the plague, preferring the challenge and excitement of the big cities. He held her hand and manipulated her wrist carefully. A shiver dashed up her spine. Just the after-effect of the fall.

"A minor sprain, I'm afraid," he said, smiling into her eyes. "But it will heal quickly." He wrapped the offending appendage in a long bandage.

"How quickly?" she asked.

"Keep it fairly still for a couple of days and it will be right as rain before you know it."

"I really have to use my left hand," Joanna said, "all the time. I type on the computer. All the time."

He looked at her intently. My, he has caring eyes, she thought. "A sprain like this can get worse, if you don't give it a chance to get better." He finished wrapping and released her hand. "Now, come back and see me in a week and I'll check it out again." He shook his finger at her. "But don't let me find that you haven't been looking after it."

She smiled. For some strange reason her knees felt weak.

"You haven't been in here before. Are you new to the area?"

"Yes, I am. I moved up here in September, from Toronto. I have a place just outside Hope River."

"How are you liking it? Different from Toronto, isn't it?"

Joanna had never been to a doctor before who asked her anything at all about her personal life. It was a nice feeling. "It certainly is. But I like my cabin very much."

"Me too," he smiled at her. His teeth were amazingly straight and white. "I've only recently moved up here from Toronto as well. It seemed a great place to settle into a practice and raise a family."

Joanna smiled back.

"My wife wasn't too sure at first. But I think that she is beginning to get used to it up here. Our first baby is due in January and I hope that when he or she comes Jennifer will appreciate living in a nice town like this."

Joanna's smile was fixed firmly in place as she hopped down from the table. "Absolutely. Thank you very much, Doctor. See you next week."

She rushed out into the street, her cheeks burning. How incredibly embarrassing.

North Ridge didn't look much like the excitement capital of

the world. But at least it wasn't Hope River. A walk along the main street before heading home would give her a chance to look around.

The biggest feature of the town appeared to be "The Last Chance Bar and Pool Hall. The Hottest Spot in the North." The crooked sign outside boasted that its specialty was "Girls, Girls, Girls!" North Ridge was dropping fast in her estimation. She gripped the bandage on her wrist, held her head high and strolled nonchalantly by.

At that moment a pickup truck pulled up to the front door and three men jumped out. One of them whistled loudly at her, they all laughed and spilled into the bar. Joanna pretended not to notice.

A group sitting in the alley by the side door she did notice. It was the same bunch of teenagers she had seen in Hope River outside the restaurant. As before they huddled together, passing around a soda can and a hand-rolled cigarette. This time the smoke did not smell even remotely like tobacco.

"Hi, Tiffany." Joanna stopped in front of the group. One of the boys snorted in amusement. Tiffany shifted her thin shoulders and took a deep drag as the cigarette, or whatever, was passed to her. She blew smoke and handed it to the girl next in line.

"I'm heading back to Hope River now. Would you like a ride?" Tiffany was sitting on the ground. She looked up at the boy looming over her and rolled her eyes.

"Get lost, lady. We don't need no ride." The boy took a step toward her and Joanna instinctively moved back.

"I'm not talking to you." She tried to catch Maude's granddaughter's eye, but the girl refused to look at her. She didn't like the emptiness in Tiffany's expression. "How about it, Tiffany? We could stop for a burger and fries on the way home."

The kids all laughed.

"A burger, oh, excitement city. And fries, whoopee, can we

all come?" The boy standing over Tiffany had hair cut like a flowerpot; it was shaved across the back and sides, leaving a few strands of greasy mop hanging down from the crown of his head. A skull was tattooed into the right side of his scalp. The others all laughed as if on cue.

"Get lost, old lady," he sneered. "Tiff's okay. She's with us."

Joanna shuffled her feet and glanced behind her. "I think you should come home with me, Tiffany. It's getting late and your grandmother will be worried."

"We'll take her home. Get lost. Tell her, Tiff," the boy ordered. He passed the toke to the girl on the ground, out of turn.

Tiffany closed her eyes and took a deep drag. Silence stretched painfully through the alley. Tiffany clutched the joint in her fingers and sucked again. "Go away, Joanna. These are my friends. I don't need you showing up here like some kind of baby-sitter. I'll go home when I'm good and ready." The group all laughed. Joanna recoiled as if she had been struck. The pain of confrontations remembered leapt up as sharply as the pain in her wrist. She stared at Tiffany. The girl passed the toke on to the next person and sunk her head into her knees. The boy with the flowerpot haircut took a step forward, his fists clenched.

"Everything okay here?" A voice from the sidewalk broke the tension like a warm knife slicing though ice cream.

"Yeah, sure man. We're all cool." The boy nudged Tiffany with a mud-encrusted boot. "Get up, girl. We're outta here." Her head nodded but she didn't respond. He grabbed her arm and hauled her roughly to her feet. The group moved sluggishly down the alley and disappeared behind the building.

Joanna made a move to follow, then stopped, caught in an agony of indecision.

"Let them go, Joanna. You're no match for them."

She turned to face the new arrival. It was Scott O'Neill. "I don't think you're qualified to be a judge of juvenile behavior," she snarled.

"No, I'm not. But you can't fight with that crowd." He reached out and touched her arm. "Come on. I feel like a cup of coffee. Join me?"

Joanna winced; he had touched her left arm. Scott noticed but said nothing. For such a large man he moved carefully, almost delicately, staring at her face while he backed out of the alley. She followed.

"Do you know that girl?" Scott asked.

"Yes, I know her."

"And…"

"She is Maude Mitchell's granddaughter. I teach her how to use the computer a couple of times a week. Don't you know who she is?"

"I heard that she was back, but I haven't had the pleasure. These kids today. Nothing but trouble. They can do anything they want, and the law doesn't touch them. Just a slap on the wrist. A good stretch in boot camp would straighten that lot out, if you ask me."

"Well, I didn't ask you. They aren't doing anything illegal, you know. It's not a crime, not yet anyway, to swear in public, or to hang around behind a strip bar."

"What the hell do you think they're smoking there, tobacco? Those kids were stoned up to their eyeballs."

Red swam in front of her eyes. "But if they were a few years older they could go into the Last Chance Bar here and drink themselves under the table, ogle a few naked women who are just trying to earn a living and then go outside and puke their guts up, and all the good-time-boys like you would slap them on the back and say what real men they were." Joanna was shouting now. An elderly couple crossed quickly to the other side of the street.

Scott dropped his voice. It was menacing in the quiet of the afternoon. "I never congratulate anyone for being such a fool as to drink themselves into oblivion. Neither desperate naked women nor gut-puking do much for me. But if you don't sort kids like that out right now, they'll be in places like the Last Chance, or worse; and let me tell you, there are lots worse, as soon as they can produce fake ID. They'll stay there for the rest of their lives drinking up their weekly pay while their wives raise ten kids on the pittance hubby has left over after the Friday night drunk."

Joanna clenched her fists to stop her hands from shaking and thrust her jaw forward. "That is no concern of mine," she said. "They can all go to hell in a hand basket, for all I care." She pushed Scott out of the way and started off down the street, her body as tight and rigid as her jaw.

Scott caught up to her. "Leave it alone, Joanna. Once a kid's gone bad, they're bad. From then on they're beyond hope."

She turned in fury. Her face was red and she hissed from between clenched teeth. "No one is ever lost, not ever. Do you hear me? Not ever. And if I give up, may it be the day I die." Joanna swiped ineffectually at him with her purse, turned on her heels and ran.

Scott stood rooted in his tracks and let her go. This was about far more than a group of punks smoking dope in the alley behind the Last Chance Bar. He knew when he was way, way, out of his league.

LATE THAT EVENING Joanna was still mad at the world, at Tiffany for being such a fool as to allow herself to be manipulated by that bunch of louts, at Scott for his blindness to the girl's innermost problems, at her daughter Alexis for exposing her family to the world of troubled and angry teenagers, and then abruptly breaking off all contact with those who wanted so much to help her. But above all she was angry with herself, with Joanna, for falling into a fool's trap of caring for other people and allowing herself to get involved in their problems.

She clattered angrily about her cramped kitchen, banging cupboards closed, rattling the crockery, scrubbing pots with a vengeance until they gleamed, drinking far too much wine. One-handed she furiously swung the mop at a speck of mud on the kitchen floor. Out of control, the mop swerved wildly and caught the side of her wineglass, knocking it to the linoleum in a crash of glass and a spray of ruby red liquid. "Oh, for heaven's sake," she groaned and tiptoed back from the shards of glass. It was a full glass, curse it. She fetched a broom and dustpan and set about sweeping up the damage. The trashcan was already filled past the brim and close to overflowing, so she tipped the glassy contents into a plastic bag and scooped up the garbage bag. Maneuvering the back door open with her good hand and with her butt propping it in place, she picked up the bags of trash with their glassy burden and carried them out into the night.

Like everyone's in this northern community, her garbage sat by the road waiting for pickup in a large, homemade wooden chest with a tied-down latch. The latch was there to keep out bears and raccoons and other large animals with dexterous fingers or claws and good brains. She placed her bags on the ground at her feet and fumbled with the latch. Sometimes it seemed as if raccoons weren't the only things locked out by human ingenuity.

Finally her garbage was stuffed into the chest and everything tightly secured once again. She walked down the hill back to her cabin, taking the time to let the beautiful evening remove the sting from her anger. The night was mild, clear and calm.

Snow crunched beneath her boots. She took a deep breath of crisp winter air and stopped to admire the display of stars above.

An owl hooted and she glanced up to see a huge great horned owl staring wide-eyed at her from a branch in a knotted old white pine. The enormous bird stared her down and Joanna broke her gaze to look back up at the star-studded sky.

It was gone. A thin layer of fast-moving clouds covered the heavens. A sharp cold wind blew down from the north and pierced through Joanna's thick winter sweater. She looked into the pine. The branch was empty.

But beneath the old tree a black shape slowly formed out of the blackness of the forest night. She stared, open-mouthed. Black was black, none lighter or darker than the other. But the shape before her was able to form substance out of darkness and a presence out of black. For a split second while Joanna stood paralyzed, the shape undulated softly before her. Then it broke from the all-encompassing darkness under the tree and moved forward. Blackness separated from blackness. It appeared to be reaching out for her, like a child reaching for a parent, a drowning man reaching for a life preserver.

Joanna squealed and ran. As fast as she could go, she dashed down the driveway to the cabin. She stumbled up the steps, slammed the door behind her and stood with her back against it, gasping for air.

She stood with her back pressed against the door for a very long time, shutting out she knew not what.

ELEVEN

THIS TIME SHE DIDN'T make it into the woods. She was barely out the door before the heaving in her stomach forced her over the porch rail, spewing the remains of breakfast onto the piles of yellow and red leaves blown up against the walls of the cabin. She remained bent over the rail gasping for breath, her stomach still trying to rid itself of its non-existent contents, until she heard the screen door creak open. She wiped her mouth on her shirtsleeve, took one deep breath and turned to face her mother.

"What's the matter with you, girl?"

"Nothing, Mama."

Her mother shoved her heavy breasts out of the way as she folded her arms across her plain housedress, washed until the fabric barely held together. "You sick?"

"Just something I ate, Mama."

Her mother planted her thick, vein-encrusted legs apart and crossed her arms tighter over her chest. Her breasts wiggled with the effort. "You think I don't hear you out here every morning these last few days? Last time I was sick like that, I was carrying your baby sister. Is there something you want to tell me?"

The girl looked at her mother's feet in their old slippers, one corn-encrusted toe sticking out from a ragged hole in the side. "No, Mama."

The woman's face softened slightly and she shifted uncomfortably. "I don't know what your papa's gonna say to this."

"Yes, Mama." She still did not look up.

"Run along now, go and wash your face. I need help in the kitchen. Your papa will be wanting his breakfast in no time."

"Yes, Mama."

The girl slipped past her mother and into the cabin. The woman gazed after her, blue eyes sad and thoughtful. Then she shook her head and straightened her shoulders; breakfast wouldn't cook itself. She returned to the kitchen, just in time, as the porridge bubbled over the edges of the pot.

Soon enough the sickness stopped, and the household slipped into a strained silence. Mother and daughter, who rarely exchanged words at the best of times, almost ceased to speak. The mother watched her daughter with heavy, troubled eyes. The girl took to wearing her older brothers' old shirts, stolen out of the rag box.

"Where have you been, girl?" Her father stumbled from the back room, unshaven for days, bleary-eyed, his slate-gray hair standing on end, his huge belly draped over stained and torn boxer shorts.

"Out." The girl stared at the floor as she held in her breath and attempted to pass into the kitchen.

"Out, I know all about your 'out.' Out drinking you mean, out carousing with every no-good drunk in town." He grabbed her by the arm and his voice rose to a fevered pitch.

One by one the boys crept out of their beds and gathered silently to watch the show. They didn't ever have the money to go to the pictures in town on a Saturday night. This would have to do. It usually did.

She lifted her head and stared her father in the eye. *"Not every no-good,"* she said, *"I didn't see you there."*

With a roar the man lashed out and struck her in the face. The girl fell to the floor and wiped gently at her mouth with *the back of her hand. "Did you enjoy that?" she asked in a soft voice.*

He pulled back his foot and aimed a powerful blow into the girl's exposed stomach. She could see his wrinkled, flabby balls though the gap in the boxer shorts as the foot connected with its target.

Through a haze of pain she barely heard her mother's thin voice shouting from the kitchen, "Stop it, stop it." As always her father paid no attention. The boys grimaced but couldn't turn away. Once their father's anger was directed it wouldn't turn on them, as long as they kept quiet.

He reached down and dragged the gasping girl to her feet. He punched her in the face, once, twice, three times: blood spurted from her nose, and dripped down the front of her brother's plaid shirt.

From the back room a thin cry cut into the silence. With a gasp the mother slipped out of the room. She grabbed the baby from her crib and rocked the child furiously in her arms. She hummed a lullaby, dimly remembered from her own childhood, but scarcely comforted by the frantic rocking and unsettled by the tension in the cabin, the baby cried all the harder.

Once again the girl wiped her face. She stood up straight. "As I said, old man, did you enjoy that?"

The youngest boy gasped and the father, suddenly aware of his silent family watching the scene, turned on him. "Get out of my sight, you lot, this is no business of yours. Get out of here before I tan the lot of you." He lunged for the nearest boy.

The boys ran for the door, falling over each other in their haste to get out of the reach of their father's thrashing fists. Like a pack of young wolves they disappeared into the snowy woods, dressed only in their nightclothes with nothing on their feet.

Distracted by his sons the man forgot his daughter the

moment his back was turned to her. He stumbled forward and collapsed in a filthy heap on the nearest chair. He closed his eyes and began to snore. From the back room, the mother's voice singing the lullaby cracked on the notes and the baby cried harder.

The girl cleaned her face from a bucket of water beside the sink. Tears stung her eyes and slipped down her face but she did not make a sound. Once her face was as clean as she could make it, she gripped her stomach and limped past the snoring mess in the chair to collapse in her own bed.

When all was quiet in the rest of the cabin, the woman carried the now screaming baby into the kitchen and sat down at the table. She opened the front of her dress and placed the baby to her swollen and cracked nipple. The baby took one last gasp of air and settled down to feed. Her mother looked down at her in silence.

JOANNA'S EYES FLEW OPEN and remnants of the dream crashed around inside her head. She was instantly awake. The dream was strangely disturbing and she lay still, huddled under the quilts for a very long time, simply staring at the ceiling. She was still awake when the first weak streaks of daylight peeked through her bedroom window.

Combined with last night's experience in the woods, the dream left a gnawing feeling of discontent that permeated deeply. The strange appearance in the woods played itself out over and over again in Joanna's head. When she pushed it aside, the dream took over. She told herself continuously that she was imagining things, then she was scared that she was going "bush crazy." Which was worse, a ghost outside or a ghost inside? She couldn't decide.

Throughout the day, her hand continued to ache despite

large amounts of wishful thinking. She tried to work through the pain, but Dr. Richardson's warnings to keep her hand unoccupied kept coming back. Shifting black shapes were popping up in every unlit corner; lights remained on all day. Finally, in desperation, afraid for her sanity, she picked up the phone and dialed Toronto.

"Fred, I have to know now," she demanded. "Do you people have a contract for me or not? I have a really big offer from a major software company," she touched her nose to see if it was growing, "and I have to make up my mind. If I go with them I won't have time to do your work at least until the summer. So what's it gonna be?" She scarcely dared to breathe.

"Joanna, I was about to call you. Of course we want you. You must know that." He oozed charm through the phone. "How about Friday, two PM? Does that suit you? I can set up a meeting with all the principles for then."

"Let me check my calendar." Joanna watched a squirrel digging in the snow under the pine tree for a few moments. He came up with a prize nut and rushed off happily, the treasure clutched in his teeth. "Looks free for now," she spoke into the phone again. "I'll see you at two o'clock Friday, main board room. Oh, and Fred, be prepared to talk money." She hung up with what she hoped was a decisive click.

Breathless, she collapsed back into her chair, amazed at how out of character she had behaved over the phone. Demanding decisions, confrontation, lying. She chuckled nervously, then threw back her head and broke into a full-throated laugh. Felt good, too.

Friday morning she set off before dawn, deathly afraid that something would happen to delay her arrival. Joanna knew that she had a reputation for always being early. Rather than look efficient it made her look as though she had nothing better to do.

In her personal life it was worse. En route to a party once she stopped at the library, browsed the stacks, and checked out a few books. Yet, to her embarrassment, she was still the first to arrive.

In the few short months that she had been living up north she forgot how bad the Toronto traffic could be. There was a major accident on the 400 and everyone was screeching to a halt. From then on it was stop and go all the way into the center of town.

She forgot also, how much it cost to park downtown. For someone whose cash flow wasn't up to much lately the twenty dollars for underground parking in the center of the business district was a blow.

Nevertheless, Joanna emerged energized into the excitement of the city streets. Black shapes, haunting dreams and empty bank accounts were forgotten. She was pumped and ready to do business.

The offices of her old company were located close to King and Bay Streets, the financial heart of Canada. Serious-faced corporate employees dressed alike in their matching power suits, differing only in a choice of skirts or pants, scurried through the streets intent on the next deal.

On a very rare day Toronto would forget that it was almost winter and break out into warm winds and bright sunshine. Secretaries, office clerks and CEOs alike rushed out of their air-conditioned, sealed window offices to bask for a few brief moments in the faux-spring sunshine and munch on a hot dog purchased from the ubiquitous street-corner vendor. This was such a day and Joanna moved through the crowded post-lunch-time mob as if she belonged once again. Except that she felt terribly provincial in her heavy winter coat (it was minus ten degrees in Hope River this morning) and last year's suit.

The security guard at the front desk was new. He didn't recognize Joanna so she had to take a seat and cool her heels in the lobby while they tried to locate Fred. She watched groups of employees returning from over-long Friday lunches. There were a lot of new faces. The majority was dressed in semi-business wear—jeans and running shoes, a few in tracksuits. Joanna tugged at the hem of her skirt and glanced ruefully at her high heels. She forgot all about "casual Fridays," she'd look totally out of place.

"Joanna, there you are!" Fred Blanchard strode across the lobby, beaming widely. She got to her feet and accepted the out-stretched hand.

He pumped her hand enthusiastically. He was dressed im-maculately, as always, in light gray slacks and white open-necked shirt with a tasteful, thin stripe exactly matching the color of his pants. His salt-and-pepper hair was perfectly groomed, not a strand out of place. A large gold signet ring graced the little finger of his left hand, side by side with a huge wedding band. Joanna knew that he went for a manicure once a week.

He hustled her past the security guard and into the elevators. The moment the doors opened on the executive floor, a secre-tary was summoned to divest Joanna of her winter coat. She was an attractive, young blond dressed in skin-tight jeans and a short pink sweater that barely reached her waist. Open toed-pink shoes with three-inch heels would never be Joanna's idea of suitable footwear for casual day.

They watched the secretary totter off to the coat closet. "Where is Anna? I was looking forward to seeing her." Anna had been in charge of the executive floor for as long as Joanna could remember.

"She decided to take a package. Left about a month ago."

"That's funny," Joanna said. "When I spoke to her at my farewell party she told me she never planned to retire. 'They'll have to carry me out feet first in a wooden box,' is what she said."

"Well, people change their minds all the time. Bring in the coffee now," he ordered the returning secretary.

He held the door to the boardroom open with mock ceremony. Joanna looked around her with interest. As a lowly employee she had never before been through the hallowed portals. It was pretty disappointing. The prints on the wall were cheap and unimaginative, dirty coffee cups and saucers and a plastic platter containing the remains of a breakfast meeting's half-eaten muffins and bagels still sat on the side table. A tattered fake palm tree in dire need of a good dusting drooped against the window.

"Well, I must say, Joanna, you look marvelous. Absolutely marvelous," Fred gushed. "It's wonderful to see you again."

"It's great to be here," Joanna lied again. *I wonder if that hair is real,* she thought. *It always looks exactly the same.*

He noticed her bandages. "But what have you done to your wrist?"

"It's just a sprain. I fell skiing." Sounds a lot better than saying she slipped on a bar of soap in the shower. "But I can't use it much."

"Well, I hope it gets better soon."

The secretary arrived bearing a tray with a carafe of coffee and two sets of cups and saucers. They sat in silence while the coffee was poured.

The woman closed the door behind her as she left. Joanna wished that she would take the dirty dishes with her. She glanced at her watch. It was ten past.

"Who else will be joining us?"

Fred cleared his throat and opened the folder already in place on the table in front of him. "Just us today. I know that you and I can come to a reasonable deal."

"But I think we need input from all the department heads.

If I'm going to put together a truly comprehensive package, the more opinions the better. Don't you agree?"

Fred shuffled his papers and laughed nervously. "I think it's best to proceed slowly at first. We've decided not to go ahead with the entire package for the time being." He drummed his carefully manicured fingernails on the wooden table. "I think we could start with a user's guide. Sort of an introduction to the system, for now."

Joanna listened to him in mounting horror. This was not what she was counting on. She kept her face smooth and her voice steady as she sipped at the weak, tepid coffee just to give herself a chance to recover. "You know that in the long run it's a good deal more expensive and time consuming to try to do each piece as a separate unit rather than creating a strategy that covers all aspects of the entire product." Her voice sounded strong and steady, while inside she was screaming.

"Yes, we've discussed all that. But this is what we've decided to do."

She pretended to shift through the papers he passed to her, her mind racing. Her contract would be a lot smaller than she was hoping for, smaller than she needed to keep herself afloat.

"You worked so closely on drawing up the sales desktop, Joanna," Fred droned on in the distance. "You shouldn't have too much trouble writing it all up." She could turn it down, and try to find something bigger. But what if nothing else came up?

"How much?" She folded the papers neatly and smiled up at Fred.

He named a figure. Joanna shook her head. "That would cover one portion of the whole project," she said, "but if there is no whole project this will have to cost you more." She named a counter-figure. It was almost half as much again as she would reasonably expect.

Fred agreed without hesitation. She should have gone higher.

They covered off the details quickly. Fred handed her a slip of paper with the name and numbers of the technical analyst she would be working with, Francis Fukuyama. Another new name. "Unfortunately, he's not in today, or I'd take you down and introduce you. But you can give him a call when you're ready and he'll upload as much of the system to you as you need."

Fred walked her to the elevator. He gripped her hand firmly and held it too long. "So nice to see you again. Next time you're in town perhaps we could have dinner."

She pulled her hand away. "Perhaps." She stepped into the elevator and stabbed at the ground floor button. The doors shut firmly in front of her face.

Joanna visited her favorite bookstores to stock up on the latest mystery best sellers (of which the nearest library to Hope River was sadly lacking), and to check out what was happening in the world of computer books and periodicals. She stared at the rows of titles but registered very little. She tried to push the day's events aside but the disastrous meeting keep replaying itself in her mind, like an out of control video. Either Fred was out of the loop and he couldn't get approval for his project; or, he could be trying to shut her out. Offer her only a portion of the job in the hope that she would go away. Either way she was back into the hateful world of corporate politics that she moved to Hope River to escape.

She tossed a handful of paperbacks and magazines onto the cash counter with no idea of what she had chosen.

Joanna strolled up and down Queen Street West but she was far too tense and upset to fully enjoy the warmth of the late afternoon sun on her face. The locals were out in all their finery to celebrate the sunny day. The street was a veritable sea of black leather, nose rings and multi-hued hair. Before long she was experiencing a feeling of mild discomfort. It was apart from her frustration over the meeting with Fred, and it wasn't something she could put a name to. She felt uncomfortable and out-of-place in the crowded streets. Her winter coat was weighing heavily across her shoulders and her feet were aching in the unfamiliar pumps.

She was due to meet Elaine for dinner at six o'clock. Long before time she turned south on John Street and pushed her way through the crowds to one of her favorite eateries. The restaurant was still empty, staff milling aimlessly about waiting for the expected Friday evening rush. She asked for a table beside the window, and was given the best in the house, overlooking the street. The setting sun streamed in through the window and glittered gaily on the glassware. Joanna opened her bag of books and browsed through her purchases while sipping slowly at a glass of Merlot. Some of the titles she didn't ever remember choosing but as usual the unconscious had done a great job. She would love them all.

With a flurry of fur coat and squeals of delight Elaine burst into the dining room. Spotting the coat, the waiter rushed over immediately to escort her to the table and presented large, elaborate menus and a smaller, more discreet one for the wine list.

Once settled, they kissed each other enthusiastically and exclaimed, with total sincerity, over how well the other was looking. Elaine slipped on her reading glasses, a necessary embarrassment, and studied the wines carefully. "Shall we order a bottle, dear?"

"Nothing more for me," Joanna said. "I have to nurse this one all night."

Elaine dismissed the waiter with a wave of her hand. "Whatever for? Aren't you celebrating tonight?"

"Not exactly. And I've decided to drive straight home after dinner."

Elaine peered at her intently over the rim of the glasses. "I thought you were staying with Wendy."

"I didn't even mention to her that I'm in town." Joanna opened her menu. "I think there is some trouble between her and Robert. So I don't think this is a good time for me to impose on them. Besides, Wendy is worried about me enough as it is. I don't really want her to see this," Joanna held up her bandaged wrist, "and start worrying all over again."

"You could come home with me. You know you're always welcome."

Joanna smiled. She knew. "Not tonight, but thanks."

"Won't it be a long drive home?"

"Yes. But believe it or not, I miss it up there, and I've only been away since this morning."

They studied their menus in silence for a few minutes. "Everything looks so wonderful," Joanna laughed. "I can't decide. But I think that I should have something fairly light with that long drive still ahead of me. Seems like a waste, though."

"Well, I'm starving. So I'll make up for you."

The waiter took their orders: a small serving of pasta with roasted vegetables for Joanna, and for Elaine, mussels to start, followed by the veal with wild mushrooms.

"What do you mean, you're not celebrating tonight?" Elaine returned to the subject as the waiter slipped a basket of fancy breads onto their table. "Don't tell me you didn't get the contract!"

Joanna explained the details. "This is going to make it tough," she said. "I've going to have to drum up more business than I was expecting."

Elaine broke off a slice of pita bread and chewed thoughtfully. "Maybe you should go back. Try for the whole job. You know the work is there to be done."

"What do you mean? Fred said…"

"Never mind Fred. Fred's a jackass—I've always said so." Joanna smiled. That was certainly true. "There's a lot happening over there. Rumors are flying left, right and center all over town. That company is facing some major changes and if you want to do business with them you have to make some changes, too. So dump Fred. Go straight to his boss and make a pitch to him for the rest of your contract."

Joanna sat back as the beaming young waiter arrived with a plate of steaming mussels. "That seems awfully disloyal to Fred."

Elaine wrestled the tender meat out of its shell. "All you know is what Fred is saying. You don't owe him anything. So if Fred isn't telling you what you want to hear, find someone who will."

"Maybe. I'll have to think about it."

"You do that." Elaine bit happily into a mussel. "Heavenly."

Their main courses arrived and the women tucked in with gusto. All the tension of the last few days slipped away as Joanna rolled a length of pasta onto her fork and speared a roasted red pepper. No more troubled teenagers, or far-too-sexy artists, or strange dark shadows.

They finished the meal discussing Joanna's children, mutual friends and Elaine's business adventures. When the waiter brought the dessert tray, Joanna regretfully refused. "I'll never stay awake on the drive home." As always, Elaine demurred loudly that she "couldn't possibly" but soon relented and allowed herself to be talked into a huge slice of chocolate cheesecake.

Coffee was served in brightly colored giant cups with mismatched saucers: decaf for Elaine, regular for Joanna.

Watching her best friend sighing over a thick forkful of cheesecake, Joanna considered mentioning the sudden storm and the scratching noises and then the black appearance in the driveway. She was opening her mouth when Elaine pushed her dish back with a sigh and said, "I must tell you about the fiasco around this amazing fly-by-night mining firm. That people would buy into this half-baked adventure is beyond me." She chattered happily for several minutes and then waved for the check.

The women slowly walked back toward the center of the city, Elaine to catch the subway, Joanna to get her car. While they were in the restaurant the brief taste of summer had disappeared and winter winds were back with a vengeance. Joanna was glad to be able to wrap her coat around her and pull up the hood.

The drive home was long and dark and tedious. Not long after one AM, Joanna gratefully turned into the road leading to her cabin. And none too soon—she was getting too tired to be driving.

The forest closed in all around her, the only light provided by her headlights as they cut a thin beam of illumination through the encircling blackness. Along the sides of the road a seemingly impenetrable barrier of dark trees stood, guarding the depths of the forest beyond. Naked branches with thick snow-covered fingers reached out into the road, some of the taller trees linked hands to form a canopy overhead, reducing the world to a compact circle of Joanna, her car, the snow and the trees.

Joanna shivered; her imagination was getting the better of her. The car followed a bend in the road and the headlights caught the shape of a dark figure standing by the entrance to her driveway. Her heart leapt into her throat. He turned into the lights. It was Luke, holding up his hands to shield his eyes from the glare. She allowed her heart to settle back into her chest.

Joanna pulled up beside the old man and rolled down her window. "You really startled me, Luke. What on Earth are you doing out here in the middle of the night?"

Luke pulled off his cap and nodded, politely. "Evening, Joanna. Nice night, tonight."

"But, what are you doing here?" Joanna repeated. "Does your brother know you're up here?" She peered intently out the side window. Snow was falling thick and heavy. Her windshield wipers could barely keep up.

"Sure. Larry dropped me off before dinnertime to cut some wood up at Maude's place. I had dinner with Maude, then walked over to my place to do some chores what needed doing."

She was confused. "But no one is living at your place now. The house is gone. What sort of chores are there to do?"

"I was cleaning out the old barn," he explained. "Been meaning to do that for years, just never had the time. Tonight seemed like a good night, is all." He placed his cap back on his head and stood upright. "Night, Joanna."

"Wait, Luke. Would you like a ride somewhere? Can I drive you home? I mean, it can't be too safe out here this late."

The old man looked at her with an expression of bewilderment. "Not safe? I been walking these woods all hours of the day and night my whole life. Larry will be by soon, to pick me up. I'm just walking a bit up the road to meet him. Night."

She watched as Luke walked off down the road. The dark forest swallowed him up and he was gone. An owl hooted and the trees rustled in the wind as if in answer. She gratefully turned the car into her driveway.

As the front door swung open to let her into the cabin a slip of paper fluttered lightly down to the ground. She picked up the note and moved over to the desk light to read. "Where are you?" it read in thick, childish scrawl. "I was here for my lesson. T."

Joanna groaned. She had completely forgotten to tell Tiffany not to come today. Well, maybe forgot wasn't entirely the correct word. After the confrontation in the North Ridge alley she didn't think Tiffany would be back. She crumpled the note into a ball and tossed it into the wastepaper basket under her desk. No basketball player she: it missed and rolled into the corner.

THE NEXT MORNING she phoned Tiffany first thing to apologize for missing the lesson. Can't afford to offend a paying customer.

"Why, isn't Tiffany there with you?" Maude said, suddenly alarmed. "She told me that you said she could stay over last night because you were going to play computer games until late."

"Oh, Maude," Joanna said, "I am so sorry. I mentioned to her in passing that we would do that one Friday night and I would drive her home later. But I didn't say what Friday night. And I wasn't here yesterday. I had a business meeting in Toronto."

"Then where can she be?" Maude's voice was rising into hysteria.

"I'm sure there is no need to worry," Joanna said, attempting to sound calm. "She probably just stayed over at a friend's place. Why don't you call all her friends and I'm sure you'll find her."

"Yes, I'll do that. I'll start now. Good-bye, Joanna."

"Good-bye. And, Maude, if you need anything, please give me a call."

She drove into town to pick up her mail. She wasn't worried about Tiffany. The stupid girl jumped at the chance to have a night out without her grandmother knowing.

She sat in her car outside the post office, sorting through her mail. One envelope bore the return address of a major computer magazine. With nervous fingers she opened it and peeked in. The letter very politely informed her that her proposed article on *"Fighting Computer Viruses in your Home Based Business"* was not suitable for publication in their magazine at this time. They invited her to submit more articles at her convenience.

Joanna tore the letter over and over until all that was left were handfuls of large confetti. She stomped out of her car and dumped the paper into the garbage can on the side of the road. When she looked up, Tiffany was standing in the doorway of the post office, watching her.

The girl looked like hell. Her black eye-makeup had carved rivers down her cheeks. A family of rats appeared to have taken up residence in her hair. She wore only a light sweater over her jeans and shivered in the cold morning air.

"I need a ride home," she mumbled.

Joanna bit her tongue before she could insist that the girl say "Please." This was probably not a morning for a discussion of manners. "Get in the car."

Tiffany wrenched open the passenger door and slid inside. She crouched down low in the seat and chewed at her fingernails.

"Where's your coat?" Joanna started the engine, and turned the heat up full blast.

"Lost it."

"How can you lose your coat?"

"It happens, okay," Tiffany snapped.

"Your grandmother knows that you weren't at my place last night. She's very worried."

"Then stop yakking and take me home, okay!?"

They drove the route in silence. Joanna concentrated intently on the road, as if a vast chasm would suddenly open up and swallow the car, and its passengers, should she let her attention be distracted for one brief moment. Tiffany wrestled the last of the black polish off her nails.

Finally the endless ride was over. Joanna pulled up in front of Maude's neat house. "Do you want me to come in with you?"

"No, I don't want you to come in with me," Tiffany snapped, leaping out and slamming the door shut. Without a backward glance she ran up the steps into the house. The curtains were open and Joanna could see Maude cross the room hurriedly, arms outstretched. She turned away and backed the car out of the driveway before witnessing anything more.

As soon as she got home she made a cup of tea and collapsed into her chair to read the rest of her mail. The pile included several bills and a long letter from her ex-mother-in-law, now living in Florida, with whom Joanna made a special effort to remain on good terms. Then she fired up the computer to check her e-mail. There was one from her son, James, away at the University of British Columbia.

The stress that enveloped her whenever she was in Tiffany's company eased as Joanna gave herself in to the sheer enjoyment of her son's letter. She was laughing out loud at his efforts, wholly unsuccessful so far, to impress a young woman in his psychology class, when she heard a car turn into her driveway. This place was becoming more like Grand Central Station all the time.

She opened the door to face a very tired and tense looking man, well into late middle age. He twisted a black toque roughly in his hands.

"Ms. Hastings, I'm Larry Snelgrove, Luke's brother. Sorry to bother you but I was wondering if you have seen my brother since yesterday?" He blurted the question out before she could even say hello. "I know he does some work for you."

"What's the matter? Is he missing? I saw him last night. He was walking down the road. He told me he was on his way to meet you."

"Well, he never showed up. I was supposed to pick him up at the old property right after the bar closed at two. I was pretty late, got talking to some of the boys out in the parking lot."

"Come on in." Joanna stepped back. Belatedly, she held out her hand. He stuffed the toque into one pocket and shook her hand.

"Nice to meet you, Larry. It's too cold to stand outside. Perhaps he ran into a friend and spent the night somewhere else. Luke knows everyone around here, from what I understand. Would you like some tea? I've just made a fresh pot."

"Yes, please. Maybe that's what happened." Larry nodded eagerly at the thought, stripping off his coat and boots.

Joanna poured another cup of tea and set it on the table, then went to fetch hers and joined Larry.

Luke's brother gripped the mug so tightly in his hands, Joanna was afraid it would shatter. "It's just that he…Well, I worry about Luke, you know? If he did go to someone's place for the night, he probably wouldn't think about calling me. But anyone else would. They know I have to look after him. He's a lot older than I am, but ever since we were kids I have always sort of had to look out for him.

"I really don't want him hanging around the old place anymore. But I can't stop him. He belonged to that old house, you know. In a way that the rest of us can't comprehend. He's scared without it. He feels like he doesn't belong in the world any more. Can you understand that at all?"

"I can't imagine what it must be like," Joanna replied, honestly. "But I think I can understand on some small level. He told me last night that he was there to clean up the barn."

Larry laughed dryly. "As if anyone cares. No one will ever want to buy that property, and if they do they'll just rip down all the out buildings."

"Luke cares."

Larry loosed his grip on the mug and looked in her eyes. "You're right. Well, I'd better get going. Vera's at home, calling all the people around here. Hopefully he's sitting at someone's kitchen table right now, eating bacon and eggs. I'll drive around a bit. He wouldn't be lost. He knows every bush and tree in this part of the world, but he might have fallen or something. Keep your eyes open when you go out, will you please, Joanna?"

"Of course. Good luck."

She stared out the back window while washing up the teacups. A cold shiver crept over her as she remembered the night she heard the scratching at the door, and the sense of something watching her in the woods. Luke Snelgrove may have walked these woods all his life, but he was only a human after all, and no human ever truly belonged if nature decided they didn't.

TWELVE

THE NEXT MORNING panic spread throughout the area as Luke's whereabouts continued to be unknown. At last, Larry formally contacted the local police to report his brother as a missing person. Of course they knew about it all along.

Constable Jenkins settled himself at Joanna's kitchen table as she, once again, set out the tea things. She picked the mug that looked so much like Luke out of the cupboard, stared for a few moments at its funny/serious face, and put it back in the rack. Instead she selected one with "I love my Mommy" written in a pseudo-childish hand, a gift from countless Mother's Days ago.

Joanna related her story while Jenkins sipped his tea and slathered a freshly baked blueberry muffin with butter.

"You're sure of the time?" he asked through a mouth full of muffin.

"Reasonably sure. It was a very long, tiring drive back from Toronto. But I remember that the CBC news was ending as I drove through town. So it must have been about one or quarter past when I saw Luke."

"He didn't say anything about going to visit a friend or anything?"

"No. It was such a short conversation. I remember it pretty well. He was going to walk along the road until Larry drove up. That's it. You don't think that he could have just decided to leave? His home is gone, remember—burnt to the ground.

Maybe he just took off." Joanna thought of Luke's kind old face and didn't believe a word she said.

"Maybe," Jenkins mumbled reluctantly, "but remember, the man can't drive. Ain't many people to be passing by at one o'clock in the AM. And what there are ain't gonna pick up no old man they don't know."

"Yes, you're right."

"Seems like you're the last person who saw him. No one else has come forward yet. The whole county knows about it by now. You'd think if anyone knew anything they would be in touch with us."

She nodded in agreement. "Have you searched the area? Maybe he met with some kind of accident." She grimaced at the thought of kind old Luke lying helpless in the cold snow unable to call for help.

At her words Jenkins' worn face tightened. It was obvious that his thoughts were an echo of Joanna's.

"We'll be forming a search party later today. But there's a lot of land out there. Keep your eyes open, Ms. Hastings. If you'd like to help with the search, we're meeting over by the Number Three Concession Road at noon." He patted his belly and pushed the chair away from the table. "Nice muffins those. Didn't think you city folk could cook like that."

Joanna didn't know if she had been complimented or not. She decided to take it that way and showed Jenkins to the door.

AT THE APPOINTED HOUR, she drove slowly past the field where the search party was gathering, watching out for an open parking space. A line of vehicles, mostly pickup trucks, snaked along both sides of the road. The majority of the searchers were men and only a very few arrived singly, like Joanna. They formed into small groups, shifting from one foot to another uncomfortably and rubbing mittened hands together in an effort to generate some warmth.

The snowfall was tapering off, but it had fallen steadily since late last night, and a fierce wind was still blowing. The wind carved the snow into wild patterns across the landscape. Everyone knew that all traces of footprints would have long since disappeared.

She was standing uncomfortably at the edges of the crowd, feeling like the outsider she was, when she heard a piercing voice calling out her name. Nancy Miller waved wildly as she made her way through the small clusters of people. She was wearing the ugly fake-fur coat, this time with matching earmuffs. Her nose and cheeks glowed in the cold, but she smiled warmly at everyone she passed. Joanna looked around, searching for an avenue of escape, but she was too late. Nancy reached her, puffing steadily from her walk up from the road.

"It's nice to see so many people out, isn't it?"

Joanna nodded.

"Poor, dear old Luke. Most folks around here liked Luke very much." Nancy brushed a small tear away with her mitten. "God, I hope he's all right."

All around them people were getting restless. It was quite simply too cold to be standing around waiting for instructions. Eventually the Senior OPP Officer, whom Joanna recognized from the night of the fire, raised his voice and called for attention.

"You all know why you're here," he said. The crowd stood at attention, listening to every word. "We're looking for Luke Snelgrove. Most of you know Luke well. Now Luke was last seen Friday night around one AM, Saturday morning that would be. He was walking down this road. About an hour and a half later his brother Larry drove by and didn't see him. Luke talked to Ms. Hastings that night. Ms. Hastings, would you come up here and tell the folks what Luke was wearing?"

Joanna flushed with embarrassment. Every eye watched her make her way up to the front.

She described Luke's appearance as well as she could remember: heavy black overcoat, his usual brown cap, black or brown mittens. The police officer thanked her and she slunk back into the crowd.

"Now, I want this here half of you," with his arm he created an imaginary line down the center of the group, "to look on the south side of the road, and you others to take the north. Form a line and start into the woods. Keep the people on either side of you in sight and don't go any faster than the rest of your line.

"If you find anything, call out 'Over here' and an officer will come over. I don't want everyone else breaking the line to rush over and have a look." He glared at the crowd daring them to break the line. Everyone nodded solemnly.

"Don't you decide what is important and what isn't—that's our job. Is everyone sure of what they're supposed to be doing?"

Once again they all nodded, a few men mumbled their agreement.

"Let's go," a man shouted.

"Mind if I walk with you, Joanna?" Scott O'Neill stood off to one side by himself. He stepped forward as Joanna and Nancy passed. She hadn't noticed him arrive.

"If you want," she replied. As Nancy was regarding Scott with undisguised interest she felt obliged to introduce them.

"I knew your parents well." Nancy smiled at Scott. "They used to come into the store all the time. Real nice they were, too. I was very sorry to hear about them passing."

"Thank you," Scott said simply.

Nancy shouted greetings at several of the searchers and

fell back to talk. The moment she was out of earshot, Scott turned to Joanna.

"I've been meaning to call you," he said quietly, "and apologize about the other day in North Ridge. I'm sorry if I offended you. I don't know any of those kids and perhaps I was a bit quick to judge."

"Apology accepted," she said. "I think I was pretty much out of line as well."

He smiled at her, his teeth white and even. Snowflakes were sprinkled lightly among the salt and pepper of his hair, worn loose today, soft, thick curls touching his shoulders.

They were among the searchers assigned to the north side of the road. Fortunately it was still early in the season so the snow accumulation wasn't too thick, although in a few places it had drifted into soft piles that clutched at the searchers' knees. But it was still tough going—very tough. They plowed through wet, sticky snow, stumbled over broken logs and stumps and were sideswiped by low hanging branches. It was a dull, monotonous afternoon. Occasionally they heard a shout of excitement from further down the line, but it always came to nothing and the line carried on resolutely. Fingers freezing, nose running, eyes watering, sprained wrist throbbing, head to the ground, she walked on. The monotony was broken only once by a flash of excitement as shouting burst through the trees to her right. As instructed Joanna and her group of searchers resisted the urge to rush to the source of the commotion and reluctantly carried on along their assigned path. Their ears were stretching almost out of their heads as they tried to catch a whisper of what was happening. But soon enough word spread down the line; it was only an old high-topped Nike basketball shoe that, half-buried in the snow, the searcher had over-enthusiastically mistaken for one of Luke's winter boots. Even before the officer looking after their section arrived to inspect the find, everyone shrugged and carried on. Luke would never own a pair of shoes like that.

The December night descends early and fast in the North. By the time the search was called off due to fading visibility Joanna was tired, hungry, cold and cranky.

In ones and twos and small groups, they slowly returned to their cars, calling to each other not to give up hope, surely tomorrow something would be found, some indication that Luke was alive. Joanna marveled at their optimism. She, herself, had absolutely no doubt that after a few nights in the winter wilderness, no matter how much of a woodsman Luke might be, he was dead. She thought everyone understood that they were looking for a body, plain and simple. Obviously not.

Engines sputtered loudly to life and headlights broke through the dark, lighting up the heavily trampled clearing like a Wal-Mart parking lot on December twenty-third. The few groups of people who remained behind blinked and raised their hands against the harshness of the lights, and carried on gossiping quietly among themselves.

Joanna and Scott stood just outside a circle of men into which Nancy Miller had thrust herself. Joanna shuffled from one foot to another uncomfortably. She was more than ready to go home. Images of a hot bath, a glass of slightly chilled red wine and a beautiful dinner danced tantalizingly through her head. She glanced sideways at Scott. He grinned and smiled speculatively.

She was afraid he was about to ask her what her plans were for the evening, then she was afraid he wasn't.

"…said it was good riddance to bad rubbish and he didn't care if Luke was ever seen around these parts again." An elderly man with a massive gray beard and twinkling blue eyes paused to draw deeply on his pipe. He looked so much like a child's vision of Santa Claus it brought a ghost of a smile to Joanna's frozen blue lips.

"What a thing to say," Nancy Miller tut-tutted crossly. The others in the circle nodded in agreement. "If he doesn't watch his big, flapping tongue, people may start to think he has something to do with all of this."

"Who are you talking about?" Scott asked.

They were only too happy to fill him in. "Roy McMaster. Old guy lives over the other side of Hope River. Him and Luke have been enemies ever since they was in grade school. Only this morning Roy was sounding off to everyone who would listen…"

"And some what didn't want to," Nancy cut in.

"…that he wasn't sorry about Luke being missing."

"Pretty mean talk," a man agreed. No prizes for guessing this must be Santa Claus' son, Joanna thought. He was a paler image of the older man. His face was less lined, still a bit of black among the gray hair, beard not quite so bushy, eyes not quite so blue and they didn't seem to know how to twinkle. He resembled nothing so much as a cheap photograph of a famous painting. The reproduction may try to capture the colors, the lines and the image of the original, but could never achieve the depth or the power.

"Have the police spoken to this McMaster yet?" Scott said.

"Don't know," Santa Claus' son replied. "Roy and Luke been enemies ever since they was in grade school together. By now it's just a habit. Don't reckon as anyone pays any attention to them any more." He offered his hand to Scott. "Hugh Murphy."

Scott shook it. "Scott O'Neill, pleased to meet you."

Joanna smiled, all ready to shake hands and introduce herself as well. The men ignored her. The smile faded and she clasped her hands behind her back.

"You up to a couple of beers, O'Neill?" Hugh Murphy asked. "I'm too wired up to go on home. How about you, Pop?"

Santa Claus, presumably Mr. Murphy, nodded.

"Good idea," Scott said.

Joanna was appalled. Could her radar be that far off? She was so sure Scott was sending her getting-to-know-you-better signals that she was busily debating the pros and cons of accepting his offer before it was even extended.

"You ladies okay to get yourselves home?" Hugh asked, already moving toward his truck. She wondered what he would do if she said, "No." Ignore her, probably.

"Of course," Nancy tittered. Joanna's fingers itched to strangle her.

"Good night then." Scott waved over his shoulder. "See you soon, Joanna." Without a backward glance he followed the other men to the road. They were immediately swallowed up by the night.

Nancy and Joanna stood alone in the clearing. "That's a nice looking man," Nancy said with a bit of a leer and a sigh. "Wouldn't kick him out of bed for eating crackers."

"Do you mean Scott?" Joanna asked. "I hadn't noticed. Uh, do you feel like going out for a drink or something?" She was horrified to hear the words coming out of her mouth but they couldn't be stopped.

"Oh, I'd love to. But I really can't. I have to be getting home. Bill's gonna be wanting his dinner—I've already been later than I said I would. He's like a bear until he gets his dinner. You know how it is."

Joanna nodded, she knew exactly how it was. That was why she had never remarried.

In silence they walked each other to their respective cars. While they were talking, the night had closed in completely.

Snow was no longer falling. The moon was so bright it cast ghostly shadows among the trees. A shooting star flashed overhead and plunged to earth somewhere in the far distance. Nancy pointed and exclaimed with delight, but Joanna was so lost in gloom over the disappearance of Luke, the humiliation of Scott's departure, worries about her work, even Nancy's rejection of her offer of friendship, that she didn't even glance up to notice the beauty of the heavens. She climbed heavily into her car, started the lights and switched on the engine. Out of habit she watched Nancy until the other woman's pickup truck roared to life, and then she shifted into gear and drove slowly home, alone.

THIRTEEN

JOANNA STOOD UP from her desk and stretched lazily. After a few false starts the work for Fred was going well. Her wrist was feeling much better, with only the occasional twinge to remind her that she was supposed to be resting it. She worked hard all day, practically straight through with only a brief stop to make a tuna sandwich and a cup of tea for lunch. If she could keep this pace up she might be able to finish well ahead of schedule. The phone in the living room was unplugged and blissful silence filled the cabin all day.

The late afternoon sun was moving west, faster and faster toward its nightly bath in the icy waters of the lake. The soft winter light glistened brightly on thick white layers of ice and snow. Without checking the answering machine, Joanna slipped on her boots and coat and strolled down the hill to the lake. The caress of the fading sun, gently resting on her face, but not quite warming it, felt wonderful.

She stepped off the bank hesitantly at first, then with more confidence. The lake ice would easily hold her weight; people living around here turned the lakes and rivers into roads as soon as there was a sufficient thickness of ice.

She walked for a long way, lost in her own thoughts. It was almost a week now, since Luke's disappearance, and not a sign of the old man was to be found. The search parties were moving further afield, but people were losing their enthusiasm for marching through the winter woods in deep snow. Try as they might, it was hard to keep up the optimism.

High overhead a hawk circled lazily, his sharp eyes on the lookout for any movement crossing the sweep of white below. He dismissed Joanna as too large to take and broke out of his pattern, climbing higher and higher until he disappeared from sight.

The expanse of frozen lake was wide and untouched. She looked behind her to see only a single line of tracks disappearing back to the horizon. Before her the terrain was unbroken. She placed one boot carefully into the snow and withdrew it to create a perfect footprint.

"To boldly go where no one has gone before." She laughed at the thought.

The shoreline loomed to her side, dark and foreboding. The forest grew thickly right down to the edge of the water. Signs of human habitation were rare: the odd cabin in a clearing in the trees, a few boathouses boarded up tightly for the winter. Several docks had been crushed and twisted by the force of the ice—the annual repair job awaiting the owners who would return with the spring thaw.

She walked on, enjoying the silence and the solitude. She came up here, to the North, to get as far away from life, from people, as she could; yet over the last few months she had become caught up in the maelstrom of those around her. If she set up residence in an igloo at the North Pole, some lost soul would no doubt parachute right into her frozen front yard looking for a cup of tea or computer lessons.

But could she really survive, if everyone did leave her alone? Probably not. Humans were supposed to be social animals. Although some were certainly more social than others. Joanna always thought of herself as solitary; although people were constantly seeking her out, trying to offer company.

She and Wendy once went to a lecture on orangutans in Borneo given by the famous Dr. Brute Galdecus. Dr. Galdecus devoted her life to first studying, then trying to save, the wild orangutans and their forest environment. According to Dr. Galdecus, who should know, orangutans are truly solitary creatures. They move through the jungle alone most of the time. A mother and her child might not feel the need for the company of others of their kind for as long as eight years. Sounded good to Joanna.

An image of Scott smiling at her through the thick brush as they trudged on with the search for Luke leapt unexpectedly into her mind. She pushed it away roughly, then reconsidered and called it back. She had been divorced for a very long time now. At first she eagerly sought out another mate, but as time passed and the perfect man didn't present himself she came to rely more and more on herself. As the children got older she felt that she could never expect anyone to venture into the trauma that constituted their family life. The years passed and Joanna forgot that men could, sometimes, be fun and also be friends. Several men approached her, but she either ran in terror or simply didn't notice their intent. The effect was the same: he thought he was rebuffed and did not try again.

She shook her head and chased Scott out of her mind once again. He was too young. Probably just wanted to be friendly to the old woman living all by herself. After the night of the search, it was clear that he was not really interested in her.

A small plane roared overhead, startling Joanna out of her reverie. She glanced at her watch. It was getting late and she didn't want to be out on the ice once the sun went down. It would be awfully difficult, maybe impossible, to locate her cabin in the dark. There were few landmarks along the shoreline and she couldn't remember if she had left any lights burning in the cabin.

She followed her footprints most of the way back, although they were fading beneath the long, tireless brush strokes of the wind. She rounded the headland and the frame of the dock sprung into sight. Joanna let out a deep sigh of relief. She had been unaware of how much she was keeping her worry in check, afraid that she would be unable to recognize her bit of land when she came to it.

She clambered up the rocks onto the shore and sat for a moment to catch her breath. The dock was designed to come apart for winter storage. The planks were stacked in orderly rows on the rocks behind her. An old boat lay face down beside the pieces of dock. At her approach a squirrel popped up from under the wood and ran for cover.

A sudden gust of wind picked at a piece of fabric trapped under the boat. It waved at her and then flopped back down to lie still. She leaned over to get a better look. She was about to dismiss it as a cleaning rag when some instinct made her move in for a closer look.

It was a sleeve—of a coat. She tugged on the cloth. It was stuck under the boat. She lifted the boat slightly and the coat pulled free.

Joanna stood up to examine her find. It was in good condition; it hadn't been lying on the ground for long. In fact, it looked somewhat familiar. It was black and gray. She turned it over to see a large Bulls logo stitched onto the back. Rusty brown stains covered the hood and the front of the jacket.

It was very much like Tiffany's. The jacket she claimed to have lost. Carrying the garment, Joanna started back up the hill. She would call Tiffany and let her know that her coat was found.

Halfway to home she stopped. What was it doing out here? She walked back down the hill and stood hesitantly beside the boat. Tiffany may have dropped something else. She should really have a look. But anything could be under there. Dead animals; or worse, a live animal not happy at being disturbed.

She crouched down and pushed the boat a few feet to one side. A human hand, unnaturally white, flopped out. It lay on the ground, palm up, perfectly still.

Joanna screamed and fell back, rolling down the hill to crash to a halt up against a tree. A broken branch ripped through her coat and sliced into her back but in her shock she didn't feel the pain. She scrambled to her feet, gasping for air. The boat had fallen back to the ground, trapping the hand under it. Images from all the horror movies she had ever seen flashed through her mind. It looked as if someone was trying to crawl out from under the boat.

She gathered her breath calmly and with nerves she didn't know she possessed, walked slowly back to the boat. She took a deep breath and placed both her hands firmly on one side. With a burst of strength pulled from heaven-knows-where, she threw the boat over onto its back. A flurry of activity erupted as beetles and mice scurried out of the unexpected light.

Old Luke lay face down. She knew all along that it must be Luke. She couldn't see his face but the clothes were clearly his and the size was right. There were no visible marks but the black hair on the back of his head was thickly matted with a dark brown substance.

Joanna moved slowly up the hill, clutching the jacket to her chest. Behind her the beetles and mice crept out of their hiding places to resume their gruesome task.

FOURTEEN

JOANNA HUGGED a steaming mug of red zinger tea tightly in her hands, seeking to draw some warmth into her shaking body. She stood at the living room window and tried not to watch as poor, old Luke was carried on a stretcher up the hill to be laid in the coroner's van. But like a moth to a flame she was unable to turn away.

The two men carrying the stretcher slipped and slid on the snow and ice covered path. The front man tripped on a tree root and dropped his end of the load. It crashed to the ground accompanied by loud curses. The thick blanket they placed loosely over Luke's body flopped aside revealing the blood-encrusted head. The man at the back of the stretcher bit his tongue as he caught sight of Joanna standing stiffly in the front window, watching them. He flipped the blanket back into place; they resumed their burden and continued up the hill, out of her sight.

"Ms. Hastings, why didn't you search your property before this?" Constable Jenkins turned away from the window to resume his interrogation. "Everyone around here was looking for Luke."

"Well how was I supposed to know that," she snapped, the shock of the discovery breaking through her composure. She had to find someone to blame. "You didn't tell me to. No one told me. I'm from Toronto. We don't regularly search our property for dead bodies in Toronto. Maybe it's a rural custom I've missed."

Jenkins scratched his head. He didn't quite understand what being from Toronto had to do with anything but he knew that if this tea-drinking city lady had done what was expected it would have saved everyone a lot of time and trouble.

"It's all right, Jenkins. Why don't you go down and see if the forensic boys need anything. I'll talk to Ms. Hastings here." Bob Reynolds came into the cabin, stomping snow off his boots.

Jenkins agreed eagerly and slammed the door on his way out.

"Come over here and sit down." Reynolds motioned to Joanna. "You've had quite a shock."

She looked at him suspiciously, but slid into a seat.

"I don't think we've met, properly. I'm Bob Reynolds. Staff Sergeant in charge of the OPP detachment in these parts." He held out his hand.

Joanna shook it, still suspicious.

"We're interested for now in that jacket you found." The garment had been carefully bagged and taken away by one of the fresh-faced forensic "boys" from the nearest city. There appeared to be no "girls" in law-enforcement in this part of the world.

Reynolds was watching her. "Have you seen it before?"

"Plenty of times," Joanna replied before she could think it through. "Half the men and boys in Toronto are wearing jackets exactly the same as that one these days. Why they are so loyal to the Chicago Bulls, whoever they may be, I have no idea."

"Great basketball team," Reynolds said.

"What's the matter with Canadian sports teams?"

"What's that? Oh, well, nothing I guess. But didn't you say that a jacket just like that was on one of the people you saw running away from the Southland's property?"

"The what?"

"The break-and-entry you saw. It was at Mr. and Mrs. Southland's summer cottage."

"Oh, right. I just didn't know the name. Yes, I thought I saw one of those Bulls jackets, but as I say, every man and his dog is wearing one these days."

"But not every man in Hope River or even in North Ridge," Reynolds answered. "We'll be looking for someone who owns one of those. Well, thanks for your time, Ms. Hastings. I know how difficult all this is for you. But I'm afraid I'll have to ask you to stay away from the lake front, for a day or two, until we've had a chance to look over the area in the daylight."

Joanna nodded dumbly. As if she would want to venture back down to the lake any time soon and face the canoe, the stains underneath it, and the little animals and insects digesting who-knows-what. She fell into her chair. It was much more than she could take in. All she wanted now was to go to bed. She would process it all in the morning.

Sleep had little chance of coming. She could hear the shouts of the men as they worked, the steady rustling of dead and decaying leaves as they carried bags, full of evidence presumably, up the hill. Far off in the distance Joanna heard the deep growling of dogs. The police must think the—culprit? scum bag? perpetrator?—was still in the area. The thought didn't bother her, with the woods full of police officers and dogs they wouldn't be around for long.

She popped the cork on a bottle of French wine, her very best, the one she was saving in expectation of one day having a big contract to celebrate. She poured a glass almost to the rim and swallowed without tasting. She served herself another, forced thoughts of sweet sleep out of her head, ignored the lateness of the hour and picked up the phone to call Maude.

"It's Joanna. I want to come over and speak to Tiffany. Is she there?"

"Why yes, she is." Concern crept into the elderly woman's

voice. "What's happening up there? We saw all the police cars go by with their lights flashing. Are you all right?"

"Me? I'm fine. I'm coming over. Tell Tiffany I want to speak to her." She poured the full glass back into the open bottle and placed it in the fridge.

Maude was anxious, Rocky enthusiastically friendly and Tiffany characteristically defiant when Joanna arrived. Maude was wearing a heavy, red velour housecoat, fluffy pink slippers peeking out from under the hem. Masses of hairpins held her hair into tight gray rolls. Despite the urgency of her visit, Joanna was fascinated—she hadn't seen pin curls since she was a child visiting her grandmother for a sleepover. Tiffany was still fully dressed, watching the television with a steady, unblinking stare. Rocky danced about in delight—nighttime visitors were a rare treat. He sniffed at Joanna's crotch, a proper display of good manners, but was pushed aside with a snarl. Offended, the big dog crept off to his blanket by the fire.

Joanna got straight to the point—she was well past polite. "Tiffany, turn off the darn TV. I have to talk to you and I have no intention of competing with whatever rubbish that is."

Tiffany looked up in astonishment, but she leaned over and pushed a button on the machine. The yellow cartoon character with the big eyes was cut off in mid whine and the picture faded to black.

Joanna walked across the room until she was facing the girl. "Tiffany, I want to know where your jacket is. The Bulls one. And don't lie to me. It's in your interest to tell me the truth."

Maude opened her mouth to protest, but one look at Tiffany silenced her.

"I told you, I lost it." The girl sunk back into her chair, crossed her arms over her thin chest and glared.

"I've seen you wearing that jacket. I thought it might be you

I saw a few weeks ago. Someone very short, probably a girl, with a jacket just like yours was breaking into the Southland's cottage to steal liquor. And her companion looked a lot like that scruffy boy I've seen you hanging around with in town. But I wasn't about to accuse you."

Tiffany's eyes widened in surprise, and she started to chew at her fingernails.

"But I don't want to talk about that now. That jacket is about to get you into a lot more trouble than a break-and-enter. So I will ask you again, where is your winter jacket?"

Indecision wrestled behind the girl's eyes. Joanna stood her ground but didn't say a word. She left it up to Tiffany to struggle with her own demons. If the girl rejected her, Joanna would leave the room and never come back. Maude glanced from Joanna to her granddaughter and back and remained silent.

The defiant set of Tiffany's shoulders deflated and she sunk further into her chair. "Okay, I was wearing it when you saw us at the Southland's place. They're just a couple of rich city jerks. Christ, they can buy out the whole liquor store and not care a bit. If they leave booze lying around all winter they're just asking someone to come in and take it, you know." She glanced at her grandmother, begging for the older woman's understanding. "It was just for fun, Grandma, really. What the hell else is there to do in this stupid place?"

"Watch your language young lady," Maude spoke sharply. "You know I'll not have that sort of thing in this house." It hurt Joanna to see the pain etched into her face.

"Sorry, Grandma," the girl mumbled into her flannel-coated chest.

"And after that," Joanna persisted. "What happened to it after that? Do you know why I am asking you this, Tiffany?"

The girl's head snapped up. "No, I don't. It's just a jacket.

There are hundreds like it." Tiffany's voice lowered to a whisper. "My mommy bought it for me. Once she started on the booze she didn't buy me much. Didn't have any time for me then. But one day we were in the store and I told her how much I liked that jacket. That I wanted one like it.

"So she bought it, right there. It cost over a hundred dollars. She didn't make that kind of money working at Tim Horton's, you know. It was a great jacket."

"So, where is it now?"

"I lost it. What is it to you, anyway? I lost my jacket. Some jerk stole it."

"Tell me how you lost it."

Tiffany opened her mouth to tell Joanna to mind her own business but the look in the woman's eyes stopped her.

"My mom bought it for me. But I lost it. We went to the pool hall in North Ridge. I left it alone for a few minutes and some jerk stole it. It wasn't there when I came back to my seat. I'm sorry, Grandma. I know you don't want me going there, but sometimes there isn't anything else to do."

Maude fell back into her chair. Rocky walked to her side and whimpered. The dog licked her outstretched hand, love reflected in every movement of his big head.

"Was that the Friday night before I found you in town?"

"Yes."

"What is all this about, Joanna?" Maude interrupted. She scratched behind Rocky's ears. "Why are all these questions so important?"

Joanna ignored her. "Where were you that night, Tiffany? And tell me the truth. Please. Don't lie. I've had more teenage lies told to me than you can imagine. If you lie to me I'll throw you to the wolves."

Tiffany stared at her, frightened by the worry in Joanna's

voice. "All right, I'll tell you. I spent the night in the alley behind the Last Chance Bar."

Maude gasped. Rocky whimpered.

"I'm sorry, Grandma, but that's the way it was. I went to your place, Joanna, to play computer games, like you said we would. But you weren't there." Shades of the child she still was crept into her voice. "So I came home and called Rick. Grandma was out. Rick and a bunch of the gang picked me up and we went to North Ridge. We played pool, had some wings, then some jerk stole my coat. The other guys left and Rick wanted to have sex. But I didn't wanna. I didn't want to bother you, Grandma, so I slept in the alley behind the 'Last Chance Bar'. The next morning I hitched to Hope River where Joanna found me and I came home. That's it."

By now Tiffany's nails were bitten down to the quick. Her voice toughened once again. "I've told you what happened," she said defiantly, "so now you tell me why it's so important."

"I found Luke," Joanna said simply. Maude gasped again and Tiffany looked up from her fingernails. They all started at the loud cry of the police dogs as they made their way along the lake and into the woods. Rocky's ears twitched, but well trained, he did not leave Maude's side.

"And…" the old woman asked.

"He's dead. Poor Luke. Murdered, almost certainly. Left under a canoe on my property. That's why all the police are up at my place tonight. But you see, Tiffany, what I found first was your jacket. Nicely tucked in with the dead body."

"No, not mine." Tiffany leapt out of her chair. "I didn't kill Luke. Why the hell would I do that?"

"Sit down, girl." Maude's voice rang out sharply. "You haven't been accused of killing anyone, yet. But I want to hear the rest of Joanna's story."

Tiffany sunk back into her chair. Joanna continued, "It was one of those stupid Bulls jackets. Like you have, or had. There are a lot of those jackets around. I didn't tell the police that I know you have one, Tiffany. But I'm not going to lie to them either. If they ask me right out, I will tell them. But up to that they can do the leg work themselves."

Tiffany was crying now. "I didn't kill Luke. Someone stole my jacket, I told you that. You can't say I killed Luke."

Joanna rose to leave. "I'm not saying you killed anyone, Tiffany. Because, to be honest, I don't think you did. But you had better stay out of trouble for now."

Maybe for the first time in her life Maude let a visitor leave without offering tea. Instead she followed Joanna to the door. Rocky whimpered anxiously at her heels. He was terrified, something was happening, he was being ignored and he couldn't understand why.

Maude gripped the other woman's arm tightly. "Tiffany didn't kill Luke."

"I know that. Though why I know it, I don't know," Joanna said. She hugged Maude fiercely then turned to go.

A thin, childish voice piped up from the other side of the room. "I'll be over Friday, Joanna, for my lesson. Can I stay late and play Tomb Raider?"

"Yes." Joanna patted Maude's hand, which was still clinging to her own. "Why don't you plan on staying overnight and I will drive you home in the morning. Is that all right with you, Maude?"

Maude nodded stiffly and Joanna said her good-byes. She walked heavily to her car, as the flashing red light of a police car drove past.

NEWS OF THE DISCOVERY of Luke's body spread through the district like wildfire. To Joanna's dismay phone calls to the cabin resumed in earnest. She briefly considered moving out for a few days, at least until all the excitement passed over. But she was making good progress on her work and was afraid to break the momentum, so she settled for hiding the phone in a drawer and curtly dismissing the few visitors who popped by to discuss it with her in person.

She knew she was developing a reputation in the town of being "unfriendly," a position she didn't mind one bit. She had moved up here to be alone and she was getting altogether too little of that.

Try as she might, however, she couldn't ignore the attentions of the police. Staff Sergeant Reynolds returned the next morning, bringing with him a homicide detective all the way from the big city.

To Joanna's considerable surprise, the detective was a tall, slight, crisp, stern-faced woman, one Detective Inspector Erikson. Although she was well on her way to middle age, the inspector's hair was still a natural ash blond, a remnant of her Viking ancestry, along with the cool blue eyes. A few strands of gray were barely visible in the thick mass, which was tied tightly back into a severe bun. She was dressed in a somber brown pantsuit with a plain white blouse, tiny gold earrings and cheap pantyhose bunching around her ankles. She carried an unattractive, heavy brown purse from which she pulled out a tiny ring-bound note pad, and a pen.

They sat in the living room and went over the events of the previous day in tedious detail. Erikson wrote everything down in her notebook. Joanna explained, once again, about her late-afternoon walk on the lake and how she came to the unfortunate discovery of Luke's body under the boat. She was already thoroughly sick of telling the story, and knew it would be much worse by the time all of this was over.

"When was the last time you were down by the dock?" Erikson asked. Her voice was surprisingly high-pitched.

"More than a week, I would guess," Joanna said. "Two weeks, maybe."

"And you saw nothing out of order at that time?"

"No. Nothing I can remember."

"Tell me again about this jacket you found, the black one," Erikson said.

"It was lying under the boat, with just the sleeve sticking out."

"Too bad you moved it." Staff Sergeant Reynolds was standing at the window with his back to the two women. Up to now he had not joined in the conversation.

Joanna bristled at the criticism and glared at the staff sergeant's broad back. "Well how was I to know what else was under that boat?" She turned back to Erikson, in time to catch a sparkle of laughter in the detective's eyes before it was quickly extinguished. Joanna found herself liking the woman. She had enough experience working in a man's field to know that you sometimes had to submerge your own personality in an effort to belong.

She looked at the staff sergeant again, standing ramrod straight, back to the room, staring out the window. She suspected that he resented having to tolerate a big-city detective moving in on his case, and the fact that she was a woman probably made it all the worse.

"You didn't see any other loose clothing? Other than the jacket?" Erikson continued the questioning.

"No, nothing."

"Did you hear any unusual sounds in the last few days? See any signs of people on your property who aren't supposed to be here?"

Joanna shuddered and shook her head. Until now the thought simply hadn't occurred to her: someone either killed Luke by the lake or carried the dead body down the hill. Either way they were close to her—too close. She considered telling Erikson about the dark shape under the trees, but she had seen it only that once, and was afraid the inspector would think her nervous and over imaginative.

The police didn't stay for much longer. Erikson folded her notebook and returned it and the pen to her cavernous purse. She handed Joanna a business card. "If you think of anything else, give me a call at that number. If I'm not there, leave a message."

Reynolds grunted and Erikson quickly added, "Or call the staff sergeant here, of course." The twinkle flashed through her blue eyes again.

Joanna turned the card over in her hand. "I will."

She stood at the open door for a moment as inspector and sergeant made their way down the steps. She caught only two words of their conversation.

".. Mitchell, now…" Erikson said. Reynolds nodded.

Joanna stood in the doorway until she heard their car drive off. She grabbed her coat and ran out to her own car.

She drove slowly past Maude's, straining to see the house through the dark woods. As expected, the police car was in Maude's driveway. Joanna parked her car and sat for a moment deep in thought, watching Reynolds and Erikson knock politely on the front door.

She didn't particularly like Tiffany, didn't want anything to do with the girl and her problems, so why did she feel the need to interfere, to protect the teenager? Joanna couldn't find the answer, couldn't put it into words. It existed somewhere in her own past, in her own dark years of dealing, or rather, not dealing, with teenage angst. Of trying, and failing, to get through to an angry and troubled young woman. She had failed the last time, perhaps that was why she was drawn to try again.

She switched off her engine and marched decisively up to Maude's home.

A look of absolute relief flooded through Maude's aged and worry-lined face when she saw Joanna standing in the door. She eagerly invited the younger woman to come in.

"Oh, sorry. I didn't know you had company. Am I interrupting anything?" Joanna handed her coat to Maude and pulled off her boots, without being invited to stay.

This time Reynolds sat in the prime chair, the one closest to the fireplace, while Erikson rummaged through her bag for the notebook and pen. Neither one of them looked happy to see her.

"If I'm interrupting anything, I could come back later." Joanna smiled sweetly at Maude.

"Not at all, dear. Please come in," Maude replied, as Joanna knew she would. As he did every time, Rocky sniffed at her crotch in welcome. There was no sign of Tiffany.

"We'd like to speak to your granddaughter, Maude," Reynolds said. "Is she here?"

"Yes, but she's in bed. What's this about? Can't it wait?"

"Would you get her up please, Mrs. Mitchell," Erikson said firmly. "We'd like to talk to her now."

Maude hesitated and glanced at Joanna. Joanna nodded. This was going to be rough, might as well get it over with.

The group waited in silence while Maude went in to get Tiffany. Reynolds shifted uncomfortably in his seat. Erikson casually reviewed her notes. Rocky paced. Maude returned to sit on the edge of her chair. Rocky paced some more. Maude picked up a piece of knitting from the coffee table beside her and turned it in her hands.

"While we're waiting, I would like to ask you some questions, Mrs. Mitchell," Erikson said. "The night of Friday, December second, were you home all evening?"

Maude placed the knitting needles in position and selected a length of wool. Her hands were shaking. "I'm not sure, that was a while ago."

"Try to remember, please—take all the time you need."

Maude glanced quickly around the room. Her eyes flickered but didn't settle on any one person. She returned to her knitting and studied it carefully.

The silence stretched into minutes. Maude put her ball of wool down. "I went out about five or so, I think."

"Where did you go?"

"To Nancy Miller's place. I'm knitting a sweater for her husband." She held up the unfinished garment as evidence. "I went over to pick up the wool she bought for me to use."

"Did Tiffany go with you?"

"No."

"What time did you get home?"

"Around seven."

"Was Tiffany here when you got home?"

"No."

Tiffany marched into the room. She had dressed quickly and had pulled a brush through her purple hair. She stood with her hands on her hips, legs spread apart.

"Hello, Tiffany," Reynolds nodded at her. "Why don't you sit down."

"I'll stand," she said, biting off the words.

Maude continued to stare at the wool on her lap. No one introduced Tiffany to Inspector Erikson.

"Do you know where she was?" Erikson returned her attention to Maude.

"At Joanna's. She told me she was spending the night at Joanna's. They were going to play computer games."

Erikson flipped back a few pages in her notebook. "But Ms.

Hastings told me she was in Toronto that evening until late."
She sounded confused.

Maude shrugged, mute.

"If you weren't at Joanna's, where were you, Tiffany?"

Tiffany shifted under the inspector's icy blue gaze. Silence
hung like a razor-edged sword through the comfortable room.
Rocky whimpered in confusion and nuzzled Maude's leg, seeking
comfort. In the fireplace a log collapsed in a flurry of sparks. A
finger of bright red flame danced higher. Tiffany, Joanna, Maude
and Reynolds watched the fire. Erikson watched Tiffany.

"Joanna didn't tell me she was going out." The girl glared
at Joanna. All this was her fault. "There was no one there. So
I came home."

"Did you stay home all evening?" Again Erikson consulted
her notes. Joanna was sure that the detective remembered every
word written there. "Your grandmother didn't see you when she
came home."

"I called some friends. They picked me up and we went into
North Ridge."

"What did you do in North Ridge?"

"Look, Inspector," Joanna asked, "is there some reason for
these questions? This girl is only fourteen years old, you know.
Perhaps you should get to the point." Joanna knew all there was
to know about juveniles and the law.

"The point, Ms. Hastings?" Erikson cast her cool gaze on
Joanna. The twinkle was definitely gone from her blue eyes. "I
will get to the point soon enough. What did you do in North
Ridge, Tiffany?"

"Hung out—no crime in that is there?" The girl shifted her
weight and planted her feet again. Joanna wanted to shout at
her that her attitude wasn't doing her any good. But even if she
dared to find the words Tiffany would pay no attention.

"That depends, I think, on what happens when one is 'hanging out,' don't you? What time did you get home that night?"

"Don't remember."

"Mrs. Mitchell, do you remember what time it was that Tiffany got home?"

"No."

"Was it after you went to bed?"

Maude continued to knit. She was dropping stitches all over the place. The whole thing would have to be ripped out and started all over again. "Yes, it was after I went to bed."

Joanna knew that she should speak up. She waited to be asked a question. It didn't come.

Instead Inspector Erikson turned her attention back to Tiffany. "Can I see your Bulls jacket please?"

Tiffany's face registered the first reaction of the day. "My jacket? Why do you want to see it?"

"I have been told that you own one. Can I see it, please?"

"Who told you that?"

"I hardly think that matters. Can I see it, please?"

"Unfortunately the jacket has been lost," Joanna interrupted. "Tiffany told me it was stolen. Happens all the time with these sort of trendy clothes."

"Yes, I know. When was it stolen, Tiffany?"

"Don't remember."

"You don't remember? That seems odd. Not to notice that your jacket has been stolen in the middle of winter."

Tiffany shrugged.

Inspector Erikson shut her notebook firmly and rose to her feet. Reynolds scrambled to follow suit.

"I'll be in touch," the detective told them, "and if your jacket should somehow show up, I would suggest that you contact the police immediately." She crossed the room to place one of her cards on the table beside Maude. The older woman sat stiffly in her chair, staring at the mess of knitting in her hands. She did not get up to show them to the door. Once again, no tea was offered.

"I wonder what your interest in all this is, Ms. Hastings," Erikson turned to Joanna. Reynolds had already escaped and was hurrying down the path, the very picture of a man in agony. He had accepted a posting back to Hope River, where he grew up, happy to spend the few years before retirement in his hometown. He had known Maude all his life.

"The girl is only fourteen," Joanna reminded the inspector. "I think sometimes we forget that they are still just children, don't you?"

"I never forget what a fourteen year old can do." The twinkle was gone and the blue eyes had turned slate gray, as gray as the snow-filled clouds filling the sky outside Maude's carefully kept home.

Joanna left immediately after the police. Tiffany marched off to her room with a loud slam of the door. Maude sat stunned and mute in her chair. She looked very old. Unable to help, the huge malamute whimpered at her feet.

WORK ABANDONED, Joanna wrestled most of the day with her own better judgement. It was folly to get involved in Tiffany's life. Clearly she had not endeared herself to Inspector Erikson. She must remember that she found Luke's body on her property. That alone must put her high on the suspect list, although she had no motive.

Motive, she thought as she paced the small living room. Who would have a motive to kill Luke? Maybe there was no motive, just a random killing, something to do on a Friday night for kicks. She threw another log into the stove. That was a truly terrifying thought for a woman living alone in a cabin in the woods. Much preferable to concentrate on trying to find a motive.

The dwindling stack of firewood reminded her forcefully of Luke and the very few times they spent together. She remembered that he spoke of people, of music and parties, in the woods at night. Teenagers, he had said. Tiffany Jordan among them. He had confronted them and chased them away. She sat at her desk the remainder of the day, too deep in thought to do much work.

FIFTEEN

A FEW DAYS LATER, Joanna stood at the open fridge, warily eyeing the sparse contents. Dinner tonight was a choice between a leftover pasta dish, which was completely tasteless to begin with, a boring salad, or the ubiquitous peanut butter sandwich. As she was contemplating which was the lesser of all evils a horn sounded in the driveway, announcing a visitor.

She slammed the fridge door shut with a groan. Another busybody with nothing more interesting to do than nose around the murder site.

"Yoo-hoo, anybody home?" Nancy Miller's piercing voice sounded from the front porch. Joanna wondered why she didn't simply knock.

Nancy stood at the door looking uncharacteristically shy and insecure. She held a casserole dish out in front of herself like an Inca Priest at the sacrificial offering. "I brought you a little something," she said shyly. "Everyone is talking about Luke's body being found here and all. So I thought you might not want to come into town for shopping and all." She thrust the offering at Joanna.

Joanna accepted it. She had no choice. And it did smell quite wonderful. "Thank you, thank you very much. Won't you come in." The words escaped before she could stop them.

Nancy visibly relaxed and smiled as she stepped through the doorway.

"It must have been quite awful for you, Joanna," Nancy said. "But even worse for poor old Luke. Do the police have any idea who did it?"

Joanna kept her thoughts to herself. "No, I don't think they do."

"I heard they brought in a hotshot detective from Toronto," Nancy went on. "A woman. Can you imagine that?"

"Actually, I can," Joanna replied. "There are lots of women in the police now, you know. I had better put this in the kitchen." She nodded at the casserole dish. "Have a seat, please, and I'll be right back."

"It must be quite wonderful," Nancy chattered as she followed Joanna into the kitchen, "to be a policeman, or woman I guess I should say. I wonder sometimes what I could have done, if Mamma hadn't died when she did so that I had to come home to Hope River to look after my daddy and the family."

There was nothing Joanna could say to that. She filled the kettle with water and put it on to boil.

"Maybe I could even have been a writer like you. You could write about this, you know. About the murder I mean. You could write a detective story about Hope River."

"Well, I'm not a fiction writer. I think I told you that. It's very different."

"People are saying that it's Tiffany Jordan."

"What's Tiffany?" Joanna demanded, although she knew the answer already.

"The murderer. They're saying that Tiffany, or one of her no account friends did it. Tiffany's jacket, or one just like it, was found with the body, I hear."

Joanna bristled. She was about to terminate this conversation when Nancy sighed and continued.

"People don't have enough to do sometimes. I know that Tiffany is into a bad crowd, but that doesn't make her a murderer, does it? Sometimes I think that teenagers get accused of everything these days. But they're no different than when we were girls, are they, Joanna?"

In fact Joanna thought that they were much different, but she nodded in agreement.

"I remember Tom Krozenski that I was in school with. He set fire to the principal's office once." Nancy laughed at the memory. "He didn't mean to burn up the whole office. Just thought he would start a fire in the wastepaper basket, make a lot of smoke and have everyone running around. Instead, the fire got away from him and pretty near burnt down the whole school. All us kids knew it was Tom, of course, but no one let on to the police. Tom's a professor at some big city university now, I hear. Did all right for himself, just had a lot of steam to let off when he was young, is all." Nancy accepted a cup of tea, added a splash of milk and three spoonfuls of sugar, and they carried their cups back into the living room.

"So when people come into the store and say that Tiffany and her friends killed Luke, just because they don't like the way they dress or the way they do their hair, or the way they talk, I have to fight really hard not to tell them to mind their own business. I started to argue with John Dietrich this morning, right in the store. John says that Tiffany sassed him once, and he thinks that makes her a murderer. Damned fool. Uncle Jack got real mad at me. Told me to mind my mouth, that the customer is always right. Maybe so, but it makes me real mad. And it's not as if Uncle Jack isn't above sassing a customer if they get in his way." Nancy's pudding face was set with fierce determination and her eyes flashed with the injustice of it all. She took a deep breath and sipped carefully at the hot tea.

With a pang of reproach, Joanna saw Nancy in a new light. She had been far too stuck up to venture beyond this woman's country-peasant exterior to even try to guess at the emotional depths of the person beneath.

Nancy finished her tea quickly and rose to her feet. "Anyway, I hope you enjoy the casserole. I have to be getting home now. Bill will be wondering where his dinner is. He gets right annoyed if it isn't on the table smack dab at six o'clock."

Nancy bustled off in a flurry of good-byes and furious honking of the overworked car horn. Joanna watched her until the headlights of her car disappeared down the road and the engine faded into the distance. Only then did she push her guilt to the back of her mind and rush back to the kitchen to inspect the casserole pot. She lifted the heavy lid and waves of warm, fragrant steam rose up to greet her. It was a dish of chicken, cooked in a thick mushroom sauce with bright splashes of red and green peppers, bathing in a bed of fluffy white rice. She took a deep breath and sighed with contentment.

She popped it into the oven to stay warm and went into the bedroom to check for messages on the answering machine.

The light was blinking angrily, chastising her for ignoring it all day, but the messages were all hang-ups, except for Fred Blanchard anxiously inquiring how the work was going, and Scott O'Neill asking her to return his call.

Fred could wait. She called Scott.

His voice was warm and deep, sounding genuinely pleased to hear from her. It wrapped her in a nice comfy feeling, which she decided to ignore, for now.

"We didn't get much of a chance to talk," he said, "the day of the search for Luke. I heard that you found the body and all…and I was thinking that must be pretty hard to take…so I was wondering, if you have the time that is, if you would like to go into town for a burger or something? I could come by your place and pick you up."

She was bone tired. As nice as it would be to go out on a real date she was about to say no, explain that she was too tired to go out and hope that he wouldn't take it as rejection. But a whiff of Nancy's chicken and mushroom casserole floated tantalizingly through the cabin. "I have something in the oven right now. There's plenty for two. Why don't you come and have dinner here with me?"

"Great," Scott said with enthusiasm. "Let me know how to get to your place and I'll be right over."

Joanna gave him the directions quickly and hung up the phone. She rushed about the cabin, picking up discarded clothing, tidying her desk, putting away the remains of the breakfast dishes and mopping the floor.

Once the living room and kitchen were moderately tidy she stood at her bedroom closet, staring blankly at the contents. Not a single thing looked suitable. She had one or two business suits, far too severe for a spontaneous dinner at home, or jeans and track suits, too casual. She finally decided on a pair of jeans matched with a crisp white blouse and a denim vest. She dabbed a bit of makeup on her eyes and cheeks and fluffed her short curls. Too late to wash her hair now. She stood in front of the long bathroom mirror. Perfectly dreadful, but it would have to do. At the last minute she added a dab of perfume. A Christmas gift from her former mother-in-law, hardly ever used.

Fortunately there were plenty of fresh vegetables in the fridge. She tossed them together in a large wooden salad bowl to serve as the first course. Nothing for dessert. Couldn't be helped. She placed fresh candles on the table and arranged her favorite CDs in the player.

All too soon she heard the familiar sound of a car pulling into her driveway. She fluffed her curls one last time, straightened her smile and went to open the door.

She watched Scott make his way down the hill. An hour ago she was dead tired, mentally more than physically, but now she was pumped and energized.

Scott passed her a bottle of wine prior to discarding his heavy outdoor clothing. His very presence filled the tiny cabin to overflowing. "Not a very good bottle, I'm afraid," he said, "but the best I could do at such short notice."

She smiled. "I have something we can start with." She produced a bottle that she had opened earlier to decant and poured them each a glass. Scott nodded in appreciation and they settled in the living room before the old wooden stove. A Beethoven sonata clicked into place on the CD player. Perhaps she should have chosen something less romantic.

"I heard what happened," Scott said, stretching his long denim-clad legs out toward the fire. "Of course everyone in this part of Ontario is talking of nothing else. Must have been rough. Finding the body, I mean."

"Yes, it was. And the police have been nosing around ever since. Along with every busybody in the district."

"It's a small community. Hard to get used to at first if you're from a big city or the suburbs. What brought you up here, anyway?"

They chatted casually for a while, avoiding anything serious, about Scott's art and Joanna's attempts to set up her business.

His eye settled on the group of family photographs arranged on the table. "Are those your children?" he asked. "Nice looking kids. What are they up to now?"

"Dinner should be ready." She hurried into the kitchen to pull the casserole out of the oven, hoping it wouldn't be cold. She had turned the oven off an hour ago, afraid that it would overcook.

It was perfect. Once they finished Joanna's bottle she opened the one Scott had brought. When the meal was finished and the last of the wine poured, he helped Joanna carry the dishes out into the kitchen and washed up while she tidied the table and put the salad ingredients back into the fridge. She ground beans and put the coffeepot on while Scott went to stand by the big front window looking out over the lake.

"It's a lovely night out," he said. "Why don't we go for a walk and have coffee later?"

"Sounds like a great idea."

A full moon shone heavy and white in the clear night sky, reflecting enough light off the snow to give the appearance of a ghostly sort of daylight. A scattering of stars twinkled high above, only the brightest able to pierce through the brilliance of the moonlight. There was no wind.

In contented silence they walked down the hill toward the lake. Remembering what she had found there, Joanna turned sharply from the path and they cut through the woods to come out at the water's edge close to the boundary of her property. They climbed over the rocks at the shoreline and walked out onto the thick layers of ice that now constituted the lake. The howl of a wolf could be heard very faintly in the distance.

"Are you happy up here?" Scott asked, talking her mitten-wrapped hand in his. "This is quite a change from your life in Toronto."

"That it is," she said, "but I'm very happy. At least I think I am. After all that's happened over the last few years, it's hard for me to tell what's happy, and what's just feeling numb." She briefly considered confiding in him about the darkness in the woods and the scratching at the cabin door, but as with Inspector Erikson, she feared that he would think her weak and frightened, a hysterical woman not able to cope with life on her own. So she said nothing.

They walked on.

"Except for all this horrible business about Luke of course." Joanna broke the silence. "I really came up here just to be alone. I was sick of the corporate rat race, of spending as much time playing politics as doing my job. I knew that if I set up in business on my own, I couldn't earn enough to stay in the city, at first anyway, so I wanted to find someplace where I can live really cheap, at least while I see if I can make it on my own or not. So I took this place. And it suited me to come up here. I was also tired of people making demands on me all the time. I've always been a bit of a loner, but with three children and a house in the suburbs that's pretty hard to do. So, now that my children don't need to be living with me any more I wanted to really experience living alone." Joanna breathed the night air deeply. It filled her lungs, clear and crisp and cold. But all she could think of was the bulk of the man beside her, of how his beard was filling with crystals of ice, of his tender brown eyes and soft understanding voice.

"We'd better turn back," he said. "It can be hard to find your way out here in the dark."

"What about you?" she asked. "Do you like it up here?"

"Yes, I like it very much. Like you, I need to live someplace cheap and the surroundings are a good deal more pleasant than in some starving artists' community in the city. I need the quiet to work. A lot of artists can just block everything else out and get on with making art. But not me—I get far too distracted when things are happening around me. I guess I'm a loner, too."

Scott stopped walking and dug into the snow with the toe of his boot. "Look, Joanna," he mumbled, suddenly a tongue-tied little boy. "I want to apologize again about what happened the other day in North Ridge. I really don't know what I said to make you so mad at me, but I am sorry that I upset you."

Joanna mumbled back, "Never mind, it was nothing."

"It wasn't nothing. I want to understand. I got the feeling that we were talking about more than Maude's granddaughter. Am I right?"

She reached out and took his hand. "It's not something I talk about, okay? I overreacted, so can we just leave it like that. Please?"

He squeezed her hand through two pairs of thick mittens. "If that's the way you want it."

They smiled at each other and continued walking. All too soon the lights from Joanna's cabin shone through the bare trees. Scott climbed up onto the rocks and reached down to help Joanna up after him. When she stood beside him again, he did not release her arm. They looked at each other for a long moment. Scott placed one arm behind her back and bent down. He kissed her gently on the lips; she lifted her arms and held him close, returning the kiss. She had never before kissed a man with a beard—it was rough and scratchy against her face. Scratchy, but thoroughly pleasant at the same time.

"Ms. Hastings, are you down there?" Inspector Erikson's voice cut through the forest silence like a gun shot. Scott and Joanna leapt apart like a couple of naughty teenagers caught saying good night in the back seat of the family car.

A beam of light from a powerful flashlight danced down the hill and came to rest on them. The light remained fixed firmly on their faces as they climbed the slope.

"What could you possibly want at this time of night?" Joanna snapped on reaching the cabin. Inspector Erikson and Staff Sergeant Reynolds stood on the porch waiting for them.

"I have a few more questions, if you don't mind," Erikson said, politely. Joanna knew that whether she minded or not amounted to absolutely nothing. Grumbling, she led them all into the cabin.

"I don't believe we've met." Erikson smiled at Scott and held out her hand. Joanna introduced them. She did not ask the police to sit down.

"I think one detail was overlooked the other morning," the detective said. "Tiffany Jordan told us that it was after her grandmother went to bed that she got home that night. Do you know what time it was, Ms. Hastings?"

"Why are you asking me?"

"Because I think you might be able to tell us."

Joanna sighed. She wanted to protect Tiffany but she was not about to lie to the police. She had read somewhere that they never asked a question they didn't know the answer to…or was that a lawyer? "I found her in Hope River the next morning, about ten o'clock. And drove her home."

"So she was out all night?"

"She told me she was, yes."

"Thank you. I was just wondering. We found a gun on your property, by the way. You haven't lost one, have you?"

"Of course not. I don't own a gun. Never had and never will," she felt obliged to add. "Do you think that it's the murder weapon?"

"We won't know until we've run some tests. But it hasn't been in the woods for long, and it's clean and recently used. So I would say that's very likely." Erikson stared at Joanna. Scott and Reynolds stood by, watching. The silence was so thick it was almost a physical presence.

"Well, then I guess that proves Tiffany Jordan couldn't have done it," Joanna said with considerable relief. She forgot that Tiffany had not been accused.

"Why do you think that?" Erikson answered, cool and crisp as ever.

"Well, the gun, I mean." Joanna fumbled for the words.

"This is Hope River, for heaven's sake. Fourteen year old girls don't exactly pack heat in Northern Ontario, you know."

"Unfortunately, we never know these days what fourteen year old girls, or any girls for that matter, are carrying, or of what they are capable," Erikson replied coldly. "It's an unfortunate byproduct of feminism."

A life-long feminist, Joanna bristled at the comment. "Perhaps," she said, "but along with that goes the willingness and the ability to defend themselves rather than humbly submit to a 'fate worse than death' and I think that's a fair trade. Wouldn't you agree?"

Erikson lifted one pale eyebrow. "It may well be from your perspective, but it makes my job considerably more difficult."

Joanna stretched herself to her maximum height, but she still came no where near to matching the inspector's imposing Viking form. "Rather my life than your job."

"We'll be in touch, Ms. Hastings." Erikson turned and left the cabin without another word. Reynolds nodded to Joanna, said good night to Scott and followed.

"Dammit all." Joanna stomped her foot. "Why have I gotten myself mixed up in this business?"

"I think maybe I should be going," Scott said.

Joanna looked at him. He was a good-looking man. "If you don't mind," she said reluctantly.

"I understand." He bent down to kiss the top of her head and shut the door on his way out.

SIXTEEN

JOANNA WAS A CITY GIRL. Until now she had lived her entire life either in downtown Toronto or out in the suburbs. In those environments people kept to themselves, for better or for worse.

When she was first starting both her career and her marriage, Joanna and her husband Mike lived in a high rise apartment smack in the center of downtown. She praised city living to anyone who would listen: the closeness of the shops, the theater, the museums, the galleries. Friends. On a bitter Canadian winter's day you could live your whole life and not once venture outside. True civilization. But she knew her neighbors only from standing together waiting for an elevator.

One Christmas they were invited over for a seasonal drink by the couple at the end of the hall. Joanna was entertained all evening by the wife's descriptions of the charity ball she organized, single-handedly of course, while the husband attempted to seduce Mike in the back bedroom. The canapés were delectable, the wine was excellent and the music superb. They declined to attend the New Year's Party.

When she was a young mother, at home looking after three small children, they lived in a row of brand-spanking new homes all cut like cookies from the same cutter with not a tree over five feet tall to be seen. She nodded at her neighbors over chain-link fences on weekends in the summer when they were all out fertilizing and planting and weeding their tiny lots. They discussed the weather and how their gardens were coming and insisted that she drop over for a glass of wine on the deck "anytime." But no firm invitation was ever forthcoming and she was always reluctant to just drop in on anyone. Her only friend lived two blocks away, a woman she met by chance in the park one day when their toddlers got into a fight over who should be first to climb the ladder to the slide. Rare was the invitation to neighbors' parties, and then only because the party-giver invited everyone in earshot lest the uninvited call the police to complain about the noise.

One day Mike announced that he was leaving. Family life was not for him, he told her. She and the children could have the house—he understood that children needed a stable environment. She was grateful, truly, for his generosity until she found out that he was living with the 22-year-old daughter of one of the biggest mining magnates in Canada.

The party invitations, rare as they were, dried up the minute Joanna attained the status of "single mother." Whether it was because the wives were afraid she would be after their husbands (as if she wanted someone's leftovers) or that they just didn't know what to do with her (maybe the numbers at the dinner table would be off), Joanna never found out.

But her playground friend stuck with her, and they remained fast through it all until the friend died of breast cancer at the all-too-young age of 31. Broken-hearted, her husband took his children and moved to Calgary seeking the support of his huge extended family and she never heard from him again.

Like everyone brought up in a big city, Joanna was raised on stories about the legendary friendliness, and inquisitiveness, of country neighbors. She only half believed it until she walked into the grocery store for the first time after the discovery of Luke's body.

Nancy was right. The culprit was discovered, tried and found guilty.

Joanna stood by the pile of shiny red tomatoes, trying to find one or two that, it being December, looked like they had matured in the pleasant fall sunshine. A woman she had never laid eyes on before slid up to her.

"So sorry to hear about poor, dear Luke," the woman said, beady little black eyes looking her up and down.

Joanna smiled in agreement. *Who the hell are you?* she wondered.

"The poor dear man." The woman's voice dropped, her eyes moved closer together. She whispered, "Won't be long before they charge her, I hear."

"Charge who?" Joanna asked innocently.

"Why that Tiffany, of course. Maude's granddaughter. I hear that her jacket was found with the body. Imagine." She shivered with delight at the thought.

Another shopper joined them. Obviously the same unimaginative stylist cut their hair. *Probably a two for one discount,* Joanna thought meanly.

"Poor Maude," the newcomer agreed. "It must be so hard on her."

"But there are lots of those jackets around," Joanna clutched her tomatoes and protested feebly. "They're very common, you know."

"Well, I hear that the police are about to arrest Tiffany," the first woman announced. Her multiple chins shook in indignation.

"Fat lot of good that will do. These young offenders, they get away with murder. Let me tell you."

"That's not true," Joanna interrupted. "Are you aware that young offenders actually get more jail time than adults convicted of the same offence?"

The women stared at her, not expecting a bit of disagreement. To her dismay a third woman joined them. "Don't know why they haven't arrested her by now."

"Maybe because they haven't any proof," she snarled. Despite the heat of her near-boiling temper a chill settled over the produce aisle. Belatedly, the women realized that Joanna was not agreeing with them. In unison they lifted their chins and sniffed.

"Well, we all know that you're friends with her," the first woman said. "Everyone knows she gets her computer lessons from you." Her tone made "computer lessons" sound like "urban terrorism lessons."

"Girl like that doesn't need computer lessons. She'd be better off learning how to cook and clean and keep herself looking nice. Have you seen her hair?"

They all agreed Tiffany's hair was frightful.

Her mother's daughter, Joanna had never knowingly said a nasty thing to a person in her life. But all the memories of a troubled teenager and her confused and angry friends flooded back and broke through a lifetime of self-control. "Perhaps you mean that she should learn how to be just like you? God help us all. That would be a fate worse than death, I'm sure." She grabbed a handful of bruised tomatoes, shoved them into her cart and backed out down the aisle.

The three women stared after her, mouths hanging open like happy whales feeding on a huge batch of krill.

In a black rage Joanna grabbed packages of Fruit Loops and Pop Tarts off the counter and plunked them into her cart to join the tomatoes.

She neatly sideswiped Jack Miller who stood stone faced and stiff blocking her path at the end of the aisle. Joanna glared at him and struggled to maneuver her cart out of the way. He held his ground, watching while she wrestled with the unwieldy shopping cart. The back right wheel was sticky so that she was forced to press down on one hand to overcompensate and wrench it back into line. Jack stood firm, his expression blank as he watched her struggle with the cart. It was all she could do not to fling her purchases to one side and storm out of the store. She could always drive to North Ridge and shop there. But, determined to retain some last shred of dignity, she unloaded the cart onto the conveyer belt at Nancy's cash register.

"Hi, how are you today?" Nancy said, cheerful as ever. For a change her hair was dyed an attractive auburn.

"Fine, thank you." Joanna spoke through gritted teeth.

Nancy dropped her voice as she continued checking things through. "That Roberta McCallum. She hasn't said a word of sense since nineteen-forty-nine. Don't pay no attention to her. And a lot of the ladies in this town, they just follow along like a bunch of parrots repeating whatever Roberta says, just because her husband owns the best piece of farming land this side of Gravenhurst." Nancy laughed. "And that ain't saying much." She packed Joanna's purchases carefully into plastic bags, emblazoned with the store's logo. "Give Maude and Tiffany my regards, now."

Joanna smiled at Nancy. "How is your husband…Bob, is it?" Overcome by the woman's sympathy she struggled to find something nice to say.

Nancy smiled back. "Bill. But that's okay. He's just fine, thank you. And the kids are doing real well. Coming up to exams soon, you know. These exams are real important for my Jenny. The results will go to the university, you know."

Joanna was about to ask where Jenny hoped to go, but at that moment Roberta McCallum and her posse pulled into the end of the line and with a shrug of resignation, Nancy turned to the new arrivals and smiled brightly.

Joanna placed her packages back into the cart for the trip out to the parking lot. A box of Pop Tarts looked up at her. *What on earth am I going to do with those?* Her stomach cringed.

THE NEXT MORNING, she was struggling to find something barely edible to eat. Her cupboard was almost empty. It contained not much, in fact, but bruised tomatoes, Pop Tarts and fruity cereal. The very thought made her teeth ache. For breakfast she was reduced to two slices of stale brown bread toasted with a bit of supermarket jam.

She was working like a demon and the project for Fred was gradually nearing completion. A few other people had called over the past few weeks, given her name by either Maude or Scott, to ask her to do small jobs for them. Install software, a bit of training, fix minor problems or point out a more efficient way to use their computers. All easy and stress-free and a welcome bit of much needed money.

By lunchtime her stomach was growling in an attempt to attract her attention. She thought fondly of the days when she could just dial up pizza or deli sandwiches and carry on working through lunch. She remembered that Nancy had told her they would deliver. She made a quick mental list of all the things left behind on her last shopping expedition and called the store. Nancy took the order over the phone, and promised delivery in one hour.

It was closer to three before Jack pulled into the driveway and carried her box up to the front door.

"This is great," she said, opening the door and showing Jack into the kitchen. "I must order this way more often."

"There's a charge, you know." He handed her a slip of paper and held out his hand.

"Well, yes. I do know that." Joanna read the bill. "Let me

get my purse. Just a moment." She hurried into the bedroom and rifled through her jewelry box for some bills.

When she returned to the living room Jack was standing by her desk. He watched her eyes as he casually dropped her black address book back on the desktop. He had been going through her things.

She handed him the money, holding back the tip she was about to offer, and thanked him tightly.

Without a word Jack left the cabin, pulling the door shut behind him. Joanna watched as the store van backed out of her driveway and disappeared down the road.

SEVENTEEN

TIFFANY ARRIVED PROMPTLY for her next Friday afternoon lesson. She carried a battered, black school bag over one shoulder containing, Joanna assumed, her night things. The bag was thickly marked with the names of popular heavy metal groups interspersed by swear words and death symbols. Joanna found the bag unsettling and pushed it under the desk.

The girl had reverted to her "I don't care what you think" appearance and attitude. Joanna just hoped she was possessed of enough common sense to drop the act in the presence of the police, but she doubted it.

They worked on Mrs. Beeton for a short while. Joanna soon realized that the typing tutorial was only boring Tiffany and was no longer necessary now that the girl knew the basics.

"I think we can leave Mrs. Beeton for a while, you're coming along so well. Have you been working on the computer at school?"

"A bit," Tiffany mumbled out of the side of her mouth as if it were something of which to be ashamed. "They let me back in the computer class when Grandma phoned and told them that I was taking private lessons."

"That's great!"

"It's stupid. I really hate it. I hate the teacher so much—she's such a miserable old lady. She can't stand me. She didn't want me in her stupid class, but the principal said that she had to have me."

Joanna nodded dryly. Not too difficult to image why the

teacher doesn't like Tiffany. "Well, I thought that we would do something more practical now. I'd like to teach you a word-processing package. Word is the most popular. Do you know anything about it?"

"No."

"Well, it's used mostly for writing documents. Letters, school papers, and things like that. You will find it very useful for doing essays and reports for school."

"But I don't have a computer. And I don't do essays and garbage like that."

"Oh, I would have thought that in Grade nine you would have projects to do?"

"I didn't say we didn't get projects. I just said I don't do them."

"Oh, I see." And she did see. This was all ground she had covered with her own rebellious daughter. You can make the child go to school, but you can't make them do the work if they don't want to. Feeling that any effort on her part would be useless, she nevertheless forced a bright smile and struggled on "Well, if you would like to, you can use my computer sometimes. Just phone ahead and make sure that I don't have any urgent work to get done."

They worked for a couple of hours as the winter darkness deepened and the mercury in the thermometer hanging by the front door continued its downward progression.

Tiffany leaned back in her chair and stretched: "Don't you think I've done enough? Can we play Tomb Raider now?"

"All right, you've done very well."

Tiffany beamed at the compliment. It was amazing, Joanna thought (and not for the first time), how these teenaged girls could so quickly drop the tough girl persona and become just a tousled little child eager for praise.

"You play for a while. I'll start the dinner."

Before beginning the game Tiffany went outside for a smoke. Although the girl protested furiously every chance she got, Joanna had flatly forbidden smoking in the cabin, regardless of the weather. While chopping onions and green peppers for the meat sauce and placing a heavy pot of water on to the stove to boil, like every non-smoker, she marveled at what a smoker would go through for their regular fix.

Tiffany stood under the light on the front porch, shivering in her coat (probably an old one of Maude's—the only thing available to replace the much sought after Bulls jacket), puffing furiously. The light cast a halo around her, edges softened by the falling snow. Except for the demon weed, she looked like a lost child, cold and alone in the winter darkness. Or maybe a 14-year-old Madonna caught in a beam of heavenly light. Without warning Joanna's eyes filled with tears and a sob caught in her throat. Whether for her Alexis, or for Tiffany or maybe even for her own lost youth she didn't know, but unbidden, warm, salty tears drifted silently down her cheeks. With a gasp she pulled her hand off the handle of the old iron pot as it heated up. She shook one burning hand and with the other wiped the tears from her face.

Cigarette finished, Tiffany stomped back into the cabin, teeth chattering, nose and cheeks a painful red.

"It's really cold out there, even colder than when I arrived. The snow is sure falling now and the wind is something fierce. I think it's going to storm tonight. Glad I'm not out in it." Tiffany crossed the room quickly to warm her hands by the old stove.

"Boots off in the house," Joanna reminded her.

Tiffany threw Joanna a dirty look but pulled the Doc Martins off and kicked them across the room.

They dined on spaghetti with meat sauce, salad and store-delivered chocolate cake for dessert. Joanna poured herself a glass of wine but refused to share with Tiffany. The girl's protests were only half-hearted.

She cleared the table and did the dishes while Tiffany eagerly started up the computer game. They sat in companionable silence late into the night. Tiffany played Tomb Raider with determined concentration; Joanna read the computer magazines she bought in Toronto but hadn't yet had time to get into. Outside the cabin, the temperature dropped further and a full-force northern winter blizzard arrived.

Joanna finished the last of her magazines and glanced at her watch. To her surprise it was long past midnight. "Hey, look at the time. We should be getting to bed," she told Tiffany. "I'll put out blankets and sheets and you can make up the couch."

Tiffany yawned. "I'm not tired. I'd like to play some more. Can I?"

"Sure. Play as long as you like, but I'm going to bed." On her way to the bedroom, Joanna stopped to peer out the front window. The snow fell thick and heavy, tossed madly about by the wind. She could only just make out the porch light trying to break through the curtain of swirling white. "Wow, it's quite a storm outside. Not a fit night out for man nor beast." A sudden gust of wind crashed into the window and the old pane groaned loudly. She leapt back in shock as the glass settled back into its frame. It had survived a great many worse storms than this one.

Tiffany grunted, but didn't take her eyes from the screen.

Joanna was half across the room when a soft scratching at the front door stopped her in her tracks. She turned slowly and looked around. Tiffany sat at the computer, head bent in concentration; a second gust of wind rattled the windows but otherwise all was silent. Joanna sunk slowly into a chair. Sounds in the night had never bothered her before; she was a woman living alone and well used to the creaking and settling of an old house. But this night was different. This night an overwhelming sense of dread gripped her chest. She tried to shake it off, she told herself that she was imagining things. But the terror would not go away.

Again she heard the scratching, and again it fell silent. So far away it might have been in another world. Computer keys clicked rapidly. Tiffany groaned as Lara Croft plunged to a bloody death in a pool full of starving piranhas.

"Don't you hear it?" Joanna whispered softly.

"Hear what?" For once Tiffany tuned in to another person's emotions and, alarmed, abandoned the resurrection of Lara and turned in her chair to look at Joanna. "What's the matter with you? Are you all right?"

"Don't you hear it?" Joanna repeated.

"Hear what?"

"Just listen."

The two women strained to hear. Again the windows groaned and again the steady scratching echoed throughout the cabin.

"There, that noise. At the front door."

"Sounds like a cat or something wanting in." Tiffany jumped up and threw the storm door open before Joanna could stop her. She peered through the glass in the still-closed wooden door. "Nope. Nothing here but a pretty big pile of snow." The girl looked outside, her head turning from left to right, up and down. Nothing caught her eye and she shut the door firmly. "Must be just the old wood rattling." She took one look at her friend's white, stricken face. "These old places make all kinds of funny noises. You should hear our house. When Rocky walks around in the night anyone would think the whole floor is going to collapse. That's all it is, I'm sure. God, you look like you've seen a ghost." Tiffany knelt down in front of Joanna. "The door is creaking, that's all."

Joanna shook her head wordlessly. The scratching sounded once again, louder this time.

"It really does sound like someone wants to get in." Tiffany stood by the window, holding her hands in front of the glass, the better to see out. "I can't see anyone, though. You don't have a cat, do you? Wonder what it is. You don't look too well. Can I make you a cup of tea or something?"

Joanna shook her head.

"Another glass of wine?"

Joanna nodded.

Tiffany poured the wine carefully. No one was watching her, so she took a cautious sip. Still Joanna didn't look in her direction; Tiffany gulped half the glass down. She topped it up, wiped her mouth with the back of her hand and carried the drink over to Joanna.

"It's just a noise in the wind, really."

Joanna ignored the offered glass and gripped Tiffany's arm tightly. "Don't you feel it?" she whispered. "The cold, can't you feel it?"

"It's cold outside. But I'm nice and warm inside. Should I put another log in the stove?"

"Won't help," Joanna croaked.

Tiffany pressed the wine into a trembling hand. The older woman was raising the glass to her lips when the scratching once more echoed throughout the cabin. This time it was accompanied by a soft moan.

The glass shattered in Joanna's hand. Bright blood seeped from the gash on her index finger and dripped steadily onto the wooden floor. It mixed with the spilled wine to form a glistening red pool. Joanna simply stared at the mess, unable to comprehend what was going on.

"There is someone out there." Tiffany leapt to her feet. "They must be lost in the storm." She threw open the storm door and unlocked the heavier wooden door behind it. She began to push the door open, but a sharp gust of wind slammed it shut. Tiffany wrestled against the wind in an attempt to force the door back open. As the wind softened and Tiffany began to win, Joanna roused herself and leapt from her daze. She knocked Tiffany aside and pulled the door shut. The girl's foot caught in the area rug and she fell heavily.

Tiffany shook her head and rubbed absently at the wrist that had taken the brunt of her fall. Joanna stood resolutely against the force of the storm and whatever it carried, her back pressed tightly against the door.

"For God's sake. What's the matter with you? There's someone out there. We have to let them in."

"No," Joanna gasped. The scratching started again. One long moan sounded through the night. She dragged Tiffany to her feet.

"Do…Not…Open…That…Door…Again." She wrapped Tiffany tightly in her arms. They listened as the scratching continued, then fell still. The wind shook the windows one last time, and then it moved on. All that could be heard was the crackle of burning logs on the fire, the roar of the wind outside and the women's breathing.

Slowly Joanna's heart took up its regular rhythm and the unnamed terror cleared her chest. With a sigh she released Tiffany and collapsed into a chair.

The teenager turned to face her. Her thin face was hard and accusing. "What was all that about, Joanna? There was someone out there. You can't just leave them alone out in the night."

"Yes, there was someone out there. There was. But didn't you feel it, Tiffany? It wasn't right. Whatever was out in the storm tonight shouldn't have been there. It did not belong here. Didn't you feel it?" This was all beyond Joanna's comprehension; she didn't even understand what she was talking about, yet the words, like the horror, seemed to form out of the dark by themselves.

Tiffany sank to her knees in front of Joanna, and grasped the woman's hands in her own. "I felt it," she said, "I know that it was no cat, no one lost in the storm at night. But it wanted in, it wanted us to let it in. Why couldn't you do that?"

"Didn't you fear it, Tiffany?"

"No. I don't have anything to fear from it."

"You've felt it before, haven't you?"

"Yes. Twice before. At night and always when it's cold. I've been in the woods, coming home very late. The first time was last winter. I was just drinking and…well, just drinking, when I realized that it was late and Grandma would be worried about me. So I left the group and started home. I hadn't been living here long, so I wasn't too sure of the way. I saw something moving through the trees, drifting slowly ahead of me, like, so I followed it. I didn't have a better way of getting home. Soon it disappeared and there I was, right in our front yard.

"The next time was this year, just before you came. Again we were out drinking and having a party, like. Down at the lake by Luke's place. One of the boys was really bothering me so I left. But he came after me. I could hear him following me. I started walking faster and faster but he kept on after me. I didn't see him, but I knew that he was there. I was really scared. He stepped out of the woods and knocked me down, he was drunk and I was so scared. Then she was between us. I didn't see her, but I knew she was there."

Joanna stared at Tiffany, speechless.

"He turned and ran. Took off, just like that. And I walked home.

"That boy never said another word to me again. I still see him at school. But he always looks away. He doesn't ever come out drinking with my crowd any more either. Everyone wonders what's gotten into him. They think maybe he's found religion or something, but he doesn't talk to anyone any more."

"Why do you say, 'she'?" Joanna asked.

"Eh?"

"Why do you say 'she'? You said, 'she was between us.'"

Tiffany shrugged. "I don't know. I just did. I guess I just know."

Joanna shivered and wrapped her arms around herself, she was chilled right through to her bones. "What is she?"

"I don't know. But I'm not afraid of her, I have never been afraid of her. I wonder why you are."

JOANNA WOKE EARLY the next morning, her head thick and confused. The previous night's storm was over; soft winter sunshine drifted in through her bedroom window. She had slept heavily, not daring to lie awake or to dream. She lay in bed for a few minutes watching the early morning sunlight play with swirls of hard frost decorating the bedroom window. Like illustrations in a child's picture book, the windows looked as if Jack Frost had stopped by during the night, to paint them with patterns of ice and frozen snow.

Tiffany was still asleep on the couch; a gently breathing bundle of blankets, pajama-clad feet and tousled purple hair.

Joanna slowly got out of bed and moved to the kitchen. She put the coffee on and pulled a packet of cinnamon buns from the freezer. After placing the buns in the oven to defrost and warm, she went for her shower. She stood under the hot water until it turned cold, then quickly turned the knob off. She forced herself not to think about the events of last night. There were no ghosts. Her city-bred, computer-educated mind knew that.

Tiffany was a wild young teenaged girl with a healthy, overactive imagination, and that was all there was to it.

When Joanna emerged from the shower, carefully using her uncut hand to rub her hair in a towel, Tiffany was up and standing by the front window. Her flannel pajamas were the one-piece kind with feet and a design of happy little animals. The smell of warm cinnamon and sugar and fresh coffee filled the tiny cabin.

"See anything out there?" Joanna asked.

"Nothing but a lot of snow. There are some small animal tracks on the lawn, maybe a fox."

"Anything on the porch?"

"Not a mark."

They looked at each other, but neither had the words.

"You'll have to wait a bit for a shower." Joanna shied away from any talk of last night. "I used up all the hot water."

Tiffany sat at the table in her strange pajamas and watched while Joanna tossed eggs with milk in a bowl and slowly poured the mixture into a hot frying pan. When the eggs were done they went onto the table along with steaming cinnamon buns, coffee and orange juice.

Maude pulled up as they were settling in to eat. She stamped snow from her boots and pulled off her heavy winter coat. Her cheeks glistened red and her sharp brown eyes sparkled with the morning cold. Another plate and mug were produced and the elderly woman settled into the table happily. Despite her scrawny frame she was an enthusiastic eater.

"You must know some of the history of this cabin, Maude." Joanna spoke the words before she was aware of thinking them. She ignored her eggs, gripped the coffee mug tightly and tried to control the shake in her voice.

"A bit, yes. This is the oldest cabin in this part of the county,

I believe. Why do you ask?" Maude selected a bun and dug in
with gusto.

"I was just wondering. Old houses like this sometimes have
a wonderful past."

Maude laughed. "Not this old place, I'm afraid. This has
always been nothing but a rundown cabin, on a useless piece
of land. Those buns were lovely. Very fresh."

Joanna continued to stare into her mug. Tiffany passed the
plate to her grandmother.

"Is something wrong? You seem tense, I hope there weren't
any problems last night…?"

"Oh, no. Tiffany was a pleasure to have over, really. Anytime."

Maude glanced anxiously at the two faces staring intently
at her across the table. "Though I do remember one strange
thing about this old cabin."

"Yes!" Tiffany and Joanna almost shouted their enthusiasm.

"Back in the thirties, there was a family lived here by the
name of McDonald. I didn't know them very well. When I was
a girl we lived in town, you see. My father was manager of the
paper mill in those days. He was one of the few men who had
a job through all those hard years. Anyway, the McDonalds had
a daughter a few years older than me, she was a friend of my
sister Dorothy, which is why I know something of her story. I
don't remember her name, though. Dirt poor the McDonalds
were. You can't grow much on this land and jobs in town were
few and far between. Lots of families were poor in the thirties,
but what made things so tough for the McDonalds was that the
father drank something awful. No food for the children but you
could always find Mr. McDonald in one bar or another. I
remember my mother and her lady friends were always having
tea and talking a blue streak about the McDonalds.

"Of course in those days, in this town, everyone talked no

end about the McDonalds but no one would do a thing to help the family. None of our business they would all say. No better than they should be." Maude shook her head and held her coffee cup up with a smile. Joanna rushed to put on another pot.

"Where was I, oh yes, it's all coming back to me now. The girl, whose name I don't remember, was a wild one. My sister Dorothy was pretty wild in those days too, but she was too smart to ever get caught. The McDonald girl though, she was always in trouble." Maude accepted another coffee with a smile and poured three spoonfuls of sugar into it. She stirred the drink carefully.

"I remember my father and mother talking late one night when they didn't know I was sitting under the stairs. Seems that the girl had gotten herself *in trouble.* I didn't know what that meant then but it sure sounded bad. She disappeared for a while and no one talked about her. And then the next thing I heard, she was dead."

"Dead," Tiffany said. "What happened?"

"I didn't know, not then. She was buried quickly and no one ever talked about her again." Maude stirred her now almost empty mug.

"But you did find out?" Joanna poured more coffee.

"It was a few years later, on the anniversary of her death. My sister, Dorothy, and I were in town doing some shopping when Dorothy said she needed to do something before she went home. She told me to go on ahead, but I insisted on going with her. We went to the graveyard, to visit her friend.

"It was the middle of winter, and I can still remember that day. The trees were bare and silent, snow piled up around the pitiful graves. A few dead flowers or a Christmas wreath propped up against some of the more recent tombstones. But there was nothing to decorate the McDonald girl's grave.

"Dorothy cried and cried. She placed a paper flower she had made on top of the mound of snow covering the grave. I was surprised; she hadn't said a word when her friend died. I thought she didn't care much.

"We were just starting to leave when a girl, younger than me, crept up. It was Lorraine, the youngest McDonald girl. Funny how I can remember everyone else's name, but not that poor dead girl. Lorraine thanked us for coming. She told us her papa had forbidden any of them to visit their sister's grave. She said they weren't allowed to even talk about her in the house, or to anyone else. They had to pretend that she had never lived. But her mother asked Lorraine one day, when her papa wasn't home, to visit the grave when she could and try to keep it nice. She said her mother would be glad that we also came. So her sister wouldn't always be alone."

"How did she die?" Tiffany asked, her voice breaking with a degree of empathy Joanna wouldn't have believed the girl possessed. Then she remembered: a troubled teenaged girl feels everyone's pain.

"I don't know," Maude replied, staring off into space, deep in her own memories. "No one talked about it. It was all hushed up. Even her little sister, Lorraine, didn't know. Just that one day the girl was gone and in the spring there was a grave they were forbidden to visit.

"But whatever happened she died badly, Joanna. Some would say a bad death is never an end."

"Is that what you say?"

"I say, it's time to be getting on home. Can't sit around this nice fire all day eating eggs and drinking coffee and talking about people and things long past. Come on, Tiffany, get yourself dressed, girl." Tiffany scooped up her clothes and carried them into the bedroom. Joanna tried to question Maude further but her neighbor changed the subject, firmly. The topic was now closed.

EIGHTEEN

THE FOLLOWING MONDAY, Joanna drove to Toronto, still unsettled by Maude's story. She had spent most of the weekend tossing it over in her mind, unsure of why it was bothering her so much. It was certainly not the first tragic story she had ever heard, nor was it likely to be the last. To contribute to her unease, when she wasn't remembering the story of the poor, forgotten McDonald girl, she couldn't stop thinking about the last time she left her cabin and what had transpired upon her return.

She called Wendy Sunday afternoon, expecting to be offered dinner and a bed for the night. But Wendy and Robert's plans were made already. They were taking the Monday train to Montreal, to spend a few days with Robert's mother. Wendy didn't sound at all pleased about the prospect, although Joanna knew that she had enjoyed previous visits with her in-laws.

It was now mid-December. More than two months had passed since Joanna's arrival in Hope River. A few small jobs had come in from her old contacts in the computer business. A friend of Elaine's had hired her to design a web page for his cycling club. And a bit of work from the locals continued to trickle in. But nothing substantial, nothing large enough to support her through the winter. The first part of Fred's project was finished and ready to be presented to the executives. She was desperately hoping that it would lead to something more.

As before, Fred received her with much enthusiasm. He

ushered her to an elevator and into the boardroom. She was pleased to see that, this time, the remnants of the morning's previous meetings had been cleared away. She idly wondered why it mattered so much to her.

A young man carefully dressed in a conservative blue suit, crisp white shirt and nondescript striped tie stood as they entered. He approached Joanna and held out his hand, bowing ever so slightly. *They get younger every year.*

"Francis Fukuyama, Joanna Hastings." Fred made the introductions.

Joanna took the offered hand enthusiastically. "We have met many times, already," Francis said, smiling at her, "but this is the first time, face-to-face." Joanna smiled back. She and Francis had put in some long hours on the phone, discussing the project and she had enjoyed working with the bright young man very much. His enthusiasm was contagious, always the best kind.

A PC was set up on the board table, per her request, with a large display screen so arranged to give every chair in the room a clear view. Joanna and Francis set up their equipment quickly.

They were soon joined by a small group of executives and the presentation got underway. Unexpectedly, Joanna was nervous. She tried not to wipe sweaty palms on her best suit. Of the five people in her audience, not counting Fred or Francis, she recognized only two from her days as part of the company, a mere three months past.

But despite her nervousness, the presentation went well. The equipment didn't break down and she didn't forget anything too important. Francis stepped in twice to offer thoughtful and enthusiastic commentary.

Then it was over. She thanked everyone and gratefully sat down. Questions were brief and to the point. Francis helped her field them.

"I like it all very much, Ms. Hastings." Morris Lipton, the Senior Vice President of Client Relations nodded at her through his coke-bottle-bottom glasses. He sported a hideous comb-over, which served only to emphasize the scarcity of his hair and the greasiness of the few remaining strands. Joanna stared at it. *Why do men insist on wearing that ridiculous style. Don't they know by now that women universally hate it?*

She pulled herself out of her fascination with the hair sculpture in time to hear him say, "I think we can definitely agree on something more."

Joanna let her breath out slowly. She hadn't realized that she had been holding it in.

"I'd like Mr. Fukyiama here to take me through it all again, at my own slow pace. But for now, I like it very much." He stood up and gathered together his papers. "We'll be in touch soon." He shook Joanna's hand and left the room, the rest of the executives nodding and following in his wake.

Joanna and Frances beamed at each other. "Allll right." They raised their hands and highfived. Francis helped Joanna pack up, then Fred walked her to the elevator.

"A good job, Joanna," he said.

"They seemed to like it," she replied. "But I was surprised that you didn't introduce our proposal for the rest of the project. When do you think we can get together again to go over that?"

"Well, uh. Not too soon. Don't want to rush things with this bunch. I'll call you."

The elevator arrived with a ping and Joanna got on. Fred smiled and raised his hand as the doors shut in his face. It was lunchtime, the elevator stopped at almost every floor on its way down. As more and more people crammed themselves into the small space and Joanna was pushed further into the back corner, she thought about Fred. He hadn't seemed at all pleased by the success of her presentation. A massively over-weight man stepped on her toes as the crowd shifted again to let more passengers on. He mumbled an apology, but she was too deep in thought to reply. They reached the ground floor and a stream of lunchers burst from the elevator banks and through the security gates like school let out for summer holidays. Joanna was the last to leave.

She stopped at the main desk and flicked through the office directory. Pulling the desk phone over, she rapidly punched in the numbers.

"Mr. Lipton," she said, "Joanna Hastings here. I'm sorry to bother you right at lunchtime, I understand how busy you are, but I'm still in the building and I was thinking that if you have a half hour to spare I'd like to discuss some more ideas I have about client training. No, I have no plans for lunch. I'll wait right here."

She smiled to herself and placed the phone down gently before taking a seat in the lobby to await her lunch date.

IT WAS LATE in the afternoon when Joanna joined the stream of traffic escaping Toronto. As she drove, the traffic declined steadily. An hour and a half to Barrie and north, then she was one of the few cars left on the road. The weight of the city dropped from her shoulders and she enjoyed the dark panorama of the northern woods at night. Her headlights cut through the inky blackness and she thought she was the only person left in the world. It was a good feeling and she was glad, again, that she made the move to Hope River.

Her presentation had gone extremely well. Even better, she and Morris Lipton had enjoyed a pleasant lunch at a very ex-clusive restaurant. She outlined her ideas for a totally compre-hensive training plan, including manuals and documentation, classroom courses, web based interaction and sales plans for the staff who would be charged with selling the product. Morris asked her to get started on a design that he could look at after the New Year, with particular emphasis on the Internet portion. He was very interested in how training could be conducted through web pages, reducing both the cost of paper and transporting staff and teachers to and from the training site. He told her that he would be spending the holidays at his family cottage in Quebec and was greatly looking forward to her plans when he got back. He invited her to call on Francis Fukuyama for any assistance that might be needed. After lunch he invited her back to the office and had his secretary type up a contract.

But what good was all this excitement, the thrill of success, if she didn't have anyone to tell all about it? To go over every detail, to discuss what everyone said and how they reacted, the brilliance of her presentation, and particularly how enthusiastic Morris Lipton sounded about Joanna's ideas and how shockingly betrayed Fred Blanchard would be when he found out. Wendy and Robert were in Montreal, hopefully having a better visit than Wendy appeared to be expecting. Elaine was also out of town this week, on vacation in Barbados.

The drive up had been long and tiring, but easy. The roads were clear and the moonlight bright. But as she approached Hope River, the snow stared to fall. By the time Joanna reached her cabin she was driving through near-whiteout conditions. Spotting her property she swore loudly. Her driveway, perfectly shoveled that very morning, was once again knee-deep in the white stuff. To make matters worse, the ever-efficient snowplow had been by, leaving a small mountain of tightly packed snow squarely blocking the entrance.

She pulled her car over to the side of the road and dragged the snow shovel out of the trunk. Still dressed in the "dress-for-success" suit, ever so smartly accompanied by thick, salt-encrusted winter boots, she began to dig. The snowfall was very wet, she felt every shovel-full up her arms and into her back.

At long last enough of a path was cleared that she could get the car off the road and nosed into the driveway. The rest of the job would have to wait until morning.

She returned the shovel to its place in the trunk and pulled her briefcase out of the car. A thick bank of clouds covered the moon and it was very dark. The single strong light left on over the porch door reached out of the darkness to welcome her home. As she fitted her key into the lock a slip of paper fluttered in the doorframe. Joanna pulled out a crisp, efficient business card. The insignia of the OPP was printed on one corner; Inspector Erikson's name and rank filled the other.

Joanna turned the card over. "Call me. Immediately." Joanna tossed the card onto her desk. Tonight she was in no condition to engage in a battle of wits with the inspector. She could only fight one fight a day.

Instead she called Scott. It was very late but she had to share her excitement with someone. He was still up, or so he said, and sounded happy at her news. They made a dinner date for next week. As she hung up, Joanna congratulated herself on being a single woman in a time when it was acceptable to phone a man, and dragged her tired body off to bed.

NINETEEN

"A BABY! YOU DARE to tell me a daughter of mine is having a baby!" the man screeched, a thick red haze descending behind his eyes. With one quick gulp he downed the last of the beer and threw the bottle across the room at his wife. Well-practiced, she ducked and it missed her to fall harmlessly to the floor, cracking apart in a spray of beer-soaked glass shards on the worn and dirty linoleum.

"Yes, a baby, you drunken fool," his wife hissed, as she grabbed the straw kitchen broom and waved it in front of her, whether to sweep up the glass or to defend herself no one could tell. *"And if you didn't come home from O'Reilly's bar pickled every night you would have noticed months ago."*

The boys gathered silently at the kitchen door. Their eyes glowed with excitement. This was news: even the youngest of them knew what it meant for an unmarried girl to have a baby. Total disgrace at the absolute least.

"Why didn't you tell me, woman?" The man sprayed spittle through stained and broken teeth. *"I have a right to know."*

She summoned what little bit of courage she possessed. *"You have no right to know what you're too blind drunk to notice."* He pulled his arm back and she flinched, ready for the blow that was sure to follow. But instead of lashing out, his arm fell lifelessly to his side. *"I wouldn'ta known, but for John telling me hisself. John knows what a son's duty is to his father."*

He glared at the circle of boys as he dropped into a kitchen chair. Even through his drunken haze he remembered, or maybe it was force of habit, to balance slightly to the right to counteract the wobbly left chair leg. He would fix it tomorrow— tomorrow, for sure. He parted his legs and scratched his crotch.

The oldest boy, John, preened before his brothers. He was in his da's good books now, for sure. The other boys had better watch out. John knew he could do no wrong, for a while anyway, at least until their da found another grievance with the boy. Another fault, real or imagined, it made no difference.

"So now you know," the woman said, brushing absentmindedly at a bit of long-dried baby vomit on the shoulder of her worn dress. It had been a nice dress, once—full of flowers, trimmed with bits of lace, with a generous full skirt and scooped neckline. Once, when the dress was brand new out of the charity box in the church basement, the design of the flowers danced in the blue of her eyes, those eyes the exact color of the cornflowers in the soft fabric of the dress. A long time ago the color washed out of those stunning eyes and she gave up trying to keep the dress mended. A seam under her arm gaped and the hem sagged loosely at her knees.

She waved her hands at the huddle of boys standing at the kitchen door. "What you all staring at, looking like a bunch of donkeys in the barn? You got nothing else to do? Ray, you go look for your baby sister, watch that she's not into no trouble."

The man spat on the floor. "You stand right there, boy. Looking after babies is women's work, you all know that. Ain't no son of mine doin' no women's work."

Ray crossed his arms over his chest and planted his legs further apart. He grinned slyly at his brothers. He was a small, thin boy with scrawny, knobby knees and exceptionally bad eyesight, which forced him to squint most of the time. All too often his father's ridicule came crashing down upon him. It was nice, very nice, to be singled out as one not deserving of women's work.

The woman shrugged and picked up her broom. She placed it back in its place beside the sink and moved toward the kitchen door, to see what the baby was up to out in the yard.

"She's a whore. Just a common whore. And she has to be out of this house. Ain't never had no whores in this family. I ain't having it start now." The man rose to his feet and crossed his arms tightly. "You hear me, woman, you hear me? You tell the filthy whore she ain't having no baby in this house." He scratched his crotch once again.

She stood still, frozen in her path to the door, her back to the room.

"You hear me, you hear me, woman? She is to be out of this house tomorrow," he announced in a deep voice, as he imagined the old prophets they learned about in Sunday School many, many years ago, must have sounded. A belly-shaking belch ruined the effect. "I want the whore out of this house tomorrow."

The woman turned slowly. From the yard, they could all hear the thin cry of a toddler who had fallen over a rock or a rusty garden implement and scraped her knee. No one moved. "But she has nowhere to go. Nowhere. You can't throw out your daughter, your own flesh and blood."

The man bent over and took another beer out of the icebox. It was the last one; he would have to go to town tonight. Good thing he still had some money left from that job he did clearing land for the Thompson brothers. The crack in his butt peeked over the rim of his soiled pants. The boys elbowed each other and pointed, but they knew better than to laugh. The man fumbled through the kitchen cabinets for the bottle opener. He frantically tossed spoons and knives out of the way onto the floor, and at last he located his prize. With a flick of the wrist he cracked open the bottle and took a long, satisfying slug. The opener he threw over his shoulder. His wife stepped forward to catch it before it hit the ground.

The woman slowly lowered herself to her knees and started picking up the cutlery. As she stretched out almost flat to get at a spoon that had bounced under the icebox her dress rode up exposing a flash of gnarled white knees and thick thighs crisscrossed by purple stretch marks. The boys grinned in their embarrassment and shifted from foot to foot, elbowing each other once again.

"Ain't no whore gonna live in my house," the man said to his wife's rear as she scrambled under the table. "I don't teach her what's right, how'm I gonna look any man in town in the face ever again? The whore." He spat. "Who knows who she opened her legs for. Every man in town gonna be panting around here like a hound dog after a bitch in heat, word get out about this."

His wife crawled backward out from under the table. As she rose to her feet, she smoothed her dress over her hips, the dress that once had beautiful blue cornflowers and a light trimming of lace, and placed the cutlery carefully back into its place.

The sobbing baby clambered up the back stairs to the kitchen door and howled to be allowed in. The woman scooped her daughter up into her arms and held her close. Her face was a mask of dust and dirt through which bright blue eyes and white teeth still shone. A thin trickle of blood ran down from her right knee—an old scrape had reopened as she fell into the puddle of mud lying in wait at the bottom of the steps. The thick smell of ooze mixed with a well-soiled diaper assaulted the woman's nostrils. She brushed twigs out of the soft blond hair and rocked the baby to her chest. The youngest boy stepped forward and wordlessly plucked the now-howling girl from his mother's arms. His eyes caught hers for an instant, then cooing softly, he took the baby into the back room for a wash and a change of clothes. Everyone pretended not to notice them leave.

The man finished his beer and looked at the empty bottle in disgust. He threw it into the sink. "I'm going into town, I gotta get more beer. John, get the truck out, I'm going into town."

John didn't know what to do. It was a rare privilege to be allowed to drive the old pickup truck up to the road, but he didn't want to miss anything exciting. His father staggered into the front room and plucked his old plaid working jacket off the coat hook by the door. "What you waiting for, boy? You want me to get one of your brothers to go for the truck?"

"No, sir." John leapt out the front door and flew down the porch steps. Halfway down a tread cracked under his weight and he stumbled, but he quickly corrected himself and raced across the yard, his brothers' mocking laughter following him.

The woman ran after her husband and plucked at his arm. "You can't go into town, now. What's to become of my daughter?"

"Your daughter's a whore, plain and simple. I know my Christian duty. I'll give her some money for the bus to Toronto. Lots of whores there, I hear. When she's had her whelp she can come crawling back. Not before." He slammed the front door behind him. He tripped over the newly loosened step, but not as agile as his son, he fell into the yard in a tumble of waving arms. No one dared to laugh.

The remaining brothers looked at each other in dismay. Fun was fun, they would all agree, but maybe, just maybe, this had gone a bit too far. Not one of them wanted to see their sister thrown out of the house.

ONCE AGAIN Joanna was instantly awake. No light permeated her bedroom. It was still the dead of night. She lay in the dark for a long time staring at the ceiling. She thought she heard the lonely howl of a wolf far out over the lake, but she couldn't be sure. It might be some drunks shouting at the moon. She was still awake as the first feeble streaks of watery daylight broke through her bedroom window.

The day passed slowly. She should still be elated, flushed by yesterday's success, at her own audacity in snatching victory from the very jaws of defeat. Instead she prowled the cabin, beginning small housekeeping tasks and then abandoning them half-finished. She picked up books and magazines and tossed them down a few minutes later, into a growing pile on the floor. She considered going for a walk to enjoy the pure new snow, but only got as far as pulling on her boots before deciding that it was too much effort.

She couldn't get the dream out of her mind. In the past, the memory of a dream, no matter how pleasant or unpleasant it might be, would be gone almost the moment she stepped out of bed. Only these spooky images of the rebellious girl and her dysfunctional family lingered on in her mind, as clear as if she had really experienced them. Was she was going a little cabin-crazy? Would they find her emaciated body come spring, buried in a pile of unread computer magazines? Or perhaps she'd be wild-eyed and mangy-haired, wandering through the woods talking to the deer and squirrels and rabbits.

The shrill cry of the phone cut into her reverie and she grabbed at it with a burst of relief, glad to be yanked back into the world of people and technology.

"Hi, Mom, how ya doing?"

Shadows of the dream disappeared in an instant. "Great, James, just great. So nice to hear your voice, where are you?"

"At home, Mom," he said, meaning his residence at the University of British Columbia.

"Have you bought your ticket yet? You've left it awfully late. Let me get a pen and I'll jot down the details. I am so excited about seeing you again, it's only been four months since you left but it seems like forever. Hold on a sec."

Joanna moved the phone away from her ear, but he called out, "Wait, Mom, wait. I have to tell you something."

"Yes, dear."

"I won't be coming home for Christmas, Mom." She pretended to herself that she misunderstood him.

"I know, James. The house is rented, remember. But you'll like it here. We already have so much snow, it will really be a white Christmas."

"No, Mom," he said softly. "I mean I'm staying in B.C."

"Oh, but why?" A sinking feeling spread slowly outward from the center of her chest. She wanted to hang up the phone and pretend this conversation never happened. Instead she gripped the receiver tighter and held on.

"Listen, Mom, I'm really sorry. I know that you'll be disappointed, but this guy that lives on my floor, I told you about him, Eric, remember? His parents own a condo in Whistler and they go there for Christmas every year. Well, they had a big fight over Thanksgiving, the parents I mean, and they almost got a divorce over it. Eric thinks his dad was having an affair, but he's not really sure. Anyway, they want to try to work on their marriage so they are going to Mexico for Christmas, just the two of them."

"But what has all this got to do with you, James?" Joanna sank into a chair.

"Well, Eric and his brother are going to be alone at Christmas, so their parents said that they can both invite two friends to spend the week at the condo."

"Oh," Joanna said in a tiny voice.

"I'm sorry, Mom, really I am. But, I mean, a week at a

condo in Whistler. And the whole place is like fully stocked. We won't have to buy food, or anything."

She could hear the excitement creeping into his voice. He was trying to sound sorry and full of regrets but it wasn't working. Despite herself she smiled. Who wouldn't leap at the chance to spend a week in a private chalet in North America's number one ski resort? And over Christmas, no less. The village would be a wonderland at Christmas.

"How old is Eric's brother?"

"He's twenty-seven. Mom, you won't have to worry."

But I will anyway. "It sounds wonderful, James. Absolutely wonderful. You'll have a great time."

"Thanks, Mom. I'll miss you."

"And I'll miss you." *More than you can imagine.* She wiped at a tear in the corner of one eye.

"But you'll have Wendy there right, with Robert?"

"Yes, they're coming."

"Ah, anyone else?"

"No."

"You haven't heard anything?"

"No, dear, not a word."

"Don't give up hope, Mom, eh? She'll get in touch with one of us one day."

"I know, James, I know," Joanna sighed. "But never mind, you have a really great time, okay? Phone me when you get there with the phone number of the condo so I can call you on Christmas day."

"Bye Mom. Love you."

"Good-bye, James." Joanna hung up the phone carefully. She was disappointed right to the bone, but she reminded herself of what she had always known: we raise our children so they can leave us one day.

TWENTY

ON THE SPUR OF THE MOMENT, not wanting to digest James' news, not just yet, Joanna phoned Scott O'Neill to invite him for Christmas dinner. His voice sounded full of regret as he explained that he had made arrangements to spend the holiday with his brothers and their families in Florida. "I'd much rather spend my Christmas up here, but even though I don't get on with my brothers very well I try to have a good relationship with my nieces and nephews," he explained.

The phone was barely back in its cradle before it rang once again.

"Hello."

"Ms. Hastings, Inspector Erikson here."

I really must get caller display, Joanna thought. "Yes, Inspector, what can I do for you today?" She tried not to sigh too loudly.

"I came by the other night but you weren't home. Didn't you get my note?"

"No, I didn't see a note. It must have fallen off the door." Joanna winced, she was a terrible liar.

"I didn't say I put it in the door," Erikson replied.

Joanna winced again, caught. Could a two-bit crook in a second-rate TV movie have handled that exchange any worse? "What can I do for you, Inspector?"

"I have a few more small points to clear up and I would like to drop by to discuss them."

"Couldn't we talk about it on the phone? No need for you to go to all the trouble of coming all the way out here, now is there?"

"No we couldn't. And it's no trouble. I can be there in about ten minutes."

"Ah, I was just on my way out. How about tomorrow?"

Erikson's voice took on an edge of steel. "Ms. Hastings don't play games with me, please. This is a murder investigation and you found the body of the victim. I will be there in ten minutes." Without a good-bye she hung up.

Joanna stood in her living room, staring glumly at the silent phone in her hand. All she wanted was peace and quiet, to put her troubles behind her and sort her life out. Instead she was living in the Village of the Damned and smack dab right in the middle of a homicide investigation at that. It was becoming too much.

With a screech of rage she ripped the phone cord out of the wall and hurled the offensive instrument across the room. It missed her late mother's handmade pottery wall sconce by inches and fell to the floor with a dull thud. She yelled again and kicked at the computer table. This time she gasped in pain as foot made contact with wood.

She refused to give in to the self-inflicted injury and stormed into the kitchen. She poured herself a glass of wine and drank it in a gulp, then poured another. She was halfway through the second glass when the crunch of car wheels on snow and the slamming of doors echoed through the woods. She finished the wine in one swallow, then carefully washed out the glass and put it away in the cupboard. Wouldn't want the police to know she had been drinking. She pasted a smile on her lips and walked across the cabin to open the door.

Erikson and Reynolds were just mounting the steps. Staff Sergeant Reynolds reached out his hand and shook Joanna's with enthusiasm. She almost felt sorry for the old guy—the village constable was having a lot of trouble dealing with death and suspicion among his friends and neighbors.

Inspector Erikson marched past them and into the cabin. "Having a problem with your phone?" she asked dryly.

Joanna grimaced. Wisely she remained silent.

As she did at the beginning of every interview, Erikson pulled her notebook and pen out of her mammoth purse. She flicked the book open to a blank page.

Joanna remembered that she was trying to be friendly. "Please, can I take your coats?"

Reynolds moved to open his mouth but Erikson was faster. "No thank you. We won't be very long." Reynolds wiggled his coat back onto his shoulders, trying not to look as if he had been in the midst of slipping it off.

"Would you like to sit down?" Joanna persisted.

This time the staff sergeant was first. "Yes, thank you," he said, sinking into the chair closest to the fire, "that would be very nice." Erikson relented and took the second best chair.

"I want to ask you about the Bulls jacket," she began.

Joanna nodded silently. She was only surprised at how long it had taken them to come to this.

"Tiffany Jordan says that she lost the jacket. I think that you know a bit more about it than you are saying."

Joanna considered offering her unwanted guests a drink. She could use one herself right now.

"Ms. Hastings, do you know how Tiffany lost the jacket?"

Joanna got up and knelt in front of the stove, opened the iron door and carefully placed another log on the fire. She stirred the embers until they flared up to catch the remains of the last log and eagerly reached for the fresh fuel. Only then did she shut the door, return the poker to its stand and turn her attention back to the police officers.

"I know only what she told me," Joanna said. "She was in the Last Hope bar, or something with some such stupid cowboy name in North Ridge, having a few drinks. Even though she is well under age, I think that the bartender at the Last Stop doesn't worry too much about that sort of detail."

"I'll look into that." Reynolds puffed himself up in an attempt to get into the conversation.

Erikson glared at him—she did not appreciate the interruption. "And then…"

"And she says that she left her jacket on a chair and when she went to get it, it was gone. It does happen, Inspector. You know how often these sort of trendy big-city clothes get stolen."

"Yes, I know."

"And, unfortunately, these jackets are pretty common, it's not as if it is a one of a kind designer thing, is it?" Joanna hurried on. Now that she was talking, the words were stumbling over themselves in their haste to get out. "You don't know that the jacket found with Luke was Tiffany's, do you? It could well be a similar one."

"Thank you for your time, Ms. Hastings." Erikson rose abruptly with a snap of her notebook and Reynolds scrambled to his feet.

Joanna stood at the door watching as they made their way down the shoveled path. Gathering her wits at last, she raced after them as they climbed into their car.

She tapped furiously at the passenger window as Reynolds, who was driving, put the car into reverse and glanced over his shoulder to back out of the narrow drive. He stopped suddenly and Erikson rolled down the window.

"Was it Tiffany's jacket?" Joanna gasped, bending over to peer into the inspector's face. "The one found with the body, I mean? I have invited this girl into my home, I think I have the right to know."

Erikson looked at her solemnly, undecided. Then she nodded, to herself more than to the two people watching her. "There are no identifying marks on the jacket, no personal labels or name tags or anything of the sort. It is extra large but we all know that most people today wear that type of jacket as baggy as it can get. No, Ms. Hastings, I have no proof that it is the Jordan girl's jacket. Although, it would be very nice indeed, if hers turned up." She rolled down the window and nodded to Reynolds. He took his foot off the break and backed carefully up the snow-packed driveway.

Joanna watched as they turned into the road and drove slowly away.

As she walked thoughtfully back into her cabin, the first thing that caught her eye was the hole in the wall marking where the phone cable had so impulsively been freed from its constraints. The telephone itself lay on the floor on the other side of the room, broken into a jumble of small pieces. It was dark outside now, probably too late to use the cell phone to call the phone company, not if she wanted to get a real, live person on the line. And tomorrow was Sunday; highly unlikely anyone would be around to take her call then.

She wondered if perhaps she should get a TV. She had hardly ever watched the one the family had in the city. But how long and lonely the nights were proving to be. She poured herself another glass of wine and stood in the kitchen doorway, looking around her cabin, as if seeing it for the first time. Her eyes came to rest on her desk and then they lit on the scrap of paper containing the rough notes she was randomly jotting down as ideas popped into her head for the training manual. As if out of nowhere, a great concept for the format of the graphics on the web page popped into her head. A burst of excitement propelled Joanna forward to her desk. She looked once out the window into the impenetrable darkness of the forest and the unseen lake beyond. The wind was high tonight and she could hear the naked branches of the trees rustling together. She reminded herself that this is what she had been wanting for many years. So let's get to it. The disturbing dreams, the police and the missing jacket forgotten, she worked late into the night.

Fortunately for her peace of mind, she did not dream that night, or if she did, the ghostly images disappeared at the moment they were experienced, as dreams so often do.

SHE CHEWED HER breakfast bagel and sipped her coffee with something approaching enthusiasm. Her work last night had gone well and she was pleased with the results. She would have to read it all over very carefully; work done late at night was known to take on a particularly rosy tinge, but she knew that she had done well.

The police were aware that Tiffany's jacket was missing, that was probably not a good thing, but at least they could not positively identify the one found with Luke as the same one that belonged to Tiffany Jordan.

Her mind shifted to the problem of the dead phone. She was hoping Wendy would call tonight after they got back from Montreal. Joanna was anxious to discuss Christmas plans with her eldest daughter. She used her cell phone for outgoing calls only, and no one, not even Wendy, had ever been given the number.

As she ate, she remembered the small sign posted in the grocery store in Hope River. "Electrician available" was all it said. She probably didn't need the phone company to fix the connection; after all, it was only a few wires coming out of the wall. The shattered phone itself would be a problem, though. She finished her bagel and popped another into the toaster. A surplus electronics store occupied a piece of land on the side of the highway leading out of Hope River: they might have telephones.

Good mood forgotten at the necessity of leaving her cozy, warm home in pursuit of an errand that was, indeed, entirely her own fault, she grumbled the entire way into the back room to get her purse and car keys. And she was still grumbling to herself on the short drive into town, in search of the number of someone she might be able to call to come and fix the blasted phone.

Fortunately, the electrician answered on the first ring and was more than happy to come out to Joanna's cabin, for special Sunday rates of course, to repair the phone wiring. She made an appointment to meet him later and set off in search of the surplus hardware store.

It lay on the outskirts of Hope River, apparently too disreputable for even that none-too-opulent small town. From the outside it resembled nothing more than an old-fashioned junkyard dealer and Joanna almost gave up the search for a phone right there. But thoughts of another drive into North Ridge to search for a more reputable store had her gliding to a stop on the side of the highway. What bit of a parking lot there was, was jammed to overflowing with broken appliances and strange parts, large and small, for she knew not what.

She pushed open the door and a bell clanged in cheerful announcement of her arrival. To her surprise the store was almost full, not only of assorted bits and pieces of almost any type of electronic or mechanical equipment one could hope to find, but a good number of the town elders as well. The men lounged against the counter, smoking steadily and watching her approach. All conversation ceased.

Joanna smiled greetings to Jack from the grocery store and two of the other men whom she recognized from her visits to town. All the men nodded politely or mumbled hello, save for

Jack who spat a large wad of chewing tobacco onto the floor at her feet. Gracious fellow. She ignored him and spoke directly to the one man standing behind the counter. Younger, much younger, than the rest, full of smiles and false charm, he led her to the back to investigate rows of surplus telephones. As they walked down the crowded aisles Joanna was surprised again. There were piles upon piles of spare computer equipment, monitors and motherboards, modems and SCSI cards, and boxes filled with assorted chips. She promised herself to return another time and see what she could pick up, hopefully without an audience watching her every move. There looked to be enough here to build an entire computer from scrap. Maybe she could put together a machine for Tiffany, not the most up-to-date, but a decent working computer at little cost.

As soon as she moved off down the aisles the men picked up their conversation where it had been cut off.

"…drugs," she heard the oldest of them exclaim, coughing around the words. "Drugs and them single mothers. Nothing but trouble."

"Don't think there are any single mothers in Hope River." His duties done, the clerk settled back into the conversation.

"Don't matter," the old man replied. "City folks and drugs done old Luke in."

Joanna pricked up her ears and replaced the telephone she had chosen, pretending to search through the bin for a better one. She peeked over the dusty shelf and saw the other men nodding their agreement.

"These big city drug dealers are coming up to Hope River, you mark my words." Jack waved his finger at the circle of men. "These teenagers will do most anything for drugs and those types know it. I seen a couple of them myself, hanging out around the store. Pants hanging down to where it ain't decent, hats on backward, giving girls the eye and waiting for my back to turn to make their deal."

The assembled men growled in appreciation. "So what did you do, Jack?" the oldest resident asked.

"Why, I drove them off, of course. Told them we don't want their kind in Hope River." He sighed theatrically. "Not that it do much good. They'll just move on down the street and sell their drugs somewhere else."

Selection in hand, Joanna approached the counter. She doubted if Jack would know a drug or a drug dealer if it rose up to bite him in the ass. Assuming of course that tobacco and alcohol, the most persistent drugs of all, didn't count. But the old men were hanging on to his every word and that was probably all that mattered, to Jack at any rate.

"I hear there's some mighty strange goings on in the woods to the south of town." Joanna recognized the man she had dubbed Santa Claus from the search party. He bobbed his bushy white beard in emphasis.

"You live right near there don't you, Ms. Hastings." A man she had never set eyes on before addressed Joanna politely as she fumbled in her purse for her wallet. She probably shouldn't be surprised that they all seemed to know who she was. She was no doubt the talk of the town. "Do you hear wild drug parties and such goings on in the night?" he added.

Joanna turned a full wattage smile on them all. "If I did, I would probably assume it was just a bunch of good old boys out for a night of drinking. Good day, gentlemen." Shoulders back she sailed out of the store, a few scratching heads bobbing in her wake.

CHRISTMAS WAS COMING UP awfully fast. Amidst all the chaos of the last few weeks, she had barely given the holiday a thought.

She glanced around her cabin. It was definitely sparse and certainly cheerless, and a bit of decorating would help. At home Joanna had always gone all out for the Season. As well as a huge live tree, which rose up to touch the ceiling and was covered with decorations the children had proudly carried home since nursery school, she filled the house with candles and ribbons and armfuls of greenery, and the outside she draped with swags and wreathes. Evergreen boughs and stark winter branches and rosehip in clay pots lined the walkway. The children would dig the old outdoor lights out of the garage and carefully sort through them all, discarding broken ones and those with the colored paint almost completely chipped off. Then with much pushing and shoving and laughter one or the other would climb up the ladder dragging strings of brightly colored lights behind them. Inevitably the lights would sag and some would loosen and then flicker and grow dark but the children were always so excited by the display and their own part in arranging it all.

But nothing had been the same for the last few years. Christmas was just such an effort. The spirit of the season was hard to maintain in the face of Alexis' mounting anger. Joanna tried halfheartedly, but before long Wendy and James would prefer to escape their mother's and sister's continual conflicts in the homes of their friends, even if it was Christmas.

She was thinking that it would be nice to decorate the cabin a bit when the electrician arrived, right on time. The broken wires were fixed and the new (second-hand) phone installed, the electrician paid and waved off, only minutes before Wendy called with the welcome news of the timing of their arrival for Christmas.

Hanging up the phone with a smile Joanna wanted to recreate

some of the gaity of Christmases long past. She struggled to remember if she had seen a nursery anywhere in the vicinity.

Getting the tree should be no problem, there were plenty of tree lots to choose from. But a wreath would be nice on the front door; maybe some swags on the wall. She stepped out onto the porch and gazed absentmindedly into the woods. There were no florists anywhere near Hope River. She didn't feel like driving for hours in search of decorations.

Her bark of laughter crashed through the silence of the late afternoon. A large chipmunk, about to venture out of her little nest under the woodpile in search of a few over-looked acorns, got such a start she thought better of the expedition and pulled swiftly back into the shadows under the porch.

Laughing at herself for a city-bred fool, Joanna gleefully rushed back into the cabin. Grabbing a sharp vegetable knife and slipping on her boots, she ran out into the woods not bothering with a coat or sweater. All the Christmas greenery one could possibly hope for right here in her own front yard.

She spent the rest of the day's light rambling through the woods filling her arms with thick pine boughs, red dogwood branches, winter berries and all the pine cones a woman could carry. She carted load after load back to the cabin and then set off again, searching for still more. Only when it became so dark that it was impossible to distinguish a lush evergreen branch from a dead one did she stop.

The accumulated pile had assumed near-monstrous proportions. Joanna flicked on the overhead light and knelt in the snow on the porch to sort through her bounty. She selected a few of the best pieces and carried them proudly into the cabin.

She had brought most of the family's Christmas decorations with her to the north. The memories they held were far too precious to consign to storage. Rooting through the box, she pulled out bright red and gold bows, homemade decorations and long strings of wooden beads.

She worked late into the night, tying evergreen branches into shapes and decorating them with bows and beads, dried berries and pinecones. She stopped only once to add more fuel to the fireplace. When she was finished a huge wreath hung proudly on the front door, swags bounded across the front porch and draped gracefully across the brick wall behind the fire. Tomorrow she would go to the hardware store for some clay pots to fill with more pine branches and stalks of huckleberry and dogwood to mark the entrance to the driveway.

Tired and happy, Joanna staggered off to bed. Pine needles and bits of bark, too-small cones, cut ribbon and a few broken wooden beads littered the kitchen table and spread out across the linoleum floor.

Outside the cabin a sudden wind stirred the branches on the porch and clouds rushed to cover the moon. A light snow was falling, swirled into eddies by the wind. Barely distinguishable from the night beneath the blowing snow, a thin black shape moved across the lawn to drift without sound up the old porch steps. It crossed over the broken wooden step but for once the tread lay silent. It swayed silently in front of the large wreath hanging in pride of place on the front door. An insubstantial shifting of the blowing snow in the air around it was all there was to mark any movement as it reached out for the cheerful red bow hanging from one side of the wreath. It hovered in the air for the briefest of moments until a gust of wind whipped up the falling snow. When the wind again died down, nothing more remained to be seen.

A large-eyed owl sitting in the nearest tree blinked just once before resuming its eternal, silent scan for a flash of movement through the dark, snow-covered woods.

"YOUR PLACE LOOKS GREAT, Joanna, really great." Tiffany shrugged out of her coat, still her grandmother's cast-off, and looked about the room. "That thing over the fire is fabulous. I guess you bought it in Toronto, eh?"

Joanna grinned. "Believe it or not, I made it myself, with stuff I gathered from the woods outside my very own front door."

"Wow. Maybe you could make something like that for us."

"Doesn't your grandmother decorate for Christmas? I would have thought she did. She certainly seems like the type."

"Oh, sure. We have all kinds of plastic wreathes and dime store Santas, but nothing, you know, nothing real."

"It's not hard, not really. Why don't you make one yourself? You'd be surprised at how easy it is."

"My mom started making a real wreath once, it would have been nice but then her jerky boyfriend came over and wanted a beer and we didn't have any in the fridge so she had to go out and get some and then she never finished it. She even had some real berries, like you have on yours."

Joanna thought desperately for something to say. "All the more reason for you to give it a try."

"I'm no good at stuff like that."

"I won't really have time, anyway," Joanna said. "My daughter and her husband are coming tomorrow to spend the holidays with me."

"Yea, I guess." Tiffany's shoulders drooped and the girl retreated once again into her slumped posture.

Joanna decided to ignore her and pulled a chair up to the computer table. "Let's get started. I thought that maybe we should get into presentation software. Something that you can use to make nice-looking projects and reports for school."

"Oh, yea, like I'm going to do reports," Tiffany snorted.

Joanna looked up in surprise, taken aback by the abrupt

180-degree change in the girl's mood. She had had more than enough of teenagers and their moods in her life. "Oh, stop whining and sit down," she said sharply. "Let's get started."

The lesson was strained enough as it was but today of all days the computer decided to act up. They had to reboot the machine twice and Tiffany was full of disparaging comments about the state of the computer industry in general and this machine in particular.

Joanna bit her lip and held her tongue. She was accepting money to teach this girl, so she would put up with it.

At last the endless hour was over. Tiffany scrambled to the door and pulled on mitts and boots the instant they heard the tooting of Maude's car from the road. She rushed out without a backward glance.

Joanna sighed as she pulled up the computer chair to return to her own work. Tiffany's moods could swing like a weather-vane in a hurricane and she did not intend to spend any more time or effort figuring them out.

Hours later, she looked up from the computer monitor and let out a low groan as she stretched her arms into the air and twisted her back in a futile attempt to wiggle the kinks out. Rising stiffly to go into the kitchen and make a cup of coffee, she noticed Tiffany's long, red, hand-knitted scarf peeking out from behind a cushion on the sofa. She groaned again, and pulled the scarf from its hiding place. She hung it on the coat rack by the front door and walked into the kitchen to make her coffee.

TWENTY-ONE

THE MOMENT SHE HEARD a car slowing down on the road and turning carefully into the driveway, Joanna launched herself down the steps of the cabin. With a squeal of joy Wendy leaped out of the car before it had come to a complete stop and ran into her mother's arms. They hugged each other and jumped up and down in delight as Robert carefully parked the rental car behind Joanna's Toyota and came over to join them. He kissed the air beside his mother-in-law's cheek and said, "Why don't you two go in and relax? I'll bring in the suitcases."

Joanna and her eldest daughter needed no further encouragement. Their arms wrapped around each other's waists, they virtually danced into the cabin.

"Oh, Mom, everything looks absolutely fabulous," Wendy gushed. "Just like when we were children. For heaven's sake there's the pottery Santa Claus that I made, must have been a hundred years ago."

Joanna laughed, "Not quite, but sometimes it seems like it's been that long."

Wendy rushed to open the screen door as Robert stumbled up the steps, his arms laden with brightly wrapped parcels. "Where shall I put these," he gasped. He spotted the fully trimmed tree. "Oh, never mind, I think I can guess."

Laughing, Wendy took the presents out of his arms and placed them under the tree as Robert went out for another load.

Joanna directed her daughter's husband to put the suitcases in the back bedroom. "Sorry, but it's pretty cramped and there is only the one bedroom," she apologized, aware of how inadequate the cabin might appear to others. "You can hang your clothes up in my closet. I made some room."

She followed Wendy and Robert into the back. "You two will sleep in here, of course. I will be quite comfortable out on the couch."

"Good Heavens, Mom, we can't kick you out of your bedroom," Wendy said.

"I insist. I will be perfectly comfortable out there. In fact, you will soon find that it is the only warm room in the place. I won't suffer. Besides, if I force myself to stay awake tonight, I might see Santa Claus himself sliding down the chimney with all those presents. He comes extra early to us in the North, you know. First thing."

Wendy laughed. "Do you remember the year we went for a drive on Christmas Eve to look at all the lights before bedtime and we saw Santa getting out of a van on our street?"

Joanna smiled at the memory. "You were starting to wonder if maybe Santa wasn't a real person after all. That fixed you for a couple of years."

"What," Robert gasped in mock horror, "you mean Santa isn't real?" He clasped his hand to his heart and rolled his eyes in despair. "My life is ruined, what else is there to believe in. Next you'll be telling me that the tooth fairy didn't really give me a dollar for every tooth I lose."

"A dollar!" Wendy shrieked. "We only got twenty-five cents for a tooth. You cheated me, Mom. Pay up, now."

With a chuckle, Joanna left them to unpack. It was great to laugh again.

Because Wendy had been unsure as to when they would be

able to get out of Toronto or what the traffic would be like, Joanna had prepared a dinner that would be quick to reheat once they were ready to eat. She popped the lasagna back into the oven as Robert went out to the car for another load of Christmas presents, and put together a quick salad. She poured herself and Wendy a glass of wine and a beer for Robert, put a new log into the fire, plugged in the tree lights and finally settled back into the living room couch with a sigh of contentment.

"There seem to be an awful lot of presents here," she said, eyeing the tree once her guests had picked up their drinks and snuggled up on the floor beside the fire. "A lot more than you would expect for just three people."

"Some are from Dad," Wendy said, swirling her wine in gentle circles. "He gave me presents to bring to you."

Joanna was surprised. "Really. After all this time." She studied the reflection of the candlelight as it danced across the ruby surface of the wine in her own glass. "I didn't send him anything. Nor to Buffy, either."

"Belinda, Mother, you know her name is Belinda."

"Oh yes, right. Belinda. Sounds like Buffy to me. Well, I had better check on dinner. Be back in a sec."

After dinner Joanna insisted on following the family custom of one present on Christmas Eve. Robert opened a tie from his mother. "She refuses to admit that I don't wear ties and a three-piece suit to class." He shook his head fondly as he held up the neckpiece for all to admire, a lovely black tie with a background of blazing stars and the original starship Enterprise boldly going where no one had gone before.

Wendy's gift was from James, an extremely nice sculpture of a breaching whale.

Joanna tentatively opened one of the gifts from her ex-husband, beautifully wrapped in glistening silver paper so delicate that the box inside virtually glowed. Of all things, it was a negligée, a flimsy peach thing in soft drapes of silk and satin. Joanna sat back in shock and then despite herself she chuckled gently. Wendy and Robert giggled.

"Okay," Joanna announced, trying to hide her embarrassment at the gift, "who's for a walk in the wilds of Northern Ontario?"

Bending to pick up the empty wineglasses she failed to notice Wendy exchange quick glances with her husband.

"Tell you what," Robert announced solemnly. "You two go out for a walk and I will do up the dishes."

Joanna looked at Wendy in mock surprise. "Did I hear correctly? Is this a model of the modern male, or what?"

Wendy shrugged into her coat and held Joanna's out in front of her. "Let's go, Mother, before he changes his mind."

THE WINTER NIGHT was clear and cold. Every star in the sky sparkled as brightly as candles dancing dangerously on a Victorian Christmas tree. Wendy slipped her arm through her mother's and hugged her close as they stood on the front steps appreciating the silence. Wendy blew quick gusts of warm air out of her lungs and into the winter chill to watch her breath turn into her own personal clouds in front of her face.

Joanna laughed and in companionable serenity the two women walked up the driveway to the road.

Wendy sighed. "I still wonder about all this, your place is just so terribly isolated."

Joanna tightened her grip on her daughter's arm. "I like it here, dear, I really do. Isolation suits me just fine."

"As long as you're not running away, trying to avoid dealing with things, I mean."

Under the cover of darkness Joanna grimaced to herself. "I am dealing with things as best I can, Wendy. As I said, this place suits me. Now tell me about your classes. How is your thesis coming along, how is Robert doing? You told me he was struggling a bit at the end of last year. I hope that everything has straightened out for him."

Wendy took a deep breath. "Actually, Mom, he has decided to quit school and take a position that he has been offered with a mineral exploration company."

Joanna stopped walking. "What do you mean, 'quit school'? What about his PhD?"

"His thesis is going nowhere, Mom, absolutely nowhere," Wendy said with a shrug, "and he jumped at the chance to take this job. So, at least for now, he won't be finishing his PhD."

Joanna was somewhat relieved: she was starting to fear that they were both turning into professional students. "Maybe that is for the best, dear, a bit of practical experience is probably just what Robert needs. What company is it? Is the head office in Toronto?"

Wendy stopped walking. Thick, light snowflakes were falling out of the black night to drape the women's shoulders in cloaks of the softest white.

"Their head office is in Toronto, but their operations are in the Yukon. That is where Robert will be working."

Joanna nodded, refusing to take in the implications. "You won't get a chance to see him very much, then. I hope that the company will fly him down regularly for a visit."

Wendy brushed snow off her shoulders. "That won't be necessary. I am going with him. I will finish my thesis by correspondence. In fact, I might start it all over again, *'The effects of long-term sun deprivation on the human psyche,'* or something similar. What do you think?"

"What do I think?" Joanna struggled to keep her voice under

control, although the words still came out harsher than she had intended. "I think you're nuts. You almost have your PhD in Psychology and you are about to throw it in and move to the Yukon, of all the God-forsaken places."

"I am not *throwing anything in,* Mother, I think that this is a great opportunity for us both. Robert needs a chance to prove himself, you know."

"But what about you? What do you have to prove to yourself? You're so close to getting your degree, what you have always wanted. Are you prepared to start it all again?"

"Look at yourself, Mom," Wendy said. "You have given up everything to move to this backwoods nowhere. People told you that you're crazy, but you went ahead and did it anyway."

"This is different." Joanna carved an ever-increasing series of circles in the snow with her boot. "I've put in my time, I've paid my dues. Now I want to do something for myself."

"Yes, it is different, we're still young. We have time to make mistakes, Mom. If this is a mistake we can go back to school or find new jobs and start all over again. You can't."

Wendy's logic was like a physical blow to the stomach. Joanna knew that her daughter was right. In her late forties, she was, quite simply, too old to make life-sized mistakes. She had cashed in a large portion of her retirement fund to make this move and start up on her own. There was no time left in her life to start saving again.

At that moment a long-legged, brown-speckled deer, as delicate as a teacup made of the finest bone china, burst out of a thick clump of bushes and bramble and crossed the road with one majestic leap. It was gone in an instant, barely making a sound and leaving not a trace behind, save for a cluster of hoofed footprints in the snow.

"Oh, my goodness," Wendy gasped, her eyes wide with astonishment. "Did you see that?"

"Oh, yeah," Joanna replied with an air of total nonchalance that covered the depth of awe she felt at the appearance of the majestic animal. "See them all the time around here."

"That is so fabulous. Maybe there is something to be said for living up here, after all."

Joanna laughed. "Maybe there is indeed."

Wendy grinned and they continued their walk.

The appearance of the deer put everything into perspective. She was disappointed that Wendy was breaking off her studies. It is a rare person who is able to pick up again once they leave university. But it did happen and living in the far north would be the experience of a lifetime, and there was no point in arguing against it, anyway. The young couple had made their decision.

She could only hope that her daughter's marriage would be strong enough to cope with the isolation of that Arctic community, the harshness of its life and in particular the long, never-ending winter nights. It would be all too easy for Robert to get wrapped up in his job. No doubt he would spend a great deal of his time traveling, and would fail to notice (or not want to notice) if his wife was lonely and depressed, away as she would be from friends, family, city-life and the university she so loved. Joanna hoped that their marriage would be strong enough, but she doubted it.

"I have sort of wondered lately, how things have been going with you and Robert," she asked hesitantly. "Is everything okay? You seem to have been a bit off lately." She cast her eyes downward and started intently at her boots as they crunched through the packed snow, leaving Wendy to answer as, and if, she wanted.

Wendy bent down and scooped up a handful of fresh snow from the side of the road. She formed it thoughtfully into a ball and tossed it several times into the air. In a flash, she assumed a baseball pitcher's classic stance, shifted her position a few times and threw the ball straight at her mother's head. Years of being the star thrower of the local girls' league softball team paid off handsomely, and the ball sailed by Joanna's ear, exactly where Wendy had aimed it.

Joanna shrieked and leapt out of the way. Whirling around, she faced her attacker who was now helpless in the center of the road, doubled up with laughter.

She waited for Wendy to recover. Chuckling they linked arms once again.

"Everything is fine, Mom," Wendy said. "It has been a tough decision for us to make and I think we were getting a bit short with each other over it all. Robert is very worried about going so far away from his mother. She hasn't been well lately at all."

"I'm sorry to hear that. What does she think about this job and the move and all?"

"He hasn't told her. When we went up to Montreal last time he was going to tell her, but she was so sick that he never got around to it. He won't say so, but I think that he thinks that it won't really matter if she believes we are still living in Toronto. It seems closer to her, but she will never come and visit so it doesn't really matter where we are."

Joanna walked in silence. It seemed so sad, Robert's mother not even knowing where her son was living. It's a mistake, she thought, not to tell. Robert's mother was much older than she herself, Robert being the youngest of 10 children, but young people often underestimate the ability of their elders to handle change and disappointment. After all, they had plenty of practice. *Listen to me,* Joanna thought, *I sound like someone's great-grandmother myself. When did I start including myself among the old people?*

"I'm getting cold," was all she could say. "It's time to turn back."

THEY ENJOYED an enormous breakfast Christmas morning. Wendy and Robert scattered the remains of whole wheat toast and pancakes onto the front porch and spent a good deal of time exclaiming in delight over the number of birds and small mammals who crept up to the cabin in order to partake of a Christmas treat.

After breakfast, they opened their gifts and then Joanna moved into the kitchen to begin slicing onions and celery and mushrooms for the stuffing. From the kitchen window she and Wendy could watch Robert chopping wood. There was a great deal to be done, and since the death of Luke she had not found anyone else to come out and do the job for her. Her pile of stove-ready logs was getting very small indeed.

"I spoke to Dad the other day," Wendy said tentatively, exploring the waters with care as she peeled potatoes over the sink.

"Umm," Joanna listened with only half an ear. She was debating whether she should add just a touch more sage to the stuffing. It was an incredibly big turkey for a mere three people. She would be eating turkey sandwiches for a month. Not that that was ever a problem.

"He went to California in the beginning of December."

Sage forgotten, Joanna stopped slicing. "Oh," she said stiffly. "Why would he do that?"

"You know why, Mom." Wendy put down the potato peeler, placed her hands in a firm grasp on her mother's shoulders and stared into her eyes. "He wanted to see Alexis."

"And did he?" Joanna was immobile under her daughter's grip.

"Yes, yes he did. But it didn't go very well." Wendy released her mother and picked up another potato. She examined it closely for eyes and bad spots. "She saw him for only a couple of minutes. There were two people there all the time, listening to every word. Dad said that it was awful, he said it was like she was in an aquarium, one of those in which you watch sharks and whales and big ocean fish swimming around in circles. It felt like he was trying to touch her through a plane of glass six inches thick."

Joanna sunk into a kitchen chair. She could hear the steady thump of Robert's axe hitting the old, scarred chopping block.

Wendy crouched in front of her mother. "She told him that she was happy living there, that she didn't want him to come and visit her again, that she wanted us all to stop writing her letters, that she had a new family now and she was happy with them."

Joanna groaned.

"So Dad left."

"He left!" Joanna shrieked. "He just left her there?"

"What else could he do, Mom? What else could he do? He couldn't force her to come with him."

"Well he should have, he should have."

"Boy, it's sure cold out there. How about a cup of hot chocolate for an old working man."

Robert threw open the back door and stood in the kitchen stomping his feet and rubbing his gloves together, cheeks flushed with the cold, eyes bright from the unaccustomed physical work.

Wendy shot him a sharp glance and shook her head vigorously.

"Uh, maybe I'll work for a bit longer before having that hot chocolate, if it's all the same to you." He backed out of the room in a flurry of embarrassment, closing the kitchen door softly behind him.

"Why doesn't she want us, what did I ever do to make her hate me so?" Joanna moaned, oblivious of Robert's interruption.

"Stop that, Mom," Wendy said. "Don't talk like that. We've been all over this before. It's not your fault."

"But it is, it is. I must have done something wrong." Joanna put her face into her hands and let tears flow.

"Why don't you go and lie down, Mom." Wendy tugged her mother's arm, trying to raise her from the chair. "You go and have a nap."

"But the dinner," Joanna protested through her tears. "The turkey has to go into the oven soon."

"Robert and I will take care of it. Don't you worry. You go and have a nap now, and we'll talk again when you get up."

Despite her misery, Joanna cracked a small smile. "Robert will get the Christmas dinner?" Both women knew that as the youngest in a family of ten children, Robert didn't know much about looking after himself, and certainly nothing about cooking.

"I'll tell him what to do." Wendy hustled her mother into her room. "He's very good that way. He doesn't know any better, so he just does as he's told."

Joanna slipped off her sweater and slippers and socks, and slid under the covers as Wendy switched out the light and softly closed the door.

TWENTY-TWO

IT SEEMED AS IF the day she turned thirteen Alexis departed her body and an invader from outer space took possession. The light-hearted girl, the one who was always the happiest, always the one laughing the loudest, was gone and in her place stood an angry, resentful teenager. Perhaps she was all the more bitter because she really had nothing to rebel against.

Everyone told Joanna that it was only a phase. "She'll grow out of it," they all said. But she never did.

Grade eight was the last grade Alexis passed. Into high school and her marks fell off the chart. She was caught skipping class time after time. She endured her in-school suspensions and as soon as they were over, she skipped class again. At first the principal and the teachers kept Joanna apprised of the situation. But gradually their calls dried up, as one after one the school staff gave up on her daughter.

Alexis' childhood friends stopped coming around. Joanna would see them in the mall sometimes, and they would nod and slink away. Alexis found a new group of friends, young people with numerous piercings, and strangely cut and dyed hair. Many nights Alexis came home late, very late, staggering and incoherent.

Joanna was beside herself with grief. They went to counseling, government funded and private, both together and separately. Sometimes the entire family went. Nothing helped. Alexis attended the sessions without too much protest, sat quietly and nodded at the therapist's suggestions and went right back to the streets with her new friends.

At work, Joanna's performance suffered. She came in late, red-eyed after driving around the neighborhood half the night looking for Alexis or waiting up until the wee hours for the sound of the front door slamming, and left early hoping to get in before her daughter got home from school (assuming that she went) and then went out again for the evening. When she was at work her production dropped down to practically nothing. One day she was going over her notes and reviewing her slides for the presentation she was about to make to a prospective client when the school called to say that Alexis had slashed her arms with a razor blade in the girls' washroom and was on her way to the hospital. It was the Friday afternoon before a long weekend and most of her colleagues had already left. Before she flew out the door, the only person in her department Joanna could find was a co-op student. She thrust the slide folios and the text of her talk at the surprised young woman and was gone. To her astonishment they got the contract, mainly on the strength of the product, not the quality of the presentation. The student was offered a full-time position and it was politely suggested that Joanna take some time off.

Wendy and James were not immune to the storms whirling through their lives. They were supportive of both their mother and younger sister for a long time but as the rebellion on Alexis' part, and the despair on Joanna's, grew they retreated into separate worlds of their own interests and friends.

Joanna's ex-husband blamed her for all of Alexis' problems. "If you were a better mother," he shouted at her on one occasion. "If you weren't so messed up, all this wouldn't be happening," was his opinion on another. Eventually Alexis

packed her bags and went to live with her dad and his new
family. She was back within a week, leaving in the middle of
the night without telling anyone and hitchhiking across town.
Belinda had some problems when Alexis tried to teach her
seven-year-old how to smoke.

Joanna crumpled the duvet under her chin and sobbed
silently into the fabric as the memories came flooding back.
Outside her room Wendy paced anxiously, unable to help, not
knowing what to do. Robert's arms were about to fall off, but
he kept swinging the axe and cutting more and more firewood
as the cold crept into his city boots and through his thin gloves.

The school took Alexis to court several times for truancy.
Joanna had to stand in front of the judge and say how she tried
to make her daughter go to school. Alexis was fined a small
amount, small enough that she could pay it herself, and a few
months later was back in court again. After she was hospitalized for cutting herself the truancy officer told Joanna that he
wouldn't charge Alexis again.

Brushes with the law escalated. Alexis got off with a warning
after her first shoplifting incident, and after she was found drunk
and disorderly in a public park. Each time Joanna took time off
work to go to court and each time as they left the courthouse
Alexis sneered at her mother and refused to account for her
behavior. One of her friends, Joanna suspected that he was
Alexis' boyfriend although Alexis never brought him around to
their house, was sent to jail for taking a swing at the arresting
officer during the public park incident. Although she was
unwanted, Joanna insisted accompanying Alexis to court for his
trial. She was there, but the boy's parents were not. He told the
court that his father was on a business trip and his mother didn't
want to expose his younger sister to the trauma of the courtroom.

Alexis was arrested once along with a girlfriend who was

selling drugs. She was lucky to be released—she didn't have any of the drugs on her, and said she didn't know what was happening. The friend got a year in juvenile custody. Alexis never mentioned her again.

Joanna lay in her bed and stared at the ceiling. There was too much light in the room to sleep. She crumpled her sheets into balls in her fists and remembered.

"I HATE YOU," Alexis screamed, "you've messed up my life. You should never have been allowed to have children."

The front door slammed as James abandoned his homework and scooted out of the house. Wendy had already left.

"Look, Alexis, Aunt Jackie and Uncle Dave are only in town for a couple of days and I want us all to have a nice dinner together, please, can't you stay home this one night."

"You can't control my life."

"I don't want to control your life, I am just asking you to stay and have dinner with us, this one night." Joanna didn't know why she was pleading with her daughter. In fact, it would be better for everyone if Alexis wasn't here. They could relax and have a nice evening without worrying about what Alexis would say next. But she was compelled to keep on fighting.

Suddenly Alexis reared back and spat right in her mother's face. Joanna was so shocked she just stood there. Sensing her advantage Alexis spat again.

Joanna wiped her face carefully. "Oh, all right," she sighed, giving in. "Do what you want."

Alexis continued screaming abuse at her mother. Sobbing, Joanna fled to the bathroom and locked herself in. Alexis pounded on the door. Eventually the house fell silent and she slowly opened the door and stepped out into the hall.

The blows came out of nowhere. Joanna covered herself

with her hands as Alexis rained feeble punches all over her head and shoulders. She shoved Alexis across the hall into the wall.

"I hate you," the girl screamed once again.

Without stopping to think Joanna ran into the kitchen and grabbed the phone. She dialed 911. "I've been assaulted by my daughter," she gasped. Alexis stared at her, unbelieving. She turned without a word and left the house.

While the police were on their way, Joanna called her sister and apologized for canceling tonight's dinner. A sudden migraine, she explained. No, she was sure it was nothing serious. Lie down for a while and it will pass. You know how these things are. So sorry about the evening.

Joanna sat on the bench by the front door sobbing while the fresh-faced young police officer listened to her story. It broke her heart as he called in on his radio and described Alexis to all listening as "the suspect."

There was nothing he could do other than call in a report, because Alexis was not there. The officer left a number for Joanna to call once her daughter returned home. A few minutes after he drove off, Alexis marched through the front door. She had been watching her house from the shadows of the neighbor's backyard.

"That was a stupid thing to do," she declared, dropping her coat onto the floor. "Don't you ever call the cops on me again." She marched down the hall, leaving wet footprints in her wake and slammed the door to her room.

Joanna pulled out the card the young officer had given to her and slowly dialed the number printed on it. He was back within minutes.

Alexis came out of her room grudgingly enough when she heard that the police were back. They all stood in the front hall, Joanna sobbing quietly, Alexis coldly defiant.

Joanna looked at her daughter, her heart aching. "No, I don't want to press charges," she told him, "I just want us to get along again."

Alexis said nothing.

"Are you going to promise me that there will be no more trouble here tonight?" the officer asked Alexis.

She crossed her arms. "I can't predict the future, you know."

His face tightened. "Look, if you can't tell me that you won't hit your mother again, I will have to take you in with me. I am not going to come back. Do you understand?"

"Okay."

"Okay, what?"

"Okay," she mumbled. "There won't be any more trouble."

True to her word, for once, there was no more trouble that night. In fact Alexis began to calm down from that point. She dropped out of school the month she turned sixteen and spent her days lying in bed, only getting up in time to go out at night. Her circle of friends changed again. Not that she ever brought friends home, but Joanna saw them occasionally at the mall or on the street and they seemed a slightly less threatening, less aggressive group.

Slowly life was getting back on track. Joanna was working hard again and starting to achieve results once more. Wendy had left for university and James seemed content to spend more time at home. To Joanna's frustration her daughter wasn't going to school and was doing nothing about finding a job but she decided to let it ride for a while.

Then one lovely summer morning, when she was enjoying the warmth of the rising sun on the back deck with the newspaper and bagels and orange juice, she heard Alexis come in. The girl had not been home the night before.

Alexis went straight to her room and rummaged through her things.

Finally she came out to face her mother. Her bulging

backpack drooped across one shoulder. "I have found The Way," she declared solemnly.

Joanna spluttered orange juice.

"I am going to live with a group of the Accepted Ones. I will not be back."

Joanna leapt to her feet. The pages of the newspaper fluttered in the breeze. "What do you mean you won't be back?"

"When we are accepted into the circle of the Believers we must cast off all our worldly ties. I will never speak to you again, it is forbidden."

Unnoticed, the wind picked at pages of the paper and carried them gently across the well-groomed lawn.

"You can't be serious," was all Joanna could say.

"I am very serious, I have never been more serious. I have found The Way and now I will be saved. Good-bye."

"Wait," Joanna cried. "Where are you going, what is this way?"

"They are a group of Holy Ones, ones who have found The Way to a life of Peace and Contentment. I have been chosen to follow them and if I am very good, I also may be able to find The Way." She shifted her pack to the other shoulder and rubbed her hands through her curly blond hair, growing out to its natural color for the first time in years. "They are waiting for me now. Good-bye," she said again.

"Who are this group, where do they live, where are they taking you?" Joanna asked.

"They are the Holy Ones, I told you that. In that their physical bodies must live on this earth, they currently have a camp outside of Toronto, but the leader, the first of the chosen ones, lives in California."

"Where, 'outside of Toronto'?" She couldn't believe they were having this conversation. The day was perfect, how could this crazy thing happen on a lovely summer day like today?

"I cannot tell you, it's secret," Alexis said stiffly. "I must go now, they are waiting. Good-bye."

"Are you crazy?" Joanna yelled, reaching out a hand to stop her. She grabbed Alexis' pack and held on. "You can't just go off with people you hardly know."

All of Alexis' composure disappeared in a flash. "I'll go where I want, where you can't ever find me. Let go of me."

Joanna held on, tighter. "Alexis, stop. This is crazy. Think about it first, then if it's really what you want I'll take you to these people."

Alexis' fist lashed out and caught her mother on the jaw. With a cry, Joanna fell to the deck. Alexis turned and ran.

Joanna stumbled to her feet. She got to the front of the house in time to see an old van turning the corner at the end of the road. Then it was gone from sight.

She immediately hired a private detective to find out what he could about this group. A cult they told her, a cult like so many others. Confused kids, powerful controlling men, rules and privacy. But nothing illegal. Nothing they could be charged with. Alexis was over sixteen, no one could force her to leave if she didn't want to. The police interviewed her at the cult compound, but she told them she was happy and not being held against her will. She refused to speak to her mother or her father or even her siblings. Their letters were returned, unopened, and the compound did not have a phone. The detective's last report told Joanna that her daughter had left with several group members for the cult's headquarters in California. They were very sorry, there was nothing more they could do for her, there was no point in taking any more of her money.

Joanna collapsed.

The next few months passed in a daze of depression and psychiatric drugs. She took her four weeks annual vacation and spent three of them in the psych ward of the local hospital, telling her colleagues and her sister that she was off for a sunsoaked month in the south of France. James went to live with his dad, commuting by bus to and from school and to visit his mother in the hospital. Elaine dropped by almost every day. She brought mounds of flowers and cards and the melodramatic gothic novels they both loved. When Joanna took notice of the flowers and glanced at the books and asked for computer magazines her doctors agreed that she was ready to return home.

One more week of vacation was spent at home and Joanna went back to work, although her doctor strongly advised against it. James returned from his dad's and everyone tried to forget Alexis and pretend that life was back to normal.

Joanna tossed and turned in an agony of memories before she fell asleep at last.

THIS TIME THE DREAM was jumbled and wildly distorted. Not clear and sharp, like the other dreams, but a confusing flash of images, of pictures and sounds and feelings.

THE GIRL WITH the peroxide hair was there, no longer throwing up over the porch rail but her swollen belly strained at the seams of her ragged dress, the one that used to be too big across her breasts and hips. It now fitted her snugly, a fact not one of her brothers had failed to notice.

Her mother was even more careworn than before, if that were possible. She gripped her baby daughter to her chest every non-existent moment that her hands were free. Anxious and confused, the baby fussed and struggled to escape the suffocating grip of her mother's doughy arms.

Even the boys were quieter now. They crept through the house like ghosts, afraid to disturb the strange equilibrium that had settled over the household. The calm before the storm.

The father rarely came home much before dawn. He was drinking more than ever and his wife and children were careful to keep out of the way of his swinging fists and scathing tongue. Only the baby still held up her arms and smiled a gleeful toothless smile at his approach. She was rarely disappointed, for he would swing her in a high arc almost at the height of his head, around and around, singing the songs of his father, until she shrieked with delight and her mother cried out in fear.

At the back of the property the oldest boy swung his axe against the tree trunks and nurtured the anger in his breast.

Then one day the dress ripped right up the back as the girl with the peroxide hair falling over her cornflower blue eyes bent over to pick up a slice of bread off the kitchen floor.

Outside the snow gathered strength off the lake and winter closed in.

TWENTY-THREE

A LIGHT TAP AT THE DOOR roused Joanna from her sleep. "Time to get up, Mom," Wendy said, peeking softly into the room. "I hope you had a nice nap."

She swam thickly up through a storm-tossed sea of memories, real and imagined, and emerged into partial consciousness. "Is that you, Wendy?"

"Yes, Mom, it's me. Time to get up. The Christmas dinner is almost ready. Robert is starving and I don't think we can keep the poor boy from the sacrificial poultry any longer. I thought that we would phone James before dinner. Imagine, spending Christmas skiing in Whistler. The little jerk. How did he get so lucky?" Wendy stepped into the room. "Are you okay, Mom?"

Joanna sat up and rubbed sleep from her eyes. It was nice to be woken up by her daughter again, funny how much she missed that. "Yes, dear, I'm fine. Now. Bit of a shock, I guess, to think about Alexis." She took a deep breath. "I'm glad, very glad, that your father tried to see her, even if nothing came of it. I guess I didn't react to the news very well. I'm sorry."

Wendy nodded, relieved. "Why don't you come out and join us now. Dinner will be ready soon." She shut the door gently behind her.

Joanna climbed out of bed and stumbled across the hall to the bathroom to wash the sleep out of her face. She stared at herself in the mirror with the silver finishing chipping all down one side, and thought about the amazingly realistic dreams she had been having. Funny how lifelike that dream was, like the other ones. She had never experienced anything similar before. Every other dream drifted softly around the edges of her consciousness as soon as she awoke but all-to-soon they were gone. Even the fun ones that you tried to remember in order to relish them again and again, but try as you might they were gone like a whiff of wood smoke on a windy fall day in the country. But this one lingered in the mind, every detail so clear, so crisp. Almost like a memory. She stared in the mirror for a long time, thinking that memories of the last few years of life with Alexis must be interfering with her dream process. She was mixing them up, perhaps that is why the dreams seemed so realistic. Though why she should confuse the woman with the faded cornflower blue eyes and the drunken husband and the pack of surly boys with herself and her own life she could not understand. "Rather you than me," Joanna said to the mirror. She splashed water onto her face and brushed her hair. Refreshed, she joined her family for Christmas dinner.

WENDY AND ROBERT left early on Boxing Day. Robert's job started in the New Year and they had all the formalities and all the work involved in relocating still ahead of them. They departed with many hugs and kisses, promises to e-mail and call often, and an open invitation for Joanna to visit anytime she was able. "Any time I just happen to be passing through the Yukon, you mean," she said to Robert as he placed the suitcases into the trunk of the car.

He laughed and smiled. "Believe it or not, Joanna. I do mean any time at all." They smiled at each other until Wendy came bustling out of the cabin with the last of the now-opened Christmas presents and tossed them into the back seat.

Joanna walked up to the road and stood in the snow watching the taillights of their car long after it crested a small hill and was gone.

WHEN SHE WAS A CHILD it was the custom for family and friends to drop in and visit on Boxing Day. Nothing was planned, everything was unannounced, but it was understood that some people went visiting and some would stay at home to receive visitors. She never understood how, but it always seemed that when they were the visitors everyone they called upon was at home, and the years that her family was at home all the visitors would find them. A quaint custom, long forgotten, especially by Joanna who planned to spend the rest of the week catching up on the work waiting for her. Nothing of any significance would be happening in any office on Bay Street until the New Year. She had more than enough time to get the work finished and be ready to show off her progress at the next meeting with her clients.

She was settling down to her computer, cup of coffee close at hand, rough notes piled high, when she heard the sound of a car pulling into the driveway. She sighed mightily and looked up. Oh, great, Nancy Miller. Joanna groaned audibly. *Just the one to spoil a productive day.*

She could barely summon up a smile as she opened the door to her unwelcome visitor.

Nancy, on the other hand, was grinning across the entire width of her pudgy face. "Merry Christmas, Joanna, and all the best for the New Year." She held out a parcel wrapped in gaudy Christmas paper: Bugs Bunny dressed up as Santa Claus. Joanna stood aside and waved Nancy into the room.

"Wow," Nancy gushed, looking around the cabin interior. "I just love your tree, and all those fabulous decorations." Uninvited, she pulled off her winter coat and hung it on the coat rack. She was wearing an oversized hand-knitted Christmas sweater with a motif of a traditional Christmas tree complete with colored balls, ribbons and piles of wrapped presents underneath. Tiny colored lights twinkled across the tree, powered by a small battery knitted into the hem of the sweater. She quickly slipped off salt-crusted boots and walked further into the room. "Your house looks so beautiful, Joanna, just like Christmas in a fancy magazine. Next year will you help me to do my place just like this?" She looked at Joanna, naked pleading in her eyes.

"Of course," Joanna said, good manners preceding thinking. "It would be my pleasure. It's nothing really, a bit of greenery and berries I gathered from the woods. Nothing much at all."

Nancy beamed. "I don't think it's nothing. Not at all. It looks so nice, so, well, so Christmassy."

Despite herself Joanna was pleased.

Nancy thrust the Bugs Bunny package into her arms. "Merry Christmas."

Joanna placed the parcel on her worktable and unwrapped it. Beneath the gaudy paper lay a froth of crinkly cellophane and bouncy red and green ribbons. "It's beautiful," she breathed, meaning it, "really beautiful."

"That's just the store wrapping," Nancy said, beaming from ear to ear. "Go ahead, open it."

Gently she peeled off the layers of cellophane and ribbon to uncover a wicker gift basket filled with aromatic bath beads, skin creams and essential oils. "This is lovely, Nancy. Very thoughtful of you." She cringed with embarrassment at the memory of her continually condescending attitude toward her visitor. "But I didn't get you anything."

Nancy blushed ever so slightly and waved her hand in the

air. "I didn't expect anything. I just dropped by because it's Boxing Day."

"Well have a seat, why don't you. Would you like something to drink? I still have a bit of eggnog left, maybe I could put a splash of rum in it, what do you think?"

Nancy laughed. "No rum for me. I still have calls to make. But a bit of eggnog would be very nice. I am always partial to eggnog at Christmas."

"Be right back." Joanna slipped into the kitchen and quickly prepared a tray. She pulled her special Christmas glasses out of the sink and rinsed them off hastily. They were a gift from her former mother-in-law, rimmed with patterns of holly and berries and a few snowflakes. She had always thought them a bit gaudy but the children loved them. She poured eggnog into the glasses, placed a few decorated cookies and some of Wendy's rich Christmas cake onto a platter, added a splash of rum to her own glass and carried the tray out to the living room.

The women lifted their glasses and toasted each other. Nancy selected a slice of the cake and bit into it appreciatively. "I do love Christmas. Don't you, Joanna?" she mumbled through a huge mouthful of cake.

Joanna smiled. "Yes I do."

"Sergeant Reynolds was in the store the other day," Nancy said. She had finished her cake and was dabbing daintily at the corners of her mouth with a napkin. "He was asking about the night poor Luke was killed. Everyone in town is really upset, you know."

"I can imagine."

"Not just 'cause they knew Luke and all, although he kept pretty much to himself. But a murder here in Hope River. Who woulda believed it?" She shook her head. "What is the world coming to?"

"I'm sure you've had problems in Hope River before," Joanna ventured to guess. "This can't be the first incident, can it?"

"Oh, we've had our share of troubles, let me tell you. But nothing that involved the police. People usually sort things out among themselves, or else keep quiet about it. But murder. Can't much keep quiet about that, I guess."

"I don't think so. More eggnog?"

Nancy held out her cup in appreciation. "Don't mind if I do. And them cookies was real nice, too. Where was I…Oh, yes. Troubles in Hope River. I guess some people 'round here can't really face up to the idea of outsiders, the police and the like, getting involved in folks' troubles. But you can't always keep them out, and sometimes it ain't right to try, I say. Why, just last week young Ethan Elderbridge was rushed off to the hospital in the middle of the night. His mama don't want no one knowing about it, let me tell you. But soon enough the whole town heard the story. Drugs, it was."

"Drugs?"

"Yup. Bad drugs and too much of them, we heard. No one's saying where the story started but it must have been Maggie Black what works at the hospital as an orderly. They woulda all tried to keep it hushed up, like, but I think it's better that everyone's talking about it. If someone's taken bad drugs you can bet that that ain't the last of them, right, Joanna?"

Joanna was quite sure that that wouldn't be the last of them.

"Gosh, will you look at the time, and me with all my Boxing Day calls still to make." Nancy brushed crumbs off the front of her Christmas tree sweater and rose ponderously to her feet. "I had better get going. Thanks so much for the eggnog, Joanna."

"You're very welcome." Joanna walked her guest to the door. "Too bad you weren't here a bit earlier. You just missed my daughter and son-in-law."

Nancy struggled into her winter boots and heavy coat. "That would have been nice," she said, departing with a bright smile and a cheerful wave.

Joanna cleared up the glasses and cake plates and placed them into the sink to wash later. She returned to her desk, sorted through her papers, and tried to get her mind back to where she had left off. Her eyes fell on the gift basket sitting on the corner of the desk and she ran her fingers across the now-discarded wrappings. She liked the sound the cellophane made as she crinkled it between her fingers. She felt a twinge of guilt; Nancy seemed so keen to offer her, Joanna, friendship. Then she reminded herself firmly that she didn't want any friends—that she only wanted to be left alone. She pounded the "Enter" key to clear the screen saver.

MAUDE AND ROCKY also dropped by to pay a social call. Maude brought a bottle of homemade jam and Rocky attempted to bring a dead twig that was caught in his long, fluffy tail. Maude had no news of Tiffany. Their Christmas had been strained; the girl's intense disappointment at not hearing a word from her mother was palpable although she tried to hide it behind a façade of indifference. From the police they had, thankfully, also heard nothing. Maybe it would all blow over, Maude said more to herself than to Joanna.

As soon as the old woman and her dog had set out for the walk home, Joanna remembered Tiffany's bright red scarf, which was still hanging on the coat hook beside the front door. She considered running after Maude to return it, but it was now snowing copiously and she was reluctant to pull on the necessary layers of clothing to venture outdoors. She promised herself that she would take it over tomorrow.

Of course, she forgot all about the scarf as soon as her back was turned and it hung on the old wooden hook throughout the New Year.

SHE ACCOMPLISHED A LOT of work in the week between Christmas and New Year. She finished the bicycle club web page and her client was wildly enthusiastic about it. The task was enjoyable and she hoped that it would lead to more. She talked on the phone with Francis Fukuyama daily and expected to have the demonstrations and models ready for Morris Lipton in plenty of time.

It snowed steadily most of the week and she left the cabin only to shovel the driveway and drag her cross-country skis out for some exercise. The iron stove was kept going all day and all night and the last batch of firewood that Robert had so clumsily chopped was almost finished.

One dark evening a dose of cabin fever descended on her with the ferocity of the plague and she drove well over an hour through bad roads and worse driving conditions to North Ridge, to the nearest available "good" restaurant. That is, one that served something more imaginative, she was thrilled to discover, than hot turkey sandwiches with canned peas and gravy and mashed potatoes. She had a lovely dinner, and then it was back to the cabin and work and more work.

Scott was not due back from Florida until the first week of January and Elaine had taken off again, this time to Mexico. Joanna spent New Year's Eve working, and scarcely glanced up when the clock reached midnight.

But the holidays were over eventually and then it was time to travel down to Toronto for another round of meetings on the documentation project. She couldn't wait to get out of the cabin and out of Hope River. She and Elaine arranged to meet for dinner and this time she felt she could afford the luxury of a night at her friend's house rather than drive all the way back up north through the winter night.

The strange, disturbing dreams had not bothered her since Christmas Eve, although they remained unnaturally memorable and fresh in her mind.

JOANNA ARRIVED AT the company's offices for her appointment only to find Francis waiting for her among the crowd of smokers puffing away outside the front doors. The young man looked tense and concerned. He was standing alone, well away from the social groups of smokers and was not smoking himself. She approached him, hand outstretched, frozen smile in place, already afraid of the news he was so obviously there to give. He did so quickly: Morris Lipton had suffered a massive heart attack on New Year's Day and would be off work for quite some time. Francis had not been at work yesterday; he was attending a family funeral in a town some distance away so he only heard the news this morning. He tried to call Joanna, but she was on her way. Overnight, Fred Blanchard had taken control of the documentation and training aspects of the project and was already causing trouble. He had called Francis in first thing and proceeded to rip their work to shreds. Francis knew that Morris was pleased with it, but he would be unable to contact him for verification until, at the very earliest, he was released from the hospital.

Francis smoothly guided Joanna away from the group of smokers at the front doors. He didn't want Fred to know that they had their heads together and news travels fast, but not nearly so fast as gossip. It was a few degrees warmer in Toronto than Hope River and the accumulation of snow was melting rapidly. Puddles of slush made navigating every street corner a challenge. Exhaust fumes and kicked up mud from countless cars and buses cast a thick black layer of grunge over the banks of snow. A light, freezing rain was beginning to fall and the sharp wind blew icy pellets into their faces.

"You should know before we go up that Fred is threatening to cancel your contract all together. He said that the work isn't up to the quality agreed upon." Francis shivered slightly. In trying to slip out of the building unnoticed, he had not stopped to put on his coat.

She groaned. "But we know that Morris was pleased. He told you so. That's right, isn't it?"

Francis nodded. "Yes, he did, last week. He came into the office for one day after Christmas and I briefly showed him all that you had done. He said that it was good."

"Did he tell anyone else?"

"Not that I am aware."

"Well, let's not panic. I have known Fred Blanchard for a long time and he can be a first class—pardon me—prick."

Francis lowered his head and the corners of his mouth turned up, just a touch.

"He's playing a power game here. With Morris Lipton out of the way for a while, it gives Fred a good chance to flex some muscle. Show everyone how important he is, how he can make the tough decisions." Joanna snorted. "God, how I hate that phrase. It's just an excuse for being mean. Oh, well, let's go on in and face the lion in his den. Thanks for the warning, Francis. I wouldn't have wanted to walk into this blind." She turned and stepped off the sidewalk into a river of slush. The cold water sloshed over the top of her low boots and rushed in through the holes in the soles. She was trying so hard to keep calm that she didn't even notice her stockings soaking up the icy water. She had circumvented Fred by going straight to Morris to get the contract. Fred would be spoiling to get even. She had always suspected that beneath the well-coiffed hair and shiny smile, Fred could be a nasty piece of work. He certainly would not have forgiven her for going behind his back to get the contract she wanted.

He made a great show of welcoming Joanna to their meeting. Shock was expressed all around at Morris' heart attack. She was surprised to hear that he was only 41—he looked a great deal older. So much for putting in endless hours and making a life-long dedication to the company. No one had any updates and of course no one could guess when he would be able to return to work.

"I spent most of yesterday going over your work to date, Joanna," Fred said, smiling like a barracuda as he got down to the business at hand. "And I must say, I didn't think it quite came up to your usual standards."

Joanna smiled tightly. Beside her she could feel Francis twitching in his seat. "What exactly do you mean?"

Fred opened the pile of papers in front of him. "Here, let me show you."

For the next two hours Fred went over Joanna's work with a fine-toothed comb. She twisted in her seat and could barely curb her impatience as he carefully pointed out supposed grammatical errors and nit-picked over every little point. At long last, he sat back with a satisfied grin. "I know that it seems like a lot to throw at you right now, Joanna, but you understand that I have to make some tough decisions in Morris' absence."

She moaned inwardly but her smile was fixed firmly in place. Good thing she had a nicely signed contract and was well into the project. If Fred fired her now, they would never get anyone else to finish on time. But he had given her a lot more work and no more time to do it in. Neither working through the nights nor explaining why her project was late were ideas that appealed to her.

It seemed like she was doomed to spend the rest of her life in that claustrophobic boardroom, smiling inanely and listening politely to reasons why her work was just not good enough, but eventually the ordeal ended and everyone rose to their feet. Handshakes and false smiles all around and Joanna escaped back into the bracing winter air.

Still coatless, Francis stood beside her on the sidewalk. "Well, Joanna, I don't know what you did in there, but we seem to have survived."

She chuckled without mirth. "There was no real battle, Francis. Fred couldn't possibly release me from my contract, and he can't bring anyone else in or order you not to help me any more because there isn't time to start anything new. He knew that all along. It was just a lot of posturing and chest-pumping on his part as he pretended to show me who's in charge." Joanna stepped to the edge of the pavement and waved furiously at a passing taxi. The cab kicked up a wave of slush over her boots and sped past. She eyed another cab bearing down in their direction and stepped out into the road as she lifted her arm. This time the taxi pulled to a halt at her feet, coughing and sputtering as if it couldn't make it for another kilometer. The driver sported long Rastifarian dreadlocks and continued to eat his fried chicken lunch from a takeout container on the front seat while he sat staring out the front window. He didn't give his potential fare the barest of glances as Joanna gripped the door handle and hesitated for a moment.

"If you want some advice from me," she said to Francis, "and I really don't know why you should, but keep your head down for a while. Fred can bear a grudge for a very long time, as I well know." She slipped into the back seat of the cab. "But I have a feeling that he won't be lasting too much longer. So hold on for a while and you'll be okay."

Francis shook her offered hand and bowed slightly over it as he had done on their first meeting. To him, it was plain to see that if Morris was out of the loop for very long, the company was heading straight down, and quickly. He intended to be long gone well before it hit the bottom. But he smiled at Joanna and shook her hand. "I will call tomorrow," he assured her, "and we'll carry on working from where we left off." He slammed the car door and stood in the muck as the cab pulled out into traffic.

Joanna gave the driver directions to Elaine's office where she had parked the car. She kicked a lipstick smeared Styrofoam coffee cup under the front seat and collapsed back into the cracked vinyl seating. The project was saved, but at the cost of a lot more work and to the detriment of any other contracts that might come in. She swore under her breath and tried to shut out the static-encrusted, blaring rap music, not her favorite at the best of times, which emanated from the cab's tinny radio. She reminded herself of all the reasons she had left the world of corporate politics in the first place. This sort of one-upmanship seemed awfully familiar. Dilbert was very, very, funny—at least until you had to live in his world.

The cab dropped her off at Elaine's building in the heart of the financial district. Still angry at the world, Joanna left a miserly tip, then she wandered around until business hours were finished and it was time to meet her friend. She wanted to buy some clothes, something new that would be smart and businesslike for all the future meetings she hoped to have, for all the contracts that should start flooding in any minute. But although she peered into endless shop windows and pawed through countless racks she could find very little that would fit her size 16 frame and nothing to suit either her taste or her limited budget.

She still had a bit of time to kill before meeting Elaine so she took a seat at a fashionable coffee bar, overlooking the street, and sipped at a frothy, cinnamon-laced cappuccino. She sat for a while and watched the parade of people passing by her window. When she first caught sight of the beer-bellied man shuffling uncomfortably down the street, quite out of place among the fashionably dressed business crowd in his plain brown cap, massive parka and heavy work boots, she thought that he would fit in better in Hope River. With a start, she realized that he really would fit in better in Hope River. It was Jack Miller, Nancy's uncle.

She had no temptation to run out into the street to greet him; she didn't like him very much, and he clearly didn't like her. Instead she watched as he walked up to a bike courier lounging on the street corner, smoking. The two men exchanged brief greetings, and then moved on, circling the corner and out of Joanna's sight.

She scooped the last remnants of delicious steamed milk out of the bottom of her cup with one finger and licked it off. Strange to see Jack in Toronto at all, and very strange to see him with a bike courier, of all people. It looked as if the two men knew each other and their meeting didn't appear to be happenstance. Maybe Jack has a secret, she giggled to herself. A long lost, illegitimate son. That bit of news would no doubt cause a gossip hurricane in the hamlet of Hope River.

She glanced at her watch, and promptly forgot all about Jack and whatever tawdry little secret he might have. It was time to go. She dashed across the slush-covered street and traveled up to Elaine's corner office high above the teeming city.

Discouraged as she was by the failure to find the perfect con-

tractor-on-the-go business suit, Joanna was even more depressed at the first sight of Elaine. Not that there was anything
at all different about Elaine; rather, as always, every stitch of
her beautiful winter-white wool suit was perfect, her blood-red
silk blouse looked as if it had been taken fresh off the store rack
that very hour. Her shoes sported three-inch spike heels and
were an exact match to the color of the silk blouse. Tiny
diamond earrings and a thin gold and diamond tennis bracelet
were her only jewelry. At the tail end of a very long and hectic
business week, every dyed and permed blond hair lay perfectly
in place; every painted, manicured nail was…perfect.

Joanna wanted to scream; instead she collapsed into her
friend's warm embrace. Elaine was the first to pull away and
leaned back to stare up into Joanna's face. "Maybe it's the
blood of my gypsy mother talking, but I have a feeling that your
meeting didn't go too well."

Joanna shook her head. "Bit of an understatement, that. But
I survived. Again."

Elaine picked up her bulging briefcase and flicked off the
office light. "I need a good drink, and I think you do too, so
you can tell me all about it at the Duke of Westminster."

TWENTY-FOUR

"CHRIST, IT'S COLD out here tonight," Tiffany mumbled into her woolen mittens at the same time she blew on them in a fruitless attempt to create some heat.

The boy looked at her lazily. "So what's your beef? The old lady asked you if you needed better gloves. You said no, so stop your moaning and let's go."

"I'm not moaning," she moaned, following her friends through the woods. "I'm telling you that I'm cold, that's all."

"Oh, shut up." The girl who had come along to pick her up hissed at them. Tiffany didn't know her name, and didn't particularly want to know it. "Ever since that stupid old man got his stupid old self knocked off near here the pigs have been creeping around the woods night after night. Can't barely take a step out of place anymore or they'll be on to you. It's getting pretty hard to score around here, I'll tell you." She pulled off her toque and scratched at her shaven scalp. A row of silver hoops marched up the sides of both of her ears, drawing attention to the tiny snake tattooed onto the side of her neck with its tail curling around to the back.

Tiffany shivered at the sight of the blue snake and stuffed her hands back into her pockets but she stumbled through drifts of fresh snow after the others. Brad and Pam she knew from school. Pam was okay; Brad was a braggart and a show off. But what else was there to do in this miserable town? She had never seen any of the other kids before. Friends of Brad. From North Ridge, he had said. No one introduced them.

Brad's car, if you could call the old barely-alive 1981 model a car, was parked further down the road. The girl was right, Luke's death was highly unusual in this community, the police continued to look into it and this group did everything possible to avoid the police.

The sharp northern wind blew gusts of snow and air so cold it was almost solid, into the front of Tiffany's exposed neck and right down to her thin chest. She held the collar of her coat closed with one hand, almost instantly her fingers began to tingle again. She couldn't decide which was worse: frozen fingers or snowdrifts piling up on the inside of her coat.

She cursed again and stumbled after her friends.

"You look like you're absolutely freezing, Tiffany," one of the girls remarked. Out of the group of six heading into North Ridge tonight, indeed out of all of the teenagers she had met since coming to Hope River, Pam was the only one who had tried to show Tiffany some real friendship. She was a tall, exceptionally skinny girl with a shock of curly hair the color of a maple tree in autumn, and masses of freckles. Tiffany knew that the boys loved the color of her hair and they particularly adored her complexion; but like every redhead, Pam absolutely hated her freckles and bore an intense dislike for her hair.

"I'm freezing, Pam, so totally freezing." Tiffany shivered and clutched the collar of her second-hand coat tighter. "Maybe I'll just go home. You guys go on without me."

"Don't be silly," Pam replied. "We're almost at the car. You'll be warm as soon as we get there. Where's your scarf, anyway? You have that really fabulous red scarf. I've always liked it. Did you lose it?"

The car was parked almost squarely in the middle of the lane.

With the piles of drifting snow Brad couldn't tell where the road ended and the ditch began. He was too afraid of getting stuck to park the car properly. Anyone else out tonight would simply have go around.

They waited for Brad to unlock the doors. "I left it at Joanna's house," Tiffany said. "But I've been so mad at her that I don't want to go back and get it."

Pam nodded. "She's a strange one. No one likes her much, she's so stuck up."

"My mom says she's a real rich snob." The girl with the shaved head and the tattoo spoke up. "Thinks she's too high and mighty to mix with people from Hope River. Nancy Miller from the store told my mom that she's here to write a book, that she's some famous novelist." The girl snorted. "I don't think so."

"She's all right," Tiffany said, blowing into her mittens again. "She wants to be left alone, that's all. And she never told Nancy Miller she was writing a book. Nancy made all that up."

Brad stood by the open car door, and whistled. "Are we going to go or are you chicks going to stand there clucking like a pack of hens all night? Get in the car. Linda, Pam, let's go."

"Why don't we go and get your scarf? Joanna's place isn't far," someone said.

Tiffany wrenched the back door open and climbed in. The others quickly followed suit. It was too cold to stand around arguing.

Several false starts had the engine grinding while the wheels spun wildly through the fluffy snow, but eventually they found a patch of packed snow to grip and the old car lurched on its way.

Brad slowed down at the curve before Joanna's house. The outline of her cabin was visible through the bare trees. Only the light over the front porch was on.

"Stop," Linda shrieked. "We can just run in and get the scarf."

Tiffany was developing a strong dislike for this Linda. Why couldn't she mind her own business? "There's no one home. The lights are all out and there isn't a car in the driveway."

"Can we just get going?" Pam groaned. "The bar's gonna be full by the time we get there."

Eyes sparking, Linda ignored them both. "You're right, there is no one home. So let's go and get the scarf, eh?"

Brad jerked the car to a stop and shut off the engine. "If it will shut you up. Let's go."

The other two boys needed no encouragement.

"I'm in."

"Sure, let's do it."

Before Tiffany knew what was happening, all the car doors were flying open and everyone else was standing outside in the snow. "She's not home. I don't need the stupid scarf anyway. This is dumb, let's go." She gestured wildly for Pam to get back into the car.

"Maybe she's at home but at the back where we can't see the light. Maybe her car is broken and in the shop for a couple of days," Linda said. "I think we should go and knock on the front door anyway. Come on, Tiffany, we'll get your scarf back."

The five teenagers set off toward Joanna's dark cabin. Tiffany sighed and followed slowly. It would be great to have that scarf back. It was a really warm one, one of the few nice things she owned, and it looked fabulous, too.

Brad was first to reach the cabin. The others crowded in behind him as he marched up the front steps and loudly banged on the door with his fist. There was no answer so he knocked again.

Tiffany stood alone at the bottom of the steps. "No one home, let's go guys."

The others ignored her. Brad continued hammering on the door. Squirrels and mice and chipmunks that had taken up residence under the porch stirred restlessly. They were not used to being disturbed in the night and were unsure of what to do. Remain in the safe, familiar darkness of their homes hoping that the fuss up above would not descend any further, or venture out into the cold open spaces? They burrowed deeper into their dens and hoped the noise would soon stop.

"Well, we have to get Tiffany's scarf," one of the boys announced to the group. "If that woman isn't home to give it to us, I guess we'll just go on in. The scarf belongs to Tiffany, after all."

The others nodded in agreement. Tiffany launched herself up the steps. She had forgotten to be cold. "She's not home and I don't want the damn scarf so let's go."

Brad smiled at her. "But Tiff, we want to get your scarf for you."

"Yeah," Linda said, overflowing with sweetness and light. "You need the scarf, honey bunch."

"If we wait any longer there'll be a line up to get in to the bar. We might get asked for ID. So maybe we won't get in at all. Let's go, eh?" Tiffany knew that argument should convince them.

Pam and one of the boys pushed past the others and started back down the steps. But Brad and Linda stood their ground. "We'll get your scarf, Tiff," Brad said. "Won't be a minute." The other kids were looking uncertain.

"I'll come back tomorrow, when she's home. No problem. Let's go. Please?"

"Maybe we can have a look around while we're here." Linda smirked. "She's probably been using Tiffany's scarf. That means that she owes interest or something to Tiff. Right?"

"Right." Brad leapt down the stairs, but instead of walking across the yard and up the hill to the road, he paced up and down in front of the porch, scooping the snow aside with his boots.

The animals scattered about in terror and confusion. One mouse, braver than the rest, made a run for it and reached the safety of the forest undergrowth in record time. Attracted by the sound of people, the old owl swooped soundlessly out of the night sky and came to rest on her favorite branch overlooking the front yard. She caught sight of the mouse's tail as it scurried into the safety of the undergrowth. Too late. The owl settled down to watch in silence.

Brad was turning the corner of the cabin when his foot came into contact with something hard and unyielding beneath the snow. He brushed the loose snow aside and picked up a heavy rock.

"Yessss." Linda jumped up and down, yipping with excitement.

"Christ, Brad," Tiffany said. Now she was scared. "Put that thing down." She lunged toward him to grab the rock. He danced easily out of her way, and tossed the rock back and forth from one hand to another.

"Pass, pass," Linda shouted in glee and raised her hands. Brad tossed the rock and she caught it easily in her gloved hands. Tiffany ran back to the stairs, but Linda threw the stone over her head.

"Touchdown," Brad yelled, making the catch. Once again he scooted out of Tiffany's reach.

Pam and the other two boys edged backward toward the road. Linda and Brad were tossing the rock back and forth while Tiffany ran between them begging them to give it to her. The squirrels and chipmunks cowered in terror under the porch. Too late to make a run for it now. The old owl snorted in disgust, humans made so much noise. They always ruined the hunting.

Tiffany was on the edge of tears. "For Christ's sake, Brad, put down that damned thing. Let's get out of here."

This time, instead of tossing the rock to the waiting Linda, Brad pulled back his arm and aimed straight at the large front window.

The glass shattered with an explosion that Tiffany was sure had to be heard in North Ridge and a spray of fine shards burst into the cabin. Pieces of broken glass littered the snow-covered porch, the reflection of the overhead light causing each sliver to sparkle and glitter like a diamond resting in a soft bed of cotton wool. "Way cool," Linda sighed.

Pam and the other two boys turned on their heels and ran up the hill as fast as they could. One of the boys slipped on a patch of ice and fell heavily into the snow. The others ignored him in their haste to get away. He stumbled to his feet and scrambled after them.

Brad whooped with delight and rushed up the steps. He wiped jagged glass out of the window frame with his coat sleeve and created enough of an open space that he could barely fit through. Gingerly he climbed over the windowsill and stepped into the cabin. "I'll get your scarf now, Tiffany."

Linda giggled and followed him. From outside, Tiffany could hear the sound of broken glass crunching under their boots. Frightened, she peered in after them. This was so out of hand. Brad had draped the red scarf around his neck and was sorting through Joanna's collection of CDs. Linda was out of sight, but Tiffany could hear her opening the fridge and rummaging through the cupboards.

"Hey, guys, look what I got here." She came out of the kitchen cradling several bottles of wine in her arms like a particularly delicate baby. "Party tonight. Oh, boy."

"No," Tiffany shouted through the broken window. "You've got my scarf now, let's get the hell out of here."

"Lousy collection of CDs," Brad announced. "Not one worth borrowing." With a disgusted sweep of his arm he swiped the CDs off the table and onto the floor, then he moved over to Joanna's desk.

"No," Tiffany screamed, as Brad grabbed the monitor. "No more." Linda had deposited her cache of bottles on the couch and was heading off down the hall in search of jewelry. She stopped and stared at Tiffany in surprise. "Come on, Tiff. What's the matter with you? I thought you hated the old broad. Come on in and pick up some stuff. I bet she has some things worth taking."

"No," Tiffany screamed again. That computer meant everything to Joanna, it was her livelihood. "Put that thing down, Brad. Right now, I mean it. You said it yourself: the cops are in the woods at night ever since Luke's murder. I bet that window breaking made a lot of noise. Maybe they're on the way now."

Brad placed the monitor back down on the desk and Tiffany let out a long, slow sigh of relief. "I guess you're right. Nothing much here worth taking anyway. Don't know why you think she's so rich, Linda. No one with money would be living in a shack like this in a town like Hopeless River. I sure wouldn't. Grab those bottles and let's split."

Linda sighed and looked once more toward the bedroom, but obediently she collected her wine bottles and climbed out the broken window after Brad.

Tiffany exhaled a huge sigh of relief and followed. Brad unwound the scarf from around his neck and tossed it to Tiffany. "Told you we would get the scarf, Tiffany. Say thank you."

"Thank you," she mumbled, gripping the warm cloth to her chest.

"Now let's go and party." He grabbed one of the bottles out of Linda's arms and held it high overhead. "No need to drink at that lousy bar tonight."

Linda giggled and danced wildly through the snow, puffs of white clouds rising under her feet.

Tiffany stared at the ground. "I don't feel much like a party any more, I want to go home."

"Are you a whiner or what?" Brad sneered. He threw the bottle back at Linda who had already started up the hill. It fell unnoticed, and soundlessly rolled into a snowdrift under the porch. "I got your scarf for you, didn't I? You don't sound very grateful." He grabbed her by the arm. "Now let's get the car and party. You can show me how grateful you are."

Over the boy's shoulder, against the black darkness of the trees, Tiffany could see an even blacker shape slowly take form and shimmer with all the fragile grace of a ballerina in the light wind. As she watched, it drifted deeper into the woods, blown by the cold winter air. Then it reversed direction and came back toward them. Brad turned to see what Tiffany was looking at; he could see nothing but the blackness of the winter forest that stood in sharp contrast to the undisturbed snow below. He tugged on Tiffany's arm. "Did you hear me? I said, let's go. The others are waiting."

Tiffany watched as the shadow retreated back into the woods. This time it silently stood its ground. With a cry, she wrenched her arm out of Brad's grip. "No, I'm going home. Good night." Without a backward glance she tossed her red scarf around her neck and marched resolutely into the woods. The dark shape melted before her and the trees swallowed them up.

Brad shrugged. "Suit yourself!" he shouted after her. He was sorry she was leaving. He liked Tiffany, although he couldn't figure out what her problem was. He had tried to impress her, hadn't he? He followed his friends back up the hill to the car.

TWENTY-FIVE

JOANNA PULLED HER CAR into the driveway and blew out a sigh of relief. Even though she would have to shovel one more tedious time, it was good to be home. She wrenched her briefcase and overnight bag out of the back seat, threw them over her right shoulder and started down the path to the cabin.

It was not until she dropped her bags on the front porch with another heavy sigh and put her key into the lock that she noticed the glass crunching underfoot, and then the gaping hole in the front window. With a cry she struggled to turn the key and burst into the cabin. A large section of the front window lay in tiny bits scattered around the living room. She stared in disbelief— surely the wind couldn't have knocked a hole in the window. There was nothing immediately apparent that might have fallen through it, such as a tree or branch. The daze of incomprehension in her head cleared slowly and then in quick succession she noticed that a rock was sitting in the middle of the rug, that her monitor was lying half-cocked over a pile of books and that large muddy tracks covered the worn floor boards.

She ran from room to room searching for signs of damage. Nothing else broken, nothing seemed to be missing. Is it possible, she wondered, that a large animal had broken through the window, knocked over the computer, tracked mud all over the carpet and then jumped back out via the route by which it had arrived? That seemed unlikely, she thought, rearranging the computer equipment and papers, and sweeping up mud and glass up off the floor.

Only much later, after the cabin was neat and tidy and well organized once again, when she reached into the cupboard for a bottle of wine to open while preparing her dinner, did she discover that her entire stash of wine was missing. In disbelief Joanna sat back on her haunches. There were a good number of bottles in here, surely she couldn't possibly have drunk them all and then forgotten about it? She rooted through cupboards and under the sink, she even opened the back door to make sure she hadn't inadvertently put full bottles out with the empties into the blue recycling box. Only then was she forced to face reality: she did not misplace the wine and no wild animal tiptoed in to steal it. She picked up the phone and dialed the police. As the distant ringing of the telephone in the OPP station echoed into her ear, Joanna's eyes came to rest on the coat hook hanging in pride of place by the door. The abandoned scarf waiting for Tiffany to come and collect it was noticeable by its absence. Slowly, she placed the phone back onto the cradle. Other than the wine, nothing else was missing, nothing but one long, hand-knitted scarf in a particularly striking shade of red. Her heart sunk to the bottom of her stomach. Still, she searched the cabin from top to bottom, all the while knowing her efforts would be futile. At last she admitted it to herself. No one would break into a person's home and leave an expensive computer, a good CD player, even her parka, untouched but take a couple of bottles of wine and one scarf. No one that is, but the owner of the scarf.

Now that she knew Tiffany had broken into her cabin, violated her space, destroyed her trust, she should phone the police. It would be so easy. They would doubtless even find the scarf on the girl. She stared at the phone but could not summon the will to make the call. All too well she remembered that teenage defiance, the wall of indifference that covered up the cowering child underneath who was trying so foolishly to stand up to so-called authority. She believed that the night she called the police on Alexis, as necessary as it was, was a turning point in their relationship. Everything was now out in the open and nothing was ever the same between the two of them again. She did not regret that frantic phone call because Alexis had struck her and she had to know that there were lines over which you did not cross. That there would be consequences. But Tiffany had not committed any act of violence toward her, Joanna. She had come to reclaim her scarf. That she could merely have walked up to the front door and asked for it back, Joanna had no doubt. She did not attempt to excuse the girl's behavior to herself; the feeling of violation vibrated through her, sharp and strong.

In all her years of living in the city she had never experienced one act of violence, not one, not one single one. Despite the fears of the women with whom she worked who rushed home after dark to cower in their houses until their husbands came home, Joanna, who did not have a husband, walked boldly and freely about the city streets. She heard many tales of houses and cars broken into, of property stolen and damaged, of burglaries and rapes and murders and she refused to give into the fear. She lived her life freely and moved about as and when she wanted. To do otherwise would be to freeze up and to die.

Yet it was here, in her tiny cabin in the north woods to which she had escaped in search of peace and of solitude, that her home was violated and her space threatened and her complacency shattered. Her rage was almost physical.

Joanna threw on her coat and her boots and set off up the road.

Maude's smile of greeting faded the instant she saw her friend's face. "Is something wrong? Come in, please." The older woman bustled the visitor into the front room. As always her home was immaculate, not a fleck of dusk on the furniture, not an object out of place. A cheerful wood fire burned steadily in the open fireplace. From pride of place in front of the flames, Rocky stretched languidly, opened one lazy eye and twitched the end of his nose to check out their guest. Recognizing Joanna he thumped his tail, grunted softly and rolled over in search of a more comfortable position.

"I am looking for Tiffany. Is she here?" Joanna asked.

Maude nodded, disturbed at the stiffness of her visitor's spine and the barely controlled fire in her eyes. She did not speak.

Alerted by the sound of the front door, Tiffany emerged from the kitchen clutching a handful of chocolate chip cookies. She was still wearing her long-legged, one-piece pajamas. Her hair was tousled and her eyes bleary with sleep. "What do you want?" she asked.

"Someone was in my house last night. What do you know about it?"

Tiffany shrugged. "I don't know nothing about it. Why are you asking me?" She took a bite of cookie and stared Joanna in the eye, chewing steadily.

"Would you care for some coffee, Joanna?" Maude said. "I have just taken cookies out of the oven. Come into the kitchen, please."

Joanna ignored her. "I think that you know a lot about it. In fact, I think that you were there. Want to tell me about it?"

Rocky rose cautiously to his feet. There was tension in the air and he could feel it, something was bothering his beloved owner and although he didn't understand it, it was his job to protect her. He growled softly and the hairs on the scruff of his neck and on his long back stood up sharply.

Tiffany shrugged and finished her cookie. She suppressed a

fake yawn with her long, black fingernails and pretended to look bored. "You're nuts," she mumbled. "I haven't been in that crummy cabin of yours since you threw me out." Her expression was of bored indifference but her eyes darted quickly about, giving everything away.

"Joanna, please explain yourself," Maude said. "If you weren't there, Tiffany would have had no reason to go into your home." Her eyes darted quickly between her granddaughter and her neighbor, afraid of what she was about to hear.

Flames engulfed a log in the fireplace and it fell apart with a crash of sparks. No one, human or dog, noticed.

Joanna ignored Maude and stared steadily at Tiffany. "You left your scarf at my place the last time you were there. I put it on the coat rack for you. When I left for Toronto the night before last it was still there. I know it was. I got home a little while ago. Someone broke a window and went into my home. That's obvious. Not much is broken or stolen, but your scarf is gone. Why is that, do you think?"

Maude collapsed in a chair. Rocky moved quickly to her side and licked her hand. He was getting worried but he did not understand why.

Tiffany shrugged again, and continued munching on cookies. Joanna wanted to slap her. Instead she simply stared the girl down.

"It's my scarf and I wanted it back, okay? You weren't home, so I got it myself." Lazily, she stirred the embers of the fire with an iron poker, avoiding Joanna's angry gaze. "So a window got broken, not as if it's your computer or anything. Easy to fix."

"Is that all you have to say, 'Easy to fix'?"

Tiffany shrugged.

"I won't call the police this time, out of respect for your grandmother." Joanna spoke through clenched teeth, her fists tight at her sides. "But you come anywhere near my home again, and I will charge you. Do you understand?"

Tiffany stirred the fire log a bit more and did not answer. The embers flared up and the pieces of wood caught in a blaze of leaping yellow flames. Rocky traced the source of the unwelcome tension in his home and bared his teeth to Joanna, growling softly to warn her away. Maude stared miserably at her worn old house slippers.

Without another word Joanna turned on her heels and marched out of the house. The front door swung loosely behind her.

When the sound of angry footsteps faded away, Maude rubbed her forehead with her fingers, but she did not look up. The threat gone, Rocky settled in front of the fire, once again content with the world. Tiffany stared at the swinging door and then moved to shut it against the winter wind.

"Tiffany," Maude said, "is Joanna right? Did you break into her home? Did you?"

Without a word Tiffany turned on her heels and left the room, tossing the remains of her cookies into the dustpan on the way by. At no time was she even tempted to tell her accusers what happened last night. You didn't rat on your friends. No matter what. Not ever.

Rocky glanced around quickly through half-closed eyes. No one was watching him. Good. He crept silently over to the trash and dug out the discarded remains of chocolate chip cookies.

JOANNA RETURNED to her work with a vengeance. She pictured herself surrounded by enemies: betrayed by Fred, arrogant as ever, determined to bring her down; by Tiffany whom she had tried to befriend. She threw herself into a frenzy of work. She would show them all.

With a flurry of farewell phone calls and barely a backward

glance, Wendy and Robert departed for the Yukon. James pronounced his vacation in Whistler as the best of a lifetime and returned to the university dreaming of the day he would drop out of school and take up the life of a snowboard bum, keen but just a bit too cautious to actually make the leap. Not a word was heard from Alexis but at least Joanna's Christmas card and letter were not returned, unopened.

Late one night, a few weeks into January, Joanna rubbed her eyes and cradled her head in her hands, and stared at the computer screen hoping for inspiration that was slow to come. She was trying to rush through a contract that involved writing the manual for a small company that had written a computer program for personnel agencies. To her surprise the owner of the accounting package that was her very first contract, was pleased enough with her work to recommend her to a friend over the nineteenth hole of the Glen Abbey golf course.

She was finding it tough to stick to her commitments to Fred Blanchard as well as keeping up the smaller projects she need to complete in order to keep her head above water.

She was nodding off at her desk, barely able to keep her head upright, when she heard the sound of car tires crunching on the packed snow of her driveway. Joanna stumbled to the window and looked out to see Scott O'Neill shutting his car door and walking slowly down her front path. He stumbled over the broken step half way up to the porch. For such a large man he was surprisingly agile on his feet. Recovering instantly he skipped lightly up onto the deck.

As she watched him, she thought, for perhaps the hundredth time since moving in, that she should do something about getting that step fixed. She took a deep breath, fluffed her hair, pasted on a smile and opened the door with a hearty, "Hello. So nice to see you."

Scott was caught off guard by the strength of her welcome. He stepped cautiously into the cabin.

"What a nice surprise," Joanna beamed. He had phoned her on his return from Florida but she hadn't returned the call. She excused herself, to herself, with the pressure of work but she was really trying to avoid him. And she didn't know why. It was nice to hold someone close, to feel his heart pounding against her chest, to sense his breath moving in and out, in and out. Before Scott it had been a very long time indeed.

She stepped aside and swept her arm back in a theatrical gesture to welcome him into her home. She took his coat and scarf and hung it on the worn wooden coat rack. She should say something, anything, but her powers of speech seemed to have deserted her.

Scott mumbled thank you as he shrugged out of his coat and sat awkwardly on a chair by the window.

"How nice to see you," Joanna said. "Can I get you a drink?"

"A beer would be nice."

"Sorry, no beer." She was embarrassed at the oversight, afraid that she would be found wanting. "A glass of wine?"

"No, no thank you." He twisted his hands in his lap. "Coffee, if you have some."

"I do." Joanna fled to the kitchen, glad for the opportunity of a moment's escape. She ground beans and poured water and poured a glass of wine for herself.

"The snow seems to have stopped for a while," Scott said. "It's nice to see the sun again."

She smiled, any uncomfortable moment in conversation can always be broken up by a discussion of the weather—what would people do without it? "Very nice," she replied.

"Did you have a good Christmas?"

They talked aimlessly for a while about her Christmas in

Hope River (fun), his in Florida with his siblings and their families (deadly boring, except for the nieces and nephews), about her work (coming along at a good pace) and his painting (a gallery showing in Toronto scheduled for the summer).

Eventually Scott got around to the point of his visit. "I called you, Joanna, and left messages." He sipped at his empty coffee cup. "I was sorry not to hear from you. I thought that maybe we could try to have something together. I would like to pick things up where we left them, see where it leads." His voice trailed off and he stared intently into his coffee cup.

She clutched at her wineglass as if it were a life preserver. She found Scott attractive, very much so. At another time in her life she would have jumped at the chance to get to know him better. After her divorce she had dated casually, but quite simply she was afraid to get too much involved with anyone. She didn't want to introduce a new man into her children's lives. She had heard far too many stories about the children of divorce trying to cope with a trail of boyfriends and girlfriends parading through their houses, fighting with the kids for their parent's affections. She made a good living and didn't need a relationship for financial security, so why bother? But in the back of her mind, in a very small part that she rarely brought out and examined, she had always hoped that when her children were grown and out of her house and moved on into lives of their own, she would be able to find someone with whom to share her "golden years." That time was fast approaching and she was still too emotionally fragile from the strain of the years with Alexis and the residue of her breakdown to take on any more emotional baggage. She needed time, lots of time, to get over the pain of the past and to rebuild her emotional core.

She looked at the big man sitting awkwardly in her living room clutching a coffee cup in one huge paw, and she sighed.

She wanted to tell him how she felt, to ask him to give her a bit of time, but she couldn't translate her feelings into words. "I don't think so," was all she could say. "I need to be by myself now. I'm sorry."

He put the cup down carefully and lumbered to his feet. "That's okay. Just thought I'd ask."

Joanna walked him to the door. He started down the steps but turned back. "If you change your mind…" he said.

"I know where you are. Good night."

"Good night."

TWENTY-SIX

SNOW CONTINUED TO FALL through the rest of January and into February. The second week of February brought a surprise thaw as temperatures crept up above freezing. However, all too soon a cold snap froze the melting snow and turned the roads and Joanna's driveway into rivers of glistening ice. But the days were getting longer and inside the cabin the few potted plants stirred themselves back to life and eagerly stretched their branches toward the light in the windows. She had not seen either Tiffany or Maude since the confrontation over the break-in, and as far as the townsfolk knew the police were getting nowhere with their investigation into the death of Luke.

The big training manual approached completion. Even Fred Blanchard could no longer find things to criticize, at least not very much. Francis told her that Morris Lipton was sitting up at home now, directing operations from the old desk he ordered be moved to a picture window overlooking his wife's prize winning rose garden. Apparently he wasn't too happy with some of Fred's suggestions and wanted things returned to the way that he had approved them. Fortunately Joanna, despite the disorder in her personal life, was meticulous about the organization of her professional side and still had copies of all the previous revisions. She didn't even mind the extra bit of work involved; it was so satisfying to rip out Fred's petty alterations. Morris firmly believed that no matter how good their product might be, it was only as good as the person using it and he was prepared to pay top dollar for the best training and documentation. Joanna was offered a small bonus for the extra work involved. She e-mailed the final product to Francis who sent it out to be printed and bound. As the last part of her contract she would "train the trainers," when and if the software was sold, training representatives of the companies that purchased the product, so they in turn could train their staff.

To her considerable surprise the smaller project, for the employment agency software, was also well received. She had skipped through it as fast as decently possible, in order to get back to the larger contract. She was a bit embarrassed about it, considering it to be a third-rate rushed job, but the client was happy and promised to recommend her if she heard of any other contracts being offered.

Work falling to a manageable level at last, Joanna invited Elaine up to spend the weekend at the cabin and promised to treat her friend to dinner at the only trendy restaurant in North Ridge.

The day before Elaine's arrival she had tried to see the cabin through her friend's eyes. Elaine would find it drab and uninviting so Joanna bought a few brightly colored cushions and huge bunches of fresh flowers (at great expense) in an attempt to give the cabin a touch more life.

She was nervous. It was important to her that Elaine approve of her new home. As she added a large log and a fresh bundle of kindling to the iron stove she could hear a car engine slowly drive past. It continued to the bend in the road and then reversed, driving backward down the narrow snow-covered country road before it turned into her driveway.

Doubts forgotten, Joanna ran through the snow laughing and skipping all the way. She threw her arms around Elaine and hugged her close. The two women danced up and down and laughed at themselves for doing so.

"So this is it, eh?" Elaine said as they walked up the path, arm in arm. "I have been trying to imagine what this place looks like for months."

"And, what do you think?"

"It's tiny, and isolated. But I can see that you like it here and that's good enough for me."

Elaine was dressed in a fabulous red Gore-Tex parka, just the thing if one intended on camping out in the Rocky Mountains in winter. Underneath she wore a polar fleece vest with flannel shirt and khakis from Eddie Bauer and on her feet, the very best in winter hiking boots. Joanna laughed and hugged her again. Everything Elaine wore was clearly brand new. The woman who refused to visit her boyfriend's Muskoka cottage until she found out that it came equipped with a hot tub, satellite dish and gourmet kitchen, was trying to fit in to her friend's new life.

Elaine was a bit taken aback by the fact that there was only one bedroom and bath, but she did protest a tiny bit when Joanna insisted that she, Joanna, would be perfectly comfortable on the couch in the living room.

They spent the afternoon reminiscing about their days in high school and university and catching up on the more recent news. Elaine was Alexis' godmother and was brokenhearted to hear that Joanna had heard nothing from her younger daughter. "Perhaps I could go and pay a visit to Wendy," she said thoughtfully. "I have always thought that I would like to go to the Yukon sometime. Maybe I could settle there and be a, what do you call it, a sourdough?"

Joanna threw back her head and laughed. "Well, you certainly are dressed for the part."

Elaine grinned. "A bit overdone, am I? Well, I always try my best."

That night they had dinner in North Ridge at the town's best, and only, elegant restaurant. Not expecting anything quite so nice, Elaine neglected to pack a suitable dinner dress. Joanna assured her that most of the people who would eat there were no doubt staying at a hunting lodge or winter resort for ice fishing or skiing and would not be dressed for dinner.

Nevertheless, in her new Eddie Bauer getup and diamond earrings Elaine still stood out as someone worth cultivating. Jean-Claude, the owner/chef took time out from his busy kitchen to join them for a glass of wine.

He was a tiny man, with a thin goatee and delicate hands. He wore a classic, tall, white chef's hat and his perfect English was thickly overlaid with a Parisian accent. He first came to the Near North of Ontario, he told them, over 20 years ago on a canoe trip with his older brother and instantly fell in love with the wilderness. He returned to Paris, sold his bistro as soon as was possible and moved to Canada. For a while he worked in the kitchens of various cottage country resorts and lodges.

He sadly told them of his brother, as if he was telling them of a death in the family. He had returned to France and was now the husband of a fat, lazy short-order cook. They had six children, and, Jean-Claude shuddered at the thought, he worked as a laborer in a car plant.

It took Jean-Claude many years and many false starts but he slowly developed a radical new cuisine based on the freshest of fish and game and other ingredients local to Ontario. When he opened this restaurant in North Ridge it was an instant success. He had been featured in articles in *Gourmet* and *Traveler* magazines.

"So now I am a star," he declared flamboyantly. Elaine

tapped the tips of her fingers together in applause and Jean-Claude bowed his head ever so slightly. Although his attention appeared to be focused completely on his guests, his eyes were constantly darting about the crowded dining room. He seemed to be sending or receiving signals from the headwaiter, but his attention never wavered from Elaine's smiling face and her bright conversation.

"The winter is not so good," he was explaining, "it is hard, and very expensive, to obtain the fresh vegetables, so the past few years I have closed after Christmas until spring."

"Why not this year?" Elaine asked. "Although I am glad you didn't."

He nodded his head at the compliment. "I have, what do you Canadians say? I have met someone, and this year I have no desire to return to Paris for the winter."

Elaine noticeably deflated but she recovered quickly and raised her glass in salute. "Our gain," she said smiling.

Joanna joined in the toast. The silent communication between their host and the handsome, young headwaiter assumed new meaning and she was pleased for him.

Their salads arrived and with a bow, Jean-Claude excused himself to attend to the kitchen.

After dinner, reluctant to end the evening, Joanna and Elaine bundled up tightly against the winter night and strolled arm in arm down through the town of North Ridge. Not many people were about, but the night was clear and the stars hung brightly overhead. Joanna pointed out the North Star and Orion's belt and the Big Dipper, and a few other constellations she recognized.

They were turning around to walk back to the car when a pickup truck pulled to a halt beside them and discharged a load of rowdy teenagers. Tiffany jumped out of the cab of the truck, stumbling slightly as she hit the pavement and came to a stop as she recognized Joanna.

She didn't say a word and was quickly pulled across the street by her male companion. She tossed her hand-knitted red scarf around her neck and they disappeared into the Last Chance Bar and Pool Hall without a backward glance.

"Uh, Ms. Hastings, can I talk to you for a moment?" A young girl Joanna didn't know stepped out of the shadows and approached them hesitantly. Her face was a mass of soft freckles. Red tendrils escaped from underneath her winter hat. Beside her, Joanna felt Elaine tighten her grip on her purse.

"Yes?"

"My name's Pam. I'm a friend of Tiffany's."

"Yes?"

"I know that you told her you didn't ever want her coming around your place again," the girl mumbled into her chest. She was highly embarrassed and her red complexion flamed with the effort, but she forced herself to stand her ground.

Elaine looked confused, but she relaxed her grip on her purse. There were no other pedestrians in sight, but a steady line of cars passed by, most of them headed for the parking lot behind the Last Chance.

"That's right," Joanna said sharply. "I befriended her and she stole something from me."

Pam hesitated and glanced toward the open door into which the others had disappeared. More than anything she wanted to cut and run into the safety of the noisy, anonymous bar and the comfort of her friends, but she forced herself to stand in front of this stuck-up woman and her snooty friend. "Tiffany didn't break into your house," she mumbled.

Joanna could barely hear over the noise of cars cruising the street, the roar spilling out from the bar and the girl's whisper. Elaine was fascinated, this was the first she heard of a break-in.

"I know she did, there is no point in you trying to defend her."

"But she tried to stop them," Pam cried. "Really she did. I was there. I didn't stop them either, but I didn't go into your house, I swear I didn't," she added quickly. "It was a couple of others, they said they would get Tiffany's scarf for her. Tiffany tried to stop them, really she did. I didn't see what happened after that, 'cause I got out of there. But Tiff told me that they were going to wreck your place and she made them stop." Pam paused for breath and turned to run.

"Why do you care?" Joanna stopped her. "And why are you telling me this?"

"Because I like Tiffany. She's a nice kid, but no one will give her a chance. She likes you, you know. She really liked those computer lessons you gave her. She talked about them all the time; she told me I should ask if I could have lessons too. But my dad would never pay for them. Tiff is really broken up that she can't work on the computer any more. She is really broken up, you know, because you don't like her any more." Pam shuffled her feet and glanced across at the beckoning bar door. "I had better go. She'll be mad at me if she knows that I talked about this to you."

"Wait, please, just a minute." Joanna put out a hand and grasped the girl's sleeve. "If Tiffany tried to stop the others from breaking into my cabin, then why didn't she tell me? Why did she let me believe that she did it?"

Pam looked at Joanna as if she didn't have a brain cell in her head. "She wouldn't tell on her friends. No one would ever talk to her again her if she did that. And I gotta go or they won't talk to me neither." She ran across the road and barely managed to be missed by a pickup tearing through town at over 100 kilometers an hour. The boys hanging out of the back of the cab whistled and yelled obscenities at her, but the truck swerved wildly and kept on going.

They watched the car careen through town. A beer bottle launched from the driver's window crashed against the wall of a run-down hardware store. It bounced off the bricks and clattered down the street before coming to rest in the gutter.

"Now what was all that about?" Elaine asked.

Joanna didn't answer. She resumed the walk back to her car, hands stuffed in her pockets, head bent in thought, kicking aimlessly at the dirty piles of snow lining the sidewalk. As they neared the restaurant they could see warm yellow light spilling out onto the deserted street and hear bright laughter and the cheerful clink of crockery and glassware. The wonderful smell of garlic and roasting meat drifted through the cold, crisp winter air.

"That was a great meal," Elaine said, melting at the memory of it. "I would definitely come all this way just to eat there again. Let's come in the spring, and see what Jean-Claude has on the menu then. It will be totally different, I expect."

Lost in thought, Joanna didn't hear her. She had misjudged Tiffany badly. She, of all people, should have remembered that to a teenager loyalty to one's friends, often sadly misplaced as it was, was the highest virtue. Although Alexis' steadfast refusal to hear a word against any of her friends sometimes brought Joanna to tears, she had always had a degree of respect for her daughter's faithfulness. And if she had misjudged Tiffany about the scarf, what else was there she might have failed to notice? "I have something to do before we go home," she announced to Elaine. "Come with me, quickly." Joanna turned around once again and marched firmly down the street. Confused, tired and cold, Elaine followed.

A blast of over-heated air hit them full in the face as they

pushed open the heavy, scarred wooden door. The inside of the
Last Chance was as seedy as the outside promised. The lighting
was poor; several light sockets held long-burned out bulbs that
no one had ever bothered to replace. A thick pall of cigarette
haze hung overhead and the air was redolent of smoke, greasy
food, thawing boots, wet woolen mittens and unwashed bodies.
Wallpaper of indeterminate color hung in tatters from the walls
and the wood floor under their feet creaked with every step.
Large water stains covered the ceiling. Country and western
music blared from the old jukebox. A collection of musician's
equipment was arranged on a small stage, presumably the live
band was taking a break. The room stretched off into darkness
and there was no sign of Tiffany.

"You ladies looking for something?" A short heavyset man
with a shaved head and bushy beard approached them. There was
nothing friendly in his greeting. His arms bulged with tightly
packed muscle, a long snake tattoo ran up each arm to disappear
under the sleeves of a short-sleeved, very grimy T-shirt, souvenir
of a visit to a strip club in Toronto. A tiny silver earring glittered
in each ear. He looked over both women slowly and puffed lazily
on the last half-inch of a non-filtered cigarette.

Joanna stepped forward. "I would like to speak to the
owner, please."

"That's me, but I don't think you ladies," he sneered the
word, "have any business with me." He blew a cloud of smoke
into Joanna's face.

Elaine disdainfully waved her hand in the air, but Joanna
ignored it. "I wonder if we could go somewhere and talk."

He leered at her. "You want to talk, do you?"

Joanna flushed but held her ground. "Yes, I do want to
talk, for a few minutes." The door flew open and let in a
breath of fresh cold air, as two men sauntered into the bar.

They glared at Joanna and Elaine suspiciously and stopped to exchange handshakes and some undecipherable greeting with the owner before continuing on into the bar. The man watched them go and then turned back to Joanna. He spat onto the floor, barely missing the toe of Joanna's boot. Elaine cringed but said nothing.

"You two don't look like cops," the man said.

"We aren't," Joanna said. "Look, I only want a couple of minutes of your time." She took a deep breath. "I want to ask you about something that happened on the night of December second."

His dark eyes glittered with a spark of interest, but it quickly extinguished. He tossed his butt onto the floor and ground it out with his toe. The floor was littered with the remains of cigarettes, the wood heavily scarred with burn marks and ground-in ash. "That was almost two months ago. How'm I gonna remember one night, eh?"

A middle-aged woman, dressed in a short flared skirt, high heels and a frilly, scooped-neck blouse that displayed a good portion of over-abundant breasts, looked over. She opened her mouth to speak but shut it again and stood behind the bar owner, watching the interlopers.

"December second," Joanna repeated. "You must remember that night. A man disappeared from Hope River that night. Everyone would have been talking about it the next day."

"Look lady, the cops have been here asking me questions about that. I'll tell you what I told them—nothing." He paused to drag the last cigarette out of a crushed and broken pack and tossed the empty carton onto the floor without a glance. "Now if you want a drink, come on in. But I ain't got time to talk." He pushed past the waitress who was waiting to speak to him and returned to the bar. The band, a scruffy group of local boys dressed in cowboy hats and boots and large, shiny belt buckles finished their break and clambered up onto the stage amid equal parts cheers and boos.

The waitress eyed Joanna and Elaine, her excessively made-up eyes tinged with suspicion.

"What are you wanting to know about the second?" she asked.

"There was a group of teenagers here that night, most of them are back again I think…" Joanna said.

In front of the long bar a waitress dropped a tray of empty beer bottles and full ashtrays. Elaine almost jumped out of her skin as the crash echoed through the large room. The patrons hooted and clapped and stomped their feet with enthusiasm. "A big hand for the juggler," someone shouted to appreciative cheers.

"I can't talk here," the woman said. "I can take my break soon, give me about ten minutes, I'll meet you out front." She ran to help the red-faced waitress scoop up broken glass and wipe the floor.

On the way out Joanna bumped into a man so thickly swathed against the cold he could barely see where he was going. She mumbled an apology and he looked up. It was Jack, from the grocery store in Hope River. Joanna opened her mouth to offer a greeting, but Jack merely glared at her and pushed his way past.

"For God's sake, Joanna," Elaine said through her teeth when they were back out on the sidewalk. "What on Earth can you be thinking? We aren't going to stand here all night and wait for that horrid woman are we? We could freeze to death out here—that's if we don't get murdered first."

Joanna pulled her friend away from the lights spilling out from the bar. The capital "C" in the sign over the door was flickering frantically, about to go out. Soon it would be the *Last hance*.

"Now where are we going?"

"I want to get out of sight as best we can," Joanna said. "We can wait over here."

"We're not going to wait for that woman are we? Are you out of your mind?" Elaine grumbled. "We had such a lovely dinner, how did it turn into this?"

Joanna couldn't explain. "Please, Elaine. This matters to me. You can go back to the car if you want. I'm sure she will be here in a minute."

"Oh, I guess I had better stay. Wouldn't want you to be tempted to go back into the place and join the boys in a drink."

Joanna grinned. "Thanks."

It was cold out on the street; they marched in circles to generate some heat. A steady stream of patrons flowed in and out of the bar. A police car drove slowly past but it didn't stop. Joanna and Elaine retreated back into the shadows. They didn't want to have to explain what they were doing there. A boy flew out of the bar and took off down the street, two men fast behind him screaming obscenities. The boy leapt lightly over a patch of ice but his followers were too heavy and slow to miss it. One of them skidded on the surface and with arms and legs flailing wildly, crashed into the sidewalk. His companion tried to jump him but missed and tripped over the falling body. Realizing that he was no longer being chased the boy turned and laughed at his pursuers lying in a heap on the sidewalk. He jeered loudly and danced a few wild steps to announce his delight, then he disappeared around a corner and was gone. The two men struggled to their feet and limped back to the bar, their prey forgotten, cursing each other with every painful step.

Joanna and Elaine were so occupied in watching the antics on the street they didn't hear the woman slip up behind them. She had come out the back door and down the alley. "Mind if I smoke?" she asked, already lighting up. They both jumped at the words. In the harsh light from the street lamps Joanna could see that the woman was much older than she appeared in the gloom of the bar. Her head was a rat's nest of bright red, over-teased hair. A small scar ran down the edge of her right cheek and she was missing two side teeth. Most of her harsh red lipstick had been chewed off and her mascara was smeared under one eye.

She stepped into the alley, high heels sinking into unshoveled snow. "I'd rather no one saw us talking. Bob wouldn't be too happy with me. He doesn't like people coming around asking questions about what goes on in our bar."

"Is Bob the owner?" Joanna asked. She sniffed their surroundings, beside her Elaine shifted uncomfortably. Even in the freezing night air the smell in the alley was rancid. Patches of yellow dotted the snow along the side of the building. She hoped they were from a dog.

"He's my husband," she replied. "We own it together. Now why do you want to know about December second? You're not cops, are you? You sure don't look it."

Joanna had the vague idea that she had been insulted but let it go.

"Bob said the police came around. Did you talk to them?"

"I don't talk to the cops, not if I don't have to."

"Well, I want to know about a group of teenagers who came in that night. You might remember them, I think that they're regulars, in particular a short, thin girl with purple hair and a nose ring. Did you see her that night?"

The woman stared at her and puffed on her cigarette. "I might have. I'm not really too sure."

"Oh, for heaven's sake," Elaine muttered and dug into her purse. She pulled out a fifty-dollar bill and held it up in front of her. "Did you see the girl my friend is asking about?"

"Yea, I saw her." The woman reached out and snatched the pink bill. Joanna half expected her to stuff the money down the front of her blouse, but instead it was slipped into a coat pocket.

"The girl was here. She comes here a lot. That's a no account bunch of kids she hangs out with. Up to no good the whole lot of them." The woman peered at Joanna. "She your daughter? Don't look much like you."

"No, she's not my daughter. She was wearing a jacket that night. A big black one with a Chicago Bulls logo on the back. Do you remember it?"

"Yea, I've seen her in that jacket before. It was a nice jacket, she always seemed right proud of it." The woman took a deep drag of her cigarette and coughed. She choked on a thick blob of phlegm and spat it into the nearest snowdrift. Elaine grimaced in disgust.

"What you staring at, Miss Hoity-Toity?" The waitress glared at Elaine. "No one forced you to come here, you know."

"Do you remember if anything happened to the girl's jacket that night?" Joanna asked.

The woman paused and tossed her cigarette into the alley. "Hard to remember, it was a long time ago."

Elaine pulled another fifty out of her purse. She knew well that she was paying for her disdain. "This is all I have on me," she said. "Answer the rest of my friend's questions, then I'll give it to you." The woman eyed Elaine's black leather gloves, soft as silk, with a bit of fur peeking out of the cuff. Her own hands were red and rough from the cold and knotted with age and hard work. "Nice gloves you have there," she said.

"Thank you," Elaine replied.

"Give her the gloves, Elaine," Joanna said.

"What!"

"I'll buy you another pair, just give her the gloves."

Elaine handed over the money and her gloves.

"Okay." The woman slipped the gloves over her hands and stroked them lightly. "I know what you want to know. The girl's jacket was stolen. She left it over the back of her chair and went to the bathroom. When she was ready to leave the jacket was missing. She was real upset about it, too. I remember 'cause I helped her look for it. Thought maybe she misplaced it. But it was gone. I felt sorry for her, it was mighty cold out that night."

"Didn't the police ask you about the jacket?"

"They asked Bob."

"Why didn't you tell them what you've told me?"

The woman stared at Joanna. "Lady, I don't tell the police nothing."

Joanna didn't understand. "But you could have saved that girl a lot of trouble. This is important."

The woman lifted her new gloves up to her face and stroked the leather gently against her cheek. "Lady, you and your friend look like you've had a nice soft life, so why don't you just go back where you belong." She dug another cigarette out of her pocket and held it between her fingers for a few moments. She decided against talking off the gloves to light a smoke and put the cigarette back. She looked at Joanna's blank face and at Elaine trying to hold in her disgust at their surroundings and she laughed. "Listen, ladies." She gave the word the same sneer as had her husband. "I'm nice and comfortable in this town now. Bob may not look like much to you, but he's good to me and we run a good business. But I've spent my time on the streets. I can tell you stories would make your hair curl. And one thing a girl learns real quick on the streets is that you don't tell the cops nothing. That girl with the purple hair what comes in here sometimes, she reminds me of me at that age. All bluster and know-ev-erything and headed straight for trouble. I'm telling you about her jacket getting taken 'cause I don't want to see the girl in trouble when she don't have to be. But I don't offer nothing to the cops." She grinned, in the faint light from the street lamps the gaps in her teeth aged her about twenty years. "Besides, the cops don't offer me nice presents like this." She stroked the gloves again.

As if on cue a police car drove slowly past once again. This time it stopped and two officers, one male and one female, got out. They both shifted their hips and adjusted their gun belts as they crossed the street.

"I gotta go now. I'll be needed back inside." The woman slipped around the back of the building and was swallowed up by the darkness.

Elaine let out a long breath as they watched her go. "Well that was a real treat. I feel like an extra in a seedy private eye movie. The dumb blond who hasn't a clue what is going on. Not a hard part to play. Are you going to tell me what all that was about?"

"Let's go home—I'll tell you on the way." Joanna led them out of the alley. "I'll pay you for the gloves and the hundred dollars."

"Forget it," Elaine said. "I'll consider it the cost of admis-sion. It seems to me that offering bribes must have been a lot easier in the days before debit cards, when people carried cash. What might she have wanted off me if it was summer? My sandals, my sports bra, maybe?"

Joanna laughed and linked her arm through her friend's. "Thanks for being here with me."

They crossed the street, but in the winter darkness Joanna did not recognize the shrouded shape of Nancy Miller scurry-ing down the street and into the bar.

SHE WAS WELL FAMILIAR with teenaged girls and their habits so it was not until late the following afternoon that Joanna asked Elaine to entertain herself for a while, and drove the short distance to Maude's house. Maude was out doing the weekly grocery shopping, and Tiffany was just getting up. Rocky greeted Joanna with much enthusiasm. Tiffany was considerably more subdued.

"What do you want?" The girl stood in the doorway still wearing her pajamas, hair tousled and eyes heavy with sleep. "My grandma's not home now. Come back later."

Tiffany started to close the door but Joanna pulled it back. "I would like to talk to you, if you have a few moments."

The teenager shrugged, but stepped out of the way. "If you want, I'm not doing anything else right now."

Rocky ran the length of the living room to greet the visitor, tail wagging in joy. Tiffany plopped into a chair and sat sideways, her knees hooked over the arm. She glared at Joanna. "So talk," she said.

It was difficult to find a place to begin; Joanna did not want to betray Tiffany's friend's confidence. "I want to talk to you about the break-in at my cabin. I have a feeling that you weren't responsible. Am I right?"

Tiffany looked up, her eyes glimmered with interest, but she remained silent.

Joanna sat down opposite Tiffany and held out her hands. "I would like us to be friends, really I would. But we have to talk about this."

Rocky ran up to Tiffany, a tennis ball clutched firmly in his massive jaws. He dropped the ball at her feet and scooted away, glancing over his shoulder as he ran. She picked up the ball and tossed it against the far wall, the dog leapt after it as it bounced and quickly snatched it up.

"Don't tell my grandma," Tiffany said. Rocky dropped the ball at her feet and danced back to await another throw. The girl scooped it up and feigned a throwing action. "She doesn't want me and Rocky playing ball in the house."

Every part of the big dog shivered with excitement as he awaited the throw, his tail wagged with delight and his strange blue eyes gleamed. Tiffany let go of the precious object. It sailed over Rocky's head to bounce off the fireplace wall. Long toenails scrambled for purchase on the wooden floor as the dog took off in pursuit of the toy.

He attempted to stuff his bulk under the antique piecrust telephone table in pursuit of the ball. Joanna opened her mouth to reprimand Tiffany for giving the dog the chance to wreck the delicate table, then cursed herself for a fool and sat silently as they both watched the dog's antics. His ample rear stuck up in the air and his back legs were stretched almost flat as he wiggled his muzzle into the furthest reaches of the table in search of the prize. That the girl would ask her to keep a confidence, not to tell Maude about a secret game of catch with the family dog, overwhelmed her with a tidal wave of emotion. Tiffany was reaching out, trying to make an ally of Joanna, and almost treating the older woman as a friend. One wrong word now would spoil everything. "I won't tell," she said. "Would you like to come back to my computer lessons and some games as well?"

Rocky secured the ball and managed to get out from under the table without breaking anything. He proudly carried his prize over to Tiffany. She wrenched the ball out of his massive jaws and wiped the animal's saliva onto her pajama pants. For the first time that day she looked into Joanna's eyes.

"Why do you want me back? Why do you all of a sudden think that I didn't break into your cabin? You were pretty quick to accuse me in the first place." She tossed the ball from one hand to another, Rocky whimpered in frustration waiting for another chance to play.

"I had a chance to think about it. I have some experience with teenagers, you know. When I thought about it carefully, I realized that you wouldn't do that to me, would you?"

Tiffany shrugged, and rolled the tennis ball across the room. Rocky scrambled after it. "I'm going to make myself something to eat. I'm hungry." She swung her legs off the chair onto the floor and stood up. "You want something?"

"A cup of tea would be nice, if you're making." Joanna followed Tiffany into the kitchen. Like the rest of Maude's home the kitchen was immaculate. The appliances were old, the Formica table and vinyl chairs dated from the sixties, maybe even earlier, but everything was spotless. Linoleum designed to look like brick was worn until the pattern had almost disappeared in some places, but it shone as if it had been laid yesterday. Joanna would have happily eaten off the floor. Yellow tieback curtains hung over the kitchen sink and a crisp row of African Violets in full bloom lined the windowsill.

Tiffany pulled strawberry jam in a mason jar and margarine and homemade bread out of the fridge. She sliced the bread into thick slabs, popped them into the toaster and filled the kettle with water and placed it onto the stovetop to boil.

Joanna sat down at the kitchen table and watched the girl work; her movements were compact and organized. She methodically laid out tea things on a tray and immediately wiped up a few breadcrumbs that had fallen off the loaf.

"Your grandma keeps such a clean house. I wish I were more like her. I have never been able to get myself organized."

Tiffany shrugged and spread margarine onto her toast.

Joanna cursed herself again. Babbling on about the tidiness of one's kitchen is not the best conversational gambit with a re-

bellious teenager. Tiffany's invitation to breakfast was a break-
through, a sign that the girl wanted to talk. She was desperately
afraid of blowing it, of forcing Tiffany back into her shell of
indifference.

Rocky brought the ball into the kitchen and dropped it at
Tiffany's feet. Noticing that the preparation of food was
underway he forgot the game immediately.

"You remind me a lot of my youngest daughter, Alexis,"
Joanna spoke hesitantly. "She also liked to experiment with different colors, for her hair and her nails. She would have loved
that purple shade of your hair. Some of the things she did. Her
hair was a lovely dark blond, but she hated it."

"Is she dead?"

Joanna was startled. "No, no she's not dead."

"Then why do you talk about her in the past tense? You said
her hair was blond."

Joanna had always been the most private of people, she had
few friends, she rarely spoke of her emotions and she never
allowed anyone too close, except for Elaine. But she wanted to
confide in this confused, troubled girl. Her voice took over and
she felt like a stranger standing by watching someone speak.

"She's not dead, but sometimes, I think that she is dead to
me. She lives in California now, with some sort of a cult. The
day she left she told me she never wanted to see me again, and
she hasn't. I only found out where she was because, strangely
enough, she sent a birthday card to her brother, James. Just one
card, that one time. She hasn't contacted anyone else. I have
written, many times, sometimes they come back, unopened,
with 'NOT WANTED' scribbled on the envelope, in what I
think is someone else's handwriting, but I can't be sure. Some
letters are not returned, and I hope that she reads those."

The kettle emitted a shrill whistle as steam poured out the

spout. Silently Tiffany removed it from the stove and poured the hot water into the waiting teapot. It was a traditional old brown betty, beloved of antique collectors everywhere. She slid a plate of her breakfast toast, thickly coated with homemade strawberry jam on the table in front of Joanna.

Joanna picked up the toast absentmindedly. She chewed carefully. The heavenly homemade jam might have been sawdust for all the taste she noticed. "I worry about her all the time, I feel so helpless."

"Maybe she's okay." Tiffany carried the teapot to the table and poured a cup for Joanna. Unasked she added milk and several teaspoons of sugar.

"I hope that she is. But I hear all the time about these cults and what they can do—look at Waco, look at Jonestown. They have taken control of her heart and her mind, she wouldn't even talk to her dad when he tried to see her in December." Rocky sat on the floor beside Joanna's chair whining for a bite of toast, tail thumping loudly. They ignored him and he whined all the louder.

"What's so scary about these cults is that they do take control of the person. She might not even know her own mind any more. I keep asking myself why she would get involved with people like that. Why would she give up control, I mean. I tried to bring up my kids to be strong and independent. Where did I go wrong?" Joanna sipped her hot, sweet tea as silent tears welled in her eyes.

"What was she like before she went away?" Tiffany asked. "You said she was like me. Was she?"

Joanna smiled through her tears. "Oh, yes. Very much like you. Not just the hair and the clothes and all the external things. But the attitude, the personality, the hostility, the anger. You have a lot to be angry about, your father and your mother deserted you,

I can imagine how tough that must be, but your grandma loves you very much, Tiffany, I can see that so clearly. Please don't break her heart the way that my daughter broke mine."

"I don't want to hurt my grandma." Tiffany got up from the table and put more bread into the toaster. Joanna had eaten all of hers. Rocky thumped his tail in anticipation.

Joanna wiped her eyes with the back of her hand. "Well, I'm glad to hear that."

"Why don't you go and see her?"

"What, see who, what do you mean?"

"See Alexis. Why don't you go to her?" Once again Tiffany buttered and spread jam on the toast and put it on the table. Once again Joanna ate it without thinking. Tiffany tossed a piece to Rocky and sliced more bread.

"I...I couldn't. Suppose she wouldn't talk to me. I don't think I could face that. I guess that's what hurts the most, that after all those years she could turn her back on us and never want to see us again."

"Maybe she would talk to you. I think that you were a good mother, Joanna. I wish you were my mother," Tiffany mumbled into her chest. Joanna failed to hear. "Don't beat yourself up too much. Some kids go wrong, you know. Not that your Alexis has gone wrong, I don't mean that."

Joanna smiled. "I know exactly what you mean."

The front door slammed and woman and girl jumped, as if they had been caught doing something wrong. Rocky ran to greet Maude and Joanna and Tiffany both got to their feet.

"Goodness me," Maude exclaimed, "company. I hope you haven't been waiting long, Joanna. I just popped into town for a few groceries." She plopped two bulging shopping bags down on the kitchen table with a sigh.

"Let me help you, Maude. Do you have any more groceries

in the car?" Joanna said. Tiffany poked through the bags looking for treats.

"Thank you, dear, that would be very nice of you. There are just a few." Maude sunk into the chair recently vacated. "Is that tea fresh? I would love a cup. For some reason it was so busy in the store today. I don't know where all the people are coming from. Poor Nancy was run off her feet, her Uncle Jack didn't show up at work this morning. She told me she tried to hawl him out of some bar last night, but he would have none of it." As she talked Maude scratched Rocky lazily behind the ears. The dog wiggled in ecstasy.

Joanna carried in the last of the groceries. She said her good-bye's quickly, somewhat embarrassed by her emotional display in front of Tiffany. She paused on the doorstep, fastening her coat and pulling on mittens. "See you on Friday, Tiffany. At the regular time, okay?"

Tiffany nodded and flashed a broad smile. Maude looked back and forth between them. "You mean Tiffany is going back for the computer lessons. That's wonderful. But what brought that on?"

"It appears to have been nothing but a little misunderstanding." Joanna returned the smile. "All sorted out now."

She drove home full of cheer. Funny how she had hoped to get Tiffany to open up a bit, but in the end she, Joanna, was the one to do all the talking.

TWENTY-SEVEN

First thing Monday morning Joanna called the North Ridge police station and explained to Staff Sergeant Reynolds all that she had learned about Tiffany's jacket and its disappearance at the time of Luke's murder. Reynolds listened to the details and told her that he would report her story in full to Inspector Erikson.

It was hard to settle back into routine after Elaine's visit. Joanna wondered if she was really suited to this life of solitude that she had chosen. After the shared laughter of her friend's visit, the isolation seemed oppressive. It was difficult to concentrate enough to settle in to work and she wandered aimlessly about the cabin, searching for something to do. She never would have believed it possible in her past life, but she was getting tired of reading. She remembered all the years when her children were young, how she could imagine nothing more like heaven than to be able to read book after book to her heart's content.

What do people do all day in heaven, anyway? Sitting around on clouds and strumming harps must get deadly boring after a while. She looked at her pile of computer games but nothing held any interest, she logged on to the Internet but her favorite sites seemed endlessly repetitive. The weather had been lovely for the weekend of Elaine's visit, sunny and warm with temperatures hovering around freezing, but Elaine had taken the good weather back to the city with her. Temperatures

plummeted and heavy snow fell for days. The radio held out
no hope of anything better for the foreseeable future, just snow
and more snow and ever colder, drearier days. They might even
receive record-breaking accumulations, the announcer said
cheerfully.

Joanna considered digging out the car and making a trip to the
library, even a visit to Nancy at the grocery store and a piece of
pie in the restaurant would be welcome. But she couldn't summon
up the energy to drag out the shovel once again and trudge up the
hill to clear the driveway. She had better call and get someone to
come and plow her out, or she would be stuck here until spring.
Enough of trying to be a tough and independent countrywoman.

SHE SLEPT BADLY, night after night, tossing and turning as the
wind howled outside her window and the cabin shook to its
foundations and the snow continued to fall.

*The old truck rattled to a stop in front of the five-and-dime
that also served as bus depot. The day had been fair, a welcome
cheerful sun glimmered on snow-packed roads and frozen
farmers' fields, holding out the promise of spring soon to come.
But it was a false promise and all too quickly the sun disappeared under a blanket of fast-moving storm clouds that would
bring nothing but snow and more snow and finger-freezing
temperatures.*

*Inside the truck, no one moved. Three people stared reso-
lutely out the front window as if by the force of their will they could
wish the snow and the cold and the town and themselves far away.*

*The man reached under his seat and pulled out a bottle of
beer, and across the women to fumble in the glove compartment
for a bottle opener. With a flick of his wrist the cap flew off the
bottle to land among the debris at his feet. The women continued to stare straight ahead, at nothing.*

The minister's wife chose that moment to step daintily out of the five-and-dime, two paper bags filled to overflowing with party decorations tucked firmly under her arms. Her sensible black cloth coat was trimmed with gray lamb, just a touch of extravagance, and a lamb hat perched atop her tight gray curls. The man raised his hat to her as she passed the truck, the bottle of beer still clutched firmly in his hand. She lifted her chin higher and gripped her shopping bags even tighter to her chest and snorted as she stared forward and continued on her way.

He pretended not to notice. "Ain't got all day to be sitting around here, girl. Got chores to do, get out now."

The girl sitting between the two adults threw him a look of utter contempt, but he was still watching the retreating figure of the minister's wife as she carefully checked the road before crossing. He missed the force of the girl's glare but not her words. "Chores," she snorted. "Like you've ever done a lick of work in your life. Drinking to do, more likely."

He snarled and drew back his hand but for once the woman intervened. "Not now, for God's sake. Leave her alone this one time, can't you." She fumbled to open her door and spilled out into the muddy street.

"Come on now, it's almost time," she said softly. The man lowered his hand and the girl sneered at him over her shoulder as she slipped out of the cab. She clutched her worn, cheap, cardboard suitcase to her swollen stomach and walked slowly into the grocery store to wait for the bus.

The woman watched her go, her strength was almost enough to call the girl back, to run after her and envelop her in her arms, to stroke her back and say that everything would be all right. Almost strong enough, but not quite.

The man leaned across the seats and shouted out the open door, "You remember now, when you're good and married you

can come back. Not before. You hear me?" The girl continued
walking. She did not look back.

The man spat on the floor of the truck. "Storm coming, let's
go, woman."

Slowly the woman climbed back into the cab and slammed
the door after her. Overhead, thick, black storm clouds
gathered. Flakes of snow swirled wildly to and fro in the winds,
unable to decide in which direction to fall. With the instincts of
northerners, the few people out on the streets quickly finished
up their business and headed home. Tossed about by the wind,
an old garbage can lid clattered down the street, narrowly
missing the minister's wife as she turned into the neatly
shoveled path leading up to the church. Tonight she was in
charge of the semi-annual charity bazaar and bake sale to raise
money for those less fortunate than the good citizens of North
Ridge. She said a quick prayer that the snow would blow over
and not ruin the evening. So much work had gone into planning
this event; she was positively worn out. Someone would have
to venture out once again to clear off the church entrance. A
thin layer of snow was already covering the tidy walk.

The old truck turned and drove slowly down the street. The
woman twisted in the cab and watched the five-and-dime
receding into the distance until they turned the corner and it
was gone. With a sigh and a quick wipe at her cheeks she settled
back into her seat. She had left the baby at home with the boys.
She hoped they hadn't forgotten about her and gone off to play.

TWENTY-EIGHT

SIMULTANEOUSLY THE SNOWPLOW arrived to do the driveway and a truck pulled up with a load of chopped firewood. Joanna didn't know which of them she was more excited to see.

The driveway and the entrance to the road were cleared in a matter of minutes and with a wave the plow operator drove off to his next job. He would send Joanna a bill in the mail. The deliveryman stopped to talk after he had stacked several cords of firewood in orderly rows under the cabin and covered them with a tarpaulin.

A combination of the increasingly threatening weather, the sense of desperate isolation after the warm companionship of Elaine's visit, and the reoccurrence of the strange dreams, the most recent only last night, had Joanna jumping at every creak of the old cabin floor. She was all too glad of the chance for the deliveryman's company and warmly invited him in for coffee. As he thawed out in the warmth of the kitchen a small puddle formed around his chair. The man apologized profusely but she waved his protests away.

His knuckles were so gnarled they rose up like tree stumps out of his old hands and Joanna could hardly help noticing that he was missing two fingers off his left hand as he wrapped them gratefully around the steaming coffee mug.

He looked around her home with interest. "How's old John McKellan doing?" he asked. "We don't hear nothing from him since he moved over to North Bay."

"Sorry, I can't tell you anything," she said. "I rented this place through an agency. I didn't deal directly with the owners themselves."

The man politely but vainly attempted to suppress his surprise. No doubt every time he did business he talked face to face with the persons involved. No man would want a stranger knowing his affairs.

He bit eagerly into a chocolate chip cookie. In her restlessness Joanna had accomplished an amazing amount of baking over the last several days, most of which she would never manage to eat.

"Terrible thing about Luke. Sorry to hear about what happened. Good man, Luke. You found him, I hear."

Joanna nodded. "Unfortunately, yes. I did find him. Poor old guy."

The deliveryman sipped his coffee in silence for a few moments out of respect for Luke's memory. She waited for him to speak again.

"I hear that the police are asking lots of questions about Roy McMaster. Good cookies these."

"Please have another." She pushed the plate toward him. "Have as many as you want. What do you mean? Do they suspect McMaster had something to do with it?"

"Well." He seized a cookie in one massive three-fingered paw and swallowed it whole. "I shouldn't be telling tales out of school, if you take my meaning…"

"I won't tell a soul," Joanna breathed. No lie that, she didn't have anyone to tell anything to.

"My sister, what works in the police office part time, answering phones and doing paperwork and what all that I don't really understand, she tells me that Luke and Roy McMaster had a real set to about a week before the murder. Uh, any more coffee?"

She leapt to her feet and grabbed the coffeepot. "I saw that fight. It was nothing really, just a lot of bombast and bluster. I've been told that Roy and Luke were always fighting. People said that they had been enemies ever since they were in school."

He nodded thanks to the refill and chuckled. "That's right. I was there myself that day. Roy called Luke's sister, Jean, a real nasty name. Won't repeat it to you, ma'am." Joanna covered a smile. It was a long time since a man had watched his language around her. Come to think of it, had any man, ever?

"Luke come after him like a bat out of hell, excuse me. Beat the tar out of Roy. I guess it would have all blown over 'cepting that Roy figured himself for a real fighter, told everyone that he would be a heavyweight contender some day. And there in front of the whole school, skinny little Luke kicked him into the dust. Roy always was a nasty piece of work, even then. None of us kids were sorry to see him get it." The man smiled at his memories.

"Was Jean Nancy Miller's mother? I think Nancy told me that she is his niece."

"No, ma'am, they was a large family, like most farm families round here in those days. Jean was the oldest sister, Betty, the youngest, she were Nancy's mother."

"I know that Nancy's mother died sometime in the sixties," Joanna said. "But Jean? What happened to her?"

"Nice girl, Jean." He continued talking and eating cookies. "Real pretty she was, and smart too." His deeply lined and weather-beaten old face took on a soft, sad glow and thirty years dropped from him in an instant. Joanna had only kept him talking to make conversation, to pass the time of day. But she could see that he was leaving her warm kitchen and reaching back into the past. This story would not have a happy ending.

"She became a nurse, went off to one of them foreign places,

one of those places having trouble all the time. The whole town
was so proud of her." *And you, most of all,* Joanna thought.

"Somewhere in Africa, I think it was. Died there. We heard
she caught some disease and just up and died."

"How sad." Joanna reached out her hand as if to touch his,
but she quickly remembered her place. This proud old man
would not want her sympathy. She leapt up to refresh the cookie
plate in order to give him a moment to recover himself.

She put the cookies down on the table and refilled his cup.
"So the police think Roy McMaster killed Luke. Seems a pretty
far stretch, that he would finally kill the man who humiliated
him some, what, thirty years later?"

Back in the present, he shook his head. "No one thinks he
been waiting all those years, and let me tell you little lady, it's
been much more than thirty years since I was a schoolboy, to
do the deed. Nope they had a big fight right behind the liquor
store in Hope River. Must be ten, twenty people heard them.
Luke said Roy was having parties on his property at night.
Said Roy was bringing in all his liquored-up friends and
running wild through the woods at night."

Joanna laughed. "You can't be serious. Roy McMaster
running through the night like a Shakespearean wood nymph."
An image flashed through her mind of the fat old drunk dressed
in garlands of leaves and flowers, performing piles among the
trees. She laughed again. "I can't believe that."

He looked somewhat offended at her laughter and Joanna
quickly brought herself up short.

"Well, I don't reckon I know what a *nymph* is, but that's what
they fought about and that lady policeman is pretty interested
in Roy McMaster right now, let me tell you."

"Have they arrested him?"

"Not yet, my sister tells me they don't have enough

evidence." He pushed his chair back from the table and lumbered to his feet.

"Thank you for your hospitality, ma'am. Right nice to sit a spell. You need more wood, you let me know. Thanks for the cookies."

Joanna quickly laid out a strip of aluminum foil and wrapped the rest of the baking into a bundle. She thrust the package at her guest. "Please take some home with you."

He accepted the gift with a nod.

She stood at the front window and watched the old man plod up the driveway to his truck, a silver package containing homemade cookies tucked under his arm. The snow continued to fall, softly and steadily. Already the tracks of the snowplow were disappearing under a soft white blanket.

If the police had another suspect, then Tiffany should be in the clear. Joanna certainly hoped so. But she couldn't imagine a feud of, what —forty, fifty years?—suddenly erupting into murder. She had the impression that Luke and Roy enjoyed their reputations as crusty old men who never forgot a slight to their supposed honor. Neither of them were exactly pillars of the community, but they both enjoyed a position of some respect, a position earned in large part because of the long running vendetta.

The woodcutter had placed a large stack of ready to use firewood neatly beside the old iron stove. Joanna stoked up the embers and laid the fire once again. The dry wood caught quickly and a lovely warming blaze spread out to fill the room.

THE NEXT DAY as she was settling onto her hands and knees to scrub the old kitchen linoleum, Joanna had a visit from the police. It had been so long since they had bothered her that she was daring to hope she had been forgotten. No such luck. She peeled off her plastic cleaning gloves and opened the door to Inspector Erikson and Staff Sergeant Reynolds.

Reynolds was crumpled and relaxed in his standard issue winter uniform. He tucked his state trooper-style hat under his arm and sat down with much huffing and puffing to pull off his galoshes. Erikson slipped off her delicate ankle boots and refused Joanna's offer to take her coat. She merely unbuttoned it in recognition of the warmth of the room. Underneath she wore a severe and highly unflattering suit in a shade of brown best described as mud. No scarf or pin broke the stiff perfection of the tailored jacket. Her blond hair was fastened into a sharp, shapeless bun at the back of her head. Idly, Joanna wondered if the inspector ever let her hair down or if she slept at attention, every hair properly pinned into place, panty hose primly pulled up, knees crossed.

As usual Erikson left Joanna's mouth gaping open, about to offer coffee or any other hospitality, and proceeded straight to the point.

"I was going over your previous statement this morning, and wanted to clear up one minor detail."

Joanna snapped her mouth shut and smiled stiffly. "Yes?"

Erikson flipped open her methodical notebook and consulted it in silence for a few moments. "When you found the body of Luke Snelgrove down by the lake, it was partially under an overturned canoe. Is that correct?"

"Yes."

Erikson looked up from her notes. "Did you at any time turn the body over?"

"Of course not," Joanna spluttered. She wondered what they were getting at. The police had not been around for more than a month now and she was very happy about that. No matter how completely innocent she knew herself to be it was disconcerting to have this authoritative, no-nonsense officer questioning her movements and her motivations. She took a deep breath and tried to control her shaking voice. "I'd like to say that I didn't touch him—it—because of my sense of civic duty, but unfortunately I was just scared out of my tiny mind."

"Did anyone else come along after you found the body? Perhaps while you were up here, phoning the police?"

"I didn't see or hear anyone. Anything could have happened, but I don't think so. Why are you asking me this? Did you get the information I phoned in about what I learned about the Bulls jacket?" Joanna glared at Reynolds, daring him to tell her that he had forgotten to pass on her hard-earned piece of intelligence. Instead the staff sergeant smiled with satisfaction. For once he had done something right and the inspector had been pleased.

"Your information was very helpful," Erikson admitted grudgingly. "We went to the bar and spoke to the staff, and they did admit that the Jordan girl was there that night and that she did complain that someone had stolen her jacket. So Tiffany was missing the jacket sometime before you spoke to Luke Snelgrove on the road after one AM."

They asked her to go over her movements on the day she found the body, one more time. Erikson snapped her notebook shut in the aggressive gesture that Joanna had come to recognize as marking the end of the interview. Before the police could get to their feet, she interrupted with a question of her own.

"Why are we going over all this again? I would appreciate it if you could tell me what's going on. You can't believe that Tiffany did it," she couldn't bring her self to say the word *killed,* "not after what we found out about the jacket."

Erikson tucked her notebook and pen back into her bag and marched briskly to the door to slip on her boots. "That the jacket was reported stolen on the date in question proves very little. Maybe the girl simply misplaced it and found it later."

Joanna opened her mouth to object, but Erikson raised one hand. "However, I don't think that is the case.

"Of more significance, we are sure that the body was moved after Mr. Snelgrove was dead. We do not know where he was killed, but it is unlikely to have been anywhere on your property or the surrounding land."

Joanna felt a rush of relief so intense she staggered and barely kept herself from collapsing back into the chair. She managed to keep both her posture and her voice. "How do you know that?"

Erikson slipped on her leather gloves and pressed each finger into place. "Absence of blood, mostly. The wounds that he suffered would have produced quite a lot more blood than that which was found in the vicinity of the body."

Sergeant Reynolds had his coat and boots on now and was holding open the door. He shifted from foot to foot as tiny snowflakes drifted lazily into the room, to melt wherever they chanced to fall. The women ignored him.

"After death the blood settles in pools on the body, on the underside as any liquid would.

"The autopsy report shows that Mr. Snelgrove likely fell onto his face when he was killed and remained in that position for some time after he was dead. Not onto his back, the way in which you found him."

"And the jacket that was with him?" Joanna forced herself to remember the terrible moment that she found Luke. She drew the picture carefully in her mind's eye. One part of her subconscious tried to put up a veil, to keep her from seeing it all again, but she forced herself to concentrate. She was determined to understand. If the body was moved after death then the jacket couldn't have been torn off…torn off who… whoever…the killer… And anyone who had the presence of mind to cart a dead body God knows how far was very unlikely to accidentally leave evidence the size of a winter coat lying behind them in the snow for all to see.

Erikson smiled ever so slightly. "I think you are following me, Ms. Hastings. Because the body was moved after death, we suspect that the jacket was deliberately placed with it. I hope we've answered all your questions. Now we must be going, good day."

She turned abruptly and almost bumped into Reynolds who stood behind her as he continued to hold the door open, still letting in the snow, because he couldn't think of anything else to do.

Joanna watched them leave with a growing feeling of elation. She did a clumsy pirouette across the living room floor and jabbed one fist into the air. "Yes!" she shouted. This was great. Not only was Tiffany not the prime suspect any longer but there hadn't been a murder committed right outside her front door. She felt like celebrating, but instead refreshed the soapy water in the kitchen bucket and settled back onto her knees to finish the floor. She was getting back into a careful rhythm when a horrible thought thrust itself through her elation. She dropped the sponge in shock. Luke may not have been killed on her property, but someone put him there on purpose. No one could think her cabin was still deserted; signs of habitation were everywhere. Surely there were a hundred easier places to dump a dead body, Luke must have been placed there for a reason. Joanna shivered, kitchen floor forgotten. She hoped those reasons didn't have anything to do with her. Dirty floor and damp rag abandoned, she rose abruptly to her feet and rushed to lock the front door and check the latches on the windows.

TWENTY-NINE

THE SNOW CONTINUED TO FALL and the temperature outside the cabin dropped along with it. All Joanna could see when she peered out her front window was endless white stretching off in every direction. White sky, white trees, white ground, white air. She prayed that it would stop snowing. At long last it did, but after a few days of coal-black clouds, threatening skies and stark brown and gray forests she found herself wishing the snow would come back. At least the snow could be pretty, provided it was falling gently in thick fluffy flakes, and not the sharp, brittle clumps more like ice pellets than snowflakes that seemed to have been falling for months. Color would be nice, she thought dreamily, a bit of red or blue or leafy green. Anything but this endlessly monotonous white and gray and brown. She forced herself to go for a walk or a short ski everyday, in an attempt to keep in some sort of shape.

She received a nice note from Morris Lipton, full of praise for her work that went a long way toward keeping her spirits up. That, as well as the last substantial deposit into her bank account which she confirmed through Internet banking. If only the dreary days weren't so long, if only the clouds would break and let the sun out, even a few minutes of sun would be a relief.

She well knew she couldn't afford it but nevertheless she called up Caribbean and South Sea vacation spots on the Internet. She gazed with green-eyed longing at the vista of a

Hawaiian island: blue sky, azure seas, green palm trees and masses of flowers, red and yellow and purple and pink. Smiling people dressed in flowery dresses and short shorts and tiny tank tops and almost-not-there bathing suits. Not a snow suit or a mitten or toque in sight. Heaven. If she was having this hard a time in Northern Ontario, how on Earth would Wendy and Robert survive a winter in the real north?

The crunch of wheels on the driveway and the sound of a truck door slamming brought Joanna swimming up through visions of her tanned self draped in a beach wrap and grass skirt, body baking slowly on a beach of pure white sand (better make the sand yellow, enough white on the ground around here), a handsome waiter with a smile full of shiny white teeth offering a fruit-laden cocktail. She opened the door to find Jack, his regular scowl fixed firmly in place, clutching a single bag of groceries under his arm.

He grunted at her in his usual friendly fashion and thrust the bag forward.

In a reflex action Joanna took it. But she recovered quickly. "What's this?" she asked. "I didn't order anything."

"You must have. I brung it, didn't I?"

"Well, yes." She thrust the bag back toward him. "But I didn't ask for anything. In fact I was thinking about calling Nancy with an order."

The bag hung in the air between them. Jack eyed it suspiciously and Joanna made pushing gestures with her arms and smiled encouragingly. Finally, Jack grunted and took the bag back.

She stood in the doorway, still smiling, wondering why he was standing there. Jack seemed to be making up his mind about something. "Saw you at the Last Chance the other night."

Joanna nodded. Her cheeks were starting to ache from

holding the smile. It seemed very much unlike Jack to be making friendly conversation.

"Asking questions, I heard." He didn't seem so friendly any more. He bared his stained and broken teeth at her. Joanna took an involuntary step backward.

"I don't think a city lady," he fairly spat the words, "ought to be hanging around asking questions where she don't belong. Why don't you just mind your own business and don't be interfering with God-fearing folks around here?"

Joanna made a clumsy effort to explain. "I wasn't trying to interfere, I wanted to clear up something that was bothering me, that's all."

Jack turned his head and spat, when he looked back, his eyes were narrow with malevolence. He shifted the grocery bag to the other arm and took a small step forward. Joanna shut the screen door firmly between them.

"Just stay away." He spat once more then turned on his heels and stepped off the porch. He stumbled on the broken tread and dropped the bag as he attempted to keep his balance. Tins clattered down the steps and rolled into the snow. He glared up at Joanna, still standing astounded behind the screen door. He kicked a can of spaghetti in tomato sauce out of the way and returned to his truck.

Joanna watched him go, her heartbeat slowly returning to normal. Cans of spaghetti and pork and beans and processed meat lay on their sides, partially covered by the snow into which they had fallen. The entire scene left Joanna completely baffled. She could not imagine what she had ever done to Jack to make him turn so hostile. He was angry that she saw him the other night at the Last Chance, but if he was trying to cover up some deep, dark secret, he really shouldn't be doing the nasty deed at the bar in the very next town. Good thing he didn't see her in Toronto, the day she saw him on the street with the bike courier. She decided not to order groceries over the phone again. She looked at the loose plank on which Jack had tripped. "Good step," she said as if she was praising a faithful guard dog. "Keep up the good work."

FRIDAY EVENING, as arranged, Tiffany arrived for her computer lesson. With some excitement Joanna had planned homemade pizzas for dinner. Her children had always loved homemade pizza with do-it yourself toppings on a Friday night. She had driven all the way into North Ridge to do the shopping. She didn't know if she would ever dare to venture back to the store in Hope River.

As soon as she arrived, Tiffany tentatively pulled a homework assignment from her battered old backpack and held it out for Joanna's inspection. Joanna read it over quickly. She was delighted, Tiffany wanted her help this time. The project was to pretend that she was setting up a new restaurant, and she was to design the menus, business cards and advertising for the venture. Joanna introduced the girl to the elements of Microsoft PowerPoint and then left her to use her imagination. While Tiffany was hard at work, Joanna started work on the pizzas. She sliced onions, green peppers, mushrooms and pepperoni and grated huge mounds of cheese. Only when she ran out of ingredients did she realize that she had prepared enough vegetables and cheese to provide the entire town of Hope River with homemade pizza. Joanna knew from long experience that teenage girls tended to eat like a bird on a bad day. They were so afraid of overeating that a couple of hours after a meal they would be back, filling up on bread or cake to try to get some of the nutrients they should have had with dinner.

She stretched store-bought pizza dough into rounds in a

couple of cookie pans and turned the oven on to heat up. Then she went to have a look at Tiffany's progress. The advertising brochures were almost finished, and to her amazement they were first-class. Although she was limited to the collection of graphics that came with the computer, Tiffany had designed a real work of art. Her imaginary restaurant was a sports bar, one that could be found in any town in Ontario, probably any town in North America, but Tiffany brought it to life with a catchy slogan, clever use of graphics and a bold dramatic font.

"This is amazing, Tiffany. It really is. I had no idea you were so talented."

Embarrassed, the girl mumbled into her chest.

"I'm serious," Joanna said. "Have you considered a career in graphic arts, or maybe even computer animation? It's a rapidly growing field, you know. Great potential."

"It's just a poster. Nothing much," Tiffany mumbled, her cheeks turning pink.

"Well, I like it." Joanna placed the slip of paper onto the desk. It was difficult, but she managed to control herself from going overboard in her enthusiasm. The girl's work was excellent. If this wasn't a one-time fluke then maybe Tiffany had real talent. Joanna would try to encourage her to develop it.

"Come and make your pizza, and then you can work a bit more while they're cooking."

They ate dinner in companionable silence. Tiffany ate a great deal more than Joanna would have expected, then she rose from the table, put a new CD into the computer and clicked her way into the magical world of *Tomb Raider*. Joanna tossed a pile of kindling and logs into the stove to blaze up into a brilliant source of light and heat. With a sigh of contentment she snuggled into the couch, picked up a glass of wine and her book and drifted off into a world of foggy gas lit streets and rattling carriages.

Outside the circle of light cast by the windows of the cabin, the forest mammals stirred restlessly. Those still exposed to the elements scrambled in search of shelter while the fortunate ones, who had already found a place of safety and comfort, dug themselves in deeper. The ancient great horned owl retreated deeper into the tree hollow she had found for her nest. Creatures of the forest all, they knew what the humans, content in their artificial world, did not: a winter storm was coming the likes of which had not been seen in these parts for many long years.

The rattle and clank of an old pickup truck turning into the driveway broke the silence of the woods as it held its collective breath waiting for the descent of the storm. The sharp, harsh lights cut through the heaviness of the night like the alien presence they were. The forest animals burrowed deeper into their nests and dens and placed paws tightly over sleepy eyes.

Joanna looked up lazily from her magazine and blinked in an unconscious imitation of the old owl watching over her home. The book she was reading, a Victorian murder mystery that had started out so strong and full of promise, was plodding endlessly to a dull conclusion. The warmth of the fire and the gentle music on the CD player had her nodding off where she sat.

She struggled to her feet and lazily opened the door, blinking impending sleep from her eyes. The truck engine was running, and the lights lit up the hillside.

An arm pushed the screen door aside and shoved Joanna back into the cabin. Her knee cracked against the edge of a table and she barely caught herself before falling to the floor.

Tiffany was happily immersed in a thrilling world of magic and mystery and adventure. One more leap and she, in the overabundant form of Lara Croft, would be safely across the temple ruins and onto the next level. It took a long time for her to tear her attention from the computer screen and climb back into reality. She saw Joanna crouched over the telephone table grimacing in pain and a heavy black form silhouetted in the doorway.

The form slowly came into focus as it moved into the room.

"For Christ's sake, Jack. What the hell do you think you're doing?" Joanna shouted. "I haven't ordered any groceries and anyway, it's a little late for a delivery, isn't it."

Jack seemed surprised to see Tiffany; he must have expected Joanna to be alone. In confusion he stared from one woman to the other. Behind him the door stood open and snowflakes swirled in around him, only to melt instantly under the force of the heat emanating from the old iron stove.

Tiffany carefully saved her game, then moved to Joanna's side and helped her friend to stand straight.

"What the hell do you want?" Joanna repeated, screaming into Jack's face. This had gone beyond eccentric, country folk behavior and she was thoroughly fed up. "I think that you had better go, now. Get out of my home. If you want to talk to me, come back tomorrow, but make an appointment first."

As if she hadn't spoken Jack strolled casually into the room, not bothering to shut the door behind him. He still glanced uneasily at Tiffany but his focus was on Joanna. He had not yet said a single word.

Suddenly Joanna was frightened. She grasped Tiffany and retreated, pulling the girl along with her. Aside from the fact that this was no time for a delivery from the grocery store, there was something in Jack's eyes. Something deep and terrifying yet vacant at the same time. She always knew that he, for unknown reasons, hated her, but now she could see it burning in his face, reflected in his eyes. Years of Wen-do failed her as Joanna skittered backward across the room, dragging Tiffany with her.

Jack grabbed the telephone cord and yanked it from the wall. If Joanna still clung to any illusions that this was just a misplaced social call, they vanished in a flash. She gaped at the phone cord, dangling uselessly in his hand. Her cell phone was in the bedroom. There was no doubt that he would get to her before she got to the phone.

"You stupid old man, what did you do that for?" Tiffany shrieked. "My grandma is going to phone to check on when she should come to get me. Now she won't get an answer so she'll come right away and I'll have to go home."

Behind her daze of fear and confusion, Joanna admired Tiffany's words of defiance: Maude would not be calling. She knew that Tiffany was here for the night.

She pulled herself together. This man was a country hick, after all. And an old one at that. She breathed deeply and attempted to remember all that she had learned in self-defense lessons. Nothing came to mind.

Tiffany stepped forward, full of teenage bravado and the arrogance of those who thought that they would never die. "What do you want, you stupid old man? Just tell us, then get the hell out of here." She shoved him in the chest. Caught by surprise, Jack staggered backward. Women weren't supposed to fight back. They were supposed to take what you gave them. Then clean up the mess afterwards.

Tiffany read the confusion on his face and shoved him again. "Get the hell out of here," she repeated. Joanna edged toward the hallway. Unaccustomed to violence, she did not know that she should be backing up her ally. Rather, she would try to get to her cell phone in the bedroom. That was the first of her mistakes tonight.

Jack lashed out and struck Tiffany across the face. With a cry of surprise, sharper than any pain, the girl fell to the floor. Joanna forgot her plan and rushed to help Tiffany up.

"You stupid bitches," Jack growled. It was the first time he spoke since arriving at the cabin. "Why can't you just stay out of what don't concern you?"

Joanna dragged Tiffany to her feet. *This can't be happening,* she thought, *this is totally crazy.* This demented old man must be talking about a misplaced grocery order.

Tiffany rubbed her cheek but her voice remained steady. "I think you should leave now, Mr. Miller. Come back in the morning and we can talk about this, okay?"

In answer, Jack casually reached into his jacket pocket and pulled out a gun. Joanna gasped. She had only ever seen a handgun on TV. It looked very small. Small and shiny and insignificant nestled in Jack's big, callused hand.

He shifted from one foot to the other, nervous and frightened, but his hands were as steady as rocks. "You stupid bitch," he spat the words out. In an idle part of her mind Joanna wondered if he knew any other words for women.

"You have to go and poke your nose where it ain't wanted." He waved the gun in the air. "I warned you off, but you wouldn't listen."

Joanna attempted to inject a note of reason into the whole ridiculous conversation. "Really, Jack. I don't understand what you are talking about. Why don't you put that silly gun away and we can talk about this. Like Tiffany suggested."

Tiffany causally wiped a spot of blood off her lip with the back of her hand. "It's no secret that you're the big shot drug supplier around here."

Joanna gasped.

"I've seen you plenty of times, creeping around parties, hanging out where the big druggies can find you. All the kids know where Cliff and Rick and that bunch get their supply." Tiffany turned to Joanna. "They buy the drugs and sell them to the rest of us. No big deal, Mr. Miller. Nothing for you to make a fuss over." As she spoke Tiffany stepped slowly forward and held out her hand. A gust of wind rattled the big front window. No one noticed.

"Nothing to you, maybe." Jack raised the gun a few inches higher, warning Tiffany to stay back. "But to an uptight city bitch like her…" he waved his empty hand at Joanna. "She'll run to the cops as soon as look at you."

"No, I won't," Joanna squeaked. "Let's forget all about this. I won't tell anyone." She looked steadily into his eyes trying to convince him of her sincerity. He stared back, his eyes black and cold and empty. Joanna shivered, this was totally ridiculous. She didn't even know that this crazy man was the local drug dealer, but he had burst into her home in order to tell her so? Nothing made any sense. Unless…"What do you know about the death of Luke Snelgrove?" Her mouth worked faster than her brain and the words were out before she could stop them.

Jack's eyes narrowed even further and he tightened his grip on the gun. Joanna realized that her words had struck home. But he didn't look at all defensive, or even surprised. Tiffany stared between them, dumbfounded. She shut her mouth firmly as she absorbed the knowledge of what she had just heard.

"That clumsy old man," Jack said. "He kept snooping around, didn't know when to mind his own business, just like you."

Tiffany spoke slowly, "Luke was always mad at us for hanging around on his land. But it was a great place for a party, so we just tried to keep out of his way. We knew he didn't have any time for the cops. He would never report us, guaranteed. He caught Cliff once, and really scared the hell out of him. So the gang pissed off to party somewhere else for a while. I was leaving the scene around then, Joanna, really I was. It was just so juvenile. But I can tell you that they knew old Luke wouldn't have called the cops, no way, even though he threatened that he would. He wouldn't have told the cops about you either," she told Jack.

"He might have told his brother, though." Jack kept his eyes firmly fixed on Joanna. He did not notice Tiffany off to one side, moving slowly toward him as she spoke, inch by deliberate inch. "Couldn't take the chance."

"So you burned down his home."

"Damned old fool, still kept hanging around in them woods. Weren't no home there any more, but he was still poking around in the woods."

"So you killed him." At last Joanna realized what all this was about.

"'Course I killed him," Jack said casually as if confessing to an accidental placement of meat into the dairy case. "Damned old fool. And now I have to kill you. I wouldn't have bothered you, you know. If you had just kept out of it."

"I did want to keep out of it." Joanna kept on talking as Tiffany continued to slide around Jack's side, trying to move so slowly as not to be noticed. She picked up the only thing that came to hand, the small Haida statue that was James' Christmas present to his mother.

"But you put the body on my property, how was I to stay out of it after that?"

Jack shrugged. "I didn't know where the property line was. Musta got confused in the dark. Thought that stretch of shore was government property. Sorry."

"My jacket," Tiffany shrieked, launching herself across the room. She brought the statue down with all the strength of a short lifetime's rage onto Jack's outstretched arm. The gun flew out of his hand as he whirled to fight her off. Tiffany struck again with the statue and continued yelling. "You stole my jacket and tried to frame me. You moron."

Jack wrenched the sculpture out of Tiffany's hands. Joanna ran for the gun, but it had slid under the sofa. She was scrambling on her hands and knees trying to find it when she heard a sickening smack as Jack struck Tiffany across the temple with the figurine. He stood over her, the statue raised high overhead about to bring it down on Tiffany's dazed head. The gun forgotten, Joanna leaped to her feet. At last she remembered something from her self-defense lessons. She launched her heel firmly into Jack's kneecap. With a cry he dropped the statue and fell to the floor.

Joanna dragged Tiffany to her feet and pulled the dazed girl out the door. Together they stumbled down the porch steps and across the yard. Behind them they could hear Jack screaming his rage as he fumbled under the furniture for his gun.

An ear piercing explosion and a shower of glass from the front window told them that he found it. Joanna fell to her knees and pulled Tiffany down beside her. Together they crawled into the relative safety of the trees.

They lay in the snow, hearts pounding, ears straining. Jack burst through the door and stood on the porch firing his gun wildly into the air, screaming abuse with every shot. The women huddled together, arms clasped around each other.

From her perch in the spindly white pine the old owl grunted in disgust. Bad weather and now this: would she have to go without dinner yet again?

"In the movies they only have six bullets in a gun, do you think that's right?" Joanna whispered into Tiffany's ear. "He must have fired six shots by now."

"I don't know, but I'm pretty sure guns have improved since the days of the cowboy movies."

"If you can call it improved," Joanna mumbled.

At that moment Jack stepped on the broken old porch step.

The rotten wood finally gave way and the tread collapsed with a crack and a shower of wood and splinters. Jack screamed as his foot and half of his left leg crashed through the steps.

"Now, run! He won't be stuck for long." Joanna dragged Tiffany to her feet and set off through the dark woods. Behind them they could hear Jack swearing as he smashed the rotting wood to free his leg from the remains of the porch steps.

Joanna's heart was pounding with a strength she didn't know it had. Any moment it might burst right through her chest. She had never known such fear. A quick glimpse of Tiffany's white and terrified face reflected her own panic back at her.

They reached the bottom of the driveway. For a second she hesitated, unsure of which trail to follow, upward toward the road, or down the hill to the thick boreal forest and the frozen lake beyond.

Jack shouted a cry of victory as he pulled his leg out of the broken steps. He fired the gun once again, and stumbled to his feet.

Tiffany was already turning up the hill toward the road, but Joanna grabbed her arm. "This way," she gasped. "I don't have the car keys."

For a moment Tiffany resisted. "The road. If we head for the road we may find help."

"No, he'll think of that. Let's go."

Tiffany took one last look up the hill and then turned to follow Joanna. She trusted this woman now.

ALTHOUGH THE FIVE-AND-DIME was fairly new, it already looked old and worn out. In this town, in these times, there was not very much money to be wasted on the sort of frivolities the store stocked. Hair clips and frilly blouses and toilet water and cheap costume jewelry sat on the shelves accumulating dust from one year until the next. The floor was grimy underfoot and water stains spotted the ceiling. Lighting was poor on the best of days and with the gathering snowstorm the room was gloomy to the point of despair.

The store was empty except for the heavily made up and substantially overweight clerk standing beside the ladies' gloves and the acne-cursed boy in a tall white hat and apron who served the soda counter. One other passenger flicked through a magazine as he waited for the bus. The girl ignored them all and took a seat at the soda counter, setting her suitcase on the floor beside her. The bus passenger looked like a traveling salesman: shiny suit, balding pate and false teeth, an overlarge sample case at his side. Fuller brushes maybe, she thought without interest. The man glanced at the girl's extended belly protruding out of the front of her tattered winter coat, the buttons no longer meeting at the front, and with a sniff he returned to his copy of Life magazine. She glanced at the picture on the cover: two tiny men stood at the bottom, dwarfed into insignificance by the colossal concrete pillars of the dam filling the photo.

Behind the counter, the clerk mopped up the floor. He would let the girl sit there as long as no one else came in for a soda. If they did, she would have to go and stand outside. But with one look at the street he knew that there would be no more customers today. Might as well close up the shop once the bus to Toronto passed through.

The clock over the cash register clicked the minutes slowly. The bus was late, thrown off schedule by the approaching snow. The salesman flicked through his magazine, the girl looked at the floor, every few minutes she checked in her pocket to be sure that the bus money and the directions to the home were still there. With a cheery good night the overweight woman waved to the soda jerk and rushed out into the night. The boy wanted to lock up and go home, but he'd get real trouble if he didn't wait for the last bus.

Eventually they heard the heavy sigh of the bus pulling to a stop in front of the store. As usual only the bus driver got off and stumbled in for a cup of coffee.

"Hell of a night out tonight," he mumbled to the clerk and the salesman. "Hope we can get out of the way before it really hits. Going to be a big one, I can tell you." He finished his coffee in two gulps and returned to the bus. The girl and the Fuller brush salesman climbed on after him.

The girl stifled a moan as a sharp pain ripped through her stomach and handed the bus driver her money. "Toronto, please," she mumbled. The pain subsided and she breathed deeply with relief.

The bus driver stared at the money in her hand. "That's not enough to get you to Toronto."

She looked at him not understanding. "But this is all I have."

"Well, it's not enough."

"Please, I have to go to Toronto. Maybe I can send the bus company the rest of the money after I get there."

The man laughed and stared at her belly. She pulled her coat tighter around her but it still did not meet at the front.

"Yea, right," he sneered. "Pay up or get off the bus."

She didn't know what to do. "But my da said this was the fare to Toronto."

"Well, your da obviously don't know nothing. Now get off the bus. Ask your da for more, the next bus comes through on Friday." He looked past her. "Can I help you, sir?"

She lifted her cardboard suitcase and pushed past the man in the shiny suit. He stepped quickly out of her way as if she were a bad smell. "If you'd kept your legs together, you wouldn't be needing to go to Toronto."

The bus driver laughed and handed the salesman his ticket. The girl stood on the sidewalk, cardboard suitcase in hand thin coat flapping open in the wind. In the short time she had been on the bus the store clerk had turned out the lights, locked the door and escaped for home.

As is the way in the north in winter, night had fallen in a matter of minutes. All the storefronts were closed tight. There was no one in sight; everyone was seeking shelter from the approaching storm. Not that she would have ever approached anyone for help in any event. She was a McDonald; she knew not to expect kindness from people.

She picked up her suitcase and set off down the street. She would just have to walk home and hope that her da would give her more money so she could catch the next bus. Probably be in for a beating first, but that could be endured.

She passed the brightly lit windows of the church hall but didn't spare them a glance. Inside, the minister's wife and the bazaar committee had finally come to the realization that no one would venture out on a night like tonight.

"I am only sorry for those poor unfortunates so in need of our Christian charity," the minister's wife exclaimed to the ladies of the committee, patting her iron gray curls into place. "We must pray that our next bazaar will be a success, for their sakes." The ladies nodded as they gathered up their cakes and squares. Bending over to pull on heavy boots, they groaned in unison.

THIRTY

ALL AROUND THEM the storm continued to build. As if it were a living, thinking being, it had been gathering its strength into itself all day and now it burst forth in an excited frenzy of wind and snow.

Tiffany could barely see Joanna through the depths of the blizzard. She was nothing but a vague, ghostly shape, drifting in and out of focus against the undulating landscape. There was no day, no night, no sky, no earth. Only shifting, living white. The feel of the snow-covered ground beneath Tiffany's feet changed as they burst out of the woods and onto the frozen lake. They were no longer tripping over barely covered rocks and fallen logs, the snow on the lake was thick and smooth and unbroken. Joanna grabbed Tiffany's hand. "I can barely see you," she gasped. "Hold on or we might get separated." Gratefully Tiffany clung to Joanna as if she was a life preserver and Tiffany was drowning, drowning, not in water but in snow. A slower death perhaps, but just as final.

In blind panic the woman and girl ran out further onto the frozen lake. The snow was up past their knees but they pushed on as if they were human snowplows. They were digging giant furrows behind them, such as a farmer might make to prepare his fields for seeding. But so harsh was the wind and so heavy was the falling snow that their path disappeared almost immediately. Within seconds, no trace of their panic driven passage remained.

It seemed to Tiffany that they had been running through the white night, hands clasped tightly together, for hours. But all too soon the strain on her panicked heart and the effort of plowing through the virgin snow forced Joanna to a halt. The older woman was in better shape than Tiffany, thanks to regular exercise, good diet and no smoking, but none of that mattered compared to the difference in their ages.

Joanna bent over, hands on her knees, desperately trying to pull oxygen into her starving lungs. Tiffany moved close and absentmindedly rubbed Joanna's back.

"I don't hear anything, do you?" Joanna gasped.

Tiffany strained her ears. All she could hear was the howl of the wind. "No, I don't think he followed us."

For a split second Tiffany felt nothing but overwhelming relief: Jack was gone, it was over. Then she took in her surroundings. She could see absolutely nothing, nothing but endless shifting white. It was night, but the sky and the stars were gone. It wasn't even black, as night should be, just a darker shade of white. Lashes of wind blew frozen pellets of snow into her face. She couldn't begin to make out a trail marking the direction in which they had come.

"Joanna, where are we?"

Joanna looked up. She was still breathing deeply, but the gasping had stopped and she was able to stand straight. "I don't know." She looked around. "We must be out on the lake. I'm sure if we just turn around and walk back in the direction in which we came we will get back to the edge of the lake. Then if we follow the shoreline for a bit we will come to the Reynolds' place and we can ask them for help. Hopefully Jack gave up on us long ago."

Tiffany knew that Joanna was as confused as she was, but she was trying to put up a brave, adult front. Simultaneously the two women started the return journey across the Lake. They headed in opposite directions.

Joanna's resolve collapsed and she burst into tears. "Tiffany, I don't have any idea which way we came, do you?"

Tiffany glanced about wildly. There was not a single landmark to be seen. She remembered her geography teacher telling the class how the Inuit built large groups of standing stones, that they called *Inukshuk,* to mark the landscape and give travelers some point of reference in the vastness of the Artic desert. Too late now to build an *Inukshuk.*

Joanna cried silently. The tears froze to her eyelashes and cut icy rivulets down her cheeks. Now that the frenzy of their dash to freedom had passed, Tiffany slowly became aware of just how cold she was. She was wearing only running shoes on her feet and a thick wool sweater, lovingly hand knitted by her grandma. She gratefully pulled her hands up into the sleeves and with a flash of shame remembered how she refused to be seen wearing it in public. She only put it on to go to Joanna's because the cabin was always cold and she knew that Joanna wouldn't even notice if she was a geek wearing a homemade sweater. At least she was better equipped than Joanna, who had taken her own sweater off when she built up the fire. She was dressed only in a flannel shirt and jeans. Tiffany put her arms around Joanna, who was shivering uncontrollably. "Come on," she muttered trying to keep her voice full of nonexistent enthusiasm. "We'll go this way."

She half dragged the older woman after her, but all too soon Tiffany knew that they were lost. If she didn't find shelter, and soon, Joanna would freeze to death. And she, Tiffany, wouldn't be very far behind. Already her fingers and toes were numbing.

"Look, over there," Tiffany shrieked. "A light. We must be going the right way. Come on, Joanna. It looks really close. Maybe we're almost at the Reynolds'."

"I don't see a light." Joanna's teeth rattled so badly, she was barely able to get the words out. Tiffany hoped that wasn't a patch of frostbite she saw on the older woman's nose. She didn't know how long it took for frostbite to develop. But like anyone living in the north, she knew it was a very bad thing.

"Well, I see it, Joanna. Come on, follow me. Not much further, I think." She slipped her arm around her friend's waist and half dragged the woman after her. "Just a little bit more. I hope they have a fire going, and the kettle on to boil. I'd love a cup of hot chocolate right about now. How about you?" With a pang Tiffany thought of her grandma, the warmth of their house, the blazing stone fireplace, lazy old Rocky snoring in front of the hearth, his feet moving as he dreamt of his glory days, chasing squirrels and chipmunks deep into the woods. Warm chocolate chip cookies and a steaming hot drink ready when Tiffany got off the school bus. She had never told her grandma that she loved her, she had never thanked her for taking her in and looking after her so well. Please, please, let her see her grandma one more time, then she could die.

With a sigh Joanna collapsed to her knees into the snow. She was buried up to her thighs. "I'll wait here. You go on without me and come back with help. I'll be okay. I'll just have a rest while you're gone."

Tiffany grabbed Joanna as she was about to pitch forward onto her face and hauled her back to her feet. "I don't think so, Joanna. I think we'll stay together. I need you, you know."

Joanna smiled, her lips ice blue. "That's nice."

Tiffany could still see the light ahead of her, a bright beacon cutting through the gloom of the snowstorm, but it wasn't getting any closer. Surely they had traveled enough by now that they should be almost there. In fact, the light wasn't getting any brighter either. It was almost as if it was moving as they moved.

She plodded on, every step an effort, either lifting her foot high enough to get over the mounds of snow, before placing it down again, or pushing through the thick drifts. It would be a lot easier if Joanna would follow behind in the trail she cut, but Tiffany dared not relax the death grip she had on the woman's arm. If only she had a rope or a scarf, something to tie them together. Instead she steadily pulled Joanna along beside her.

The light bobbed silently ahead of them, neither growing nor dimming, it just moved steadily. Snow was melting inside of her shoes, wetting her feet, which immediately turned to ice. Icy crystals stuck to her hair and to her eyelashes. The wind reached arctic tentacles down the back of her sweater, feeling for the warm, dry spots between her shoulder blades. Her hands were frozen solid. Without caring much she wondered if she would ever be able to feel them again. *This is useless,* Tiffany stopped so suddenly that Joanna pitched forward. Tiffany let go of her arm and Joanna fell face first into the snow. She didn't move, the first soft snowflakes melted against her still warm body, but soon they formed a mound all around her.

Tiffany sunk into the snow beside Joanna. *I'll close my eyes for a minute, and then we'll carry on. I wonder where my mom is. She always wanted to go to Hawaii; maybe she's there right now. I'd like to go to Hawaii one day. Maybe I can find my mom there. She'll be glad to see me.*

Her eyes flickered shut, then flew open again. The light was closer now, much closer. So close that it was almost in her face. It cut through the gloom of the winter night like a brilliant, old-fashioned paraffin lantern. Tiffany reached out a hand to touch it, but the light swayed gently just out of her reach.

She strained to make out the undulating shape faintly visible behind the glare of the lamp. Shifting white hair, and a face so pale that when Tiffany blinked it was gone, blended back into the snow. Only the flash of a red scarf, decorated with soft blue flowers, and the gentle glow of the lantern were visible in the expanse of the frozen world. *Almost there.* She abandoned her dreams of the blue beaches and green palm trees of Hawaii and once again lumbered to her feet, pulling Joanna up beside her. The woman was almost a dead weight, but at least she was beyond resistance. They stumbled forward and the light bobbed on ahead.

So faintly she wasn't sure she saw it at first, a gray line of brooding snow-encrusted trees loomed out of the vast whiteness. Tiffany shouted with joy, although her throat didn't make a sound. The shoreline began to take shape and then she could see the rough planks of a dock, left bare for the winter.

"We're safe," she gasped. "Come on, Joanna, we're back on land."

"Good," Joanna mumbled. "I'll lie down here for a minute."

"No way, not after we've come this far." Tiffany released her grip on Joanna for just a minute as she clambered up the bank on her hands and knees. When she was safely on land, she reached down to offer her friend her hand. The moving light had disappeared the moment she touched land, and Joanna was nowhere to be seen as the snow swirled around her in ever decreasing circles.

"Joanna," Tiffany screamed into the wind, all the pain of her short, harsh life pouring out through her voice. She had come so far, and tried so hard, she would not give up now. "Where are you? Joanna!"

A stark white hand reached out of the moving snow and gripped Tiffany's arm. Joanna groaned once, and pulled herself onto the shore. They lay in each other's arms for a moment before Tiffany struggled reluctantly to her feet. "We'll freeze here just as well as on the lake. Let's get moving." Once again she dragged Joanna upright.

They were standing on the stretch of rocky beach right below Joanna's cabin. Tiffany could see the porch light burning faintly through the trees. As they struggled up the hill the wind died and the snow ceased to fall. Overhead a full moon and galaxies of brilliant stars were coming out. The old owl hooted once in greeting. Tiffany remembered Jack, but pushed the thought out of her mind. If they didn't get to shelter, Joanna would die. If Jack was waiting, well, she would deal with him then.

The front door flapped open, back and forth, back and forth. Tiffany shoved Joanna into the cabin and struggled to shut the door against the mound of snow piled in the entrance. She gave up and dragged Joanna over to the fireplace. Fortunately several logs lay beside the stove and Tiffany tossed them in along with a pile of magazines sitting on the coffee table. They caught almost immediately. Tiffany hoped that Joanna wouldn't be mad at her for burning her magazines before she read them. She propped Joanna up against the couch in front of the fire, legs splayed out in front of her, head lolling to one side. Only then did she stumble into the bedroom, grab the cell phone, dial first the ambulance service and then the police. Once they assured her that help was on the way, she called her grandma, and burst into tears.

EPILOGUE

JOANNA PLUGGED IN the last power cord and switched on computer and monitor. She stood back to watch the machine whirl to life. The monitor glowed and the famous logo appeared.

"This is so exciting," Maude exclaimed clapping her hands. "I really feel that I've joined the twentieth century."

"It's the twenty-first now, Grandma." Tiffany reminded her.

"That's too science-fictiony for me get my old head around." Maude smiled.

"Well, you remember," Joanna said, "I'll be back for my computer soon. If you decide you like using it, then you'll have to buy one of your own."

Tiffany sat down at the keyboard and clicked mouse buttons. Her hair was growing out, brown roots reaching up about 3 inches into the purple hair. The attitude was gone, and she smiled fondly and full of confidence at her grandmother and closest friend. "Look at this, Grandma. You can find out anything you want on the Internet. Think of something, and I'll look it up for you."

Maude chuckled, "Later, dear, we do still have a guest, remember?"

Joanna smiled and hugged the old woman tightly. "I'm not a guest any more, am I? I hope I'm more than that."

Maude gripped Joanna in return, and then released her to wipe tears from the rough, old cheeks. "Much more than that, dear. Much more than that."

The old woman sniffed, still trying to hide her tears. "Now I hear the kettle, so while I go and get the tea things, will you please let Rocky in. I think he's about to break down the front door."

Joanna opened the door wide and the dog bounded in, a faded old tennis ball, half ripped to shreds, clutched between his teeth. "Look, Rocky's found a toy. It's probably been sitting outside all winter."

"Don't you play with that dog in the house, Joanna. Throw that horrible old ball back outside and come and have tea."

Joanna and Tiffany exchanged grins before Joanna tossed the ball through the open door. It rolled down the steps and came to rest in a pile of soft mud under the crocuses. Rocky threw Joanna a dirty look and then trotted into the kitchen at the sound of plates and cups rattling. He was not disappointed, and soon returned with a dog biscuit clenched between his powerful jaws. Ball forgotten, he settled down to enjoy the treat.

Leaving Tiffany to open up the exotic world of Lara Croft, Joanna joined Maude in the kitchen. The brown betty sat in pride of place on the old Formica table, surrounded by dainty glass containers for cream and sugar and a plate of sugar cookies. Joanna took a cookie with pleasure. Sunlight streamed in through the kitchen window and the African violets stretched themselves eagerly toward the rays.

"Tiffany is going to miss you, a lot." Maude poured tea and eased herself into a chair. "As am I."

Joanna stretched her hand across the table. Maude squeezed it with affection. "And I'll miss you as well."

"I hope not to be gone for too very long." Joanna smiled at her friend. "Even if I wanted to I can't afford to be not working."

"If you're short of money…"

Joanna cut her off. "I'll be fine. Don't you worry about that." She had squirreled away most of her fee from Morris

Lipton's project and tried to live off the other small jobs that she managed to obtain. Fortunately, she had taken out disability insurance once she decided to go into business for herself and that provided some income while she was hospitalized and her hands were recovering.

"My ex-husband's paying for most of the trip," Joanna said. "He says he made a bit of money on the stock market and wants to put it to good use."

"You're very lucky," Maude said.

"I am, indeed."

The women sat in silence for a few minutes, both of them deep in thought about how just how lucky they were.

Joanna finished a cookie and stood up, brushing crumbs from the front of her sweater. Maude struggled to her feet. It hurt Joanna to see how slowly her neighbor moved and how she held her hand to her back as she struggled to stand upright. Conscious of Maude's pride, she pretended not to notice.

"Well, I'm off, Tiffany," Joanna said, taking her coat down from the hook by the door and slipping into a pair of hiking boots. "Look after my baby, eh?"

Tiffany leapt up from the computer. "I'll walk up the road with you. I'm sure Rocky would like the exercise." At the sound of his name the old Malamute pricked up his ears and trotted to the door.

The women laughed. "I think that that's a 'yes,'" Maude said.

Joanna stopped for a moment at the bottom of the steps to admire the mounds of purple and yellow crocuses that had rushed out of the cold, dark earth the very moment the snow withdrew and the first feeble rays of the spring sun warmed the ground above them. A few hardy tulips were poking their heads up, still trying to decide if it was quite time to wake up yet.

"Your grandma is going to have a great display of flowers soon."

"I guess." Tiffany kicked at a rock under her feet.

They walked up Maude's driveway and strolled down the road toward Joanna's cabin in silence, each woman deep in her own thoughts. All around them the woods threw off the oppressive mantle of the long dark winter and reached eagerly into the spring sunshine. A few of the earliest deciduous trees were sporting buds already and the pines readied themselves for another year's growth. A rabbit hopped across the road in front of them, full of the joys of spring and they could hear birds chirping in the trees, announcing that they had arrived home once again. Joanna remembered when she was a child, going to see the movie Bambi with her sisters and parents at the Galaxy cinema. Her favorite scene in the movie and the one she remembered still, was when the forest animals first woke up to spring and how they all came out to play.

"Have you ever seen *Bambi?*" she asked.

"No, I don't think so."

"Rent it on video one day, if it's available. I think you'll like it." Joanna rubbed at her right hand.

"Is your hand bothering you?" Tiffany asked.

"No, not at all. Just a bit itchy. It's perfectly fine." The frostbite on Joanna's nose and her hands, particularly the right, had been severe, but fortunately Tiffany had got her well placed in front of a fireplace, close enough to be warm but not too near to overheat the wounds, and the ambulance crew were acquainted with the treatment of frostbite, so she suffered no lasting damage. But it had been tense for a while. Elaine rushed up from the city and sat beside Joanna's bedside all the long days. She called James in Vancouver and Wendy in Whitehorse to assure them that their mother was fine and was in absolutely no danger. Scott O'Neill came as soon as he heard the news, his huge head and bushy beard almost hidden behind an enormous bouquet of flowers. He returned every day to visit and with Elaine's encouragement he and Joanna gently resumed their budding relationship.

Tiffany was the hero of the day and the entire town was abuzz with the news. People who had never before done anything more than glare at her on the street now offered to shake her hand and declare how they had known all along that there was plenty of good in that girl. Maude, steadfast and resolute as always, made sure that Tiffany knew she was no more than a nine-days-wonder and before long those same people would be back to criticizing her clothes and her hair and everything else about which they could find to complain.

Jack Miller, the townsfolk exclaimed as one, they always knew he was up to no good. Never could trust Jack, they assured each other. And look at the way he always treated that poor wife of his. Roy McMaster, enemy of Jack (as well as Luke and apparently most of the men of similar age) for forty long years, became a local hero, second only to Tiffany Jordan. Only Nancy Miller showed any grief over her uncle.

Once help arrived Tiffany allowed herself to collapse into hysterics. It was a while before she managed to calm down enough to explain to the police what had happened. An all-out search then began for Jack Miller. It didn't take long before his frozen body was found in the deep woods across the road from Joanna's property. Losing sight of his prey, apparently he floundered through the winter's night in the wrong direction thinking he was still after them. Eventually he tripped over a rock and simply lay where he fell and let the cold move in.

The police searched his house and found tens of thousands

of dollars in cash hidden in the garage and garden shed, places Jack's wife never ventured. They also pulled out brochures featuring vacations in Bali and Tahiti, which Jack's distraught and confused wife confessed to never having seen before.

Inspector Erikson and Staff Sergeant Reynolds visited Joanna in the hospital to keep her up to date on the winding up of the investigation. Erikson gently took Joanna's wounded hand in her own and thanked her for her assistance. Joanna didn't know what assistance she had offered, but was happy to accept the thanks anyway.

Nancy Miller soon followed, cheap flowers clutched tightly in a sweaty hand. She confessed to Joanna that she had always disliked her Uncle Jack, but he was, after all, her uncle. It was painful for Joanna to watch Nancy's expressions of guilt, as if she, Nancy, had something to do with all that had happened. Joanna accepted the flowers with thanks and told Nancy with a bright smile that they would still be friends. But as she watched Nancy slink out of the hospital room she feared that they would never be comfortable in each other's company again.

Deep in remembrance Joanna was startled to find that they had already arrived at the cabin in the woods. As soon as she was home from the hospital Joanna arranged to have the broken step on the front porch mended. It's fresh, bright wood stood out among the rest of the weatherworn house. A few tired old crocuses struggled vainly to push themselves up out of the mud across the front of the cabin. Joanna made a mental note to put fresher bulbs in, come autumn. A flash of sunlight on glass under the porch caught her attention and she bent to pull out a bottle of wine, a very nice Australian Shiraz. She studied it for a moment, wondering from where it had come, and carried it into the cabin.

She put the wine bottle in the rack under the sink, then went to get her purse and suitcase. When she came out Tiffany was standing on the ridge, looking out over the lake, sparkling and blue in the spring sunshine. Frantic barking, high-pitched quacking and much splashing announced that Rocky was threatening a pair of ducks who had dared to venture too close to shore.

Joanna tossed her belongings into the back of the car. She faced Tiffany awkwardly. "You'll be sure to watch the cabin, now. Water my plants and…"

"Yes, Joanna, I'll remember."

"I'm scared, you know." One hand on the door handle, Joanna paused and faced the girl. "I'm afraid that she'll reject me, again."

"Maybe she will and maybe she won't. But if you don't go, you won't have given her the chance. And wouldn't that be the saddest thing of all?"

Joanna nodded. "That it would. Take care of my things. I've put my house in Toronto up for sale and when it goes through I intend to buy this run-down old place, so it had better be here when I get back."

"It will."

"Now, you have Scott's number, right? If there are any problems and anything that needs fixing he'll come out and look after it."

"I know, Joanna."

"Do you want a ride back to your house?"

"No thanks. I think Rocky would like the walk."

They hugged each other tightly, as if they were holding on to a lifeline. Tiffany was the first to break the embrace and awkwardly Joanna climbed into the car. Waving frantically she backed up the driveway and turned into the road.

Before putting the car into drive, she noticed a huge, lifeworn owl sitting in the tree above her car. It was unusual to see her out in the daylight, so Joanna watched for a moment. Then she shifted the car into gear, tooted the horn in a chorus of good-byes and pulled away.

As Joanna drove off down the muddy old road, she glanced in the rearview mirror for one last look at her young friend, who stood waving from the top of the driveway. Rocky dashed across the road, jaws snapping in pursuit of a butterfly. Before she rounded the bend and they all disappeared from sight, Joanna had one last glimpse of the great horned owl as she caught a thermal and soared away above the forest.